AFTER

THE

SUCKER

PUNCH

A Novel

LORRAINE DEVON WILKE

AFTER THE SUCKER PUNCH by Lorraine Devon Wilke

ISBN-13: 978-1497596306
ISBN-10: 1497596300
LCCN: 2014906941

Cover design by Grace Amandes
Cover photographs by Lorraine Devon Wilke

www.lorrainedevonwilke.com

For Pete and Dillon
My heart and soul

.

ONE

January 5, 2002 – the journal of Leo Curzio:

One is obligated by moral duty to love one's child. One is not obligated to like them. A conundrum when it comes to my fourth, my third daughter, Teresa – or Tessa, as she insists we call her now.

Recently I searched through my journals of the past several years looking for an entry about her but could find nothing. Perhaps that's not so strange; she has been an enigma to me since she finished high school. As I look back, it seems her senior year was the pinnacle of her life...from that point on little has happened to bear out her great promise.

Convinced of her own abilities, which do seem apparent or, at the very least, measurable, she decided to try for a job in the movies, TV, or perhaps the recording business out in Hollywood. She insisted that if after two years she had gotten nowhere she would try something else. Well, it's been more than three years and she has nothing to show for it except some amateur acting classes and self-produced plays. In September she will be twenty-five.

So what's the problem with Teresa? For sure, I don't know. She is a great disappointment. Not simply because she's failed up to now, but that endowed with so much talent she hasn't employed it for anything useful and doesn't show signs of improving.

On a day when all she wanted to do was mourn the father so

1

often longed for and buried just hours before, Tessa Curzio sat on the bed in which she was surely conceived and felt posthumously sucker punched. She looked down at the twelve-year-old journal splayed across her lap and realized it truly was a Pandora's box come to life, a dubious gift from a dead man who had little to say while living but clearly plenty upon departure. She snapped it shut and threw it across the room with enough force to shatter her mother's purple vanity lamp.

A clock that followed to the floor doggedly kept ticking time. 5:17 pm.

It was the beginning of the next uncomfortable phase of her life.

TWO

Because no tantrum could go unnoticed in this house, the door flew open and oldest sister Michaela, tight chignon and Ann Taylor classics all in place, swept in with a frown and a large tray of hors d'oeuvres. She and Tessa, though only four years apart, were opposite in so many critical ways they struggled to be even marginal friends, a status they'd admirably put aside to "rise above" during this challenging week. Noting the purple shards on the Oriental she'd vacuumed earlier that morning, Michaela stifled a retort only when she caught the look on Tessa's face.

"Oh, honey, I know, I know," she whispered, miscalculating the motive behind the lamp's demise. She left her tray on the dresser and came to Tessa with sympathetic arms. "It's so hard to lose him...I know."

With Michaela patting her rigid shoulder for what seemed far too long without comment, Tessa finally took a deep breath. "Um, Mickie...thanks, but I think I just need to be alone for a while, okay?"

Relieved, Michaela quickly pulled away. "Absolutely, I understand. Just do me a favor and clean up the lamp before you come down. Mom doesn't need anything else to be upset about today." Rising from the bed, her eyes caught the box of journals Tessa had pulled out from underneath; the tone shift was sharp and immediate. "Wow, really? Well, don't let her know you're already rifling through Dad's stuff. She'd actually like to look through everything first, if you wouldn't mind."

"It's just some...books," Tessa glared. A swift jerk of her ankle kicked the box back under the bed. Michaela picked up her tray and, with an icy shot back, swept out as she'd swept in.

Tessa had found the box of mildewed date books at the behest of second eldest sister, Suzanna, a sibling of a totally different color and an ass-kicker whom Tessa adored. Suzanna was the agent provocateur of the family, a role sparked decades earlier by their parents' inflamed response to her ill-conceived, if accidental, premarital pregnancy (a blessed event that jumped her wedding by less than a month). The word "whore" was invoked, her divorce a year later was "God's retribution," and Suzanna was never able to forgive them for it all, even years later when they offered awkward apologies about dogma and overreaction. Revenge was exacted by her phenomenal success in business, far exceeding that of her father's, and by raising a lovely boy despite his one fetal month of bastardhood.

In her self-assigned mission to keep the family legacy honest, Suzanna, exasperated by an uncharacteristic bout of Daddy-idealizing on Tessa's part the night before, had suggested her little sister find the box of journals he'd so copiously recorded over the years and read at least one of them, "particularly *2002*" with its insights about Tessa specifically. "You need some perspective," Suzanna had ominously declared.

So Tessa dutifully looked and regretfully found the box under the bed. Apparently there were other boxes somewhere, no one knew where, but this one held at least twelve or thirteen years of minutia spilled onto the pages of yearly date books given to the employees of the bookbinding company where Leo had spent the bulk of his adult working life. Date books meant for appointments and note keeping but utilized by Leo for his introspective ramblings over the last fifty or so years. As instructed, Tessa found *2002*, which now lay on the floor amidst dust and purple glass.

Suddenly exhausted, she curled up in the perfumed sleep habitat of parents who now seemed intangible, realizing, after many years of wondering, that she finally knew what her father thought of her. Interesting how a dead man could so easily suck breath from a living solar plexus, like the mythical cat and unsuspecting baby.

A quick rap at the door snapped her reverie. She sat up, fluffed her hair and trilled, "Who is it?"

"It's me, Tess. What are you doing? Got someone in there with you?" Ronnie, Tessa's younger brother and closest sibling, was already slurring as he cracked open the door, his face goofy with a grin. "Are you having sex on Mom and Dad's bed to assuage your fear of death?"

Tessa couldn't help but smile. There was just something about Ronnie. "Go away, idiot."

"Okay, sis, I got it. You're processing your grief by rolling in Dad's sheets. Gross but strangely titillating."

"Ronnie!"

"Hey, who am I to judge? Just don't take too long, whatever you're doing. Mom's tilting and Michaela's about to snap. It could get ugly."

As the door clicked shut and he stumbled back down the hall, Tessa sighed at the second interruption of the hour, realizing, mostly, that she didn't want to go back down there...down into the swirling eddy of sobbing, dramatic folk seeping into the small Chicago brownstone to mourn a man who now felt like an imperfect stranger. The rising cacophony was unavoidable, however, signaling the arrival of aunts, uncles, cousins, siblings, surely a priest or two, and plenty of neighbors. No choice but to postpone internal combustion for a more solitary time.

Straightening the bed, she was perversely pleased to see mascara streaked across her father's starched pillowcase. That would have annoyed him. She went to the vanity. Examining herself in the mirror, Tessa noted that her smeared eye-makeup lent a sort of punky irreverence to her face, appropriate, perhaps, to her new assignation as Failed Daughter. She left it.

She picked up the family portrait that held center stage in this private corner of her mother's world and studied it as if for the first time. It had always been one of her favorites, all of them lined up in birth order, for those, her mother once scoffed, who struggled to keep the six Curzio children straight. Suzanna once joked that they should wear permanent nametags but Audrey, the indomitable matriarch, insisted it wasn't the family's obligation to facilitate the memory of others. "People ought to take the time to differentiate." The most she would accede to was their positioning. Still, people typically mixed them up, especially the girls.

But there they all were, matted, framed and in proper order: oldest brother Duncan was on the left, then Michaela, Suzanna, Tessa, Ronnie, and the baby of the family, Isabella, whom they endearingly called "Izzy." Audrey stood with her arm around eighteen-year-old Duncan, chin raised in Joan Crawfordian aplomb, eyes sharp and a smile wide as the sky. Leo, the stern patriarch, stood on the other end, Izzy leaning slightly into his side, his handsome face set in a cool, inscrutable expression. Michaela and Suzanna were tall, mature young women gazing calmly at the camera, while Tessa and Ronnie appeared to be giggling at some private joke. It was a perfect image; an exact distillation of her family, and Tessa couldn't help but smile as she put the frame back under the amber lights.

She bent down and retrieved the assaulted journal from the floor, opening the pages once more to Leo's crinkly handwriting: "*She is a great disappointment. Not simply because she's failed up to now, but that endowed with so much talent she hasn't employed it for anything useful...*"

At least he said she had talent.

THREE

Chaos reigned downstairs. Children, large and small, ran about screaming and laughing without thought to the somber theme of the event. The adults crammed into every corner of the house and the ambiance was oddly electric, as if they were waiting for a rock star who would never show up. Mounds of food covered the table, Leo's favorite Sinatra loudly soundtracked the proceedings, and a significant crowd huddled around the weeping Audrey who, despite honest grief, was reveling in the white-hot focus of her nascent widowhood. Michaela and Suzanna whisked about making sure everyone was taken care of, while older brother Duncan, now "man of the house," as Audrey had anointed him the night before, held court in the dining room, expounding on his father's virtues to a rapt circle of church groupies. Izzy, red-eyed and reverted to "baby girl" status, tucked against her mother's shoulder, while Ronnie slumped in a corner chair taking it all in with cynically dry eyes. He was the only one who noticed Tessa coming down the stairs with a look that signaled the plates had shifted. She squeezed into the chair with him and he gave her a blurry once-over.

"Why do you look like that?"

"Like what?"

"Like you wanna throw up."

"I was reading."

A long pause until it struck him. "Is *that* what you were doing up there? You found the box?"

"Yep."

"You read *2002*?"

"The first page that had my name on it."

"Damn, let's get you a drink."

"It'll just give me a headache."

"Aw, sissy, don't you already have one?" He put his arm around her and squeezed. The shot of empathy threatened to unleash a crying jag or some other unseemly bout of hysteria but Tessa thought better of it. Michaela approached, again with the hors d'oeuvres tray.

"Is that thing attached to your arm?" Ronnie asked as he stuffed a crostini into his mouth.

"Someone's got to help around here, Ronald, you might want to try it sometime. Hungry, Tess?" Tessa's grimace was apt response. Michaela reached down and patted her shoulder, still convinced of the shared nuances of their grief. "We all miss him, Tessa, it's just going to take time."

Ronnie lurched from the chair, stomping off to the bar set up on the breakfront. Michaela looked after him, bewildered. "What's wrong with him?"

"He's turmoiled."

"More like loaded. Little shit. Have you talked to Mom yet?"

"What do you mean, *yet*? Of course I've talked to her. "

"I mean, since we got back here."

"No. Why?"

"She's on her fourth drink, carrying on that it wasn't a stroke."

"Oh, really? What was it then?" This was not a new conversation.

"Well, let's see...'the doctors don't know what they're talking about, the last meds probably poisoned him, maybe we should sue'...you know the drill. I wish Duncan had been quicker to put out that fire."

Their brother Duncan was a highly successful product liability attorney who'd made a name and several million in a case involving a child's death caused by a drug later recalled by the FDA. He had become somewhat of a celebrity and certainly an expert, garnering a pulpit style that often edged toward high-pitched pontification. There was talk of politics and much consensus that he was a bold and righteous crusader. Tessa thought he might just be an ambitious prick but odds were that was sour grapes. Duncan's financial and general life success stirred bona fide envy in her, as did his inexplicably close relationship with a father who seemed far less interested in her. Her current pique had to do with his receptiveness to certain church folk who had ridiculously queried, "What *really* happened to Leo?" as if some grand conspiracy was at work rather than a simple, unfortunate stroke. Duncan's brief consideration lent it weight, foolish in light of Audrey's predilection for drama, and though he ultimately quashed the theory, the damage had been done. Audrey was rolling.

Tessa looked over at Duncan, still on his jag in the adjoining room, and sighed. "He can't help himself. Ask a question; get a speech. And what's wrong with dying of a stroke anyway? Is there some shame in it? Would the man be any less dead?"

"She'd prefer he not be dead at all," Michaela remarked, not without sympathy.

"She'd prefer he not be so *mundanely* dead. A faulty drug, some exotic disease, anything to get the saint one more paragraph in the obits. He'd still be dead so what the fuck difference does it make?"

Michaela threw her a sharp look. "A little harsh, don't you think?"

"Sorry." Tessa sank deeper into the chair. "I'm not enjoying the hoopla."

"Our father just died; hoopla is required."

Suzanna swaggered up with a drink and a scowl. "I may just embrace the family legacy and become a drunk."

"Why?" Michaela retorted. "Out of Oxy?"

"Don't be a bitch, Michaela. I only indulge in Oxy when there's opportunity to enjoy the buzz. Suffice it to say, I'm drug-free at the moment." Suzanna plunked into the chair across from Tessa. "She just asked me for the tenth time if I'd thanked her lately."

"Yes, for 'giving you the perfect father,'" Michaela knew the thread. "I got that a few times myself today."

"She better not ask me," Tessa growled.

Both girls looked at her with surprise; Suzanna took the bait. "Are your teeth actually grinding?" Before Tessa could answer Suzanna squealed, "Oh my God, you found the box! Did you read *2002*?"

"What are you talking about?" Michaela had missed that particular conversation.

"The journals, Dad's journals. After that ridiculous wake with Duncan's homage and all the rest of that hearts and flowers bullshit, I figured Tessa could use a reality check. She'd never read any of his journals so it seemed the opportune time."

Michaela was genuinely horrified. "Jesus Christ, Suzanna, can't you even let your little sister grieve without pulling her down into your muck?"

"Have you read any of them, Mickie?"

"No, and I don't intend to. Sneaking into private journals after a man dies is pretty close to unconscionable in my book, but maybe that's just me."

"Don't be an ass. He wanted us to read them."

"Really? Who told you that?"

"He did! It's even on the cover page, read it! It says, 'I want my children to know me better than I knew my own father, these journals are my gift to them.' Or some bullshit like that."

"Why do I find that so hard to believe?" Michaela snapped.

"Because you're a denier. I can show you, for God's sake. Stop chasing the good daughter award for five fucking minutes and I'll show you."

10

Michaela picked up her tray and huffed off.

Suzanna looked at Tessa and rolled her eyes. When no reaction was forthcoming she put her drink down and took Tessa's hand. "Is this going to completely screw with your head?"

"What, Dad dying?"

"No, reading the journal."

"I don't know. It could, I guess. I hope not." A pause. "Probably."

"Then I'm sorry I suggested it."

"Yeah...me, too."

"Well, and Dad dying *is* a bit of a mind fuck."

They shared a rueful smile. Suzanna squeezed Tessa's hand as they both got up and walked into the fray.

FOUR

As funeral nights go, this one was apocalyptic.

After the buffet was depleted, speeches were made, and one last tearful sing-along to "I Did It My Way" came to a resounding crescendo, the friends, family, associates, husbands, wives, children, and priests made their protracted exodus. Once it was down to the six siblings, their mother, Audrey, and Aunt Joanne, Leo's younger sister (who had the distinction of being a bona fide nun, albeit a "non-habit forming" one, as Izzy had cutely pointed out in third grade), the façade came tumbling down.

Audrey, who'd imbibed as heartily as she'd wept, had, as Ronnie warned, gone into full-tilt meltdown, screaming through tears that she'd been abandoned by her husband, by her father (who'd fatally crashed into a tree shortly after Duncan's birth); by God Himself. Ronnie was practically unintelligible at this point, while Suzanna and Michaela maintained their ongoing snit about pretty much everything. Izzy, always a weeper, was sobbing, if less vociferously, along with her mother, and Duncan, exercising his newly ordained role as family spokesperson, offered redundant speeches about love, letting go, and the meaning of life, until Ronnie said something about puking all over everyone and Tessa almost did, having ultimately joined him at the bar. Ronnie's slurred vulgarity seemed to pry apart the tacit détente between various factions and all hell really did break loose.

"So you're just going to be a shit every day of your life, even the night of your father's funeral, is that it, Ronnie?" Michaela hissed.

"Hey, at least I'm keepin' it real instead of throwing bullshit on top of more bullshit. Which is more than I could ever say for you...or him."

"Oh, lovely, here we go. Which baseball game did he miss that's behind your tenth drink tonight...or that idiotic comment?" Michaela slammed a magazine hard on the coffee table.

Ronnie turned with some admiration. "Whoa, feisty, Mick."

Suzanna rose from the couch to pull a cigarette from her purse. "You know, Michaela, not everyone chooses to revise history as a general coping strategy."

"Don't you even *think* of lighting that thing," their mother barked, breaking from tears long enough to enforce house rules.

Suzanna sat back down with the cigarette dangling defiantly from her lips, but Ronnie waved off her interjection. "Thanks for the assist, Suze, but let me get this." He turned deliberately to Michaela. "Mickie, I love you like a sister, but you are one kiss-ass, brainwashed, daddy-damaged motherfucker."

This ignited an explosion of response, some more horrified than others, with Audrey shrieking about foul language, Michaela charging out of the room, and Duncan stepping up to defend his sister. Aunt Joanne broke through the din most successfully. "Jesus Christ, Ronnie, I know you're upset but –"

"Wow, Auntie, you just kinda swore right there," he grinned.

"Yes, fine, but let's please keep this civil. Everyone has their way of dealing with loss and there's no point in attacking each other when we could be offering solace of some kind." Aunt Joanne was a counselor at the St. Anselmo Catholic Center in Thousand Oaks, California, where she provided therapy and heartfelt facilitation to wayward nuns, frustrated students, and other Catholics in need. At the moment, she was a less-than-effective family interventionist. As

Audrey sobbed louder, carrying on that Leo's departure doomed the clan to imminent disintegration, Suzanna jumped back in.

"Auntie, let's get serious. How do we offer solace when no one really knows what we lost?"

"What does *that* mean?!" Audrey roared. "You lost your father, YOUR FATHER, for God's sake! If there ever was a saint on this bloody earth, it was that man. You should be on your knees thanking God for him and I will not sit here and listen to you ungrateful punks –"

"Oh, now we're punks?" A red cape trigger to Ronnie, the grin was gone. "You and Dad bitch-slapped us our whole lives but *we're* the punks?"

It was *on*.

Audrey started screaming that Ronnie was the Devil's kin and God had punished her by his birth; Izzy, a hard-as-nails lobbyist who could steamroll with the best of them was now blubbering into her mother's shoulder as if it was all beyond her (which it was). Aunt Joanne was stunned into silence, while Michaela went in and out of the kitchen, loudly gathering every dirty dish she could find. Suzanna continued to dangle her unlit cigarette from her lips, watching the battle like the tennis match it had become, and Tessa sat in shock as Ronnie shook his finger in Audrey's face, matching her decibels with, "What's the point of having so many kids if you have no fucking idea how to parent them?" To which Audrey shrieked, "Satan, Satan, Satan!" like a street corner madwoman.

Duncan finally roared from across the room, "ENOUGH! Dear God, everyone shut up and take a deep breath!" Oddly, they did. Clearly there was something to this spokesperson business. "We're all tired and sad and some of us have had too much to drink and this is *not* the time to analyze our family history."

"Oh, that's what this is, analysis?" Suzanna snorted.

Duncan shot her a look so fierce she actually shut up. He continued, "Look, we love each other, we loved Dad, and we've had a rough week. Let's leave it there for now. I'm going home to get some sleep and I advise everyone else to do the same. I love you, Mom, but you need to go to bed. Everyone else, good night!" He gave them each the "stern headmaster" look Tessa particularly hated, grabbed his camel trench and marched out.

Audrey stood dramatically and announced, "I, too, am off to bed. My heart is shattered and I hope I wake tomorrow to find my children back to their lovely, sweet selves." Wobbling, she took Izzy's arm and they slowly and precariously made their way up the stairs.

Ronnie yelled after them, "'Night, Iz, good talkin' to ya!" Izzy responded with a raised middle finger. He laughed. "She makes a good point, doesn't she?"

"Ronnie, you really are a royal pain in the butt." Suzanna sighed. "Please go up and go to bed; you definitely should not be out on the streets."

Ronnie tottered to his feet, smartly saluted his sister, and stumbled up the stairs. Michaela finished in the kitchen and, without a word, put on her coat and stormed out the front door, slamming it hard behind her. Suzanna collapsed across the couch and said, "Well, wasn't that a nice little party?"

Aunt Joanne gathered herself, clearly shell-shocked. "You are one rough bunch, that's for sure. I'm going to have to think some about all this, but I'd say there are some things here that really need talking about." She looked at Tessa, who had remained strangely silent throughout. "Tessa, you're here for the weekend?"

Tessa nodded.

"Let's be sure to talk before you go, all right?"

Tessa nodded again. Words continued to elude her.

Aunt Joanne looked around the old house, shook her head, and said, "Good night, girls," as she headed out the door.

Suzanna finally lit her cigarette.

FIVE

The stillness of creeping dawn was oppressive. Tessa lay in the twin bed of the basement spare room, the only bunking quarters that offered single occupancy, and felt as if she couldn't breathe quietly enough to keep pace with the silence. The last thing she wanted was to alert anyone she was awake, potentially triggering a sibling onslaught of some kind. This was not the time to talk and they were not who she wanted to talk to.

In the dim light she could make out the washer and dryer area with its long folding table and ironing board where she'd spent many an afternoon sorting laundry and ironing her father's shirts. The memory was oddly sweet – music blasting and Ronnie bouncing around the basement making her laugh. Some of it had been sweet; in fact, it had all started out fairly optimistically, this life of hers. How had she landed here, in this basement, on this night, in this state of confusion?

Tessa reached down to the floor and fumbled through her purse until her fingers landed on the 2002 journal. She'd read a few pages before bed but unable to keep her eyes open at the time, didn't get very far. Now, unable to sleep, she flicked the light back on to read.

March 4, 2002 – the journal of Leo Curzio:

When I think of our first three daughters, Michaela, Suzanna, and Teresa, I feel that in intelligence, beauty and talent, Teresa outstripped the others – personality, too. To paraphrase the Biblical parable of the servants and the talents, I think Teresa got many more gifts but rather than bury them, she squandered them. What a waste. But should I have expected more, given her general frivolousness and superficiality?

Simply put, Teresa has succumbed to the sin of sloth. It became easier to let others do things for her rather than struggle to do them herself. She really has little to show for her life, much less her artistic career – her current resume includes her high school credits, for God's sake! There'd be mortification in that if she were here in Chicago but as it is, she's somewhat out of sight, out of mind. To put it bluntly, she's made her own bed in a corrupt place and she must lie in it.

Somehow in the space of two paragraphs he'd insulted her sisters, handed her a compliment that was promptly slapped back, concluding with a humiliating devaluation of her life. So like him; economy of destruction.

Tessa was stunned by her father's clear lack of awareness of just who she was and how hard she worked for what she wanted. His religious zealotry, with its judgmental and unforgiving filter, seemed only to find her wanting – not young, not hopeful, not impetuous; just wanting. She wondered if he'd ever made note of her many accomplishments beyond that year: the plays that replaced that first naïve resume, the writing accolades, the bands, the good reviews. Had any of her hard-won success convinced him of anything redemptive or found its way onto his later pages?

Someone was rustling around upstairs and Tessa quickly curled under the covers as if to ward off detection. Even in silence they could somehow tell when one of them was up, a kind of psychic bugle that had often rallied the troops on post-fiasco mornings. Comforting in childhood, all she wanted now was solitude. Finally it quieted down and she relaxed again.

Laying in that rickety bed in the musty, familiar basement made her feel little again, as if the woman she'd become in the years since had regressed back to the anxious girl who'd so often hidden in this very place, desperate to find sanctuary from the sheer volume and intensity of a family that swirled in ways good and bad. They'd each made their mark: the siblings with their quirks and conflicts, their turbulent mother with her wild mood swings and propensity for rage, and certainly the enigma of her taciturn father loomed large at the moment.

There was a sudden creak at the stairs and Tessa was startled to see Izzy midway down. "God, Izzy, you scared the shit out of me!"

"Sorry, Tess; I was in the kitchen and saw the light on. I got worried about you. Are you all right?"

Tessa couldn't help but smile at her little sister's concern, particularly since she'd been the one crying all week. "I can't sleep, obviously. How are you doing?"

"Exhausted, cried out...and Mom's snoring. You want to talk?"

"Thanks, but I think I better try to get back to sleep. I have a feeling it's going to be another long day."

"Yeah...true." Izzy started up the stairs then turned back. "It's weird, isn't it, to think about not having a father anymore?"

Tessa gave her a sad smile. "It is." Izzy blew her a kiss and went up.

It *was* strange to think of him as dead. But it was even stranger, right now, to think of him as alive, sitting at his desk, his door shut to the noise and entreaties of his children, writing. Writing in his damn journal. She felt a flush of both rage and sorrow. Her father...her stupid, dead father.

Tessa reached back into her purse and found her cell phone. It was early on the west coast but she needed David. David Bowers: five years her senior, tall, handsome, capable; two years divorced, successful in business; her lover, friend, and the man she'd been living with for the past eight months in a relationship thankfully void of the Sturm und Drang so prevalent in those previous.

She pressed "2" and waited for his sleepy voice to answer. It always struck her as curious that David never attempted to sound convincingly awake when her calls pulled him from sleep, even in the afternoon when a stolen nap should hardly seem a thing of such depth. He'd mumble and sniff and act as though he could barely achieve consciousness, all while assuring her it was okay that she'd called. It always compelled the thought, "If you're really that asleep, why did you answer?" She almost hung up but, suddenly, there he was.

"Mmmm...hey, baby...how you doin'?" he whispered. Hearing his voice, warm and intimate, struck an internal chord. Tears flowed.

"I miss you."

"I miss you, too, sweetheart. How was the funeral?"

"Hideous. Sweet. Pathetic. My family."

"I'm sorry I'm not there...I should've been."

He should have been. But that was David, too. He loved her, he shared his house, his bed, his thoughts and dreams, but he sometimes didn't see a big enough picture. And this past week he hadn't seen that life could sometimes be asked to adjust for inconvenient death, and the seminar he had to conduct on the day of her father's funeral *could* have been rescheduled. It could have. He did, however, send her mother an expensive bouquet of lilies, a gesture that sent Audrey gushing; he paid for Tessa's flight, bought her a new black blazer, and sent condolence cards to each of her siblings. It helped. But still, he should have been there.

"It's...I understand," Tessa offered weakly. "I'm just really sort of – I don't know – lost."

"Isn't that to be expected? It takes time, sweetie, he just –"

"He wrote shitty things about me in his journal."

"What?" He suddenly sounded more awake.

"I found a journal. He basically said he didn't like me. He wrote all sorts of other shitty things about me too. And he left it there for me to find. There are boxes of journals. He probably wrote horrible stuff about all of us, but Suzanna found this one that's mostly about me. It's awful. He never told me one thing he felt about me my whole life but – "

"Wait, are you sure?" David was stunned.

"Am I sure about what?"

"Well, I don't know, that it's about you? That it wasn't just some random vent he didn't mean or forgot to erase?"

"No, he meant it. It was about me. It's lots of entries."

Silence. For too long.

"Okay, then," Tessa said, immediately annoyed at his lack of response. "I'm going to go."

"I'm sorry, Tessa, I just don't know what to say. Obviously it's awful, but I'm trying to think if there could be some sort of explanation that makes sense."

"There isn't. I already thought about that. He was just an asshole and died before I could tell him."

"Oh, come on, babe, you don't mean that. You're just sad and now this. There's got to be an explanation, I just gotta think that."

She was too tired to fight. Besides, David was always better in person than he was on the phone and she didn't need to be mad at anyone else right now. "Yeah, maybe. I love you, David. I want to come home...I hate it here."

"I love you, too. And you'll be home in a couple of days. I'll be there to pick you up and we'll go somewhere and just talk about it all, okay?"

"Okay." They would, too. They would talk and as wanting as he was on the phone, he would be perfect in person. She would hold on to that. As they hung up, Tessa knew she wouldn't be able to wait until Monday.

SIX

Walking into the dining room three hours later, Tessa felt as if even the day had a hangover. The typical early December sky, gray and heavy with clouds, had an unforgiving palette that accentuated the worn corners of the house. The sibs were crowded around the table eating a familiar Sunday breakfast of dry cereal and coffee cake and no one was talking. Ronnie slumped in a chair by the stove looking a shade of gray himself, wincing as Izzy snapped through the pages of the *Tribune* while sipping coffee and picking at streusel as if it were just a normal day. Michaela and Suzanna did their usual scurrying and mug filling, while Duncan shoveled Cheerios into his mouth, reading the back of the box as if it actually had something to say. Audrey was nowhere to be found and none of the extended family was present, which was just as well.

Everyone glanced up as Tessa entered the room. Nods were exchanged without comment or a break in the action, a morning-after ritual in a family for whom explosive nights-before were routine. Tessa set her suitcase near the front door and filled a bowl of cereal before a word was spoken.

It was Michaela who first took note of the suitcase. "I thought you weren't leaving until tomorrow," she said, hands on her hips as if even Tessa's schedule was an affront to the weekend's expectations.

"I was, but it turns out I have to get back. Some things came up at work that need my attention before Tuesday, and I won't have time if I wait to fly back tomorrow."

"I was under the assumption we were all going to participate in the family Mass for Mom this afternoon. This is, after all, a once in a lifetime thing, the death of a father. But, of course, if you can't work it out, I'm sure Mother will understand." Michaela went back to the dishes, her shoulders slack in defeat as she slammed another bowl in the sink.

With that, Duncan commenced. "All right, gang, let's talk." Activity shifted to attention. These post-apocalyptic speeches, particularly from Duncan, were also part of the family ritual. "I came over this morning when I could be spending the day with my family, and asked Mickie and Suze to do the same, because we need to clear some things up. It got really ugly last night and I do not want to remember my father's funeral as yet another family debacle. We've had far too many of those over the years and, frankly, I'm tired of it." He stood up, put his bowl in the sink, consciously creating dramatic pause. No one bothered to fill the gap. "We're all on the same side, that's the main thing. But there's been a lot of sniping at each other and talk about Dad and these journals, and I feel like we've all gotten a bit off-message. I'm not sure I fully get what's going on, but I think we should try to conclude it before we go our separate ways."

Dead silence. A beat, then Izzy looked around with a perplexed frown. "Okay, I'll ask, since I seem to be the only one left out of this family secret: what journals?"

Exasperated, Suzanna couldn't contain herself, "Oh, baby, do you really not know? We've only been talking about them for years but you really know nothing about them? How is that possible?"

Before Izzy could respond, Michaela pulled up a chair, and, like the good teacher she was, educated her little sister. "Dad wrote journals, Izzy. He wrote them his whole adult life, from before he met Mom until the day he died. There are boxes of them somewhere, Mom won't tell me where, but there were some upstairs under the bed for some reason, and Tessa read one of them yesterday. I guess he said some nasty things about her – I don't know why – but sometimes people say things they don't mean and I don't think Dad would ever say anything nasty about any of us unless he was just mad and blowing off steam. So people are upset and that's understandable, but I think we should all move on, mourn our father, and try to hold on to the good memories." She kept her attention fixed on Izzy throughout her speech.

Duncan looked at Tessa. "Did you read the whole journal?"

"Just the beginning of it."

"Was it that bad?"

"Pretty bad."

Izzy was authentically shocked. "I can't believe he would do that! What did he say about you, Tessa?"

"How he didn't like me much, how I'm a failure, how lazy and useless I am, stuff like that. I only read a little bit and, to be honest, I don't really want to talk about it right now. Suffice it to say, I feel sucker punched." Izzy reached out and squeezed Tessa's hand.

Michaela jumped back in. "Well, it *was* a journal from over a decade ago, so odds are he had nicer things to say about you since then. I just think we're making too big a deal out of it. We all know Dad wasn't perfect, but didn't we say in the last couple of days how important it was to let go of the past and just love him for who he was? That's all I'm suggesting. He wrote some journals; it sounds like he might have used them as sounding boards for his frustration about us kids – some of us are parents, we should understand that! I just don't think it's that big a deal."

"Have you read any of them, Mickie?" Duncan, ever the lawyer, kept digging.

"No, I haven't. I never felt comfortable going into his private things."

Suzanna sighed deeply. "I think we already covered that, Michaela. He wanted us to read them. *Believe* me."

Duncan noted the emphasis. "Why do you say it like that?"

Suzanna shifted her position, relishing the opportunity for center stage. "Two days before he died he asked me to help him go through his old novels and articles and all that crap he's had down in the basement for a thousand years. He wanted to make a list of what he had because he was thinking about submitting some things for publication. While we were going through all his stuff, I found a big box with about, I don't know, about twelve years of his journals, asked what he wanted to do with them, and he said to put them in the storage locker with the rest of them. I didn't even know he had a storage locker but he said Mom had the key, which, it turns out, she couldn't find, so we ended up putting that box under the bed. Anyway, he asked me that day if I'd ever read any of them and I said no, of course not, thinking that's what he wanted to hear, but it actually seemed to annoy him. He made a big deal about how he meant for us to read them, about how he wrote them for us, how he wanted us to know him better than he knew his father, blah, blah, blah. So I said, okay, fine, I'm sure we'll all read them at some point. Then he did this weird thing. He rubbed his hands together like some sort of evil villain and got this snide little grin on his face and said, 'And I'd like to be a fly on the wall when you kids *do* read them.' It actually kind of creeped me out."

"Oh, for God's sake!" Michaela rolled her eyes.

Suzanna continued, ignoring the interruption: "I took a few of the journals home with me that night and read them. Most of it was dry and really boring: inane details about the politics at his job, Catholic crap, some really amateurish reviews of books he'd read, that sort of thing. Dad was not a great writer; I think we all know that. But there was also a lot of personal stuff about some of us, too. In the ones I read the really shitty, insulting stuff was particularly about Ronnie, Tessa, and me. Not sure how anyone else would feel about it, maybe it is no big deal, as Michaela insists, but I think it was unbelievably cruel for him to leave those for us to read."

Izzy was incredulous. "Why would he do that? It's just...sadistic."

"Who knows?" Michaela responded dismissively. "Maybe he didn't even remember half the stuff he wrote." She got up and started clearing the table.

"Think again," Suzanna shot back. "He told me he transcribed each of the handwritten journals when he got his computer three years ago and after transcribing them all by year, typed up a condensed version of the entire lot. He knew *exactly* what was in them."

Even Duncan appeared stunned. Izzy kept shaking her head. "Why would he *do* that? Why?"

"He was an asshole, sweetheart!" Suzanna retorted.

Duncan snapped back into character. "Come on, Suze, let's not get into all that again. It might be more useful if we try to frame this in some way that allows us to deal with it and move on, like Mickie says." Duncan was now perched on a kitchen stool affecting a sort of professorial mien that annoyed the crap out of Tessa. She could sense something patronizing about to bubble up from under his controlled demeanor and there was no part of her that could stomach that right now. But too tired to move quickly, she decided to wait for his magnanimous statement about forgiveness or whatever it was going to be and then make her exit. He didn't disappoint.

"I think basically we have two choices. We can dredge it all up and read the journals, get ourselves deeper into the dark side of this family. Or we can simply realize this was a flawed human being probably working off an ego concept of himself that played out in those pages, none of it the total of who he was or what he felt. We know he loved us all and that should be the sustaining fact."

"You know, Duncan, that's not as easy for those of us who were the brunt of his criticism," Tessa countered tersely.

"Tessa, all I'm saying is we can't judge a man's entire life by one or two lines from an old journal. For all we know the rest of them are filled with accolades. None of us have read them all, so I'm just saying let's give him the benefit of the doubt."

"I read them all." Ronnie had been silent throughout the entire conversation; now everyone turned to him as if he just rose from the dead.

Michaela rolled her eyes again. "When did you read them, Ronnie? No one even knows where they are."

"They're in a locker at the E-Z Storage near his old office building."

"Oh, and you've been there?" Michaela was certain only she had the inside angle on all Curzio family secrets.

"Yep. He asked me to take some boxes over there a year or so ago, had Mom give me the key. He actually mentioned that the journals were there, told me I could read them if I wanted to, but I didn't at the time. Then about two months later I realized I still had the key so one day I went down and got them all, spent a long weekend reading. Over fifty books, and the transcriptions, *and* the Readers' Digest versions. All of it. *1965,* I think, to *2000* or so was in the locker. The more current stuff was in that box he had you put under the bed, Suze. I read all of that too."

Each of the siblings with their individual issues, their very particular feelings and attitudes, sat there trying to figure out what should be the next question and who should ask it. Duncan, of course. "And what are your feelings? I mean, overall?"

Ronnie slowly got up, hunched as though the weight of the week had finally worn him down. "Overall? Totally fucked. I think any guy who would spend his time writing shitty things about his kids instead of just being with them and figuring out who they really are is a true dick in my book. The rest of you will have to decide for yourself. Except for the one upstairs, I put the boxes back and gave the key to Mom. Presuming she hasn't moved them, they're all still there. Have at it, kids." He looked at Tessa. "If you want a ride to the airport, I'm headed out that way...be happy to take you."

Tessa's rescheduled flight wasn't until five that evening but the thought of sitting around further dissecting the week, the journals, and the meaning of family seemed far more tortuous than a long afternoon at O'Hare. "That would be great. Just let me run up and say goodbye to Mom." She looked around at her battered siblings. "You guys, let's just...let's just try to get on with it. I'll be fine. I'm sorry I can't stay for the Mass, Mickie, but I really can't. You and Suzanna did an amazing job this week and, honestly, I can't thank you enough for all the hard work. I love you all and maybe next time we see each other it'll be more...fun. Hope everyone has a great Christmas." She offered a wan smile and turned to go upstairs.

Duncan put on his coat. Izzy went back to the paper. Michaela and Suzanna cleaned up the breakfast table. Normal.

SEVEN

By the time Tessa got upstairs Ronnie was already seated at Audrey's bedside. The gray morning glare could find no welcome through the heavy brocade drapes and the smell of stale perfume permeated the room. Tessa was struck by the state of her mother. Audrey's face was mottled and swollen, the result of too much alcohol, too little sleep, and a night of unmitigated agony. This was a woman for whom any change was problematic; losing Leo was likely unfathomable.

Audrey was curled toward Ronnie in a fetal position, her head touching his knee, her hand in his. Somehow the bitter rage of last night was lost in the tenderness of their rapprochement, a familiar epilogue but one Tessa never quite understood. These two people who exhibited such anger toward each other also shared a private attachment that was inexplicable to anyone else. As Ronnie mumbled genuine consolations, Audrey sobbed softly, grateful for reminders of his love.

Tessa felt like an intruder. When Audrey finally noticed and reached out to invite her to the bed, she awkwardly joined them. Once in that grief huddle, though, Tessa felt a moment of something true and heartfelt. Hard to believe this fragile, broken woman was the same one who terrorized so much of her childhood. Forgiveness seemed moot.

"You know I love you both, more than I could ever say," Audrey whispered fiercely. "I don't know what I would do without you. I'm sorry I got so angry last night; it's been a horrible week and I don't know how to…" She crumbled again and Ronnie and Tessa looked at each other, powerless to offer solace when none was possible.

"You just have to give yourself time," Tessa floundered. "It's going to…take time, that's all. You can't expect to know how to feel when it's only been a week."

"How could he leave me? How could he *leave* me?" Audrey whispered, as if that question made sense or there was any answer for it.

"Mom, you've got everyone here to rely on and I'll call as much as I can. We'll all get through this, I promise." Tessa couldn't believe the nonsense she was spouting. She had no idea if any of them would get through anything.

Ronnie patted Audrey's hand, adding, "And you've got Christmas in Rome to think about; if nothing else, that's a good distraction." He stood up as though his body could no longer tolerate being there. Tessa felt the same thick impulse to leave. Audrey's grief was heavy and palpable and given her pathological dependence and strange inability to traverse her life without the guiding hand of someone, anyone, to whom she could cede authority, it was impossible to imagine her doing widowhood well. Tessa sensed the weight of this would fall disproportionately on Michaela. The guilt made her want to get on a plane and fly away.

"Mom, I've actually got to get going and Ronnie's taking me to the airport." She extricated herself from Audrey's grasp, leaned in to kiss her mother's red, swollen cheek and as she did, Audrey turned with fiery eyes and grabbed her daughter's face.

"You know your father loved you. Don't you ever forget that."

Tessa smiled tightly, squeezed her mother's shoulder and left, painfully aware that the era in which she had a father and believed he loved her was categorically over.

EIGHT

It was a bleak ride to the airport. Cold, drizzling rain had begun to fall and both Tessa and Ronnie stared out the windows as if every last word had finally deserted them. She fought the urge to ask him more about the journals, about himself, about what he was feeling, his forcefully averted eyes signaling an unwillingness to engage. At some point she leaned over to turn on the radio, something jazzy and noncommittal and, as she sat back, glanced in Ronnie's direction. He was a study in gloom: unshaven face; dark, weary eyes, unkempt hair and a wrinkled shirt stretched tight over his growing belly. She wondered which exact set of demons had led him to this place.

He had been the chubby-cheeked, bubbly baby who enchanted everyone with his indefatigable enthusiasm for everything from anthills to Thomas the Tank Engine. He talked to birds, snuggled freely, and was profoundly convinced of his own lovability. Later a natural athlete who excelled in baseball, he easily won friends, both male and female, and, though only an average student, found school to be the place where he defined his personality, in stark contrast to home where he was relegated to the role of Duncan's younger brother.

Although Audrey doted on him as *her* boy (Duncan being Leo's), Ronnie's inevitable departure from babyhood gave her pause. Infant Ronnie, with his soft skin and appealing sense of need and compliance, brought out the best in Audrey, her nurturing, gentle, attentive self. The angry toddler, the belligerent boy; the snarling adolescent sent her into spasms of anxiety. By the time he'd transformed into a frustrating teen who brushed off her affections and, later, the complicated man who challenged them, they'd both lost their footing with each other.

To Leo, Ronnie was simply a pale comparison to the gold standard of his firstborn. There was something competitive and demeaning in the way he set them upon each other, a contest Ronnie could never win and from which he'd never be free. Even when he became a starter on the varsity baseball team, Ronnie would seldom see his father in the bleachers. Leo simply preferred Duncan's debates and mock trial competitions, which any scheduling conflict made clear. Leo brushed aside Ronnie's hurt with: "It's not personal, just a matter of preference. I see no point in sitting in the stands waiting for you to catch a ball when I could actually learn something at your brother's event." It never dawned on Leo that there was something to learn in watching his younger son struggle to be a good team player or master a skill with his coach's encouragement.

Ronnie incurred further disdain from his father when he decided to marry his high school sweetheart shortly after his twenty-first birthday. "I mistakenly presumed you'd have more ambition than to tie yourself to an unremarkable girl, no doubt followed by the demands of fatherhood, all before you even know who you are," Leo declared the night Ronnie announced his impending nuptials. The fact that Leo was married at an age not much older was given no relevance in the heated discussion that followed.

Wendy Driscoll, the "unremarkable" bride, was a solid Midwestern beauty whose plans for college as a graphic design major were deferred when her father died shortly after graduation and money became scarce. Given the need to regroup, she saw the decision to marry Ronnie as a sensible one. She loved him, after all, and they could work together in the computer store he'd opened, her graphic design business a logical ancillary. Audrey thought their collaboration was a sweet idea, but Leo was disgusted that his son would eschew college for a bluish-collar job. "Well," the ever-contrarian Suzanna had pointed out, "computers and graphics fall more into white-collar territory, Pops, so you might just be barking up the wrong collar!" Leo told her to mind her own business. But over time and many family gatherings, Wendy was ultimately accepted as a beloved member, mostly because her warmth and humor seemed to enliven Ronnie in ways little else did. His father's disinterest paled next to the empowerment of Wendy's love and, for a while, he was good.

Then Wendy left him. No one was really sure why.

"I hate to gossip, but I ran into a couple of his baseball buddies and they implied there were stadium groupies Ronnie got to know a little too well," Michaela whispered in a late-night call to Tessa.

Izzy had warmed to Wendy perhaps less than the others and her take was a bit more aggressive. "She just said a few things that sounded suspicious to me. Kept referring to the fact that they were having issues and stuff but was very evasive...my guess is there was another guy."

"He's a fucking alcoholic," Suzanna declared. "I love him but who wants to live with a drunk?"

Audrey suspected procreation timing. "I know that girl wants to be a mama and I don't think she understands that Ronnie just isn't ready!"

"Maybe if he spent more time with his wife and less playing ball with overgrown boys he'd still be married," Leo tersely suggested.

But Duncan's take was probably closest to accurate: "Look, her business was doing well and his was failing...nothing kills a marriage faster than money and ego."

It seems when Wendy branched out with her own office and a small staff at the same time Ronnie was forced into Chapter 11, things took a turn that never quite readjusted. Instead of framing her success as an opportunity to keep a roof over their heads while he reinvented himself, he became bitter. As his last few clients dwindled to none, she talked about college as a way to improve her viability in the business world. When one night he found her application on the counter after a particularly trying day capped by too many beers and a burgeoning sense of despair, he put his fist through the wall very near where her head had been leaning at the time. She moved out the next day and they were divorced within eight months.

That was three years ago and Ronnie had never recovered. They split the proceeds of the house, which kept him going until he found a job, and now he was working as a computer tech with Computer Fix-It, an on-call repair company not far from where he lived. At thirty-four, he considered himself over. At least that's what he told anyone within earshot at whatever pub he was patronizing at the time.

But Tessa loved Ronnie fiercely. They'd been deeply attached throughout their childhoods and, though rarely together as adults, there remained a bond between them that not alcohol, failure, distance, or divorce could destroy.

"Thanks for the ride, by the way. I really could have taken a cab," she finally interjected.

"No problem."

She looked out at the bumper-to-bumper traffic. "I guess a Sunday to O'Hare wasn't the best idea."

"Tessa, it's fine, I offered."

She finally turned to him. "Ronnie, talk to me. Tell me what's going on. I feel like you're dying of something but I don't know what."

There was a long pause as he mulled. "It's just life, I guess. I'm dying of life. Pretty much sucks in…I dunno…every way."

"Is it work?"

"That's part of it. It's not exactly what I thought I'd be doing at this point in my life."

"I know – "

"I thought I'd be married, maybe a kid or two, building my business, planning a trip to Hawaii with my wife, whatever. I *had* a fucking plan; turns out she had a different one."

Tessa and Ronnie had talked often during the divorce proceedings, but after a while the calls grew fewer and farther between until they stopped altogether. Now she was lucky if she heard from him every few months, which had led her to believe he'd safely traversed the loss. Seeing him this past week for the first time in almost a year informed her otherwise.

"I know it sucks right now but, Ronnie, you *will* find someone again. I really believe that."

"Shut the fuck up, Tessa. You're talking out of your ass. You have no idea if I'll *ever* find someone as good as that girl. Ever. I'm not even interested in looking." A pause, then Ronnie glanced over, chagrined. "Sorry…that was fucked up."

"I'm winging it here, Ronnie. I actually have no idea what to say to you."

"Good, 'cause I don't wanna talk about me, okay? What about you? Ready to talk *2002* yet?"

"Did you really read all the journals?"

"Yeah, brutal."

"Really? Why? What else does he say?"

"I can't boil almost fifty years down to a conversation. He said lots of shit. Bullshit. Boring shit. Inane shit. I don't know. He liked the sound of his own mind, I guess. He was a weird guy."

"But let me at least ask you this – at any point in the years between 2002 and now, did he ever say anything positive about me? Did I ever get redeemed? Ever?"

He glanced over with a sheepish grin. "Okay, I did read them but *skimmed* might be a more accurate word. After getting through the first few years I realized how mind-numbing most of it was so I started speed-reading. Man, the guy was hung up on the most bizarre crap. Like keeping a running chart of how much gas his car used on every single trip or which coffee shops had the most evenly toasted bread. Oh, yeah, and at the beginning of every year he'd do this thumbnail analysis of each person in the family; a lot of that was pretty heinous. But nothing very deep and not really much about him. I remembered thinking that was weird – that he said he wanted us to know him better but he hardly ever wrote about himself. Unless you think his book reviews or his lectures on the power of Catholic dogma are the window to his soul."

"They probably are. The fact that he spent most of his time writing about dogma instead of relating to us is pretty revealing, don't you think?"

"Yeah, probably. Anyway, my point is, I remember reading stuff about all of us but mostly I was scanning for sections where my name popped up. Sorry." Then he smiled; she looked over sharply.

"What?"

"I do remember this one thing about you."

"What?" She felt a wave of anxiety.

"He got into this whole thing about when you got fat in high school. Said something about what a shame it was that you – wait, how did he put it? 'Squandered your good looks for the lure of a Snickers bar.' That might be a quote. I remembered it because I thought it was pretty fuckin' funny…or at least one of his better lines."

She'd had a rough junior year. The novelty of being the new girl her sophomore year, after transferring from the all-girls Catholic school where she'd been consigned as a freshman, had worn off. The boy she'd loved that summer had left for college, no new boys were on the horizon, and all her girlfriends were going steady. There was just something about eleventh grade that summoned her self-loathing and she responded by digging deeper into the bag of mini-bites, chunking up considerably by second semester, which, of course, did little to ameliorate her sullen state of mind. It was a brief foray, thankfully cut short by the swimsuit demands of approaching summer, an undefined hormonal shift, and the perking of spirits brought on by a certain dark-eyed poet in her English Lit class. That her father made note of this anomalous phase was telling.

"Actually, I don't find it funny. I find it unforgivable."

"Really? Then wait till you finish *2002*. You'll be looking for a stake to drive through his heart."

"God, is it that bad? Should I even finish reading it?"

"I don't know, Tess. Depends on whether your need to know is greater than your sense of self-preservation. I'm not sure I'm a better man for reading them. In fact, I know I'm not. It kicked my ass, knowing what a loser he thought I was."

O'Hare was finally in their sights. As Ronnie pulled over to the curb, Tessa felt suddenly empty, as if nothing was ever going to be the same. In fact, she was pretty convinced it wasn't. She leaned over and gave her mournful little brother a kiss on the cheek. "Ronnie, you're not a loser. You never were. He was cruel to make you think so."

"Yeah, well, have you seen me lately?" He smiled woefully.

"You're just going through a rough patch. Things will change, they always do. Call me, okay?"

"Yeah. And you call me. You might need to if you actually read that thing." Tessa rolled her eyes and got out. He leaned over as she stepped to the curb. "And don't worry about me, Tessa, I'll be okay."

She smiled, pretending she believed him. They didn't bother with "Merry Christmas."

NINE

It was somewhere over Nebraska, and after she'd plowed through both a *People* magazine and two bags of pretzels, that Tessa realized she'd gone at least an hour without thinking about her family. Then she reached into her purse and found a handkerchief scented with her mother's perfume and wondered when the addled Audrey had found opportunity to deposit that reminder. Her mother had always preferred handkerchiefs; Tessa found the idea of snot-filled fabric wadded into purse crannies to be supremely unsavory. But the embroidered cloth made her smile and, now, staring out over the clouded horizon, she thought about her mother, the searing center around which all things Curzio orbited.

In retrospect, it seemed Tessa's entire life had been spent adjusting to her mother's states of being, which could swing from schoolgirlish glee to raging hysteria in a split second, polarity that made her both dangerous and appealing. Audrey's clear narcissism was built on the notion that she'd come "from good stock," the self-described "princess-child" of a British doctor and his much younger and reportedly quite beautiful Swedish secretary (for whom he'd abandoned his first, always unmentioned, wife). This decadent if romantic legacy revealed by drunken disclosure some time after her mother's untimely death, convinced Audrey that, for beautiful women, good fortune needn't require great effort. Fancying herself a stylish if unconventional Midwestern maven, she'd made quite the splash with festive potlucks and progressive dinner parties that were the talk of the neighborhood, but the poise she exhibited socially was only a façade for her more anguished internal self. Tessa could close her eyes and conjure up any number of scenarios illustrative of her mother's duality, perspective gained on those rare days when she'd watched from the sidelines:

Audrey, dressed to the nines, makeup etched in place, stood framed in the doorway with a dishtowel thrown artfully over her shoulder. "Kids! Let's go, round 'em up, move 'em out, dinner is served," she'd holler across the street in the direction of whichever Curzio children needed wrangling.

"OK, Mom," a distant voice would answer.

Audrey's eyes would then sweep the neighborhood; back arched, hair tossed in the evening breeze, flinging salutations to passersby like so many bon mots. "Stella, that child is just too precious. When are you going to let me babysit? Oh say, Ruth, I'm not going to be able to head up the bake sale after all; Leo's got guests coming and I'll be a slave to the stove. Hey there, Dan, I hope you remembered Mary's favorite flowers this time!"

And while all this obsequious chattering was going on, she'd bounce between checking her watch and trolling the area where her non-compliant children might be, a slow burn of anger building behind her smiling face. Minutes would tick by until, in a snap of fury, all sweetness would exit and she'd scream loud enough to scatter the neighbors. "You goddamn brats better get your asses over here and cleaned up for dinner or there's gonna be blood. I'm counting the minutes and if I have to get off this porch you better hope to God I don't have a belt in my hand 'cause I'm in no mood for nice!" And the errant Curzios would come flying from every corner, clear in their goal to preempt assault.

There were countless variations to this theme but the trajectory was always the same: sunny days descending into terrified nights as everyone hid from her rage and its weaponry: belts, sticks, hairbrushes, thrown books and silverware; whatever was close at hand. It was not unusual for these events to conclude with bloody noses, bruised behinds, split lips or other collateral damage. It was a battlefield brought on, Audrey once asserted, "because you kids do bad things."

This behavior would have been wholly intolerable to her bright and sensitive children had her recovery not been swift but, once calmed, she could delight those same children with her sharp imagination and passionate – if overweening – love. A bipolar diagnosis might have been likely had she ever sought help, but even the suggestion of therapy – once made by well-meaning but clearly miscalculating neighbors – was dismissed by Leo with a terse, "Thank you, but we rely on faith and prayer rather than secular experiments." When faith and prayer left her wanting, Audrey turned to the very secular experiment of pills and drink. Those neighbors never even said "hello" after that.

Tessa loved and hated her mother with the confused loyalty of a battered child. She also wondered why her father didn't intervene to save them from her. He could walk into a room when Audrey was on a tear and disappear into his office without a word. The children felt his abdication as sharply as their mother's hand but there was no recourse and no explanation. Even as an adult, Tessa made a point of avoiding deep analysis of either her mother's rage or her father's passivity. Now it seemed unavoidable.

There was a jolt of turbulence and Tessa was pulled back to the loud, jostling present of a crowded plane on its way to Los Angeles. After alerting the flight attendant that she desperately needed both water and another bag of pretzels (regretting an earlier decision to forego the overpriced ham and cheese from Starbucks), she leaned her seat back and closed her eyes, convinced sleep was a viable option. When that proved otherwise, and noting the line to the lavatory was mercifully short, Tessa clamored across the occupants of seats B and C to make her way down the aisle. After a brief wait, the door swung open to a boy who looked to be about ten; he glanced her way as he shuffled past and uttered, "It smells like poop in there but it wasn't me."

She mumbled, "thanks," for some reason.

Once inside she discovered he was definitely odor-accurate, but her business was quick and it was only as she washed her hands that she looked in the mirror and took pause, wondering if her looks had somehow shifted with her worldview. What she saw was a reasonably pretty, deeply exhausted face, good eyes (albeit slightly red), and curly brown hair that hung straggly at the moment but had runway swing with just the right blow dry. Wrinkles had crept up at the edges of those good eyes and her frown lines were more pronounced lately (Duncan's wife suggested Botox; Tessa figured she'd just smile less). The body – what little of it she could see in the tiny mirror – was average, probably a little thinner after a week of Curzio madness, and since that was always the goal – thinner – she couldn't help but think Leo would be pleased. He'd once remarked that "a fat woman is like a cold-water dip"; Audrey, fighting extra poundage at the time, slapped his arm in a flash of real anger. He insisted he was kidding but Tessa didn't think so.

And, not unexpectedly, her brothers inherited Leo's thin bias. They never failed to make note as Tessa and her sisters, with their round Mediterranean bodies, struggled with yo-yoing shapes and sizes over the years. But other than the remarked-upon chubby stint during junior year, Tessa had been vigilant. The admiring glances when she walked into a room offered some assurance that she'd kept trim enough for cultural approval and, at thirty-six, could still be considered a babe in some quarters: last-call tables at the local pub, her gym with its preponderance of older Russian men, and at home, where David adored everything about her. Everywhere else she was probably an *aging* beauty, emphasis that left her wondering where she'd be in ten more years. David's hints at marriage occasionally sounded like sanctuary.

Okay, enough, she snapped to herself. She straightened her black skirt, buttoned her denim jacket, opened the door, and took her average, straggly-haired, slightly wrinkled self back to 31A. As she passed the boy who'd made earlier comment, she realized she hadn't mentioned the lavatory bouquet to the next person in line. Whatever. They could think of her what they would.

TEN

Sade crooned about ordinary love as a bottle of Chardonnay left its ring on the floor where they'd just made some, though surely better than ordinary. As always, David had taken his time, some moments tender, others hard and colliding, all combined to make Tessa feel precious and hot and wanted. It was only momentary balm from the chattering in her head, but David's touch was meaningful enough to bring back at least some of the wholeness of spirit she'd felt before the trip. She lay tucked in his arms on the thick chenille rug as they talked about it all: the funeral, Leo, Audrey, Ronnie...the journals.

David was genuinely perplexed. "I can't believe Leo really felt those things. I talked to the man, several times. He loved you, I could hear it in his voice; in the things he'd say. Maybe 2002 was just a really bad year."

"Are you apologizing for him?" Tessa twisted around to look at his face.

"Of course not; I think what he did was terrible. It makes me sick for you. I mean, who wants to read stuff like that coming from your father? I'm just having a hard time believing it."

"Would you like me to read some of it to you? You might find it persuasive."

"Uh...yeah, sure, I mean, if you feel like – "

Tessa leapt up, grabbed her purse, pulled out *2002*, and perched naked on the edge of the couch. David sat up and wrapped the blanket around him in a mix of dread and anticipation as Tessa fumbled toward a page.

"Okay, here, listen to this; I found this entry unbelievable: *'Somewhere in her teen years she learned that people – men particularly – will do things for her to get her favor. Guys would buy her gifts. Take her to the best restaurants. Movies. Theater. The telephone rang for her constantly, usually boys. In fact, Teresa had very few girlfriends.'"* Tessa looked up at David. "Can you believe that? I had *zillions* of girlfriends!"

"Yeah, that's a little weird – "

"*'Maybe there was too much parity for her with girls – she was mostly with boys.'* Too much parity? What does that even mean?"

"I think it means –"

"I know what parity means; what does he mean by the comment? It makes no sense. Okay, then it gets worse. *'Nothing's changed since then with her. Her trip home last Christmas was financed generously and lavishly by Trevor, who seems like a nice enough guy. I have nothing against him except that he lets Teresa fleece him – he knows it and strikes me as sharp enough to expect repayment. I have no idea if this relationship has any merit, it's hard to tell at this point and Teresa's track record with men is not impressive. It seems her recent attachment to Scientology – a pseudo-intellectualism that presents itself as a church simply for tax purposes – holds her to it. She claims she's learning how to make things go right, apparently one of the pop-tenets of the group, and intends to stick it out with this guy until the end. Personally, I'm wondering if he'll stick it out with her!'"* Tessa put the journal down and looked at David expectantly.

"Wow," he offered. "That's…"

"Stunning, right? Few girlfriends? Fleecing? Even the Scientology stuff! Unbelievable! I mean, talk about deflection!"

"Who's Trevor?"

She cocked her head. "*That's* your question?"

"I just never heard you talk about a guy named Trevor."

"I'm struck by the fact that you're less interested in my

character assassination than some asshole ex-boyfriend."

"Well, he must've been significant if you brought him home for Christmas and your dad wrote about him in a journal. "

She sat still for a moment then shoved the journal back in her purse... with feeling.

David took note. "I'm sorry. I'm just a little surprised, that's all. Not really sure how I warranted getting the lowdown on Scientology our first month in but nothing about this Trevor guy. I thought we knew about all of each other's past significants."

She got up and pulled on her shirt; nakedness suddenly felt naked. "I get it, David, it *is* weird. But now I'm tired and need a shower."

"Come on, Tess, don't be mad at me! You know I'm not good at this stuff. "

"I'm not mad, David. You're right, I should have told you about Trevor; he *was* significant. We'll talk about it later. I promise."

At two o'clock that morning they did.

ELEVEN

Trevor's significance had less to do with being an ex than being the person who ushered violence back into Tessa's life. Long after she'd left home and Audrey's rages there it was again: corporal punishment, the gift that keeps on giving.

After an unbroken series of bad boyfriends in the years leading up to her departure from Illinois, Tessa made a personal pact to never again commit to a relationship without clear conviction of the other's ability to do the same. As an addendum to that pact – and in a nod to her newly acquired affiliation with the Church of Scientology and its mantra of "make it go right" – Tessa declared, as her father noted, her own promise to make her next relationship "go right" regardless of issues, petty or otherwise, that may arise. Trevor White was not only capable of commitment, he was the sort of male who exuded an emotional gravitas that made Tessa all the more determined to sustain her promise. No matter what.

They met at a West Hollywood bar, one of those places with velvet ropes and a hot rep that months later was being hawked for catered affairs. Trevor, a successful medical supplies salesman, was a good-looking British ex-pat with an ability to be both consummate gentleman and rugged corner-boy. His classic approach – clever, witty, with her drink presciently in hand – was impossible to resist, particularly for an eager, open-hearted twenty-five-year-old ready for EXPERIENCE (in all caps). Within months they were living together in what would be a yearlong relationship. Significant.

Ironic that Leo would speak so warmly of Trevor. Most men found him pompous and off-putting. He was that guy who said things like, "Never ask a man what he does for a living. That's a private and unappreciated question," which ran counter to every conversation Tessa had ever had with a guy. He was several years older, as he so often reminded her, and she was quick to defer to his depth of experience. He did fulfill the early-relationship wining-and-dining requisite, which was lovely for a Midwestern girl from a financially strapped family, but despite her father's mischaracterization of her as a fleecer, Tessa was always insistent that they share expenses equally, something Trevor allowed and ultimately grew to expect, despite his considerably heftier income. Their compatibility as lovers and roommates was initially undeniable, and she embarked with a giddy sense of anticipation that he might be important.

Then he hit her and became important for all the wrong reasons.

They had made love. She was sitting on the edge of the bed talking about a movie she'd seen and why she liked the lead actor, when he suddenly slapped her across the face so hard she tumbled to the floor. Stunned speechless, she could only stare in horror at this man who, moments earlier, had been declaring his love and was now screaming about her "wanting to fuck every asshole in Hollywood." The twisted face and irrational diatribe were so reminiscent of Audrey's cyclical rages that beyond the pain of impact, Tessa was overwhelmed by a sense of familiar dread. That Trevor was disturbed became evident; what was not so clear was *how* disturbed, the mystery of which proved portentous.

Tessa wanted to believe the best of him, as she did with most people, as she did with Audrey, and after his tearful pleadings for forgiveness and promises to "never again do such a thing," she continued the relationship, naïvely convinced he would keep those promises.

But once initiated, like a horrible cat let out of its bag, violence moved in. It became hard to predict what would set Trevor off or how far he would go. Tessa regularly asked herself why she didn't just pack up and move out. It wasn't that she believed herself worthy of such abuse, it wasn't that she considered his jealousies evidence of love; it wasn't even that she had some syndrome that wouldn't let her out the door. It was three things:

1. As a good and compliant Scientologist she believed anyone could shed bad behaviors with desire and the teachings of L. Ron Hubbard.
2. She continued to believe in her obligation to "make it go right."
3. Her many years of enduring Audrey's violence had simply left her with a high forgiveness point.

She hated it, she wanted it to stop, she would demand that Trevor get help; she stood up for herself, said what needed to be said after the storm had passed, did everything in her power to avoid inciting it, but more than anything else, it was FAMILIAR. It wasn't the worst thing in the world. It was what families did to each other. It was just anger expressing itself in the physical realm. It was a part of life. It was the way couples fought. And so on and so he said. And just as she'd loved her mother despite Audrey's viciousness, so she loved Trevor. Until the last time.

Tessa had finally signed with a manager after almost a year of acting showcases and, as a matter of procedure, that manager, Stu Feldman, insisted on meeting the significant others of all his clients to make sure of several things: that everyone was onboard with the program, that there were no hidden agendas between his clients and their others, and, most importantly, that there were no issues between their others and him. "Can't do my job in that case," he told her.

She worried about him coming to their house, not sure which side of Trevor would show up when the time came. She'd learned after years of practice with Audrey that you could tell by the eyes which "person" was present at a given moment. With Audrey, there was an almost imperceptible tightening of the eyebrows, a puffiness of tissue around the lids that heralded the emergence of Bad Mother. With Trevor it was much the same. When Stu crossed the threshold to shake Trevor's hand, Tessa saw the tightening, heard the edge in his voice, and could almost smell the bile rising. Before Stu could even sit down, Trevor growled, "Don't most managers end up fucking their clients?" and that was it.

Tessa rushed after Stu as he sprinted to the car, desperately assuring him that Trevor was "just kidding," but he turned to her and said, "That one's going to be trouble, Tessa. You better decide if you want a career or a relationship with that prick. You can't have both."

The ensuing battle was the most brutal of all. Trevor threw all her belongings down the stairs and out the door, slammed her around the room with a ferocity she had never experienced and left her with multiple contusions and a torn rotator cuff. And as he stormed out the door and roared away in his Porsche, she knew it wasn't just that she wanted a career, it was that she wanted a *life*. And she knew now that, despite her hope, his contrition, and the ubiquitous promise to "make it go right," the next time could be a fatal blow. That was beyond even Audrey and certainly beyond her own tolerance, and before he could return with his teary eyes and redundant apologies, she packed up and moved into the den of an acting class friend whose address he didn't know. She left without one cent and never went back to negotiate her half of anything they'd bought and he kept.

This was the man her father defended against her "fleecing." The man who was "sharp enough to expect repayment." The man Leo thought was a "nice guy."

When she was done telling David the story somewhere around three-thirty in the morning, he took her in his arms and promised he would never be Trevor. But she already knew that. It was one of the reasons she'd fallen in love with him.

TWELVE

"You know that's a weed, right?" Leland, their neighbor, was concerned, as always, with Tessa's naïve attempts at gardening. He watched with arched eyebrows as she arranged a strand of morning glory around a trellis she'd found tilting in the side yard.

"You say that, Leland, and it might be true, but it's pretty and I like it so it's just fine with me."

"Okay, sister; just trying to preempt embarrassment in the event someone other than a kind neighbor makes note, that's all."

"Thank you, but I don't think anyone else in the neighborhood gives a rat's ass what's in my garden, so don't you worry your pretty little head."

As he sniffed away he threw back, "You're becoming a bitchy girl, Tessa, and that's not attractive, just so you know."

Oh, she knew. She wasn't exactly sure why, but she *was* becoming a bitchy girl. She'd snapped at the clerk in the corner market this morning because he didn't have the kind of gum she liked, the postman was somehow responsible for the dearth of "Jazz" stamps, and her car mechanic got an earful when he confirmed that the repair of her driver's side airbag was not part of her regular tune-up. It seemed lately that everyone else was responsible for whatever it was that was lacking in her life and she damn well had the right to be annoyed about it.

Oh, God, I suck. She dropped her hand spade, pulled off her yellow gardening gloves, and stomped up the stairs. Arriving in the foyer, she sat in one of the two ornate chairs framing the entryway, the only furniture she'd contributed to the house, kicked off her muddy boots and skulked to the desk. Sitting there staring out the window, she pondered her curmudgeonly state of being:

What's with all the snapping at everyone? There must be a statute of limitations on moroseness. 'Cause Leland's right, it is a weed. What idiot wants a weed in their garden? But why are you trying to make this place feel more like home anyway? Isn't it really just David's and you're along for the ride? Oh, come on now; that's not fair…is it? And why the cynicism about David lately? What happened to all the fluffy optimism that came in the door with you not all that long ago?

She'd met David at an Association of Strategic Marketers meeting in early April. She'd been there as the guest of her bosses, Vivian and Glen Benicoff, founders of *Edge+Reason*, the very successful arts/politics/culture online magazine where Tessa wrote features and a highly popular blog. David was the invited guest speaker. As the VP of Marketing at New Strand International, a hot new sneakers company headquartered in Manhattan Beach, he had a certain verve about him: creative edge mixed with corporate cool. The combination intrigued her. She was more than surprised when, in a room full of MBAs, some gorgeously female, he beelined to her table after the Q&A. By eleven-thirty they were at a bar discussing careers and favorite travel destinations and from that weekend on they'd been together.

When he asked her to move in she was originally reluctant to give up her rent-controlled, one-bedroom Art Deco in the Whitley Heights neighborhood near the Hollywood Hills, a place she'd coveted and loved for over six years. He did, however, offer a stunning two-story condo on the north end of Manhattan Beach with a view of the ocean and an easy walk to the charming town center. His logic was simple: she telecommuted and his office was just up the street; what's the argument? She was convinced, but there were times, like today, when the exhilaration of crashing surf and broad white beach did little to ameliorate her sense of displacement.

In the population of blonde, sporty, perfect-bodied tan people, her pale, brunette, unmistakably urban sensibilities often felt jarringly off-point. David kept telling her to get some flip-flops and join the party and so she did, begrudgingly embracing the Jimmy Buffett vibe and absence of the city's competitive hum. But when she discovered that not one single print shop in Manhattan Beach stocked the three-hole-punch brads commonly used to bind screenplays, she found herself breaking down at Beach Pizza, wailing, "Why am I here? I don't know any of these people!" while David looked on in dismay as his angel hair got cold and he had no good answers. She got over it eventually, mostly. Particularly because David loved her and David was here, in this blonde beach town.

Now, on this cold, gray morning in what passed as winter in Southern California, she tried to remember all that good will and stoic resolution. But when the sun finally cracked the haze that rolled over the glistening homes of paradise, turning the day into one of those picture-perfect postcards locals grew to expect and others never stopped envying, Tessa sat at her desk and gave not one good fuck.

She couldn't shake it off, this post-funeral ennui, unable to get back on track since returning from Chicago. She hadn't gotten together with anyone, even Kate and Ruby, her closest friends whose calls had been repeatedly put off. Her gym card lay untouched on the foyer table, she got her work done but without much enthusiasm and, worst of all, David seemed to be scheduling more than the usual number of "night meetings," clearly relieved to detach from her gloom. She'd caught up with everything on cable, was early with every assignment, and had blog entries so long one commenter accused her of writing a novel. Almost three weeks had elapsed since the funeral, it was just a few days before Christmas, and she shuddered at the thought of ramping up for the holidays, grateful for the pass earned by her recent loss. Maybe just a dinner or two with friends, certainly not a tree this year; a few decent gifts should be all that was necessary to commemorate the day.

Oh, God, even that's too much to think about.

Tessa clicked the mouse of her computer and pulled up the article she'd been working on. At least she liked what she did. For well over a year she'd been paid to write, a career evolution of considerable merit. After years of waitressing during her less-than-brilliant acting career, followed by years of catering during the completely exhilarating but still poorly remunerated – and ultimately unsuccessful – rock and roll phase that followed, she'd decided to reject the food industry altogether and commit to employment at something, *anything*, related to her many creative skills. She'd written a couple of well-received screenplays, one of which had been optioned by a prominent Hollywood company for a decent sum, and though it never transpired into actual production, enough people heard about it that she was able to parlay the point into the assignation of "professional writer." It wasn't quite as buzzy as "rock star" but it would do.

It had been slow go at first but after a solid year of pavement pounding around every literary circle she could find, she landed a position of substance when Vivian Benicoff contacted her after following a blog Tessa wrote at a women's site. Vivian offered an actual contract – a good offer that came with regular, meaningful paychecks and she could do it all from her desk. *Merry freakin' Christmas!*

Yet today none of it seemed particularly impressive. Tessa felt old and staid. She wished she could tease her hair and sing with a band, but instead she was gardening and writing articles about the vagaries of modern culture. She scrolled down, trying to find an entry point into her current piece, and stared at the word *redundant.* Ironically, she said it over about five times: *redundant, redundant, redundant, redundant, redundant. Is that even a word? It looks like gibberish.*

Say it enough and it doesn't even sound like anything that makes sense. Weird.

The phone rang, blessed delivery from the task of compulsive thought. It was Michaela reporting on life with mother post father. "She doesn't want to go to Rome."

"She has to. I mean, the tickets are non-refundable, right?"

"Yeah, but she says it's only going to remind her of the last time she and Dad were there and 'it won't be fun enough for all the trouble,' to use her words."

"Well, she has to go. Darlene went to a lot of trouble putting it all together."

Darlene Draskovic was a church buddy of Audrey's, a lively Serbian who was one of the few churchwomen Leo had been able to tolerate, often remarking that she was "a hoot." Several years back, after Darlene supposedly retired from nursing (her credentials were a topic of debate amongst the Curzios, most of whom believed she had none), she and her late husband, Gus, invited Leo and Audrey to accompany them on an elder hostel to Italy. They accepted and that trip forever remained a highlight. Plans were made for further adventures, then Gus died, Audrey got the shingles and, before long, enough years passed that the idea faded from conversation. By the time the upcoming Rome trip had reached the discussion stage Leo had lost his enthusiasm, particularly with Gus's male balance no longer available, but "the girls" were encouraged to go on their own. Audrey was always reluctant to do much of anything without Leo but Darlene's willingness to manage every detail ultimately proved sway. Tickets were purchased and itineraries were set. Then Leo died.

"I actually think she *needs* to go," Michaela continued. "Her first Christmas without Dad is going to be hell, so she may as well spend it looking for the Pope. Besides, she hasn't left the room for days and I can't keep going over there."

"Where's everyone else?" That came out before Tessa could stop either the question or Michaela's predictable response.

"Please. Suzanna's on a buying trip back east, how convenient;

Izzy stopped by a couple of times but she can never stay long. Duncan's in the middle of some big case so he's basically useless, and Ronnie's just useless."

"Mickie, come on."

"You can defend him all you want but the guy's made a career out of feeling sorry for himself. I get it – his life sucks, his wife left him, he's broke, blah, blah, blah; we all feel bad for him. But he's not the only person in the world with problems and it might actually help him to think about someone else for a change. Mom could use him."

"Have you called?" Another stupid question.

"About a hundred times. Never answers, never returns the calls. I'm just sick of it. Why don't you plan to spend Christmas here?"

"Michaela, I just got home and I've got a job to do. I'll visit when I can, but it's not like I'm going to move back there. Mom's just going to have to figure this out. I'll call her tonight and tell her she has to go."

"Oh, and she fainted the other day."

"What?"

"She fainted. Darlene was over there making some food, got her up and walking around, and after she sat back down on the bed, she fainted. Dropped right to the floor. It was only for a few seconds but it spooked them both. Darlene called the paramedics; they took her to emergency, the whole thing. Doctors ran tests, nothing showed up, they told her to drink Gatorade and take Xanax, which she has plenty of. Of course, now she's convinced she has a brain tumor."

"She's probably just been lying in bed too long. She's not drinking, is she?"

"No more than usual. I think the funeral was her last big bender. Though I wouldn't be surprised if she's taking more than the average nip when no one's looking. Almost can't blame her."

"But you're keeping an eye on her meds, right? No strange

new prescriptions or double doses of anything?"

"Not as far as I can tell. Darlene promised she'd stay on top on that."

"Then she's probably just going through…I don't know, whatever she's going through. Just tell her to take a walk and eat some spinach."

"You tell her."

"Okay, fine, I will. Listen, I gotta get going."

"As do I. I actually have a job, too – I mean, besides dealing with our mother."

Tessa sighed. These conversations with Michaela always seemed to end with a barb. The tension between them was usually subtle but of late it was barely disguised. When they talked it was rarely about anything besides family, and it always seemed to involve guilt-inducement and lists of who had or hadn't done what. When she really thought about it, it annoyed Tessa that Michaela never got beyond their entrenched family roles to come anywhere near the present. She never asked Tessa about her work at the magazine, never visited or showed the slightest interest in visiting, yet never failed to remark on how infrequently Tessa found her way to Chicago. Wearying.

Tessa thought about dialing Audrey to get that conversation over with, but two Curzio guilt trips in one morning were more than she could manage at the moment. She grabbed her purse and headed out the door, purposely ignoring the morning glory as she marched past the front yard. Her phone rang before she hit the sidewalk. It was David.

She didn't answer. He'd initially been sweet and solicitous after their Trevor-story night, but of late there'd been no discussion of the journal – or any seeming awareness of its impact on Tessa. David had a bad habit of thinking if you ignored something long enough it would somehow lose its sting. That might work with tantrums and bad haircuts…it didn't work with Tessa.

She turned around and walked back upstairs. Exercise, she

decided, was overrated.

THIRTEEN

"I flatlined, you know." Audrey sounded positively ebullient at this announcement.

"You flatlined?" Tessa was out on the condo deck, eating cookies with the speakerphone on.

"What's all that crunching noise?"

"Nothing, I'm eating a cookie."

"Well, that's rude, eating while you're on the phone with someone! I can barely hear anything you're saying, there's so much racket."

Tessa swallowed, hard, and put the phone to her ear. "Okay, Mother, I'm done, I'm all yours. Now, what's this about flatlining?"

"It was quite mystical. I kept waiting for the white light, looking around for your father, and –"

"Mom, I don't think you flatlined."

"Of course I did. I died and I came back."

"Really? Because Michaela said you came to pretty quickly, didn't need CPR or anything."

"I had no pulse. Darlene took my pulse before the paramedics got there and she said I flatlined. What, are you going to argue with a nurse?"

Tessa took a deep breath, reflexive action meant to stifle any impulse to argue the merits of Darlene's medical expertise. It worked. "I think if you actually died and came back to life they would have kept you at the hospital for observation – they sent you home with juice and sedatives. I'm sure Darlene probably just meant you had a weak pulse or something, but I don't think throwing around terms like 'flatlined' is particularly helpful."

There was something about Audrey's blithe exaggeration of illness and injury, a pathological insistence that had kept Leo running from doctor to doctor in earnest attempts to solve the mysteries of his wife's fragile health, that infuriated Tessa. She'd spent a lifetime rolling her eyes at the purported maladies that befell her mother and while Leo always appeared honestly concerned, the children ascertained the Münchhausen angle early on. Tessa, in particular, was stolidly unsympathetic, a trait that didn't serve her well when a boyfriend or colleague came down with the flu and she stood tapping her watch while they fevered madly.

Audrey sighed deeply. "Well, I'm sure you know more about all this medical stuff than everyone else, Teresa, and that makes you the expert, doesn't it? All I know is I'm afraid to go anywhere now because I might faint and I certainly don't want to do that in Italy of all places."

"Mother, first of all, I don't think I'm the expert, I just don't want to see you get words stuck in your head that don't apply. You already have enough to worry about as it is. Secondly, Darlene is counting on you to go and it would be really awful if you let her down, especially at Christmas. And thirdly, it seems to me if you're going to faint, you may as well faint in Italy…it has a certain dramatic ring to it. Besides, you know Dad would want you to go."

With that, Audrey burst into painful, wracking sobs; gut wrenching, authentic pain that made the veil of her hypochondria flimsy by comparison. In that torrent of grief Tessa felt helpless to say anything. She let her mother sob unabated for what seemed a very long time, occasionally uttering a gentle, "Mom, it's okay," permission that hardly seemed necessary. Finally the cloudburst passed, followed by the weight of mutual exhaustion.

"Is it just going to be this way for the rest of my life?" Audrey asked wearily. It was such a plain, simple question Tessa was taken aback. A flush of love and sympathy washed over her.

"I don't know, Mom...I don't think so. They say time is the great healer. I think you've just got to get through it one day at a time. It will get easier, I'm sure. But the main thing, I think, is to stay involved in your life. You're going to be sad wherever you are; go be sad in Rome."

Audrey flew out the next day. Tessa was as relieved as Michaela was surprised at her younger sister's inexplicable ability to affect Audrey when it seemed no one else could.

FOURTEEN

"So your dad died, you found a fucked up journal and now you want to quit writing? Why does none of this make sense to me?"

Vivian Benicoff was one of those women who did not do small talk; it was always big and usually loud. Right now it was in the bar where she and Tessa had parked during the annual *Edge+Reason* Christmas lunch. She'd ordered Irish coffees for them both. Big talk.

"I didn't say I want to stop writing, Vivian; I'm just not sure I want to write about art and politics when I feel like I could give a good shit about either."

"But why is that? What could he possibly have said twelve years ago that would stop you in your tracks today? So he didn't always like you, so he thought you were a failure...so what? You're not, he's wrong, that's fucked; get over it. You're a writer; write about that, for God's sake, but don't stop doing what you do because your dead dad pissed you off." Vivian could compose essays and articles of such poetry skin would tingle, but when it came to good old common sense, particularly of the ass-kicking variety, she was rugged as a lumberjack.

"I think I'm bored. I'm not sure where I'm going with these features and, really, what am I doing with the blog? What am I contributing to the universe?"

"Oh, dear God, we're not going down that road, are we? You want to write *War and Peace*, go for it. In your spare time. Because right now you've got an obligation to use that mind of yours to comment on life as you see it for your readers, my readers, and from my point of view, that's quite a useful service for which you are deeply valued. I'm not going to pander to you by blathering on about who thinks what about your talent, because you know where I sit with that. But I swear I'll beat the crap out of you right now if you start whining about the meaning of life and your part in it."

Tessa couldn't help but smile at Vivian's vehemence and, with that, the two women burst into laughter. Tessa raised her mug and they cheered Christmas, leaving both the conversation and the conundrum to another day.

FIFTEEN

The holidays came in a blur of intersecting calls from almost every member of the family. *Deck the halls.*

Izzy: "Our first Christmas without Dad; it's so hard to believe. I think I've been crying all week. Did Michaela tell you she cut her hair?"

Suzanna: "She looks like a Wisconsin housewife. I don't know why she thought bangs were a good idea on her particular face. Oh, and by the way, Mom fainted in Rome, the square at St. Peter's. She was in a chair so no harm done. A bunch of priests brought her wine and chatted her up so she was quite the star. She actually giggled when she told me about it, can you imagine? Said she's pretending it's not Christmas because 'there's no Christmas without Dad.' Personally, I appreciated the reprieve from Midnight Mass!"

Michaela: "Well, of course no one's heard from Ronnie; I'm sure he wouldn't have it any other way. He could be dead for all we know. Didn't even show up for Christmas dinner, our first without Dad. Selfish little shit. Have no idea if he got the cookies I sent...did you?"

Duncan: "Ronnie's gone AWOL and it's driving Michaela nuts. We stopped by her house for dessert on Christmas night, the kids sang carols and swapped gifts, it was all very nice but she wouldn't stop carrying on about little brother. Not exactly thoughtful of him, though, what with Mom being out of town and Dad gone. By the way, I hope you liked the scarf we sent!"

Izzy again: "Duncan and Suzanna found him at The Drop & Roll, you know that crappy place on Jefferson where he punched the guy that one time? Turns out he's been camping out with the closing shift waitress who lives above the bar. I'd be totally grossed out except she made him shave and cut his hair so at least she's got hygiene priorities! Oh, and don't tell Michaela I mentioned her hair…apparently she wants to grow it out a little before she tells you."

Suzanna: "Her name was Cassie or Kaylie or something like that, a real barfly. But he said she got him through Christmas…free booze and apparently she makes a great meatloaf. We're grateful for small favors."

Duncan: "Izzy went down to his office, did her sweet little sister thing, claimed he'd been out with the flu, too sick to call. She could charm Darth Vader…he still has the job!"

Izzy: "Suzanna got a cleaning crew over there to hose down his place and he's home again, sleeping off the lost weekend. Gee, can't wait till New Year's! Lucky you, in California!"

Michaela: "We're turning the page at the New Year, or so they all say. Frankly, I'm ready for spring. And listen, I know Izzy told you about my bangs…what did she say?"

Dear fucking God.

Tessa's resolve to avoid Chicago for the time being strengthened in the onslaught. She found herself annoyed with Ronnie and his endless stream of need played out in bedrooms and seedy bars but, unlike the others, refused to participate; the Curzio formula of giving the most dysfunctional the most attention was getting seriously passé. She sent him a Christmas card and a bag of California pistachios.

That done, she made a mental list of the others in her life to whom she must finally attend over this festive holiday season:

1. The girlfriends. She'd put off contact with Kate and Ruby for the three long weeks between funeral and holiday, but her hand was forced when plans were made to gather after the New Year. Love them though she did, Tessa didn't relish the thought of going over every detail of recent events in that raw, unvarnished way demanded by women who've known each other a long time, but it was inevitable. And probably useful…they had a way of shining clarity into the murkiest of matters.

2. Aunt Joanne. She had called repeatedly, concerned that they hadn't talked before they both left Chicago, but so far Tessa had managed to return the calls when she guessed her aunt would be occupied, trading messages without the burden of actual conversation. She wasn't sure there was a point to any of that right now, the whole talking to her father's sister about what an asshole she thought her father was. She did, however, send a large box of See's Nuts and Chews to the convent.

3. And, yes, David. She thought about him in a flush of affection. Limited though he was with the more emotional aspects of life, she knew he was doing the best he could. She made note to find the recipe for those powdered sugar cookies he liked, bought him a new watch and a slightly humorous sex toy, and decided to extend herself a bit more than she had. It was, after all, the jolliest time of the year.

He appeared to be of like mind. Having finally realized Tessa had all but shut him out, David became appropriately focused on remedying the situation. His Christmas gift to her was a beautiful leather bag she'd coveted, coupled with a three-night stay at a favorite Santa Barbara inn they'd stumbled on during an earlier road trip. Those three nights were, at the very least, a change. Sex. Food. Long talks. Jigsaw puzzles. Sex (he liked the toy). Quiet nights reading by the fire. Sex. He even asked to read the journal and was honestly perturbed to find she'd left it at home. She told him she didn't want the trip to be about that particular conversation, but he said it was Freudian that when they finally had time to focus on what had been bothering her for almost a month, she'd conveniently left the evidence at home. They had a fight. She slept on the sofa. He came out in the middle of the night and they made love again. But the drive back felt strained and Tessa could feel the closeness they'd managed to rehabilitate in those four days seeping slowly out of the car as they got closer to home. By the time they arrived it was like they'd never left.

SIXTEEN

June 21, 2002 – the journal of Leo Curzio:

    Frankly, both Audrey and I feel Teresa's failure is not due to any lack of talent but as a result of leaving the Church. By doing so she has become a shallower person with an inability to overcome the inevitable hurdles of life. In fact, her lack of success is likely a form of consequence for deserting her faith. I'm not sure she can reverse the trend – unless she were to come back to the Church as a prodigal daughter.

    The demon as far as I can see is her continuing affiliation with Scientology, the brainchild of a science fiction writer with a smattering of Hinduism, Buddhism and other eastern cults. It has no basis in reality and seems as dark and oppressive as any cult, but clearly it seduces its adherents as good science fiction does its readers. As much as I find it anathema to true Godly faith, had I been exposed to it when I was 19, I might have been swayed as well. I might have become enmeshed in the details in a way that would have entrapped me for years – as it has her. Though I hope I would have been wiser in extricating myself when its uselessness became clear.

    Is that happening in her case? I can only hope so because, sadly, the promised benefits she once spoke of have all fizzled into nothing and I wouldn't be surprised if she finally drifts from it as she seems to drift from any faith commitment.

    Whether that brings her home to Catholicism will remain to be seen.

I don't have a sense that she has that kind of spiritual strength, which is clearly her downfall.

It was now five days into the new year. David was off to work and Tessa had managed a productive morning ripping into the pay-for-play clubs raping the LA music scene in an irreverent piece to be posted later that week. Creatively exhausted, she sat on the deck of the condo wrapped in a mohair poncho perusing *2002*. It had been a couple of weeks since her last peruse but ultimately curiosity won over self-preservation.

At least he was right about Scientology. *How to explain that?*

Tessa remembered the day she bombarded her father with books and tapes and breathless enthusiasm for this new religion of hers. She'd been certain that a man so philosophically bent would see the benefits of a church that, as she assured him, "espoused nothing to conflict with Catholicism, just offers an addendum, a parallel path of sorts, to soul salvation." She thought that sounded properly poetic. At nineteen, naïve on the topic and convinced she had truly found the Holy Grail of eternal life, it never dawned on her that her wild embrace of this new religion would be so dismissed by her family. Frankly, they were horrified.

Duncan flipped through *Dianetics, the Modern Science of Mental Health* and shared some brief, awkward discourse, the sisters ignored her, Ronnie declared his sheer lack of interest, and Audrey stood firm her conviction. "It's heresy," she hissed. "Heresy!"

Leo had at least been willing to comment. "I can conjure up objective interest in the basic concepts but certainly there is no basis upon which to designate it a *religion*." Tessa didn't agree at the time but she appreciated his attempt. That is, until her discussion on the topic with her big sister two months later.

"You're lucky we're poor," Suzanna announced.

"What does that mean?"

"You are so clueless. Leave it to you to be the one to run off and join a cult, as if Mom and Dad need anything else to bitch about when it comes to their kids."

"Wait, they're bitching about it? Dad said he understood!"

"Of course they're bitching about it! It's a *cult*, you're all glassy-eyed, spewing jargon like some moronic puppy – "

"That is such bullshit, Suzanna! I happen to believe in something for once in my life and none of you can handle it. Could it be that what I'm saying makes too much sense, is that possible?"

"Oh, please. Spare me. We all think you're nuts. They actually had a conversation with someone about hiring a deprogrammer, that's how much sense you're making."

That stopped Tessa cold. "Are you kidding me?"

"Hells no, little sis, I'm dead serious. They called a deprogrammer. All set to hog-tie you and drag your ass back to Jesus."

"I don't believe you. Who did they talk to?"

"I don't know, some idiot from the church probably. Don't worry; they called it off. Mom got squeamish about everyone knowing you'd been bedeviled – actually said that – 'bedeviled,' like a hard-boiled egg!" Suzanna chortled. Tessa did not. "Besides, they needed the money for some roof repairs and Dad said he figured you'd come to your senses once you got your ass kicked by the apostates."

He was right; Tessa got her ass kicked and came to her senses about seven years into the experiment. But when her exit from Scientology did not prove a road back to the Catholic Church, her fate as a "lost soul," as Leo characterized her in a less than cheerful birthday card sent later that year, remained sealed.

What Leo and Audrey couldn't recognize was that Tessa's need for spiritual grounding was actually a good thing, an indication that her desire for faith, community; support, things they also valued, was intact. So stunned were they by her betrayal at leaving the Church, they could offer no guidance toward an acceptable alternative. There simply was none for them.

But Tessa, in spite of not missing the Catholic Church, *did* miss the sense of believing in something, of having an idea of what it was all about and where one goes from here. She tried Transcendental Meditation but could never sit still long enough to transcend. She explored Buddhism but was put off by the incessant discussion of suffering. She thought of looking into a Unitarian church between sophomore and junior years of college but got involved in a summer play at school and put it off. Then she met Brice Harrington. That's when Scientology happened.

Brice Harrington didn't go to the college but for some reason he was always there, hovering around the student center, sipping coffee in the cafeteria; sitting in the theater watching play rehearsals. And no one minded because Brice Harrington was the best-looking boy any of them had ever seen.

The gay men who made up the bulk of the theater department, and the dancing and singing girls who made up the rest, all found themselves swooning in his presence. He was invited to parties, private homes, and bedrooms on a regular basis. Tessa, like everyone else, couldn't keep her eyes off him and one night, after she'd wrapped a sweaty rehearsal of *Rent*, was surprised when he approached and said, "You're an awesome singer." Coffee and conversation ensued, followed by a handful of enchanting date nights, and by Week Two they were spending every night together, mostly in bed. Then came Week Three.

"Hey, sweet cheeks, I've got to get down to my job later today. You want to come with me?" Brice, all smiles and open arms, was clearly ready to move this up to the taking-the-girlfriend-to-work phase. Tessa was giddy at the inclusion, certain this would be one of many inevitable steps towards greater intimacy.

His job was at the local chapter of the Church of Scientology not far from campus. He was, as it turns out, a street recruiter for the organization, the good-looking guy out there on the front lines passing out flyers and suggesting Personality Tests to potential adherents. Or, as she later referred to him, a Scientology whore.

The church was in a bungalow that was as spit-shiny a place as

Tessa had ever seen. Smiling, happy people lurked in every nook and cranny and though the ubiquitous photos of founder L. Ron Hubbard were everywhere, the general ambiance was that of a cheerful pediatrician's office.

"I gotta tell you, Tessa, you've got yourself a good one there!" said Brice's boss, Greg-something, who led Tessa through a tour of the place, replete with introductions and hugs at every turn. There hadn't been this much hugging since middle school.

"I know, he *is* a pretty great guy!" she chirped, heady with all the attention.

"Way more than a great guy. Brice has the magic touch, you know? Just seems to have a way with the ladies..." Greg winked. "...and guys don't find him too shabby either. He keeps our recruitment stats the highest in the state. Not bad for a small local chapter! Now, I take it he's got you here to sign up for the Communications Course?"

Overwhelmed by the embrace of peers as seemingly hip, funny, and contemporary as anyone in the theater department, Tessa didn't immediately catch what was being implied. That would come later. At this point, she reveled in her role as a "new believer," as someone deigned her early in the tour, and she did, in fact, sign up for the Communications Course.

It was a quick build from there. The budding camaraderie with like-minded members imbued her with a sense of belonging she'd felt nowhere but the theater department. The cultishness implied by their nightly salutes of L. Ron Hubbard's portrait was cheerfully offset by their secular enthusiasm for Kool cigarettes and hard liquor. Tessa was so delighted by this new family she almost missed Brice's growing absence. That finally registered during her second week of attendance when he sat her down in the courtyard with the portentous, "we should talk."

"Tessa, it has been an absolute blast hanging out with you and it's something I'll always look back on and remember with a really awesome feeling."

"Um…why will you be looking back on it? I thought we were going out this weekend to make up for your being so busy lately."

"I know, we were, but, to use an old term, my work here is done." He smiled as beatifically as anyone who wasn't Jesus could muster. "You're here now, you've made the commitment to help clear the planet. We've had fun, and it's been stellar getting to know you, but it's time for me to go off and see what else I can do to get other valuable people on the bridge. That's a higher purpose we should *both* be ready and willing to kick into gear, you know what I mean?"

Tessa didn't…at least not immediately. Then, in spite of her burgeoning spirituality and deep enthusiasm for clearing the planet, she was struck by an urge to kick way more than his higher purpose. "So basically you were fucking me for the sake of recruitment statistics, is that it?" Her voice raised a notch too high – a few people from inside glanced their way. He quickly slid next to her and put his arm across her shoulders as if calming a patient.

"Tessa, listen to me. Look at me." She did and he held her gaze with an intensity she'd just learned in the first week of the Communications Course. "I know it might seem that way but it's not true. You're very special to me and we will always – *always* – be friends. But we both know my leading you and others to spiritual freedom is way more important than being your boyfriend. As much as I want to, we can't afford to be selfish when there's so much to do…I know you agree."

She didn't agree, but before she could make the point, he stood up, kissed the top of her head as if he were the Pope, and swept off to what was likely his next rapture. She wiped her tears, stuffed down whatever rejection she felt, and decided he was at least right about staying on track. After completing the first course, she signed up for whatever was next – something was always next – and began saving money for the "higher levels" with their staggeringly higher prices. There was comfort to be found in wrapping herself in the mantle of "Scientologist."

That's how it started. How it ended was less comfortable.

SEVENTEEN

"Oh God, I don't believe this; listen to this: '*Tessa had very few girlfriends – maybe there was too much parity for her with girls.*' What the hell? Where was he during the slumber parties?"

Tall, beautiful, and supremely intelligent, Kate Hamilton was Tessa's oldest friend, having met when they were both three. They'd gone to grade school, three years of high school, and one semester of college together. Her father, Roy, had been one of Leo's best friends and their parents socialized frequently. They'd had barbecues and birthday parties in each other's basements and backyards; as girls, they attended the same church, as adults, got in and out of Scientology together. They even moved to Los Angeles within months of each other. If anyone knew Tessa, it was Kate.

She flipped through the journal and read a few more of the earmarked entries, then looked at Tessa with tearful eyes. "Oh, honey…if my father said things like this about me I'd just die. I would. I don't know how you're still standing. And I don't get it. I knew Leo and I can't believe he'd actually write all this!"

"Let me see that – " Ruby Kapinos was an old acting class friend and another ex-Scientology survivor. She and Tessa had bonded over a scene from *Mary, Queen of Scots* and Ruby had remained staunchly in Tessa's corner during a particularly trying run-in with the cult shortly before they all quit. And though neither was pursuing acting or spiritual quests these days, their friendship had survived all the career, cult, and address changes that followed over the years. She grabbed the journal from Kate and sat reading in silence while Kate wrapped Tessa in her arms.

"I'm sorry, Tessa. That's unforgivable," Kate said.

Ruby read while the other two sat and watched for her reactions. She slowly leafed through the marked pages, occasionally stopping to read an entry more than once. When she was done, she set the journal down, got up and walked out the restaurant door. Kate and Tessa looked at each other in surprise, running to catch up to her in the parking lot.

"Ruby, what's going on?" Tessa panted after her.

"I hate your father. Really. I hate any man who would leave something like that for his daughter to find. As if we daughters don't have enough to endure with the Daddy-neglect bullshit and the 'just forgive him, honey, Daddy doesn't like to talk' crap and all of it. All of it! I thought my dad was bad but this, *this*..."

Kate came up from behind. "Well, your dad *was* bad but we get your point." Ruby's father had left the family when she was five and spent most of the next thirty years sending her postcards and breaking dates. Tessa always had a sort of survivor's guilt when it came to fathers, hers at least being present. And though cruel words could hardly compare to sheer abandonment, she now felt she might have been wasting that particular emotion.

They reached their cars but no one seemed to know what to do once they got there. Ruby grabbed Tessa in a hug and said, "I know this isn't about me and I'm sorry for being so dramatic, but you are one of the best women I know and if your daddy didn't know it, then fuck him." She got in the car and shut the door.

Kate gave Tessa a helpless shrug. "You know she's always been very blunt. I'll call you later. But call me first if you need to talk about anything."

"Okay. I won't. But I will."

Kate hugged her again and climbed into the driver's side. As they pulled away, waving, eyes peering mournfully from the windows, Tessa felt more abandoned than she wanted to. But there was at least some vindication in knowing her two closest friends didn't think she was crazy for being so hurt. She wished she were going home to someone who understood that as clearly.

EIGHTEEN

David fucked like a marathoner. Long stretches of paced movement and conservation of energy, alternated with enthusiastic sprints, calming interludes, until the final balls-out push to the finish line. There was something choreographed and unspontaneous about it at times, almost generic, as if she could have been any girl, any vagina; any finish line. He insisted that couldn't be further from the truth, but the first time they made love Tessa had to keep telling him to *look* at her and he would. It annoyed her how often he had to be reminded.

But he loved oral sex. Getting it, certainly. Giving it...*oh God.* He never complained about how long she took, never demanded it for himself after she was sated and spent, always conveyed to her that the act of bringing her to toe-curling orgasm with the moist, velvet coaxing of his tongue was the single most sensuous, joyful experience of lovemaking. She could not help but love him for that. Usually.

Tonight, for some reason, while he languidly carried on as if lost in a soft cloud of sensation, she found herself drifting to the point that she was actually dreaming about that giraffe at the Santa Barbara Zoo with the crooked neck and long, curled tongue. She heard it had died but there it was, all spotted and peculiar, close enough to her face that she could smell its odd giraffe breath, pungent enough that she jolted awake.

"Were you sleeping?" Still positioned between her legs, David looked up with an expression more hurt than surprised.

"Umm…no…yes! I'm sorry!"

"Is this boring you?"

She quickly sat up, stifling the laugh that was percolating just below the surface. "No, no, honey, I'm sorry, I'm so sorry. I guess I'm just tired." No longer able to hold back, she guffawed with sudden, inappropriate laughter.

He pulled away, looking at her as if she'd sprouted a third arm. "What is wrong with you?"

"I don't know…really, I think I'm just tired."

"Well, Tessa, I'm doing my best down here and I could either use a little encouragement or a reprieve."

"A reprieve? What does that mean? Is this a chore for you?"

"Oh, no, no, no. You don't get to turn this on me. You're the one who fell asleep while I was on my second fifteen-minute round. You don't get to be indignant."

She sat up further and looked at him pointedly. "David, really, *is* this a chore for you?"

"You know that's a stupid question, but if you're not in the mood, would you let me know? If I'm just keeping you up, it's a waste of a whole lotta technique." He gave her a quick grin.

"Ooooh, you are walking a fine line there, mister. I do believe you nodded off once while I was pleasuring myself at your specific request."

"That didn't involve me as a participant. A viewer can drift from time to time."

She whacked him with a pillow, they laughed, the tension defused. For now.

Afterwards, cuddled together in the dark room, a silence descended. They usually talked after sex, sometimes in their most intimate way. Tonight Tessa felt oddly distant, as if she didn't have a thing to say to him or he, apparently, to her. She finally had to break the silence. "What are you thinking about right now?" Clichéd question. She couldn't help herself.

Neither could he: "Nothing."

"Really? Nothing?"

"Tessa, please. Now *I'm* just tired."

"Okay, sorry." She pulled the blanket up closer to her neck. She waited another moment, then sat up. "What's going on, David?"

"I was going to ask you the same thing."

"Is this about the Trevor conversation? It's been weird since then. Which sucks, because, really, I didn't even want to tell you about him, it's just – "

"No, Tessa, it's not about that. I appreciated that you told me. I don't know why you waited so long, but I'm glad you did. It explains a lot."

A ping of something. "What does it explain?"

"I don't know. Maybe why you had such a hard time committing to anyone between him and me. Maybe why you have a shell around you."

"I have a shell?"

"Yeah, I think so. A little distrusting, maybe, a little sensitive. I mean, God, I totally understand why. Your mom, him, now finding out about this journal. I get it, Tess, I really do."

She lay back down. A sticky silence lasted until David spoke up this time.

"Okay, like right now. What is going on? Did I say something that pissed you off?"

"No."

"Well, don't you think *you're* acting a little strange? I feel like you haven't been yourself since you got back from Chicago and I get it, I get it, but unless you talk to me about what's bugging you, I just feel shut out. Is this just about your dad dying or work or what?"

Nothing about the journal? Really, David? That doesn't even make the list? The phone rang before she could respond out loud.

"Don't get it," he mumbled.

"I have to, it might be my mom."

David rolled over in resignation as Tessa grabbed the phone.

"Hey, Tess, whatcha doin'?"

"Ronnie! Wow, where are you?" She hadn't heard from Ronnie since the ride to the airport and was feeling less than enthusiastic about a chat right at the moment. David even less so – he threw back the covers and stomped out of the room. She looked after him helplessly.

"I'm just at home, hanging with my peeps, thinkin' about my big sis." Suzanna had relayed to Tessa earlier in the week that Ronnie had inexplicably purchased two parakeets at a farmers market and now found it hilarious to refer to them as his "peeps." Peep One and Peep Two. Tessa remarked that at least it showed he had the urge to connect to something living and figured as long as they didn't end up in a stew some hapless night, it was a good thing.

"Right, how are those two birds?"

"Keeping me alive, sis, keeping me alive." That two parakeets were all it took to keep her brother from jumping offered hope for larger things ahead. "So how're you doin'?" It was late there and he sounded like it.

"I'm okay," she lied. "Still feeling strange about not having a father, that sort of thing."

"Ah, that. I got over that years ago."

"I kept hoping for a turnaround."

"You always were more optimistic than me. Did you finish the journal?"

"Almost. I'm taking it in small doses; don't want to get the bends."

"Smart girl."

Suddenly, despite the distraction of David's annoyance, she wanted to talk to her brother. "Ronnie, I know we already talked about this but it would really help if you could try to remember something for me."

"What?" His reluctance was undisguised.

"Later on, closer to the present, after I'd won awards and made money as a writer and got into a happy relationship, did he ever say 'Hey, I was wrong, she wasn't such a failure after all'? Anything like that?"

"Okay, Tess, you *did* already ask me that and my answer is still, I don't know. I honestly don't remember – maybe, probably not – I don't know. Why does it matter? Come on, you're better than that. You don't need his approval. You know who you fucking are!"

She wasn't so sure. "I guess it's more perverse curiosity than anything. But I'm thinking of writing something about it. I'm not sure what exactly, but it's crossing my mind and maybe I could look at interviewing you as research."

"I don't know about that. Maybe you should just read them yourself. Might be good for you."

"Why do you say that? You made it sound like that was a bad idea when we talked about it in Chicago." There was a long enough pause that Tessa finally said, "Ronnie! Are you still there?"

"Yeah, yeah, I'm here. I'm thinking, Tess, trying to figure out how to put this."

Another pause. "Okay, Ronnie, just go to bed if this – "

"No, wait…here's what I want to say. Maybe you do need some perspective. I can't say I remember the details of most of what I read. I won't even try to paraphrase what I do remember. But I remember the feelings, the way it all made me *feel.* Some of it was life-changing for me in terms of my sense of myself and our family and stuff. You know what I mean?"

Tessa felt a tension in her chest. "No, I don't know at all what you mean. What kinds of things would be life-changing for you…did something happen that I should know about?"

"It's not that dramatic. It's more things said than things done. Sorting out what feelings were real with him, all the politics of our family, the church, the way he felt about Mom, all that sorta stuff.

Some of it changed how I felt about our childhoods, how I feel about myself in relation to growing up in that particular family. Look, just read them all and you'll see what I mean. Then maybe we can finally stop talking about this."

"Well, sorry if I'm bothering you – "

"Don't get all whiny-assed on me now! We can talk about it, for God's sake! Just do what you have to do for yourself and we can *all* move on, okay? I think that'd be the healthy thing, don't you?"

Ronnie talking about "the healthy thing." She felt annoyed and anxious at the same time. "Yes. I suppose."

"Oh, and hey, I think I might get out to LA soon!"

"Really? When?"

"I don't know, maybe next month or something. I need a break, need to get outta here, away from this fucking weather, away from Mickie's guilt trips, away from Mom, away from all of it, you know?"

"What about your job?"

"I'm on sabbatical," he said dryly. She had no response. "Jesus Christ, Tessa, I figured the family hotline already got to you. I was fired this week." This was the second job Ronnie had been fired from in a year.

"I'm sorry, Ronnie, that sucks."

"Not as much as the job. I'll be okay. I keep my overhead low, don't spend on much besides food and liquor."

"And why does that not make me proud?"

"Would you not go all Michaela on me, please? I'm just saying I've got enough to live on for the time being, and I'm obviously looking for another job. I'd just like a change of scenery before I lock myself in again; is that so fucking heinous?"

She suddenly felt tired. Why did everyone in her family make her tired? "No. I'm sorry. I'd love to see you, Ronnie. Just let me know when you figure it out and we'll plan some time together."

"Oh, hey, and could I crash with you for a couple of days?"

Not a great question. David had never met Ronnie but had heard enough to once remark that he "sounds like a slacker who could use a kick in the ass." Nor was David a fan of Ronnie's particular brand of victim-humor, something Tessa noticed when he answered the phone once and listened to about ten uncomfortable minutes of Ronnie riffing about the latest barroom antics. Having him as a houseguest might be a tough sell.

"Of course. Just keep me posted."

She found David asleep in front of the television. She decided that conversation could wait until another time.

NINETEEN

"Just say the word, my good man. If you want a pair of the new cross-trainers, I've got a box or two in your size and I guarantee they'll blow your mind!"

Tessa winced at David's chatter as he and Glen made their way to the patio for the men-in-one-room, women-in-the-other portion of "dinner at the Benicoff's." Vivian loved any excuse to entertain and though they had an amiable enough relationship that the two couples gathered fairly often, Tessa suspected they both thought David a conversational lightweight with his incessant sports trivia and sneaker references. As she watched the men debate the merits of a "wide toe box," she couldn't help but be grateful for Glen's easy-going personality.

Vivian hollered to her from the living room: "Get in here! I want to talk about this. I'm serious when I say you should write a book about it." Tessa walked in with refreshed wine glasses and settled into the couch. It had been days since Ronnie's unnerving suggestion that she read all the journals, something she had yet to share with David (that, along with the presumed visit), but it had been on her mind since and Vivian was the sounding board of choice.

"I'm not sure it's all that interesting," Tessa hedged.

"Really? Stern father imposes the dictates of a rigid Catholic upbringing, withholds love and communication from his children…"

"Well, some of them," Tessa corrected.

"…then upon his death leaves a lifetime of documented introspection, much of it indictments of his own children. In fact, he *bequeaths* this gift to the very children he indicts. If that ain't a page-turner, I don't know what is."

"Are you aware of how colossally insensitive you're being right now?"

"Yes, but my point is this: you can turn this sorrow into something meaningful for you, maybe even for other people who'll find something of their own story in there. Father/daughter themes are classic and resonating, and you've got something ugly but very unique to explore from that classic point of view. Use it, Tessa. It's gold."

"Personally, I think that's ridiculous. It's a private matter and I can't imagine how it would serve you or your father's memory in the slightest." David was stiff with indignation.

The ride home from Glen and Vivian's had been tense from the onset and Tessa now realized he had stronger feelings about their group discussion on the legacy of parents than he'd let on. David was very close to his own father and though he had never met Leo, had a certain admiration for the man based on their many phone conversations. The idea of dissecting and analyzing that relationship – generically or specifically – in so public a way as a book was anathema to him. "Why would you want to do that to your family?"

"Do *what* to my family, talk about something we're all struggling with? Did you ever think they might find it as healing or clarifying as I would?"

"Okay, maybe I worded that wrong, but I just think – "

"And I'm not saying I *would* write a book or that I even *want* to write a book. I just think Vivian's point about the universal appeal of father/daughter stories is valid and, as a writer, it bears some thought. That's all."

"Listen, you do what you want to do, this is your story. I just think it could be interpreted as showing a tremendous lack of respect for your family. What Leo did is wrong, I agree, but exposing and ridiculing him in a book for potential public consumption wouldn't make the situation any more right. It's a slippery slope, Tessa, and I think you're bigger than that."

Tessa felt a lump of anger growing in her throat but knew it was too big to let out right now. Her silence elicited a glance from David.

"Look, I understand, you're hurt, you're angry – who wouldn't be? I'm just saying it might be better to work it out in therapy and try to get past this with as little collateral damage as possible. The guy wasn't all that bad and out of respect for your mom, I think you should just work it out privately and hold on to the good memories. That's what I'd do."

Tessa wanted no more of this conversation. She smiled tightly and patted his hand.

Later they made love and in the quiet of darkness afterward, David held her close and whispered, "I love you and I'm on your side, Tessa, you know that, don't you?" She told him she did.

TWENTY

It was Kate's birthday and, as was tradition, Ruby and Tessa put together a dinner party for just the three of them. Ruby's husband, Ethan, and two-year-old son, Milo, had been banished for the evening, after which she and Tessa festooned their dining room with enough flowers and streamers to properly fete their friend's thirty-seventh. The three of them ate one of Ruby's extraordinary dinners followed by Tessa's marginal chocolate cake (the only thing beyond powdered sugar cookies she made passably well), and after Kate opened presents, they each took the floor to debrief on their lives. No matter what the event, no matter how dramatic the debrief, this was another tradition they'd maintained since they first gathered as adults and was as solid a thing as traditions get. Girls' Night.

Ruby went first, house rules; there was always the chance of family returning prematurely and spoiling the ability to speak freely so "the hostess always goes first." Ruby spent the bulk of her time venting about Ethan, his inability to communicate deeply, his lack of interest in sex, their growing distance, her own sense of isolation in raising Milo, and, as she had in previous gatherings, hinted at the futility of it all. Given that they were five years into a marriage with a very young child to consider, both Kate and Tessa were supportive without fanning the flames, neither wanting any onus of divorce on their hands. Besides, they liked Ethan and thought Ruby might be just a little too unforgiving in terms of what she expected of him.

Kate, next on the floor, had been married for almost twelve years to Todd Hamilton, a man they all loved and admired. There was a sense of imperviousness to their relationship, though Ruby occasionally complained to Tessa that the "fabulousness seems a bit put on; no one could be *that* perfect!" But it seemed Todd was, or at least might be with Kate, so it was accepted that one of them had gotten it right. Kate was good about not rubbing it in, particularly since Ruby's marriage was troubled and Tessa had yet to get there. She spent her time talking about the planned renovation of their house and her frustrations at work, a gift-basket company having an off year. They cheered her on and agreed to email promotional flyers around in hopes of stirring up business.

Tessa's turn. Between bites of her second piece of cake she talked about Leo, about David, about Ronnie, and in doing so, realized she sort of hated all the men in her life.

"Maybe you should get back into therapy," Kate suggested.

"Oh, thanks, now you sound like David."

"I'm just saying, you've got a lot to deal with. It might help to talk to a professional."

"I've got you guys."

"We're not professional," Ruby interjected. "We can barely make our own lives work."

"Speak for yourself, loser." Kate laughed. "Tessa, David loves you but he doesn't get how much Leo hurt you. I don't think you're going to get his agreement on that until he reads the journal. Has he even asked to read it?"

"Once, when we were out of town and I didn't have it with me."

"That's convenient." Ruby had her issues with David, who she thought was a little too conventional for Tessa. Of course, Ruby had known Tessa during the rock and roll years and it was unlikely that married life, motherhood, or their inevitable aging would dissuade her from the notion that Tessa still was, and still deserved, a rock star. "Obviously if he was really interested he could have asked again when you got home."

"I agree, but part of me doesn't want to share it with him at this point. Like, 'this is my private pain and you wouldn't understand anyway.'"

"Do you really think that? It's not like he's a completely unfeeling man." Kate had her own issues with David, who she wasn't entirely convinced was worthy of her dear friend, but in line with their philosophy about Ethan, didn't want to foment discord. "Maybe if you took the time to share it with him he'd appreciate your feelings a little more."

"I did read him the entry about how I had no girlfriends and was fleecing Trevor and that got his attention."

"I thought you were never going to tell him about Asshole Trevor." Ruby hated Trevor, as did Kate.

"I wasn't, but I was so wrapped up in the 'no girlfriends' part I forgot the Trevor mention until it was too late. But we talked about it later that night and he was surprisingly sweet."

"Well, there you go, give him the benefit of the doubt on the rest. Odds are if you opened up a bit more he'd be more receptive to what you're feeling." Kate, ever the conciliator.

"Okay, but here's my dilemma: I'm worried that he'll think it isn't all that bad. Like, 'so what, so your dad said he didn't like you, that you were a shallow, disappointing, lazy failure who used men and had no core, big deal.'"

"You really think he'd be that callous?" Kate asked.

"It's more like I'm not sure he'd think it was bad enough to crush my spirit…as it has. He might be expecting more blood splatter. Imagine that? Being worried about disappointing him because it might not be bad enough."

"Well, that's just stupid," Ruby countered. "You don't have to end up in a hospital or a psych ward to call it abuse. I think what your father did was plenty bad enough. Even David would see that."

"Yeah, maybe." Tessa was less convinced. "Ronnie suggested I read all the journals, said it might give me some necessary perspective. He was actually a little weird about it; said reading them was life-changing for him. I have no idea what that means, but if I do decide to write something I'd need to read them all. Research, right?"

"*Are* you going to write about it?" Ruby asked from the kitchen.

"I don't know. Vivian keeps encouraging me to, but I'm not sure I'm ready to tackle that."

"I don't blame you," Kate agreed. "I mean, is it in your best interest, at this point anyway, to slog through the rest of them knowing what you're likely to find based on this one…maybe even worse? I'm not sure I could survive that if it were me."

"But don't I need to know? If I'm to be really honest, I guess I want to see what Ronnie meant about its impact on him, the life-changing part. If there's something I should know, I want to know it, especially if my father ever came to believe I wasn't quite the failure he thought I was in 2002. If I knew that, I could probably forgive the rest."

And with that, the delightful Milo burst through the door with a loud, "Mommy!" and the moment was lost to a smiling boy and the handsome husband who followed.

TWENTY-ONE

July 27, 2002 – the journal of Leo Curzio:
The problem, as I see it, is not that large families have too little money, rather that childless couples and small families have too much. This creates a gulf between the two groups. What is the need for wealth? I see no purpose to it other than status and bragging rights. There is not a rich man I know whom I would call a friend or would likely get into Heaven.

We never needed more money than we had but tell that to the children whose longing for material things does nothing but make them greedy. They all ask for money but I wonder when they will ever understand its value or the hard work that goes into accruing it?

Recently Teresa called asking for $1000.00 to help her with an investment – of all things. I chose to support her effort and sent $500 but, frankly, I thought it was audacious of her to ask, knowing our family's finances. And the promised repayment never transpired, an expected result from a thoughtless child.

Didn't I repay that money? Tessa thought she had. Maybe she hadn't.

She knew finances were always a pressured topic for her parents and understood that Leo's sending a check of any amount, particularly when he thought she was "audacious" for even asking, was an act of generosity, even if his memory of it was not.

And it *had* been an investment; she'd been raising funds for the production of a play she'd written and planned to direct. She approached her mother first, excited to share her hope of getting this production off the ground, and it was Audrey who suggested she present the idea to Leo. He was predictably hesitant but ultimately sent the $500.

But he rarely asked about it afterward and he and Audrey weren't able to attend – flying to Los Angeles was as unfathomable to them as going to the moon. When Tessa sent the mostly positive reviews home, Audrey cheered loudly while Leo extended dryer congratulations. And when the play shut down earlier than expected due to slow ticket sales, Audrey cried with her daughter while Leo made note that "you chose a rough business and have to accept its misfortunes." He never mentioned the money and, given what he'd written, that must have taken some restraint.

Tessa felt a pang of remorse, wishing now that she'd been less "thoughtless," more efficient, and had made damn sure he'd gotten the money back. She went to her desk, pulled out her checkbook, and wrote a $600 check to her mother. She wrote "past-due investment refund + some interest" on the memo line. It was not nearly enough but it righted at least part of the wrong.

The phone rang suddenly and she answered before taking note of the caller ID. The minute she heard her aunt's voice, she winced.

"Are you avoiding me, Tessa?"

"No, I'm not! Really. I've just been crazy/busy and it's been hard to pin down a time when we could talk. But how are you, Auntie?"

"I'm fine, dear. I would ask if you were upset with me but I know there's no reason for that, so we'll presume this avoidance tactic has something to do with something else…your father, perhaps?"

There was a disadvantage to having a therapist in the family. There was no getting around her, try though one might. By the end of the conversation, Tessa had agreed to drive out to Thousand Oaks for a sit-down. *Christ!*

TWENTY-TWO

Aunt Joanne's office was in a cool, shaded corner of a Spanish-style building that housed the nuns of St. Anselmo Parish. Her particular order was very active in missionary work and, in fact, Aunt Joanne had spent some time in Uganda years earlier, returning only when it was determined her talents as a therapist and spiritual counselor were better used in service to the sisters of her community. She lectured at times and occasionally worked with local Catholic schools, offering counseling and guidance. She was now sixty-two and looked every bit her age, though her always youthful spirit kept her refreshingly contemporary.

Tessa didn't know her aunt well but had always liked her. Tucked now in a chair across the room, she waited awkwardly as Aunt Joanne quietly read a section of *2002*, shaking her head as she read.

"What?" Tessa asked.

"It's astonishing to me the way he frames things."

"Which part are you on?"

"Well, let me read this bit here." Aunt Joanne began reading out loud:

September 5, 2002 – the journal of Leo Curzio:
One of the most pathetic and futile vocations in life is that of a

husband-hunting spinster. It is a pitiable sight to see a woman in her mid-twenties or thirties whose appearance blares forth the desperate desire to marry. At that stage there remains little discrimination between men, and marriage in such a mental state would inevitably lead to disaster. But it doesn't stop them – lonely and bitter, they'll grab whomever they can to save themselves from loneliness.

I see that kind of charmless desperation in Teresa. Given all the boys who've scuttled around her over the years, I would guess it's her lack of any appreciable success in life that's a big part of the problem in attracting anyone of merit, particularly in terms of marriage and family.

Frankly she should have never quit college. Who makes the asinine decision to leave school in their senior year to go on the road with a theater troupe? Without even informing the parents involved? Lots of excuses about being a "theater major who's now doing the kind of work she was studying to do" but that's a bunch of crap to my way of thinking. And now her chickens have come home to roost. Her telephone calls to us are whiny and pathetic, her last visit home was depressing. She'd like nothing more nowadays than to marry Trevor, but I'm not sure that's what Trevor wants. Furthermore, I'm not sure that would reverse Teresa's decline as a person. I wonder how long Trevor would tolerate Teresa's one-wayness if he did marry her?

That's the tragedy of Teresa. I hope I can look back in ten years and see an improvement in her. It's doubtful at this point.

Aunt Joanne stopped. The room was silent as the click-click-click of the wall clock reverberated off the gray stucco walls. She put the journal down and looked directly at Tessa, who had leaned back and closed her eyes. "My brother was a difficult and very enigmatic man."

"That's one way of putting it."

"You know, Tessa, even though he and I had the same parents and grew up in the same religion, your father and I had a very different response to what we were given. If it means anything to you, I think he was wrong in the way he dealt with you and certainly in what he wrote in this journal. It must be very painful to read these terribly unkind words after his death."

That someone in her family finally grasped the impact of this event sent Tessa into a torrent of grief. There had been more weeping than usual of late and, regardless of how justified it might be, it was really beginning to chip away at her prided stoicism. She swiftly concluded the outburst, making mental note to rein it in.

"Are you okay?" Aunt Joanne asked gently.

"I'm fine. Really. At some point I'll get past all this weeping," she said, blowing her nose loudly.

"You're entitled. But listen, I want to give you a bit of an assignment."

"Really? So soon? Will there be a test, too?"

Aunt Joanne smiled. "Actually, it's a perfect first step. You're a writer; I want you to write an essay about your father. Nothing specific, just thoughts about him, anything you'd like, anything you think of. Do that for now, bring it in with you next time, and we'll continue talking."

Clearly her aunt presumed there would be a "next time." Tessa somewhat begrudgingly agreed to the task, as well as the suggestion to meet again. Given the circumstances, it seemed wise; she'd review how she felt about it after a few sessions. They hugged warmly and as Tessa walked from the convent to her car she acknowledged, with an ironic smile, that she was once again in therapy. With her aunt, the Catholic nun.

Ah. Life.

TWENTY-THREE

It was decided on the long ride home from Thousand Oaks. Tessa definitely wanted the journals, all of them. Whatever dread was in them, she wanted them. Whether it was to write, to find redemption, to uncover the mystery of Ronnie's forewarning, she didn't care. She wasn't sure she needed to know all the reasons right now, but she was sure she wanted them.

It also struck her that if Ronnie was coming to Los Angeles, he could bring the journals with him. That would save time and give a higher purpose to his visit. This plan later gave her entrée into the postponed presentation to David about Ronnie's imminent arrival.

"Fine. When is this happening?" He was getting ready to leave for the gym and barely looked up from tying his shoes.

"I'm not sure yet. I was just thinking it would be easier, rather than having all the journals sent here, to have Ronnie bring them with him since he's coming anyway, don't you think?"

"Again, I can't understand why you want to read them all, particularly since you're having such a hard time with the one you've got, but, hey, that's your prerogative."

"Well, yes it is, David, I'm not – "

"The point is, if you want your brother to spend a few days here, fine. He's your brother and I can't expect you to send him to a hotel – "

"That's ridiculous, David, he's broke *and* he's my brother!"

"I KNOW! Which is why I'm saying it's fine."

"I wasn't exactly asking permission – this is my home, too – I'm simply extending the courtesy of letting you know ahead of time."

David put his foot down with a loud, angry sigh. "Jesus, Tessa, why are we fighting so much? I don't get it. We never fought like this before and I feel like it's getting worse and worse and I don't know what to do about it. Are you pissed at me for what your father did or what is it? Just tell me."

Tessa walked to the window and stared out, reluctant to open this conversation. "Why haven't you wanted to read the journal?"

He stood, incredulous. "Are you kidding me? I asked to read it and you didn't even bring it with you when we were out of town and I actually had the time to concentrate on it."

"Oh, come on, you've had plenty of time to concentrate on it here!"

"Well, to be completely honest, I got the feeling you wanted me to leave it alone."

"No, David, I wanted you to care enough about what I've been going through to ask."

"If it was that important to you that I read it, why didn't you just hand it to me and say 'read it'?"

"Because I wanted you to *want* to read it. I wanted you to be curious and concerned enough about what's been bothering me to *insist* on reading it. This isn't the sort of thing I want to feel I'm forcing on you."

David's head was in his hands at this point. "I want to read it. Get it. Get the goddamn fucking journal and let me read it."

"Forget it. Now you're just saying that because you think – "

"Tessa, I mean it. Get the goddamn journal or I swear I'll throw this table through the wall."

So she did. She got the journal and gave it to him. And they didn't talk for the time it took him to read the marked pages. When he was done, he took her in his arms and held her close. They made love like they hadn't in a long time. But still, they didn't talk about it later and she noticed that before he fell asleep he forgot to say, "I love you."

TWENTY-FOUR

"Hey, Ronnie, second message I'm leaving. I'm wondering what's happening with your trip plans. I want to be sure I'm open the weekend you're here so let me know as soon as you can. Oh, and by the way, I decided to take your advice about reading the journals, so maybe we could talk about you bringing them with you when you come, okay? Call me."

About an hour later, he did. "Tessa, you realize there are quite a few boxes of these things. I can't exactly haul them on a plane and drag them over to your house."

Damn. Of course. "What would you suggest?"

"I would suggest you call Michaela, tell her to get the storage locker key from Mom and just ship them out to you."

Precisely what she'd been hoping to avoid.

Michaela was even less interested in that proposition. "I'm not exactly sitting around here looking for additional tasks to occupy my time."

For some reason, the tone, the implication, the sheer snottiness of it all snapped Tessa's good will. "Why do you always have to be such a bitch?"

The query resulted in Michaela hanging up and Tessa calling back three times before she'd pick up again. Tessa apologized sincerely enough to keep her big sister on the line.

"Tessa, I don't think you understand the pressure I'm under here. It's not just Mom, it's everything." Michaela was a perfectionist, always had been. And when she decided to embark upon a path – whatever path it was – it had to be done like no one had ever done it before. At school she had been a straight-A student, the Student Council President, and senior class valedictorian. She wanted to teach and, with a snap, got a full ride to Illinois Wesleyan where she got her education degree and subsequent masters with full honors, returning to Chicago to marry Randy Height, a middle-school English teacher from the north side. He inspired her to start her own school, and together they founded what had become one of the most successful charter schools in the area, at the same time raising three children, currently between the ages of five and nine. And now, on top of all that, she was the point-person for the care and feeding of their mother and the strain was beginning to show.

"Mickie, I know you've got a lot on your plate right now and I'm sorry, I really am. I wish I could do more from here but I'm not sure what that would be. Maybe we should talk about hiring someone to help deal with Mom."

"She doesn't need that kind of help; she's got Darlene to drive her all over the place and all her church friends are waiting on her hand and foot. It's just this desperate need she has to hold on to me. I honestly don't think I can take it anymore."

"Well, that's crazy and she needs to stop. You've just got to set your boundaries."

"Oh, please, I set my boundaries every day, every minute of every day. If I didn't she'd be laying on the rug under my desk."

"Can't anyone else there talk to her about it? Duncan, maybe?"

"I don't know. Suzanna tried the other day but she just kept saying I was the only one who really understood her. Which is strange, because I *don't*, not at all!" For the first time in a very long time she and Tessa shared a laugh. Brief, unremarkable, but the tension subsided for a moment. With that, they went on to talk about Randy and the kids, about how well the school was doing, the pride Michaela took in the community's support for this place she'd created.

"I hope you know how amazing it is, what you're doing," Tessa remarked. "I'm not sure I could do all that and raise three kids at the same time."

"Well, four, if you count Mom." They laughed for a second time. Then she stunned Tessa further by asking about the magazine, about David, about what it was like living at the beach. They actually had…a conversation. It was memorable. "Tessa, I'm sorry we've been so at odds lately. I think it's hard for me to feel connected to you when you're so far away and living such a different life."

"It's really not all that different. Yes, no husband or kids but, like you, I'm just trying to make something meaningful of my life and do the best I can by the people I love."

"I know. Let's try harder to not be so impatient with each other, okay?"

They agreed. Then they got back to the journals and FedEx and it all started up again.

"Michaela, please just shut up and listen! I said I'd pay for the shipping; you just have to take them to FedEx, or, better yet, have the truck come to the storage locker, and send them out, no big deal. What I'm not understanding is why you seem to have such a proprietary attitude about these fucking journals!"

"What I'm not understanding is why you have this dire need to get them all of a sudden. Ronnie said you're thinking of writing something about Dad…is that it?"

Christ. Just when she thought he hadn't been listening. "Whether it is or not, I'm one of his kids and I have the right to read them, so it doesn't matter."

"Well, it does to me. Because no matter what you think about our father and what a crappy childhood you had, he was still our father. And I'd rather not participate in letting you or anyone, for that matter, write some sort of ugly exposé about a man who isn't here now to defend himself."

"Isn't here now to defend himself? Who the fuck's fault is that, Michaela? The only reason this is being discussed after he's not here to defend himself is because he didn't have the fucking balls to tell us how he felt about us while he was still alive…when we would have had the chance to defend *our*selves!" With that, Michaela hung up again and this time Tessa didn't bother to call back.

Instead she called Duncan, who sounded very surprised to hear from her. "Wow, this is a surprise!"

"I know, I don't call very often, you don't call very often…how are you?"

Duncan was fine, family was fine, the case he was working on was fine; everything was fine. She launched. He listened. Then like the lawyer he was, attempted to reason with her.

"Yes, I agree we all have the right to read these things, Tessa, but I think you've got to have a little more sensitivity about it. Everybody grieves in their own way and I think this has hit Mickie harder than the rest of us. She's the one who stuck around there a lot longer than anyone else and, frankly, I think she sees Dad through a very different prism than you do, or Ronnie does, or, hell, even I do. So be kind. You just might have to give her a little more time before you hit her up for the ammunition to eviscerate the old man." He laughed; she hoped he was kidding.

"Duncan, I'm not even sure I want to write anything about it and if I did, obviously I'd be sensitive. Mostly I just want to get a better perspective of what Dad was thinking. It's pretty hard to read someone's distillation of your life down to one year and not wonder what he thought about the rest of them. I've got to believe he saw me more clearly as time went on and I'd like the opportunity to find that out. Is that so hard to understand?"

"No, it's not. I understand, Tessa. I just hope you're not disappointed."

"Why? Do you know something?

He laughed again. "I don't have time to read the paper much less the introspections of a very verbose man. What I mean is, given the tone of the journal you've got, plus what Ronnie had to say, I wouldn't hold out hope that the rest of them are substantially different."

"And don't you think that's shitty?"

"Yes, I do, but I also think it's not the whole picture."

"Based on what?"

"On what I saw when I spent time with him, on how he treated my kids, on what I'd hear him say about all of us throughout the years. I think Dad was a phenomenally frustrated and confused guy who couldn't figure out how to be himself and still be what his church and his family – even he himself – expected. That can make a person bitter and very critical of others."

Tessa thought that sounded remarkably wise and was a good note on which to end. Duncan agreed to talk to Michaela. By the time the conversation was done, Tessa realized it was the most she had talked to her big brother in many years and that made her sad in a way. Maybe she'd call more often. Probably not.

TWENTY-FIVE

Kate and Tessa were seated around a beige marble coffee table in a room at the Extended Stay America in Burbank where Ruby was now staying, though how extended she wouldn't say. Apparently she'd left home after some kind of melee with Ethan. Kate had been there for an hour, Tessa had just arrived, and Ruby had clearly been there long enough to moderately trash the room and get her face to a swollen, crazy-eyed state. She was now stretched out on the unattractive loveseat clutching a decorative pillow as if her life depended on it.

Kate had already put in some time trying to talk her down but seemed to have hit an impasse. "Sweetie, I get that you're mad and I get that you want to run, but obviously you can't stay away from your baby no matter what is going on with you and Ethan."

Tessa nodded, always in agreement with that basic philosophy, though she'd missed too many plot points to constructively jump in. "I'm sorry, I understand there's been a fight, but what I'm not getting is why you're here. You guys fight all the time…why's this different?"

With lips trembling so hard she could barely get it out, Ruby blubbered, "He doesn't want to be married to me anymore," then wailed loud enough that Tessa got concerned about neighboring guests calling security.

Ethan was a sound designer for a successful hour-long TV series. This was a job that demanded excruciating hours and a well-rested demeanor, and it seemed the time he had left for Ruby was relegated to exhausted moments between work, baby, sleep, and life. But after years of hand-to-mouth the job had been a boon and upon Milo's birth, Ruby had agreed, quite happily at the time, to put her retail career on hold; they didn't need the money and both felt strongly that a parent, rather than a nanny, should raise their son.

But as Milo got older and Ethan was gone longer and her own needs seemed to be less and less met, the fighting increased commensurately. Eventually it wasn't the kind that came with fantastic make-up sex and postcoital reaffirmations of love; it was the corrosive kind that soured the stomach and left both feeling toxic. It wasn't good. And tonight, apparently, it was *really* not good.

"So yeah, I screamed! As loud as I fucking could. Milo's at his grandma's so why not?"

Kate attempted interjection. "Well, maybe you could've – "

"Please don't start with what I could've done, okay? I get enough of that shit from him. He's such an ass with that controlled, arrogant bullshit thing he does; like he's so wise and I'm just a blathering, fucking lunatic, you know what I mean?"

"Yes...think I do," Kate said without inflection.

Tessa remained confused. "But this isn't new, the whole screaming thing. Isn't that basically your go-to mode?" She tended to be clumsier with these things.

"Shut up, Tessa. That's such a stupid fucking thing to say!" Ruby snapped.

"Let's not turn on each other, please," Kate stepped in. "We're all she's got right now. But, Ruby, I kind of get Tessa's point; you guys *do* fight a lot. We just want to understand what landed you here this time around."

Ruby hung her head like a shamed child. "I might have pushed it a little too far this time. I told him I didn't marry him to be a nanny and a cleaning lady, and if he expected that bullshit to continue, he'd have to offer more than a little dick and a shitty house in Burbank." She looked up with a wan smile, hoping to get a grin from the girls. Nothing. "Yeah…awful, I know. First he looked like he wanted to deck me, then he got all calm and unemotional and said something like 'being married to you is literally killing me.' Then he started carrying on about how he needed to 'rethink this arrangement for my sake and the sake of our son,' and I got so freaked out when he mentioned Milo I just screamed that he was a fucking asshole and ended up here."

Tessa liked Ethan and having seen Ruby goad many a man to near insanity with her insecurities and sharp temper over the years, wasn't quite ready to jump on the "he's a fucking asshole" bandwagon. "Wow, Rubes. You really pulled out the stops this time."

"I know; it was a hideous thing to say. He doesn't have a little dick." Still no laughter; this was all too serious.

"So what are you going to do?" Kate asked. "You can't stay here. Who'll take care of Milo when Ethan's at work tomorrow?"

"He's staying with Ethan's mom for at least the next two days. She's been wanting more time with him so I just downplayed the whole mess…she has no idea what's going on. Beyond that, I don't know. I can't tell whether I really hate my husband or I'm just unhappy but, either way, I can't do it anymore and he just doesn't get it. Something has to change."

Tessa had little to offer but Kate put in more time talking about various issues she and Todd had overcome with the help of a therapist and at some point Ruby fell asleep, leaving it all to be dealt with another day. Or at least tomorrow.

As they walked to their cars, Tessa and Kate were unusually quiet. Something about the gravity of this time hit them both. They were no longer youngsters having romantic tantrums, high-strung girls getting traction with boys by creating melodrama to keep things interesting. This was real life with kids and husbands and the very real threat of divorce and broken families. Grown-up stuff.

"How serious do you think this is?" Tessa wondered.

"I don't know; she's spent a lot of nights in our guest room lately and I don't see it getting any better." Kate's mouth was uncharacteristically tight. She'd always had little patience for the drama of Ruby's relationships, convinced that strife was wholly avoidable with calm reasoning and the occasional tune-up of a good couples counselor. Ruby was generally not amenable to either.

Tessa was struck by the fact that Ruby had been camping at Kate's so often. "I had no idea things were so bad. Odd that neither of you mentioned this to me. Also odd that neither of you felt I was a safe enough haven to offer a room now and again."

"Oh, come on, Tessa, you've had enough going on. We were just trying to keep it off your plate while you were mourning your dad. Besides, David would have been tearing his hair out with Ruby caterwauling in the room next door. You should be grateful we spared you."

But she wasn't. She was hurt and annoyed. Particularly with the David comment, which she had to begrudgingly admit was accurate. He always said the guest room was a "welcoming place" for anyone from either side of their lives but after one night of Ruby several months ago, David's repeated comments about how noisy she was left the distinct impression it was less welcoming than promised. It hadn't bothered her much at the time, particularly since the occasion hadn't come up since, but right now she found herself deeply irritated. "Well, it *is* my home too and I'd like to think my best friends know that."

They were at their cars. Kate hugged Tessa and kissed her forehead. "We know, Tess. It was just easier, that's all. Let's talk tomorrow and see if she comes around."

Tessa drove home awash with darting thoughts of Ruby, Kate, David, even her father. She pondered why he crept into every one of her mental rages, even ones in which he had no tangible connection. Some general theme of being left out or disregarded always seemed to conjure him up.

As she passed the Chevron station on the corner just below the condo, she pulled over to the curb and looked up at this place she called home. It seemed oddly foreign in that moment, distant and detached. In the warm yellow light beaming from the glass doors onto the deck, she suddenly saw David step out and look toward the beach. She knew he couldn't see her down on the darkened street and she took the opportunity to study him. He appeared tired, his expression melancholy. He briefly glanced down but never edged toward her sitting in the shadows; he turned and walked back inside. Was he wondering where she was? Was he even thinking about her?

She suddenly flashed on a childhood memory from long ago; she must have been about seven or eight. It was early autumn, in the backyard of the Chicago brownstone. Dusk was deepening into darkness and she, Ronnie, and Suzanna were playing in the yard, yelping and jumping in and out of a pile of leaves. At some point a light came on in their parents' upstairs bedroom and Tessa's eyes were drawn to the window. Leo approached and as he reached up to pull the shade, his eyes glanced down and, ever so briefly, met hers. In the darkness it was hard to determine his expression but she thought, maybe, he smiled at her. In a flush of warmth, the intense thrill of having caught his eye, she reached up to wave but before she could, he pulled the shade down, leaving her to wonder if he'd actually seen her much less smiled. She lowered her arm and rushed back to play as if nothing had happened, with only the briefest look back to the window before leaping into the pile Ronnie had made.

TWENTY-SIX

Working from home was continuing to lose its luster. What had once seemed the gift of telecommuting freedom now felt akin to exile. "I need humans," Tessa announced to Vivian in an early morning call following David's listless departure and no response from either Ruby or Kate. "I feel like I'm in quarantine but can't remember what disease I have."

"May I remind you that you were very excited about the idea of working from home? You were offered a desk here and you said you wanted to 'gaze out at the ocean and be inspired by the ever shifting tableau of nature.'"

"Fuck nature. I want people. I want to complain about bad coffee and who's getting the Costco muffins, important stuff like that."

"Sounds fun, Tessa, but I really don't need you here."

"Who said anything about need? I'm going crazy and could use some support on a solution."

"Okay, what do you want?" Vivian got serious. Tessa was her star and she wanted to keep her happy.

"I don't know. I guess I'm thinking I might be more stimulated if I was there amongst you all, feeding off the group energy, something like that. I hate to say it, but I'm bored."

"I see you haven't manned-up any since our Christmas

conversation, which is unfortunate. I don't know that sitting at a desk in this little office is going to stimulate you any more than working in that lovely living room of yours, and, besides, there *isn't* an available desk."

"What happened to the one you offered me?"

"I've got three different salespeople sharing it throughout the week and they're the ones keeping us all paid."

"Well, that sucks."

"Not if you like getting paid. Look, if you're that desperate and you're willing bring your laptop and sit wherever we can find you a spot, what the hell; come on in. I don't know why you'd want to make that drive but it's okay with me. I've always found you rather entertaining." *Thank God for Vivian.*

Before she put down the phone, Tessa checked her voice mail. Kate had called: "I just heard from Ruby and she's paid for a month at the Extended Stay. I guess we're in for the long haul."

Dammit. Why did it seem like the earth everywhere was moving beneath her feet? She'd promised Aunt Joanne she'd come in for another session today but despite her anxiety and the obvious need for a good therapeutic one-on-one, a movie sounded lots better. But when she called to beg off, her aunt insisted she keep her appointment with a tone that reminded Tessa she was dealing with a nun. Within the hour she was on her way.

TWENTY-SEVEN

<u>MY INEXPLICABLE FATHER</u>
Assignment for Aunt Joanne
By Tessa Curzio

Mystery Man. Good person but emotionally unavailable. By the time I was old enough to pay attention, I had no sense of who he was or how he felt about me. But I did believe he loved me.

He seemed dedicated to the task of fatherhood – he made school lunches, introduced us to good books, organized hikes – all that great stuff. But in looking back, there was a certain rote sense of duty to it all, as if he'd studied a manual on "how to be a good Catholic father" and implemented everything from A to Z.

And in some ways he was a good father…in that admirably dutiful way, not necessarily one that endeared him to us kids. He could be funny at times and show occasional interest, but he lacked consistent warmth or a true connection to us as individuals. Being the hyper-vigilant child I was, I watched like a hawk for any emotional generosity, always wanting more, never certain he was specifically aware of me in the chaos of our family. As I got older I took to saying, "I love you, Daddy" after every phone conversation but his stock reply was always, "I love all my kids," never, "I love YOU," as if wanting to be certain I didn't get more from the relationship than I was due. "I love all my kids." An announcement, a boundary; not an endearment.

Although he did try in his own way to differentiate. At some point he gave each of us a descriptive nickname. Duncan won the title of Best Boy (leaving Ronnie, by default, as...what? Second best?); Michaela, Little Miss Organizer; Suzanna was The Titan of Industry; me, The Drama Queen (with its passive aggressive spin I particularly hated); Ronnie, Mr. Nuts and Bolts; and Izzy was The Pretty One. I hated that too. It implied he thought Izzy was the only pretty one, which I found rankling. If Michaela and Suzanna were bothered by the slight, I have no idea. I was.

Beyond meeting you (Aunt Joanne), I felt like I knew so little about his early life. It was almost like a secret, which we all thought was very strange. All our friends had these huge extended families with cousins and aunts and uncles who seemed to come in and out of their lives, but my father and mother seemed to be keeping ours away. On my mother's side, frankly, there weren't many ancillary members to include. But on my father's side, your side, apparently the lack of interaction was due to my father's detachment from most of your family, except for you. I knew there were three older brothers; I met two, Uncle Bruno and Uncle Paul, but I was so young I barely remember them. Each of them passed away during my childhood but I don't remember hearing about funerals or related family gatherings; I certainly didn't go to any. There were various people who alluded to my father's struggles with your parents, my grandparents, who, according to my mother, were "ill-matched and fought like tigers." Since my childhood memories of them were of two very somber Italian immigrants who seemed profoundly unlike any grandparents I knew, I imagine that was true. You can clarify that for me at some point! My mother also said my father was drawn to religion as a remedy to his childhood turmoil. THAT I can believe! Here's an excerpt from 2002 that makes the point:

March 25, 2002 – the journal of Leo Curzio:

Religion, to my way of thinking, is the answer to all of life's conundrums. Would that more people viewed it that way! When others express doubt, I am only certain and unequivocal. Where life confounds and disappoints, I find my deepest comfort in knowing I'm a stalwart Catholic soldier, both in my devotion to the doctrines that guide me and the belief in the blessings bestowed, particularly that of a large and God-fearing family. When Audrey would question whether we could afford more children, make time for another child, or even produce another one, I would always assure her, "If God thinks we're doing a good job he'll give us another." Though, in truth, I do look at the parish families of ten and eleven as, perhaps, more compliant examples of quivers properly filled – more than we have been able to manage. But Audrey struggled with each pregnancy, losing two along the way, and the six we had were all we could deliver, despite our dutiful attempts in the marriage bed.

Putting aside a shudder at the thought of my parents' dutiful marriage bed, I was struck by the fact that I'd never once heard of my mom's miscarriages. They must have been deeply shaming to her or surely they would have become part of family lore, dragged out in moments of high drama. Odd, too, that my dad felt six kids wasn't enough. It certainly was for us girls in the family, considering we were obligated to be "little housekeepers" from the time we were big enough to hold a broom!

As for how my father's religion trickled down to us, it was the elephant in our lives, not just our living room. His obsession with his faith was the arbiter of everything, including his paternal decisions, often in lieu of love or common sense. Not only did he conduct his own life like a zealot, we kids were also obligated in ways that went beyond childhood duty, at least as compared to other kids we knew. While our friends played baseball and took dance classes, Duncan, Michaela and Suzanna, the "first family," as they were known, were doing internships at the parish convent (the girls) or mandatory altar boy duties (that'd be Duncan). Ronnie and I, the "second family," or "the Seconds," as my mother laughingly referred to us, were expected to follow suit but we were more rebellious than the Firsts. In fact, Ronnie literally refused to be an altar boy, which drove my parents crazy and got him knocked off the church baseball team. But he said he didn't care, less inclined to explore internal torment than me…maybe why he's now an alcoholic. I, however, did whatever was asked but always under secret protest; being around the nuns scared me (sorry, Auntie!) and our parish priest was just…well, odd, let's leave it at that.

As for Izzy, the only member of the "third family," she once told me she learned to smile and play the role of perfect Catholic daughter in whatever ways were expected, winning her the enduring adoration of our parents. Smart girl, that Izzy.

I couldn't manage the charade as neatly. Too much of it didn't make sense; I had too many questions and that was my downfall. I was always incurring the wrath of one or the other of my parents. My father, in particular, seemed to take delight in wielding his authority over me, which, at times, felt cruel and unloving. My mother's cruelty we'll leave to another essay.

So throughout my childhood and into my teenage years I was anxious, fearful of everything from my mother's outbursts, my father's disapproval, the nuns' scrutiny, the priests' doom and gloom, and just the general sense that – given all the screaming directed my way – I clearly did not have the "goodness quotient" to avoid Hell. Which was a terrifying revelation and made me all the more anxious.

My dad seemed completely unaware or unconcerned about my unnatural state of anxiety. Even when I was seven, being publicly harangued by the parish priest for waiting two months instead of the requisite one "since my last confession," my dad's only response to my anguish was, "Learn to manage your time better." I was seven!

More nights than not, I couldn't sleep, incessantly pondering what would happen when I died and how I could possibly endure Hell (where I was surely headed). When I tried to talk about it with him all he could say was, "Don't sin and you'll have nothing to worry about." So I hid my anxieties in my reading and writing and performing, focused on the countdown to leaving home for college where I thought I'd figure it all out. I didn't exactly pull that off, did I?

The fact is, it's believable to me – in retrospect – that my father didn't like me all that much. I didn't put it together at the time, but in looking back, it's clear he couldn't regard my feelings when he should have, didn't seem to know how to talk to me when he could have; rarely showed me consideration that a good parent would have. I could give you many examples but then we'd have a novel!

On the other hand, he could be sweet and unusually creative. I remember all of us circling around him while he'd play CDs from his favorite musicals, reading the dialogue between the songs, explaining what each element of a musical was about. It made me love music and art, made me love him. Those memories remain some of the happiest I have of him.

But the biggest mind-fuck of all is that I actually expected to get to know him better as we got older and time would allow. Funny how time has its own agenda. Right before he died we had this really nice conversation. It was nothing special; he just asked about my work, wondered when he'd finally meet David; he laughed at something I said, asked if I was coming home for Christmas. It was inconsequential but memorable at the same time, because it was a rare conversation with some real feeling…like he was talking to me, just me. I had a sense he was mellowing in his old age and maybe, for once, wanted to make a real connection.

Three days later he was dead. After Suzanna called, I found a picture of him and me together, put it on top of my dresser and sobbed for hours. I felt like I'd just lost the last chance to create a real, adult relationship with him. And – this is really horrible – I felt utterly pissed that it was him instead of my mom. I figured she'd go first, she was always so sick, but he had to go and surprise us all. So very Leo. I was as devastated as any daughter could be.

Until I read the journal. And then it all just disappeared. The feelings of love, the sense that we'd gotten closer, the idea that I meant something to him, that he loved me; it was all gone -- poof, like smoke in the wind. When I got home after the funeral I took that picture off my dresser and threw it in a box in the closet where it remains.

I once believed he knew who I was – the true girl, the real me – and loved me for that. I believed that until now. Now I don't know what to believe.

(To be continued…??)

115

TWENTY-EIGHT

Aunt Joanne put the essay down and looked at Tessa with tenderness. "Very thorough and illuminating. I appreciate your candor."

"I do candor well."

"Yes, you do. And where do you stand now?"

"About…?"

"About any of it."

"Well, like I said, I don't know what to believe at this point."

"About your father, your sense of your family, yourself?"

"Yep, pretty much covers it."

"And…no faith to speak of?"

"In Catholicism? No."

"What about in God, religion, a belief system of any kind?"

"I have no faith in faith."

"When did that happen, exactly? After you left home?"

"Before. When I realized how cruel it all was."

"I'm sorry to hear that, Tessa."

"Why?"

"Because I think faith sustains us, gives us something to lean on and go to in moments of need. Belief in something bigger than oneself is essential, I think, to making sense of our relatively short lifetimes on this earth. Faith in God, specifically, is a very powerful force that can actually hold us to our purpose and sense of goodness."

"That's sounds nice, it does. And I think if you really have faith, true faith, as you obviously do, it must be comforting. I wish I did but I don't."

"But you did once, didn't you?"

"Was that really faith? Doing what my parents told me, following the rules, doing what the nuns and priests said I had to do; just being a good little Catholic girl because I had no other choice? When I look back, I realize I never felt any sense of real faith the entire time I was a so-called Catholic. The other kids were burning for Jesus and experiencing transcendence or whatever it was they thought they were experiencing and I just felt a host stuck to the roof of my mouth. And it never got any better. I thought there was something wrong with me but it turns out I just wasn't one of the faithful."

"I don't know if it's that simple. I think you have to have a certain kind of spiritual mentoring that you, perhaps, never got. Maybe if you reinvestigated at this point in your life you'd find a different sort of experience in the – "

"Auntie, you're not really going to try to recruit me now, are you? Because if that's the case, we'd just be spinning our wheels and I don't think either of us needs that." Tessa's back was seriously up.

"Absolutely not, Tessa. Get that right out of your head." Aunt Joanne's eyes flashed sharply enough to make her point. "I'm not remotely interested in convincing you of anything, give me a little more credit than that! I'm just trying to understand how deep this goes and I'd say pretty deep."

Tessa softened. "Sorry. I just can't tolerate any kind of spiritual browbeating right now. I've had it from both a conventional religion and a cult and the wounds are surprisingly similar."

"Tell me about Scientology."

"Why…do you think that was the big bad wolf that scared the

Jesus out of me?" Tessa loved her aunt but couldn't forget she was someone who believed in the more orthodox expressions of religion. Scientology, with its bizarre methods and theories, must surely elude her.

"No. I actually think some of its constructs like the Communications Course and its study methods are interesting. I don't subscribe to their philosophical tenets or their methodology, certainly their antipathy towards psychiatry is misguided, but I can understand how you were drawn to it." Aunt Joanne never failed to amaze. "What I would like to know is why you left that belief system too and did that second departure have anything to do with your current lack of faith?"

Tessa told her about Brice, about how Scientology, in the early years, seemed exhilarating and exotic, so wild and fresh it completely appealed to her sense of adventure. How, once past Brice, she threw herself into it with no reservations, convinced of its purpose, its superiority amongst the plethora of religions and philosophies she'd studied. She'd been so proud and excited to be a chosen one, sorry for those "not evolved enough to be transformed by this amazing new religion," as she once put it to a non-believer, ready to do her part to clear the planet.

"The frustration was only my persistent lack of funds necessary for the never-ending list of services required for my journey 'across the bridge,' as they put it. One level was more expensive than the next, particularly the obscenely priced upper levels, but that's where we all wanted to go, to 'OT 3' with its magical, mystical powers. I figured I'd get there once my acting career made me rich and famous, so becoming a rich and famous actor became the goal. We all know how well that went."

Aunt Joanne, perplexed, remarked, "How does your acting career connect to Scientology or losing your faith? Enlighten me."

Tessa explained that, once arrived in Los Angeles, she joined an acting class run by Anthony Cabot, a moderately well known character actor who also happened to be a Scientologist. This is where she met Ruby and several of her past boyfriends, where Kate joined her upon her own west coast arrival, and where Tessa learned to teach the craft of acting herself – a heady, passionate, creative time. Most of the students were ardent young Scientologists with few acting chops and fewer credentials, driven, instead, by the fervent, if ill advised, conviction that they were destined for stardom by the sheer force of their believing. Positive affirmations (or "postulates," as they called their version of such things), particularly about winning Oscars, were rampant.

Tessa, with her bona fides as a former theater major with an impressive college resume, was chosen to be the class assistant, working alongside Anthony booking scenes, taking attendance, following up on class administration, and ultimately mentoring under him as a substitute teacher, a task for which she showed considerable aptitude. By the end of her second year she was teaching when he couldn't, her biggest test arriving in Year Five when he was off for several weeks to imbibe in some "upper level" courses out of state. Tessa felt completely prepared to run the class for the duration, and while certain students griped about paying full price for "Anthony's substitute," there seemed general consensus that everyone was on board.

Anthony was ultimately gone six weeks and during that time Tessa felt the class had gone well. Some students showed up sporadically, there was a particular group that seemed less attentive (they were the veterans who'd predated her arrival and her vault past them in terms of hierarchy rankled), but most continued to bring in scenes and adjust their work according to her critiques.

Shortly after Anthony's return, Tessa was surprised to get a late night call from him. "I need you to come down to the theater. There are some things I'd like to discuss and it needs to be done in person." Anthony's voice was oddly impassive.

"Okay, sure. When do you want to do that?"

"Right now."

Stunned, she looked at the clock. "Now? It's almost midnight and I have to get up for work pretty early…could we possibly talk tomorrow night after class?" She assumed he was going to take the opportunity to thank her for a job well done and, as much as she was looking forward to that, figured it could wait until the following night.

Strangely, he didn't. "This needs to be handled before class. I've got a busy day tomorrow so we need to take care of this now. Bring your theater keys and the attendance book with you." That instruction was alarming, as was the late hour, but she assuaged herself that it would be all right.

But upon arrival at the theater she was informed otherwise by the dour expression on Anthony's face. When he seated her at center-stage directly under a bright spotlight, a few classmates scattered in the seats behind him, she realized this was not going to be good and her stomach clenched. "Anthony, what is going on?"

He looked at her somberly, a notepad in his lap, and began. "Tessa, a number of students who've been around for a long time and have certain stature in the church have made some serious accusations about your tenure here at the front of the class, accusations I felt deserved immediate investigation."

A wave of dread washed over her, the inevitable sense of doom attached to every suggestion of sin she'd ever felt. "That's strange, because from my perspective everything went really well. In fact, I actually thought you were calling to congratulate me on a job well done!" She looked up at the surrounding students, people with whom she'd had nothing but great rapport, and asked, "Sandy, you were happy with everything, right? Kyle, did you have any issues?" But before anyone could answer, Anthony continued.

"Frankly, the accusations are these: that you consciously undermined some of the actors, that you criticized and belittled unnecessarily, and that you purposely demeaned beyond the point of good critique. What's your response to that?"

Tessa was stunned by the list of offenses, all of which were ridiculous and she adamantly denied, and was even more shaken when, from the backstage area, entering with all the drama of "surprise witnesses," came several of the accusing group. All were much higher on the Scientology food chain and that did not bode well for her, that much she knew. As her accusers gathered around Anthony in the theater seats, Tessa took note of the perverse cliché of the lighting and seating arrangement of this court. Now all they needed were the kangaroos.

Anthony gave each student the floor and, mostly without meeting her eyes, they rattled off accusations that were staggering: Tessa had been a saboteur, had shaken the confidence of several; had used negative intentions and words to diminish and demoralize certain students. One particular accuser, Richard Hielman, a man she considered a dear friend, at least had the courtesy to look at her directly as he detailed her transgressions, oddly sympathetic as he claimed she'd made him feel "so rotten" with her critiques that he'd gotten sick and no longer wanted to continue his acting studies.

"Richard, how can you possibly say that? We're *friends!* I've never had anything but the greatest respect for you and your work…I was particularly sensitive in my critique of your Stanley Kowalski. And you even thanked me!"

Richard ducked his head as if both stricken and ashamed but continued nonetheless. "Tessa, I'm really sorry, I am. Because I don't think the negative energy *is* you, but it's coming *from* you."

When this cryptic declaration with its odd emphasis was repeated several times by others, and seemingly supported by Anthony's nods, the confusion of it all finally drove Tessa to stand abruptly and holler in frustration. "Someone better tell me what you're all talking about before I go fucking crazy!"

Considering the situation, the "crazy" comment was probably unwise, but Richard took the moment to explain with some gentleness. "Clearly your OT 3 stuff has kicked up." Whatever that meant. But because OT 3 was a confidential level they'd all accomplished and she had not, Richard claimed he could say no more, other than she'd ultimately understand when she got to that level herself.

After that declarative finale, Tessa was speechless, and the group, satisfied that their grievances had been heard, waited solemnly for Anthony's verdict. Which was immediate. "Tessa, until you do OT 3, or until whatever negative forces emanating from you have abated, it's too disruptive to have you in the class, so you're out. If and when you get that accomplished you can let me know and we'll adjudicate freshly at that time. Please leave your keys and the attendance book with Richard."

And that was it. They all stood up and turned away from her in whispered conversation. She left the book and keys near Richard's turned back and, from that moment on, not one of the people in that room would talk to her...she'd been shunned by all. Well, not *all*. There were two students not present at the inquisition who immediately quit the class, though not before telling the group, including Anthony, to go fuck themselves. Royally. That would be Kate and Ruby.

At this point in the story, Aunt Joanne interjected. "I can see why these two have remained such important people in your life. I can't imagine how a sensitive young woman like yourself could have endured such a debacle without friends. I'm curious what happened after that."

"It was kind of strange. I obviously felt emotionally battered but I also felt a certain clarity move in. I couldn't help but think, if a philosophy of supposed enlightenment could turn so cruelly and unfairly against one of its own members, where was the moral high ground? How much of this could I – *did* I – actually believe? I started to really look at it and at some point I realized, once out of the 'fog of cult,' so to speak, that I didn't believe much. The technology was dubious, the elitism was arrogant and distasteful, and, given my own experience, the philosophy lacked any true compassion...much like my father's version of Catholicism. And also like his Catholicism was its cruelty." She suddenly looked at her aunt. "I'm sorry, Aunt Joanne. I feel like I'm always bashing your religion."

"No offense taken." Aunt Joanne smiled. "I believe we've covered how differently your father and I practiced our faith."

Tessa visibly relaxed. "Anyway, that's when I left. Quietly and without much notice. I guess I was too insignificant to stir any attention with my escape."

"And that was it?"

"Pretty much. But about a year later, a big magazine – I can't remember which one – ran a sensational story about this famous writer who defected, and the piece outed a lot of the confidential Scientology material, including OT 3. Obviously I was fascinated, since I wasn't going to be privy to it any other way, and I was just stunned by what I read, most of it utterly bizarre stuff about a god named Xenu and exploding volcanoes and body thetans – "

"Body thetans?"

"Yes, they're defined as something like lost spirits who attach themselves to the bodies of, say, unenlightened people like me!"

"I'm don't understand…"

Tessa explained that, from what she could interpret from the article, the negative energy the acting class accusers supposedly felt coming *from* her was actually coming from errant "body thetans," who'd attached themselves to her without her awareness and spent their time upsetting her classmates. "Hence, the 'it's not *you* but it's coming *from* you' thing. The problem was, even if it *wasn't* me, they were apparently *my* body thetans, which still left me as persona non grata. "

Aunt Joanne still looked perplexed. "I'm not sure I completely get all this."

"Don't worry, I don't think anyone actually does, even the people who've done OT 3!" Tessa laughed. "It was all so absurd I found myself laughing out loud, but also understanding – for the first time since that insane night – what sort of craziness I'd gotten myself into. I actually felt sorry for my classmates…they were good people who'd been bamboozled, just as I'd been. And it was then that I came to the not-incomprehensible conclusion that faith can sometimes be a seductive and very dangerous thing, something I'll never again embrace so freely. Hence, my current status: fatherless and faithless."

Aunt Joanne took a deep breath. "That's one hell of a story."

Tessa couldn't help but smile. "Perfectly put, Auntie."

TWENTY-NINE

On the way home from Aunt Joanne's Tessa detoured off the freeway and ended up in her old neighborhood at the base of the Hollywood Hills. Whitley Terrace, with its classic structures winding their way along the looping hillside street, embodied the gritty, eclectic Hollywood culture Tessa had loved. Buildings from the 1920s and '30s mixed with ugly '60s and '70s abominations to create a jumble of contradicting curb appeal. There was her old building, all Art Deco flourishes and pale pink stucco, the huge oak out front and twinkle lights arched over the doorway. Life here had been complicated and passionate – and not always happy – but somehow all memories remained sweet. Here was where she sang and wrote music, loved intense men who intensely loved her back, and found a part of herself that was strong enough to let go of dreams that had broken her heart. This building was surely as much a part of her life as any person or event.

What caught her eye in passing was the "For Rent" sign tucked neatly in the manager's window. She felt a rush of...what? Regret? Nostalgia? Wishful thinking? Curiosity? Curiosity, she concluded. She parked her car and went to the door, where her knock summoned a large brunette-turned-burgundy-coiffed woman who stuck her head out with a big grin.

"Tessa! Oh my God, how are you?" Martina Hernandez was

an exuberant, exceedingly warm Mexican woman with two kids, a crazy husband, and a kind heart, who managed the building with varying degrees of success and had always held the affection of her tenants. "What are you doing here, sweetie pie? Miss me too much?" She laughed loudly as she grabbed Tessa in a bear hug.

"You know, Martina, I think I have," Tessa smiled, genuinely warmed by the embrace.

They talked about the neighborhood, the latest issues with Martina's husband (he was now selling bicycles on Sunset); the woman who'd moved into Tessa's old apartment and was now, apparently, trying to break her lease.

"I'm so mad at this girl!" Martina growled. "She just begged for the place when she got here and now she tells me she's thinking about moving in with her loser boyfriend down on Melrose but, oh, she's not sure. So now I don't know what the hell to do except take some applications! You want it back? It's all yours. You don't belong down in Orange County anyway!"

Tessa reminded Martina that Manhattan Beach was still in Los Angeles County, though her assessment about Tessa not belonging wasn't too far off. They talked about the unlikelihood of Martina ever getting down to the beach given her aversion to water; they talked about Tessa's job, her "love life" (as Martina so quaintly put it), and finally about how Tessa was not actually looking to move back in. After hugs and a promise to stay in touch, Tessa headed back to her car feeling just a little bit like she was leaving home again.

*

THIRTY

By the time she got to her actual home, David had already eaten dinner and cleared the table. There was a perfunctory kiss and, before she could detail her day, he pointed to the phone with a shake of his head. "There are six messages from your mother, who claims she can't find your cell number. Apparently your desire for the journals has unleashed the hounds of hell. Good luck with that…I'm going to watch the game." He exited for the den and Tessa listened to the six messages. *Dear God Almighty.*

"Mother, you're acting like a lunatic. I have no intention of 'disemboweling' your husband!"

Audrey was in peak form, sobbing and screaming simultaneously, a feat she'd perfected over years of practice. "You are a disrespectful, ungrateful shit of a daughter! Your father was a saint, an absolute angel. You should be thanking me every day for giving you a perfect father who gave you a perfect life." *This again.*

"Mother, I – "

"Why you want to embarrass him, embarrass me, destroy our family and ruin your relationships with all your brothers and sisters is impossible for me to understand. WHAT IS WRONG WITH YOU?" This went on for about fifteen minutes, volleys of accusations and hysteria that ultimately wound down to exhausted conversation.

"Mother, it may be hard for you to understand, but this isn't about me wanting to destroy anything. I don't feel like I knew my father very well and if reading his journals would help me know him better, why would you be against it?"

"He was a saint!"

"Yes, you already said that."

"And that's all you need to know. If he isn't in heaven, there is no heaven."

"That may be true but he also had his quirks."

"What exactly does that mean, Teresa?" The snarl resurfaced.

"It means, Mother, that he wrote a bunch of stuff about his kids that he intended for us to read and a lot of it wasn't very nice. I'm not sure I understand why any father would do that, do you?"

A pause. "Well, I don't know what you're talking about but if he was angry and wrote about it, obviously you kids must've done something." Audrey had maintained throughout their childhoods that it was the "folly of obnoxious children that made good parents lash out." The concept of child abuse eluded her and she wasn't likely to see the "folly" of Leo's cutting words.

"You know, Mother, we're probably not going to see eye to eye on this."

"You are just a brat, a brat, you know that? What have I done to deserve such ungrateful children?" The mumbling of this classic inspired the urge to scream but wisdom told Tessa this would not result in the desired accommodation from her mother, who could make getting the journals an insurmountable task, particularly with Michaela's unholy alliance.

"Mom, would you please just relax and realize we're on the same side? I have no desire to do anything but read more so I can hopefully understand more. Just trust me for once…I'm not going to do anything to hurt this family. It's my family, too, so why would I do that?"

This had some success in calming Audrey, who cried a bit more, interrupted only by repeated comments about Leo's sainthood. Before long, she'd worn herself out and said she had to go to bed.

"Okay, Mom, but please give Michaela the key to the locker and tell her to send the journals, would you do that?"

"I'll see how I feel in the morning, honey, but just don't write a book. Books are a waste of time and no one will ever want to read it anyway."

Tessa couldn't help but muse, given her career trajectory, that Audrey was probably at least right about that last part.

THIRTY-ONE

True to Vivian's word, there was not a desk to be had in the *Edge+Reason* office, so Tessa sat at a workstation feeling out of place and completely uninspired. So far. She wasn't sure whether it was the novelty of being somewhere other than her desk at the beach, or if the distraction of writing in a more public setting was simply too great an obstacle, but she was getting nowhere. So far. Elaine Smith, one of the advertising salespersons who'd clearly made a home at the desk originally offered Tessa, filled the air with her rapid-fire sales pitches and the exultant tapping of her keypad. Occasionally she'd glance over at Tessa with a hearty wink – an oddly intimate gesture Tessa found creepy – but most of her time and attention was firmly fixed on the sales job at hand, something at which she clearly excelled given the enthusiasm afforded her by everyone else.

"Everyone else" on this particular morning was a copy editor named Stanley Rackett, whose eyes never left the computer screen, a perky staff writer and researcher named Meagan, who Tessa had met only that morning; an editor she was pretty sure was named Barry or Brian, and two writers named Malice and Stoney, no idea why on either name. Hovered with Glen over an apparently problematic set of computers was a tech team Tessa didn't know, one a tall, handsome fellow, the other a willowy girl who seemed attached to his hip. Cute couple, she thought.

After perusing the personnel, Tessa refocused on "Gifted Children: Cultural Phenomenon or Parental Ego Trip," her article due by Wednesday. Stuck on the second paragraph for now going on an hour, she decided it was time to exercise that favorite avoidance ritual known to office workers across the land: the coffee refill from the office kitchen. She wandered in with her lukewarm half-cup, topped it off, then stood leaning against the refrigerator wondering what the hell she was doing there.

Before an answer came to mind, Vivian bustled in, flopped down at the table, and plowed into a rather large pink pastry box. "There's an apple fritter in here with my name on it!" she announced merrily, sifting through the available options.

"How can you eat those every day and stay within an inch of slim?"

"Prodigious stress and the love of a man who forces me to yoga. Plus, I don't eat them everyday so shut the hell up. How do you like it here so far? Feeling stimulated yet?" Vivian grinned.

Tessa had to think about that. "It's…social. And that's good. I can't say I want to be here every day but I think it's good for me to be around people working on a common cause, you know? I don't have to explain myself and maybe, assuming I get used to it, I'll actually start talking to some of them and, yes, find them stimulating."

"You're such an elitist bitch!" Vivian laughed. "Listen, I don't care where you set up shop, just write. By the way, I've been thinking about this thing with your father, this journal thing and all the stuff that's bringing up, and I've got an idea."

Tessa joined her at the doughnut box. "Not sure this is something I want to hear but go ahead, surprise me."

"Seriously, Tessa, the whole subject of fathers and daughters is a big one, particularly for women as they get older and face the inevitability of losing that person they feel so conflicted about. For a lot of women it's loss mixed with tremendous confusion and hurt and I think your story would resonate – "

Tessa cut her off, a tad annoyed at where this was going. "Vivian, I appreciate that you find my story so utterly fascinating but I haven't even decided whether or not I want to write about it for myself, much less your audience!"

Vivian was undeterred. "Okay, don't write about your specific story, I get it, that's private. But either way, I want to do a series on fathers and daughters. I think it's one of those universal themes that if written well, with cutting edge stories and an original voice – that would be you, darling – would be really compelling. I mean, the idea of finding out on the day of your father's funeral that he'd written these journals about his children is one of those tragic, inexplicable things fathers do and daughters endure and if you don't want to tell that specific story, I want you to find others out there that are as provocative and tell those. A series. Interviews, great writing, graphic truth; it's a winner. You in?"

"I don't know…maybe. Where do I find these daughters?"

"I'll get Meagan on it; she has a way of ferreting out great stuff. She could find your interview subjects, you do the interviews, write the stories, we run them as a series; start an online dialogue on the page and see where it goes. Just think about it, okay?"

"I will."

And she did, all the way from Sherman Oaks to Manhattan Beach, interrupted only by her longer than usual collection of voice mail messages.

First, Ronnie: "I can't talk now, on my way to a job interview, but I wanted to say I'm still planning to get out there and I'll call as soon as I know my schedule, okay?" *Okay, Ronnie.*

Next, Kate: "Can you meet Ruby at Fiddler's Cafe? She's freaking out and I have a major job to get done before tomorrow and there's no way I can get there." *Okay, Kate.*

Then David: "Got tickets to a Lakers game. If you want to go you'll have to let me know within the hour or the ticket will be gone. I'll wait to hear from you; otherwise I'll just go and see you later." Too late. With a sigh she thought, *okay, David.*

THIRTY-TWO

It was official: Ruby and Ethan were getting divorced. Apparently after days of discussion and honest analysis of their deepening differences and inability to overcome them, the weighty, unfathomable decision had been made. Ethan would file the papers and be moved out by the end of the month; Ruby would continue at the Extended Stay until then, after which she'd move back in. They arranged for daycare so Ruby could go back to work and Ethan's mother agreed to supplement that care with regular "Grandma days." Ruby was relaying all this with uncharacteristic calm but Tessa had a knot in her stomach the size of a mountain and no amount of the supposed-logic Ruby was spouting did anything to quell it.

"So it totally sucks, obviously, but I guess it's better than the alternative…fighting ourselves to death. Anyway, it is what it is."

"What can I say, Rubes, I'm so sorry. I'd ask if you were sure this was the only solution but I trust you guys already went over that particular question, right?"

"Ethan said if we were going to do it, it's better to do it now while Milo is too young to really understand the impact. And I agree. A few more years and it would just kick his little ass." With that, the façade crumbled and inevitable tears began to pour. Picturing Milo bouncing so early between two homes made Tessa

134

almost as sad as her distraught friend. This all seemed too swift, so utterly upending without any real sense to it. How do you go from just fighting a lot to deciding your marriage is over? Something wasn't adding up and despite her internal promise to not push too hard or dig too deep, Tessa couldn't help herself.

"Ruby, I just don't get it. I know you guys have problems but this is so drastic. And so fast. Why don't you just separate for a while and see if you feel differently after some time apart? Why would you file for divorce before you've even sorted out how permanent this feels?"

"It feels pretty permanent."

"It just happened, how could it?"

"I've been sleeping with this guy from my gym." Ruby said this so matter-of-factly it almost knocked Tessa from her chair.

"What? Wait…are you kidding?"

"No. And before you get all judgie and horrified, you should also know that Ethan has been seeing this woman he works with too, so it's not just me."

"Ethan's sleeping with another woman?"

"Not yet, but I'm sure he will be."

"Wow. You guys have really done it this time." Tessa shook her head. "I don't know what to say. Who is this guy you've been sleeping with? Do we know him?"

"No, Tessa, you do not know him. And it doesn't matter; he's just a guy from the gym. A hot, sexy guy who happened to like my body and who actually paid attention to me, which is more than I can say for my husband in the last two years. It wasn't that serious, it only happened a few times when Milo was at his grandmother's, and I ended it a few days ago. But in some ways Ethan's dinners with Margo – that's the girl at work – when he should have been home with us, were a lot more intimate then me fucking some guy I barely know!"

"You just ended it a few *days* ago? Wow. Okay, well, I'm not going to get into deciding who's doing what that's more intimate,

I'm just sort of grossed out that you went down that road at all. I mean, come on, Ruby, after working so hard to get your life together, to find a good man, to make your marriage work, especially knowing how it would affect your son if it didn't...what the fuck?"

"God damn it, Tessa, I knew you were going to get all pissed off about this, which is why I didn't tell you in the first place!" Ruby slammed her coffee cup on the table so hard that brown liquid sloshed across their napkins and alerted an irate waitress who hustled off to get a towel.

"What does that mean?" Tessa snapped. "Shouldn't I get pissed off? Why, didn't Kate get pissed off?"

"Are you fucking kidding me?" Again, louder than necessary. Tessa reached out and squeezed Ruby's arm, hard; she dropped a decibel but continued in a fierce whisper. "Do you really think I'd tell Kate? Though I suppose now you will! She's even more of a priss than you are and if there's anything I don't need right now it's both my best friends standing in judgment of me!"

"Ruby, you really *are* pissing me off now. This is not about how Kate or I feel. It's about how you feel. About how Ethan feels. And about how Milo will feel when he's old enough to realize his parents couldn't keep it together long enough to get him to the first fucking grade." Tessa had officially lost her cool. Something about the cavalier way in which Ruby threw this at her was infuriating. They *did* have a good marriage and those were hard to come by. And now they'd wasted it. Tessa felt the loss as strongly as a best friend could.

Ruby started to buckle under the weight. "Tessa, please, *please* don't make me feel any worse. Don't you think I hate myself right now? I hate myself almost more than I hate Ethan. But I couldn't stand it; don't you get it? I really couldn't stand it. Month after month, year after year, feeling alone and lost and so unimportant to him. I tried; I really did, for almost two years I tried. But loving our baby wasn't enough and I just wanted to feel like someone loved *me!*"

"Oh, and this gym guy *loved* you? Right. Honestly, haven't you fucked enough guys, Ruby? Didn't you already figure out that that's not going to get you what you want? I love you, girlfriend but I gotta say, I'm having a hard time with this one. Ethan is a good guy. He was worth the struggle." She stood up, too angry to stay. Ruby could only look at her with red, sorrowful eyes.

"I know he is, Tessa. But I couldn't do it. I'm sorry." Tessa squeezed her hand and left, as turmoiled as if this were happening to her. Ruby's recklessness had too often mirrored her own throughout their lives and she needed Ruby to be stable so she could feel like stability was possible for her, too.

The gym guy. *Unfuckingbelievable.*

THIRTY-THREE

It was days before Tessa told David about the demise of Ruby's marriage. Somehow she couldn't bring herself to reveal it sooner, and she certainly didn't intend to tell him the whole story. On the few occasions they'd socialized as couples, he found Ethan and Ruby to be likeable enough but was always slightly stiff in their company, as if he were entertaining visitors from another planet – particularly with Ruby. David's life had been fairly conventional and the crispy edges of Ruby's story seemed almost cartoonish by comparison, offering them little commonality. Tessa presumed his take on their divorce would be as predictably patronizing – "Well, didn't you figure she'd screw it up?" – and that reaction was something she'd have to gird for. But he surprised her.

"Wow. That's too bad. They seemed like they had a good thing going. That has to be tough with their kid, right?"

Tessa was grateful for his compassion. "I'm sure it is. I think they're both probably in shock at the moment. But luckily Milo is young enough that he doesn't know what's going on; at least they can spare him that for the time being."

"What happened?" Exactly where she didn't want to go.

"I think the two plus years since Milo's birth finally just took their toll. Ethan's job has ungodly hours, she stopped working to become a full-time mom, and basically they couldn't find a way to spend any real time together. It all just sort of…eroded."

David tapped silently on the table for a moment then stood up and put on his jacket. "Tess, I'm going out for a quick drink with a couple of guys from work; we've got a campaign on deadline and agreed to spend some time on it tonight. But let's talk later, okay? I've actually got something I want to run by you."

His departure left Tessa immediately anxious, never a fan of the suspended tease. *What on earth does he want to run by me that requires such a cryptic preamble?* She was struck by a heart-stopping thought: what if he was going to ask her to marry him? Is that what Ruby's situation triggered: the need to close ranks and lock up their relationship? Her heart started pounding.

She thought about calling Kate but reconsidered when she remembered Kate's post-Ruby-divorce-announcement rant, a diatribe about the insanity of marriage and the greater insanity of her friends. Kate once told her she wasn't sure she liked David, later said she actually did like David but wasn't sure he was the right guy for Tessa; more recently she admitted she didn't have a "bloody clue who the fuck was right for anyone anymore." This came sometime after Ruby moved into the Extended Stay. Kate was not a go-to girl at the moment.

Nor, of course, was Ruby. They'd only spoken once since the meeting at Fiddler's. Tessa finally called to apologize for her tirade and Ruby apologized for "being a whore" and Tessa admonished her for being so hard on herself and Ruby begged for forgiveness and Tessa forgave and Ruby said she'd never have sex again and it went on and on until they were back in each other's good graces. Ruby was, however, understandably raw and in no shape to advise anyone on matters of the heart.

Tessa even thought of calling Ronnie but realized it was much too late to expect him to be in shape for anything sensible, which led her to the one person who actually *was* offering sense and was even quite effective at it. She dialed the number of a sixty-two-year-old Catholic nun to discuss whether she should marry the man with whom she'd been living for almost a year.

"Do you *want* to marry him?" Always direct, Aunt Joanne.

"I don't know. I thought I eventually would – I mean, would eventually *want* to. I'm thirty-six, I'd like to have kids some day, I'd like a normal life with a good man and David is a good man. But I don't know…I've never wanted to get married before so I don't know how it's supposed to feel. They say you 'just know' but I've never *just known* and I don't know if I know now."

"Maybe that's because you haven't met anyone you want to marry yet."

"Is it that simple? You just *want* to marry and so you know and then you do? Oh, Christ, how would you know?" She laughed. Aunt Joanne laughed too. *Thank God.*

"Tessa, I don't know, obviously. But I think marriage is a serious enough matter that if you *don't* know, you should wait until you do." Simple. Agreed. They set up their next appointment and Tessa went back to work on her article. The phone rang. It was Vivian.

"Just so you know, Meagan's already lined up two women for the father/daughter series. It's yours if you want it. If not, hell, maybe I'll write it! It's the kind of thing people win awards for and we could use a few more of those! Give it some thought…no pressure."

"I will, promise," Tessa assured her, feeling incredibly pressured.

It was another hour before David got home and by then Tessa had not only finished her article but had managed to work herself into a state of considerable panic, convinced she wouldn't have the right response for whatever it was he had to say. But she'd had a glass of Chardonnay and a bowl of soup and at least felt nourished enough to get through whatever was coming.

"Tessa, I've been thinking a lot about where we're headed and what you're trying to do with your life and I have a few ideas."

She sat like an eager child waiting for instruction. "Okay."

"We've been together for over a year now and I know it's been a tough one for you in a lot of ways. Leo's death was brutal and the whole thing with the journals didn't help, but I think you're getting past that and ready to talk about some changes."

Getting past that? Really?

He continued, "I'd already been thinking about this but what happened with Ruby and Ethan just brought home how dangerous it can be when couples allow themselves to get too far apart, you know what I mean?"

Tessa did, though she wasn't sure what *she* thought he meant was actually what he *did* mean, but until she had more information it didn't seem wise to query the matter. She simply nodded and said, "Yes."

"I feel like working from home has been isolating for you and personally I don't think that's such a good thing right now."

"I agree," she jumped in. "Which is why I decided to spend more time working out of the office." She hadn't actually told David about this yet and, so far, he hadn't noticed, so his subsequent surprise was not completely unwarranted.

"You've been going to the office? Vivian's office up in Sherman Oaks?"

"Just a couple of days this week but I think I'll make it a regular thing."

"Why would you not tell me that?"

"I just started this week. Figured I'd see if it was worth the trouble and tell you then."

"Wow. I can't imagine how driving to Sherman Oaks could possibly be worth the trouble. Why would you want to deal with that commute if you didn't have to? What did it take you, an hour, two hours?"

She wasn't loving the edge in his voice. "Actually it's not that bad if you go at off times. As for my reasons, well, they're pretty much the exact things you just mentioned. It *is* a little isolating to be working here all the time. I thought some human interaction a couple of days a week would get me going a bit, maybe get me inspired, and, in fact, it has. Vivian has already come up with a great series she wants me to write which she probably wouldn't have thought of had I not been there." Not true, but it made the point.

David was thrown off his stride. He poured himself a glass of wine and regrouped. "Okay, okay, I get that, whatever. Seems strange to me but that's your business. But anyway, here's what I've been thinking about. And please don't leap to an answer until I've said the whole thing, okay?"

Tessa nodded and took a deep breath, realizing the moment was at hand and she wanted to be careful to do it right, whatever "right" ended up being by the time he'd said the whole thing.

"Tessa, I think we do need to spend more time together. Not only that, I think we need to find more things to share, things to connect us. I know we come from pretty different places in life, but we've managed to find enough common ground to fall in love, move in together, and spend this last year pretty darn happy. I think your dad dying has been really difficult and I probably didn't handle that as well as I could have, but I really do love you and I want to keep exploring ways to keep our relationship fresh. Now, I know you love writing and being creative, I know that's a really important part of who you are – "

Wait. What? Where was this going?

"And I want you to keep nurturing that in whatever ways you see fit, whatever ways make you happy. But I also know you've been frustrated by the lack of any real forward motion. I know you hated giving up your music career, which I understand, but that's over now and this writing thing is going good, but maybe not *that* good and, frankly, I think you might be ripe for something that not only utilizes your writing talent, but could offer the kind of compensation, benefits package, and career trajectory you've been missing up till now."

Whoa. Anything with a benefits package was profoundly off-message. "Okay…"

"There's a position opening up at New Strand, in the marketing department, that you would just kill: copywriting, marketing input, social media management, creative business writing – a ton of really productive, creative stuff. It's right up your alley, Tess. You'd be working under my department but you'd have tremendous autonomy, and it would be a situation where your ideas, your words, your imagination would be the main currency. I know your first reaction might be that it's problematic for us to work together – "

Nope, not the first reaction.

"But I think we're both smart enough to know proper business decorum, so that's a non-issue. We'd both be working five minutes from the house so it'd be a convenient commute together. The compensation and benefits package is stellar – a helluva lot more than you're making now – and the potential for growth is unlimited. Particularly with the job market the way it is, this is a really amazing opportunity. And who knows? You might be running the department before you're forty and with both of us bringing in that kind of income, we could afford an incredible place right here in Manhattan Beach. And that ain't too shabby!" He took a deep breath and smiled that charming smile that stole her heart way back when. "What do you think?"

It wasn't too shabby. And she said so, winning another smile from him. He pulled her up from her chair and almost smothered her in his embrace until, from somewhere in the curve of his shoulder, her muffled words crept out: "But it's not what I want to do." He stopped hugging and stepped back with another deep breath, this one slightly more clenched.

"Okay, well, I thought that might be your first response and so I have to ask, what *do* you want to do?" Again with the edge.

"You know, David, I might complain about it once in a while but I actually love what I do. It may not be quite what I planned for my life at this point – I planned to be a rock star at this point, so I'm actually way more conventional than I might have been, which

I presume pleases you."

"What does that mean?"

"Nothing, I don't know…I just mean that whatever didn't happen led to what did and I feel like what I'm doing now is important and meaningful. And even if it doesn't make me a ton of money or come with a benefits package or whatever, at least I'm using my talents in a way I feel good about." She stopped; he had no response. "I get the feeling you think there's something wrong with all that."

"Not if you're twenty-five."

Now *she* was feeling the edge. "What does that mean?"

"Look, I get that you want to live an artist's life; I *want* you to live an artist's life if that's what you want. But there are more ways to do that than working freelance forever and hoping one day you sell a novel or something you write gets turned into a movie. You're thirty-six, Tessa, you're not a kid anymore, and I'd like to think we're headed toward something more permanent, more responsible, like…who knows? Maybe marriage, maybe kids, maybe a bigger house and a chance to travel, basically experience something more than this big, fat artistic struggle you've been in your whole life. Aren't *you* sick of that?"

This was so far from the expected conversation Tessa was reeling. "Yes! Sometimes I am! But I don't think working in the marketing department of a sneakers company is necessarily going to soothe my soul in that regard. It's a very nice offer, David, really, it is, and I'm sure a very good job for someone who wants to be on that career path, but I don't. I don't want to write about sneakers. No offense."

But David was. Offended. "So that's it? You don't even want to think about it?"

"I could tell you I would but I'd be lying. I'm sorry, sweetheart, I appreciate that you thought of me but it's just not something I want to do. I'm not sure how long I'll work for Vivian but as long as it feels rewarding and challenging – which it does –

it's what I want to do. And if I do decide to write something more substantial – like a novel or maybe another screenplay – I'll do that, too…because I'll be able to. I'll have the time and creative energy to do it. That's important to me. The money will either come or it won't, but that can't be my motivation."

David leaned against the counter with little-disguised pique. "I don't know why I'm surprised. I should have guessed that'd be your reaction. You've never tried to hide your disdain for the corporate world, so I guess you're staying true to form. I just thought you might be ready to expand your horizons and maybe make your life a little easier. Because, Tessa, if you really look at the world with brutal honesty, and you look at this creative business you're so enamored of, you have to know the odds of you making it as a writer are nil to none. If you're happy with those odds and willing to sacrifice your entire life and any other opportunities that come your way, I've got to hand it to you – you're either courageous or completely self-sabotaging. I just hope we can survive whichever way that falls." With that he turned and walked out the door.

And here she thought he was going to propose.

Later that night Tessa lay in bed, David sleeping soundly beside her, and ran through the evening's turn. He'd come home twenty minutes later seemingly free of resentment, acting as if they had never even had the conversation. That was his way: it was over, no need to beat it to death.

But things weren't as clear-cut for her. And as she lay now in the darkness of night unable to sleep, she couldn't help but ponder: *Is he right? Am I supposed to shift gears so dramatically at this point in my life? Is there anything wrong with using my talents in a more corporate, commercial setting that could actually afford me a decent income for a change? Would I be willing to risk losing David if that's what it came to? Should I be hurt or angry at his assessment of my odds of succeeding as a writer?*

Too many questions and not enough answers. It made her tired enough to fall asleep.

THIRTY-FOUR

The next morning she didn't feel like driving to Vivian's office; not sure why. Too late a start or maybe it had to do with David's comments about the commute. Either way, Tessa sat at her computer scrolling through Facebook, eating cold Pop Tarts and dropping crumbs all over the keyboard. The phone rang: Michaela.

"You can have them all. I'm sending them out tomorrow." Her voice was uncharacteristically flat.

"Why do you sound so weird?"

"Because after Mom and Duncan insisted you were going to be diplomatic about whatever it is you plan to do with them, I decided I didn't have the right to keep them from you, but I wanted to read one or two before I shipped them off. So a couple of nights ago I pulled a few out of the pack and read for a while. After that, I don't want to read one more word and I don't even want them in my house. They're all yours, Tessa. And please burn them after you're done. I don't think anyone else should read these either."

Michaela, Leo's boldest defender, then devolved into tears. Tessa felt the visceral punch of her sister's anguish. "Mickie, sweetie, what's going on; what did you read?" She could only imagine.

"The thing that got me was what he wrote about Randy and me, about how when we came back from our honeymoon and had all those souvenirs from Lake Geneva – remember those old school books and the desk chairs we got for the school?"

"Um…maybe, I'm not sure – "

"He went on and on about how we'd been 'poor-mouthing everyone' before the wedding but wasn't it interesting how we could find the money when we wanted to buy a bunch of useless junk from flea vendors…that and all sorts of other snarky comments about what small visions we had and –"

"Small visions? What does that mean? You built a school, for God's sake!"

"Yeah, well, I guess he thought Randy had a small vision because it's a small school. He said something like it was 'overly cautious and creatively limited, just like the man.' Then he said I was a 'harridan' and made some crack about what a 'soft pudgy fellow' Randy was, too soft to stand up to me. How we were both 'slack parents' and how the kids were going to turn out to be hooligans because we didn't discipline them the way he thought we should, that sort of stuff. Maybe it sounds like no big deal but the tone of it was just so – the fact that he'd make fun of my husband and diminish what we've accomplished is just…I don't know…it's hateful."

Tessa made no comment about the fact that it was Michaela who'd originally downplayed how big a deal it was, deciding to take the more charitable route. "I actually think it *is* a big deal."

"All I know is it made me feel so sick I had to stop. I knew if I kept reading I'd find something even worse about the kids and I just didn't want to go through that. I mean, he throws in a compliment here or there but the gist of it is just…mean. It's mean! These are toxic and if they could make me feel this bad, I can only imagine how they'd make anyone else feel, so I want them out of here. And, seriously, Tessa, whenever you're done with whatever it is you're going to do, burn them. For everyone's sake."

"Mickie, I'm so sorry – "

"I've been such an ass, defending him. Just this stupid little robot who believed what I wanted to believe because I didn't want to think you were right or Ronnie was right. God, I didn't want to believe Ronnie could be right about anything about Dad! Now I just feel so sorry for him. Even in the one I read, Dad said some awful things about him, about what a whiner he was, what a 'weak soul," and how he lacked quality. Our sweet little brother who never stopped smiling…I don't think he's smiled now for decades, and at this point I'm pretty sure it's because that fucked up old man destroyed him, bit by bit, day by day." She started crying again. "Tessa, I've got to go. I'll ship all of these out to you tomorrow, I promise. I'm sorry about everything." And with that she hung up.

Tessa sat stunned.

Something about Michaela's pain made hers more real. It was both a good and a bad thing. Good because she no longer felt alone, bad because she wasn't at all sure Michaela could survive it as well as she could.

THIRTY-FIVE

The next day Tessa made it into the office, sat in her little area, and set up her laptop to work. Elaine's sales counterpart, Joyce, was selling away, Barry/Brian was quietly editing, Stanley was glued to the screen proofing something, Malice and Stoney were doing whatever it was they did, and Meagan glanced over at Tessa with a collegial nod. Probably something to do with her thinking they were working together on this project, a fact about which Tessa was less sure. Glen was at another computer station across the room with the same two computer techs she'd seen there earlier and he smiled with a wave; the two tech people looked over as well. Tessa noticed the guy more clearly this time. He was looking at her with an inexplicable expression and she found it unsettling enough to look away. She noticed through an adjacent door that Vivian was off the phone; Tessa motioned to come in and Vivian nodded with a wave.

"Lonely again or are we just irresistible?" Vivian smiled wickedly as Tessa plopped in the chair.

"Sorta both. Listen, I want to talk about your series idea."

"Excellent. I'm all ears."

"The main thing is this: I think it's a great idea, I'm just not sure I'm the one to write it."

"Why is that?"

"I talked to my sister last night and she's definitely sending all the journals. That's good. I guess she read some nasty stuff about her own family and it finally shattered her Leo-delusion. That's bad. Or maybe it's good, I don't know. But when I thought about what she's going through, what Ronnie's going through, even my own reaction, I got to thinking: maybe I do need to write about it in some way. But whatever I write, I want it to be my own private journey, not necessarily in tandem with comparative stories of other women with other father issues. I'm not ready to compare or focus elsewhere, you know what I mean?"

"Is there a way to do both? Write your novel or memoir or whatever you think you should do, but maybe find a perspective that would be helpful in writing about the experiences of others. Is that possible?"

"I don't know. I was just thrown by my sister's reaction so this still feels pretty raw. All I can say is, I should get the journals later this week. Once I have the chance to go through them, sort out my thoughts, figure out what I might want to write and in what form, maybe then I could do both. Right now I can't say and if you want to get this going right now, I'm not the one. If you can wait a bit, I'd love to get back to you in a couple of weeks. What do you say to that?"

"I really don't want to wait that long, but I also don't want anybody else to write it. You've got me over a barrel."

"Vivian, that's not my intention but I can't do what I can't do; I hope you understand."

"I do, kiddo. This is tough stuff. Okay, I'll wait. Two weeks. Get back to me in two weeks and if you're not ready to leap then, I'll get someone else. You good with that?"

"Perfect. Thanks." Tessa headed back to her station and noticed Mr. Computer Tech shoot another glance her way; she suddenly felt that strange flush that comes with the unexpected attention of someone you don't know, particularly a good-looking man. She sat down and continued her blog entry but felt pulled away every few minutes to check the status of the repair across the room. At some point Glen seemed ready to wrap up whatever it was they were doing and she could tell by the way he and the tech looked in her direction that she was the object of their conversation. She got noticeably twitchy as they made their way over.

Glen began as they approached her station. "Tessa, I want to introduce you to a couple of people, part of our IT team, Haden and Cecilia Pierce. Haden is convinced he knows you from somewhere." As they shook hands all around, Tessa met Haden's eyes; she'd never seen him before but he smiled with a nod of recognition.

"Yeah, Tessa, I thought it was you! I saw your band a while back when you guys were playing Molly Malone's; I think it was about three years ago."

"Wow…that's amazing!" She laughed, truly surprised. "Actually that was almost five years ago. I can't believe you remember me!"

"I remember you." He had a way of speaking that was both earnest and playful. She found herself flustered. "I thought you guys were fantastic. I picked up a few of your CDs when I was there, gave a few away and listened to mine until I lost it, then I downloaded it from iTunes, that's how much I remember you."

Glen beamed like a proud father. "Well, we've got her now. Got talent in one arena, you're bound to have it in another, right?"

"Absolutely." Haden continued. "Are you still singing?"

"Not much. Maybe karaoke night if I've had too much to drink or family weddings if I have no choice, but for the most part I've back-burnered it."

"That's too bad. I really liked what you did."

"Thanks, me too." Tessa laughed wistfully. "Just couldn't figure out how to keep it going."

"That must have been hard. You have the talent and clearly it meant a lot to you."

She was oddly moved. It *had* been hard. In fact, it had been brutal. And after all this time it was lovely that someone remembered that part of her. She glanced over at Cecilia, a rather stunning woman who smiled sweetly throughout, clearly unperturbed by her husband's focus on Tessa…who had a fleeting thought that maybe when you're that beautiful there's little to worry about along those lines.

"Well, we'll let you get back to work. It was really nice to meet you and I hope you can put singing back in your life someday." Haden shook Tessa's hand once again then took Cecilia's elbow as the two turned and left the office.

Glen gave Tessa a playful shove. "Nice to have fans who still remember you, isn't it?"

Yes. It was. She made note that Haden looked back at her and smiled as he went through the door.

THIRTY-SIX

Tessa was nine, all gangly arms and legs, awkward in her developing girlhood. Snuggled in Leo's arms as the two watched an old movie on the living room TV, she was warmed and made safe by the encompassing embrace of her father. One of his large hands rested near her shoulder and without thought, he caressed her hair, running the curly strands through his fingers as he laughed loudly at something on the screen. Tessa was acutely aware of his touch, holding her breath for fear that even the smallest motion would cause him to stop. So seldom did she feel the warmth of Leo's physical embrace that this moment, with all its tenderness and tactile sensation, was as rare and precious as love itself and surely merited her impossible stillness. But at some point she did breathe and Leo did move and the moment was gone as quickly as it began.

Tessa woke from this dream with a pang of such loss she almost cried out and awakened David from his stony slumber. It was a version of a dream she'd had before, one that re-imagined a true and very small moment of many years earlier. In the real-life memory she'd been older than in the dream, on a college exploratory trip with Leo and one of her friends. She and Leo were seated side-by-side in a coffee shop booth with his arm stretched across the back, gently and unconsciously stroking her hair as he carried on in conversation with the girls. The awareness of his touch and the wish to not disturb it was as poignant as in the dream. And, also like the dream, it ended as insignificantly as it began.

As she sat in her bed now, so many years later, she let the sensation of that brief moment wash over her…a father who felt sweet and clear tenderness for his daughter. Real or the illusion of memory?

THIRTY-SEVEN

Tap, tap, tap…Tessa's foot manically kept time on the coffee table leg. Sitting in Aunt Joanne's office after a long day and a longer drive, she wanted to be anywhere but here. Aunt Joanne had asked her to bring the journal in to leave with her but after handing it over, Tessa could see no reason to stay. She slumped on the couch with a teenager's petulance until her aunt sighed deeply and reminded her that this was her time, intended for her benefit.

"Obviously I get that, Auntie, but can't you end these things early sometimes? Isn't that allowed?"

"It is, but why not use the time?"

"Because I'm sick of talking about myself. Aren't you sick of listening?"

"No, in fact, I wanted to ask you a question. We've discussed why you left Scientology but I never heard specifically why you left the Catholic Church."

"I'm sure we already talked about that."

"No, I don't think so. Your references about it have been general and somewhat vague and I'd like to know specifically why you made the decision you did. Clearly it had great impact on your father, it had great impact on you, and I think it might help me understand things a little better if I knew what happened."

Tessa thought silently for a moment.

"What does that question stir up?" Aunt Joanne prodded.

"Okay, well, this may sound sort of prurient to you given that you're a nun…"

"Try me."

"Okay. It was sex."

"Sex made you leave the Catholic Church?"

Tessa laughed. "Pretty much."

"You might need to be more specific."

Tessa sat up. "It wasn't just sex, obviously, it was a lot of things, a pile-on of sorts. Like I said before, I was that kid who didn't do well with unexplained rules, the whole 'mystery of faith' thing. I wanted everything to make sense and not much of the Catholic Church did to me. I was told to 'just believe' and even if I wanted to, I didn't know how. So faith eluded me and no one would help."

"Not even your teachers?"

"No, they couldn't seem to understand the problem. All I got was, 'you just *decide* to believe and then you have faith.' And trust me, *that* made no sense to a kid who needed answers. Faith seemed too important a thing to just be a decision some seven-year-old makes. But that was it. That was all I got. So with that conundrum going on, plus your basic sin terror, plus the rigidity of the rules and the nuns with their hitting sticks, it was all too much for me."

"Many adults struggle with similar issues, even in less challenging environments; it's not hard to understand the confusion from a child's perspective. And I'm sorry your school had such backward ideas about discipline; not all Catholic nuns believe in corporal punishment, I assure you."

"I know that, Auntie. The particular school my father picked was a tad more fundamental than we kids might've liked!"

"I can certainly understand that. But let's get back to why you believe sex contributed to your disenchantment with the Church. How does that connect to what you just told me?"

"Okay, how do I put this? The general confusion I just

described was bad enough during the early school years, but it was when pre-puberty hit that *everything* blew up."

"That's when sexual matters came into the picture?"

"In a way. To put it bluntly, I discovered masturbation." Tessa smiled and looked up. Aunt Joanne had no visible reaction, so Tessa adjusted in her seat and continued. She described the peculiar age with its biological tornado of hormones and sexual curiosity, when she learned there was no one – not family, not nuns, not priests – with whom she could discuss any of it. "The Catholic aversion to all things sexual, which was clear even then, dismissed me with the implicit suggestion that I keep it all to myself – my thoughts *and* my hands."

"I would have assumed your mother was fairly relaxed about sexual matters. No?"

Tessa snorted. "Oh, please! I once asked her about sex and she actually blushed. I was eleven and *she* blushed! Instead of wise motherly guidance, she gave me this little booklet to read in private, 'away from the younger kids,' she actually whispered. She made sure to emphasize that there were definitions in the back in case I had any questions, because God forbid I should ask her! But, good little girl that I was, I did what I was told. I read the book – sitting in a closet, mind you – and this is when I learned that intercourse is 'when a man's penis passes through a woman's vagina.' I remember thinking, *passes through*? Even at that age I was instinctively aware of the dead-end nature of a vagina, so the description pretty much horrified me. I kept picturing a penis 'passing through" and the damage that would wreak and I was so grossed out I never brought it up again. Obviously I figured it all out later but, at that point, the message was clear; I was on my own."

"Dare I ask if you ever considered talking to your father?"

Tessa gave her a deadpan look. "My father was terrified of the subject. When we were teenagers he actually made us break up with our boyfriends if he deemed we'd been dating them for too long, so afraid that anything past six months would lead us to sex. In fact, I missed out on my first Homecoming because he heard I'd kissed the boy I was supposed to go with. Made me break it off a week before the dance; said I was too 'libidinous' and to get my head out of my pants. Actually said that. About a kiss. Kind of clarifies his attitude on the topic."

"Yes…quite."

"But here was the problem, Auntie: I was just a normal girl; growing up, struggling through puberty, leaning into my sexuality, but so alone on the journey I thought I was anything *but* normal. So on that momentous day when I stumbled on the wonders of masturbation in a warm tub – as many girls before me have done – I was absolutely blown away, terrified and thrilled at the same time. I kept wondering, what the hell is *this*? Anything with that kind of sensation, connected to that part of my body, could only be a sin, which was later confirmed in religion class when Sister Ruth told us that 'impure thoughts and deeds' – with others or *with ourselves—* were not only sins but *mortal* sins, which would send us straight to Hell forever!"

"You were doomed."

"I was doomed. Because I couldn't stop. I don't know if you ever tried – "

"I know what masturbation is."

Tessa blushed. "Okay…sorry. The point is, I tried to stop. I knew it was a sin, but it was this maddening pull I couldn't control. Clearly my primal self had no concern about my mortal soul and you tell me how a little kid deals with *that* paradox without an adult's help?"

"Obviously not very well. Even my mother took the time to explain it to me and she was incredibly shy about sexuality. Hard to figure what was going on with Audrey."

"She was a neurotic submissive married to a fundamentalist zealot who described sex as his 'dutiful attempts in the marriage bed.' Not exactly a sexual revolution going on over there!"

"No, clearly. So, how did this resolve for you?"

"Well, suffice it to say, I bounced between the bathtub and the confessional on whatever schedule allowed my soul to be purged by Sunday communion."

Aunt Joanne was genuinely dismayed. "That must have been exhausting!"

"Yes, but I was very clean," Tessa remarked dryly. "And it was doable until my freshman year in high school; that's when this feat of time-management collapsed."

"Explain."

"I was now in an all-girls school that had *daily* Mass. Do the math."

"With daily Mass there was daily communion and a pure soul was a daily requirement, meaning daily confession."

"Bingo. And by now puberty was burnin' down the house – a phenomenon I thought was happening *only* to me because I'd not heard one other person talk about it! So like a serial felon in my quest to be good, I snuck from lunch to the noon confessional every single, fucking day of the week."

"You poor thing...."

"Yes, I was beleaguered, to say the least. Obviously it couldn't hold and it didn't. There came a Thursday, well after the noon confessional hour, when I found myself daydreaming in study hall and just sort of glanced over at one of my classmates. She was this very 'mature girl,' as they'd say, with these huge boobs that – on that particular day – were wrapped in this very fluffy white angora sweater and I just stared at them, sort of fascinated. I don't know why but I wondered what they looked like and if they looked anything like mine and it was all very innocent, but just as quickly as I had those thoughts, I realized what I was thinking and BAM – that horrible, sickening sensation of sin descended. And with no chance for confession before the next morning's Mass there was no way I could take communion, which would then out me as the sinner I was. This, as you can imagine, was overwhelming. So I did the only thing I could do. I fainted. Right there in study hall. Flat on the cold, linoleum floor."

"Oh, sweetheart."

"It was quite the drama, lots of attention and fuss, but somewhere in the chaos I realized the day had been saved."

"How so?"

"I had to stay in bed the next day."

"Ah…no Mass, no communion."

"A reprieve that could not be overstated. But it was just one reprieve and I knew I couldn't continue. So that weekend I told my mom I had to talk to her. She sat me down in her purple bedroom, closed the door to everyone else and got very real with me, not something she was prone to do. I remember her saying something like, 'This is just between us. I won't even share it with your father if you don't want me to,' and her sweetness just sort of crumbled me. I blurted out, 'I'm a mortal sinner,' and somewhere in my hysteria told her everything. She listened without a word – also very uncharacteristic of her – but I could see something going on behind her eyes, some reflection or recognition of something. When I was done, I just sat there waiting for madness to descend, for her to hit me or scream or go get my father to wreak some ungodly punishment and I swear, I thought my heart would pound out of my chest." She paused, lost in the moment.

Aunt Joanne pressed her. "What happened?"

Tessa looked up. "The most stunning thing I could possibly imagine. She wrapped her arms around me and burst into tears and, without a speck of doubt, said, 'you could *never* commit a mortal sin. *Never.*' And that was it. That was the end of it all, the end of Catholicism for me." Tessa leaned back, exhausted.

"I'm curious; why did your mother's statement have that particular effect on you?"

"It saved me."

"How so?"

"I *wasn't* doomed. It told me I was okay. It revealed the lie of our religion, the cruelty of a church that would allow any of its children to ever feel that way about themselves."

"Yes, I see."

"After I went back to school I finally started talking to other girls and it turns out a lot of them were as confused and anxious as I was. It was crazy. Granted, some of the them didn't care much what their parents or the Church thought, but some – like me – had been trying to live up to this ideal of morality that was impossible and ultimately punitive. I knew that could never be what spirituality was for me."

"Nor should it be. That kind of teaching is not true spirituality."

"Anyway, we ended up switching to a public school the next year, which was a relief, and though I kept going to Sunday Mass until I left for college, that was just to assuage my father. Once he knew it was really over, I'm sure it sent him running to his journal."

"And your mom?"

"Well, she stood as a united front with him in terms of being horrified when it was discovered I'd left, and I'm sure she'd deny any complicity in my defection, but as far as I'm concerned that moment was her finest hour."

When Tessa left that day she felt as if she'd been purged of something monumental. She went to the corner market, picked up a greeting card with a sunset photo and sent it to her mother with the note: "Hope you're feeling good today, Mom. I love you, Tessa."

THIRTY-EIGHT

Almost two weeks had passed and still no journals. *What the FUCK, Michaela?*

Tessa's answer on the father/daughter series was shortly due and Vivian would only hold out for so long. She considered calling her sister but there remained a reticence to re-engage. Their détente was a relief but Tessa suspected it was temporary. She went back to Duncan, who, of course, was busy and didn't have time to talk, though he did mention he thought the journals had gone out. He suggested she contact Suzanna, which she did.

"I think she sent them out a couple of weeks ago."

"Really? Did she mention a tracking number?"

"Yeah, like we would've discussed a tracking number. Why don't you just ask her?"

Instead Tessa called Izzy, who had nothing useful to report. "I talked to her last week and she mentioned she'd sent them out, but I don't know exactly when. But I was really surprised to hear she changed her mind! What did you say?"

Tessa ran down the whole story, but Izzy, who remained the last holdout in terms of The Truth Of Father, got testy.

"I admit I was surprised by what he wrote about you, Tessa, but I have a feeling it was only a one or two time thing. I can't imagine he'd systematically denigrate his entire family for years on end for what...for what purpose? Why would he do that?"

"You know, Izzy, I just don't know. That's why I'd like to read them, to see if I can ferret out some enlightenment to that question."

"It just seems so counter to – I don't know – to *everything*! I mean, this is the guy who spent two weekends in a row helping me paint my condo because he didn't want me to waste money on an overpriced painter. Why would a guy who'd do that for his daughter write hateful things about her in a journal? Wait, did he write hateful things about me?"

Tessa sighed. "I don't know. He didn't in the one I have. Do you want me to tell you if I find anything in the ones Michaela's sending?"

"Let's talk if you find anything, okay?"

Tessa rolled her eyes and agreed. She then called Ronnie who, of course, didn't answer, and his voice mail was full. There was nothing left to do but call Michaela. *Dammit.*

"Yes, I sent them out, about two weeks ago, right after I said I would."

"Okay, great. Could I get the tracking number so I can figure out where they are at this point? Oh, and how much do I owe you for the shipping?"

"I don't have a tracking number and don't worry about the money; it wasn't all that much."

"FedEx always gives you a tracking number."

"I didn't use FedEx. A friend of mine uses this other shipping company that's much cheaper and since she's never had any problem with them, I'm sure they're fine and everything will be there soon."

"Um...okay...but I did say I'd pay for it and I really wanted you to ship them FedEx because that's the safest and fastest way to get things across the country." She sounded like a commercial.

"Well, forgive me, Tessa, but I was trying to be considerate in not using the most expensive shipping company on earth, which I thought you might appreciate. If it takes a little longer, what's the big deal? And don't worry, you don't have to reimburse me."

"That's not the point, Michaela. There are some timing issues I'm dealing with here and if I said I was willing to pay the higher price to get them here faster, you should have just done that!"

"Oh my God, you're actually giving me grief for using a cheaper shipping company?"

"No, I'm giving you grief because you didn't respect my wishes and now I have to rearrange some things that depended on them getting here sooner."

"What could possibly be dependent on Dad's old journals getting to you sooner?"

"That's actually my business and doesn't concern you."

"Fuck you, Tessa." And once again, she hung up the phone.

With a sigh, Tessa redialed and when the voice mail picked up: "Michaela, I thought we weren't going to do this anymore. But whatever. If you could just give me the name and number of the shipping company I can try to track down the boxes. Just leave the information on my voice mail – God forbid we should try to handle this like grown ups! But thanks for sending them…however you sent them."

She hated her sister.

THIRTY-NINE

CNN blared and David was stretched out on the couch glancing between news and *The Wall Street Journal*, engrossed enough that he didn't notice Tessa's entrance. She stood in the doorway of the living room until he finally looked up…to be stunned by the vision.

There she was, in full rock and roll regalia: fishnet stockings, short black skirt, a leather jacket over a tight tee with the word "Club" stretched across the chest; her hair shellacked and more makeup than she'd worn since, well, rock and roll.

He sat up. "Wow. Why are you wearing a shirt that says 'Club' on it?"

"I'm feeling clubby."

"Yeah…the fishnets were a giveaway. I love the '80s too, but aren't we a little old for the rave scene, if that scene even still exists?"

"It still exists and fishnets have cycled back, just so you know. Look, I just want to go out, okay? I'm sick of sitting around here eating sushi and watching cable. I need to get out, I want to dance, and if you don't want to come with me I'm going by myself."

"Jesus, Tessa, relax. Fine, we'll go out. Just give me a minute. I wasn't expecting party-time tonight."

While he changed into something more festive, which for him meant better jeans and a different buttoned-down shirt, Tessa poured a glass of Chardonnay and belted it back like a shot. Fuck deadlines, journals, shitty sisters and dead fathers. Party-time, indeed.

An hour and a half later they were sitting in the sweaty, tightly packed bar of some club near the Marina wrangling a bartender for another round. The music was so cacophonous that conversation was impossible, and despite the expressed mission of frivolity, neither Tessa nor David appeared to be having much fun.

A new song, an even louder song, suddenly blasted from the speakers and the floor surged with undulating dancers. Tessa leapt from her stool and shouted to David, "Come on, let's dance!"

"Not up for it, Tessa," David shouted back.

"Why are we here if we're not going to dance?" Three drinks down and feeling fierce, she actually glowered at him.

"*You* wanted to dance; I was happy with CNN. But I'm here, we're having a drink, we're out; you want to dance, go dance." This was not going well.

Tessa slammed down her wineglass, shot him a look of defiance, and strutted out to the dance floor to join a bevy of girls much younger and hotter than she, none of whom had any compunction about dry-humping each other to the beat and for the pleasure of the surrounding, absolutely delighted, males. Tessa let loose her inner pole dancer like there was nobody watching: hips pumping, arms flapping, hair flying, sweat dripping; spinning, twerking, flailing, until one of the more appreciative fellows came up from behind to grind at her mini-skirted booty with startling enthusiasm, and, in this case, there *was*, in fact, somebody watching. David jettisoned from the bar like a bouncer and injected himself between Tessa and her oblivious dance partner who simply swept off to hump another welcoming female, barely aware of David's intervention. Tessa continued dancing in protest but David was in no mood.

"Come on, let's go. This is ridiculous."

"NO! *I'm* having fun...remember FUN?" she shouted,

threatening to lift her Club shirt, all girls-gone-wild.

"Oh, that's classy." He finally grabbed her. "Now you're just acting like an idiot."

She glared at him, turned, and stormed from the bar.

She fell asleep in the car on the way home and after stumbling up the stairs, threw up in the ficus pot at the doorway. David shoved her into bed with little finesse and her shoes still on. No words were exchanged.

The next morning he was gone by the time she woke up. Despite her head-shattering stupor she managed a text, "I'm sorry. I think I'm acting out, something about feeling powerless. But that wasn't pretty. Forgive me. Love, T."

He texted back, "We all make mistakes. Left you coffee. Have a good day. Talk later."

No "Love, D." He always wrote "Love, D."

·

FORTY

"Do you think Kate's avoiding me?"

Ruby was supervising a play date with Milo and two daycare friends and had invited Tessa to join them at the park. It was difficult for Ruby to do much of anything by herself these days and Tessa usually enjoyed these mini-moments of family life, but today, nursing a headache the size of Texas, it was less jolly. They sat on a bench as the boys made armies of Lego soldiers and commenced with full-out war in the dunes of the sandbox. Tessa had a fleeting thought about violence and young minds but decided it wasn't the time and she didn't have the energy.

"No, I don't think she's avoiding you. I think her business got busy, which is good, and it's hard for her to make the time right now."

"Really? Hasn't her business been busy before and we all still got together?"

"Rubes, don't make it something it's not. I don't see her that much either."

"But you see her?"

"Once in a while."

"Recently?"

"We had coffee a few days ago between her office and mine. It was a quick, impromptu thing around the time you pick Milo up from daycare. Stop it."

"Uh huh. Okay." Milo threw a plastic man at one of his friends. "No, Milo, no throwing! You guys play nice." *Play war nice.* "Just seems odd, that's all."

"Why would she be avoiding you?"

"Oh, come on, Tessa! She's made it abundantly clear she disapproves of my divorce. You know her, the queen of all married people. I think she's being profoundly judgmental, like somehow we should have jumped through a few more hoops before we threw in the towel."

"Do *you* think that?"

"Really? You're going there, too?"

"I'm just asking you what you think; forget what Kate thinks."

"I think we did everything we could over a long period of time and given everything we considered, not the least of which was the well-being of our son, it seemed like the best thing to do at the time."

"But not now?"

Ruby paused, her eyes filled with tears. "I don't know. I do think it was the best decision at the time but now that the fighting's done and the house is quiet and I'm working again and don't have Ethan to think about or angst over, I'm...thinking about and angsting over him." She looked up at Tessa with a sad smile. "I miss him, Tessa. I don't miss the fighting, and in a lot of ways I love being in charge of my own life again, but...I miss him."

"Have you told him that?"

"I tried, then he told me he was actually dating that woman, Margo, and that ended the conversation. But I still miss him. I haven't signed the divorce papers yet and I don't know when I will."

"Then maybe you should just wait on that. I don't know, maybe divorce *is* the best thing but I keep thinking there's another way. Can't you just stay separated for a while and see what happens?"

"In a way, that is what we're doing. He hasn't said anything about it so I don't get the feeling he's in all that big of a hurry. But he *is* seeing someone else. Not sure we could come back from that sort of thing."

"You could. If you both really wanted to, you could. Does he know about your gym guy?"

"Oh, God, no."

"Any current guys?"

Ruby shot her a look. "No. No guys. I'm a chaste, single mother, soon-to-be-ex-wife, nobly doing my job without a thought to my own physical and emotional needs. You should be so proud of me."

"Do you actually think I expect you to ignore your physical and emotional needs?"

"Kind of got that impression."

"Not true. But I am sort of proud of you." They grinned at each other. "And, hey, what do I know about relationships? My boyfriend hasn't touched me in weeks – unless you call patting me like I'm a puppy touching. And these 'work gatherings' seem to be getting more and more frequent. He's either building up major points with corporate or we've got big-time avoidance going on." She decided to abstain from mentioning the club debacle of the night before.

"Why would that be?"

"I don't know. Not sure if he just can't deal with what I'm going through or…I don't know. Maybe it's me. I am pretty testy these days. Did I tell you about the job offer he made?"

"Yeah, is that still an issue?"

"You wouldn't think so but ever since I turned him down we've been out of sync or something. Obviously he disagrees with me but since he refuses to talk more about it, he does this nice but distant thing – you know, my favorite emotional combination." Ruby nodded, eyes fixed on the sandbox. "I'm currently overlooking it but at some point we're going to have to talk about it before it gets completely out of hand."

"Oh, you guys will be all right. You're perfect for each other."

"Why would you say that? You don't even like David."

"I know, but it seems like it works. You're both independent but love being in a relationship. You share all sorts of interests, you look good together, and he's a sweetheart. You haven't had a lot of those. I'm pretty sure he's the first really nice guy you've been with since Asshole Trevor."

That was true. But on most other counts Tessa felt it was possible her very dear friend had no idea who she was these days. Suddenly Milo's military strategy escalated into the mother of all sand wars, eliciting the enraged screams of three very irate two-year-olds. Adult time was over.

FORTY-ONE

On her way up to the office, Tessa stopped at the adjacent Starbucks. Having spurned Ruby's offer of half a baloney sandwich (*people still ate those things?*) and with her head still pounding like a jackhammer, the need for hard coffee and sweet carbs was strong. Waiting in line for her order, she glanced around the room and was surprised to see Haden Pierce at a corner table sipping espresso and reading the *LA Weekly*. She took him in for a moment. Hard to say how old. Her age? Maybe a little younger? He was tall and lean, like a guy who eschewed free weights for running or tennis. And he was good looking, really good looking from her point of view: dark, longish hair reminiscent of the English rocker type, blue, sparkly eyes, and a tendency to squint a bit when he smiled. He started to look up so she quickly averted, but at that very moment the barista called her name and Haden glanced over. He smiled warmly and motioned for her to join him. After taking possession of her too-hot drink and regrettable scone, she did. It felt immediately awkward.

"Are you on your way in or out?" she asked through a much-too-big bite of scone, garbling her delivery and requiring a requisite "what?" on his part and a repeat of the question, leading to further awkwardness.

"Out, actually," he responded once they'd sorted the query.

"I've been up there since seven. There are a couple of older computers they refuse to get rid of but the latest software is too advanced to work on them so it gets tricky, as you can imagine. How about you?"

"Heading in. Sometimes I just need to get out of the house and make human contact, even if it does take me an hour to get here."

"Glen mentioned you'd just started coming in. I wondered, because I hadn't noticed you before." Flattering that he'd made note.

"It was originally my idea to telecommute and generally that works out okay. But you know how it is when you're by yourself too much of the time? Even staring at the ocean can be banal if you stare at it long enough!" He laughed as though he knew just what she meant. This was followed by several breezy minutes of where they lived (Studio City for him), how great Vivian was (comparable admiration), her latest article, all of which led them back to a discussion of music and the genesis of his awareness of her.

"Do you ever get out to the clubs anymore, even just to check out other bands?"

The mention of "clubs" almost made her wince, but she liked that he asked the question. "You'd think I would, it was such a big part of my life for so long. But I guess I kind of got burnt-out after all those years of – I don't know – trying. After my band broke up I sat in with a couple of friends every once in a while, but I missed having my own thing and just couldn't find the right players or enough money to put it back together. It was hard at first to see other people up there having a good time when I wasn't, then it just got sort of loud and unfamiliar, and after a while I didn't know anybody anymore and just drifted away. Every once in a while I get an invitation to something an old friend is doing but I hardly ever go. Seems like another lifetime ago."

"Speaking of old friends, I actually got to be good friends with your sound guy, Doug Reynolds."

"Really? Wow, Doug! What a great guy. It's amazing that you two connected."

"Yeah, we used to share geek talk whenever I'd run into him and when he upgraded his system a couple of years ago I helped get him set up."

"That's very cool. Tell him I said hi when you see him next, okay?"

"Actually, I just got an invitation to a listening party for some band he produced. I think it's next week, Thursday maybe. If you'd like to go it might be fun to surprise him…and it'll probably be a good time."

Wait. Was this a date request or just a friends-going-to-a-mutual-friend's event sort of thing? Tessa was not only surprised that Glen had clearly neglected to inform Mr. Pierce that she was spoken for, but was additionally put off by the invitation from a married man.

"Isn't Cecilia going?"

He seemed thrown by the question, which led her to believe it *was* a date sort of request, which, considering the status of both their circumstances, ratcheted up the awkwardness quotient. "Um, you know, I don't think I even mentioned it to her so, odds are, no, she's not going."

Tessa shoved her half-eaten scone into her purse and though authentically flattered by Haden's attention, sweetly but swiftly shot him down. "Thanks for the invitation, it sounds like fun, but I guess Glen didn't mention that I'm living with someone right now so it probably wouldn't be a good idea."

He shifted in his seat. "No problem, Tessa. I was just thinking of it as a friend thing. No big deal and I apologize if I made you uncomfortable."

"No, of course not, and I really appreciate the thought. I just wanted to be sure you were aware of my situation, that's all. Maybe some other time."

Some awkward parting chatter and she was on her way, cheeks a'flaming.

FORTY-TWO

Vivian's annoyance was palpable. "Well, dearest writer, I appreciate that timing hasn't been on your side, but I really need to get this series going – wanted to get it going yesterday – so, per our agreement, I am now going to pass it on to someone else."

Tessa thought she'd feel relief at this wholly anticipated pronouncement but was, instead, unexpectedly deflated. "Who's going to write it?"

"I'm not sure yet. I might ship it out to a new writer I've been talking to. Or maybe Meagan. She's already done a lot of the legwork; it might be time to give her a shot at something bigger."

"Meagan. Okay. I guess she's got the talent and experience to do a good enough job."

"Don't be a bitch, Tessa. You've put me in an untenable position and I have to move forward one way or the other. If you want the job, it's yours. If you want to wait until whenever these journals find their way to your door and you've taken the time to read them and assess your position, well, fine; that's your decision. But I've got a magazine to put out. What's it going to be?"

Damn Michaela. "Fine. I'll do it."

Vivian smiled in that wise, knowing way that infuriated Tessa, as if she'd already known the answer. "Fabulous. Let's get started after lunch, I'm starving."

They went to a nearby café and, over some very weird Monte Cristos, Vivian brought up the computer guy.

"By the way, you've got a real fan in Haden Pierce."

"Yeah, that's what Glen said." Tessa decided to leave out the earlier Starbucks encounter. "Nice that someone actually remembers me as a singer."

"Not that kind of fan; I mean fan as in *wow*."

"What does that mean?" Tessa felt herself blush. Twice in one day.

"Oooh, you're blushing...you know just what that means!"

"Well, and that's a little creepy. I met him with his wife, for God's sake!"

"He's married?" Genuinely confused.

"Isn't he? Who's the gorgeous blonde he's always with, the one with the same last name?"

"Cecilia? Oh, God, that's his sister!" Which explained the odd reaction when Tessa asked if Cecilia was going to Doug's event. Retroactive embarrassment. "She's getting into the business and he's been training her for weeks. Brilliant little shit, if I may say so myself, and a lovely girl to boot. Oh, that's so funny...you thought she was his wife!"

Vivian chortled as if this were quite hilarious and ended up sucking in enough powdered sugar to compel a coughing fit that lasted for a good two minutes. By the time she'd drawn a concerned waiter to the table, aroused another customer who thought she might need the Heimlich, and finally got enough water down to quell the coughing, the subject of Haden Pierce had, thankfully, been forgotten.

FORTY-THREE

After several hours of going over story ideas with Vivian and looking through the research Meagan had meticulously compiled (she *was* efficient!), Tessa made her way home with a full head and the sense that she was going to enjoy this project. Which was good, because she clearly needed something new to engage her attention.

It had been two days since the latest phone unpleasantness with Michaela and still no journals or any information about the shipping company. Her mother had left a chatty message that morning but Tessa put off returning the call until such time as her headache retreated. Now, caught in traffic and calmed from a day of distraction and caffeine, she felt up to fulfilling her daughterly duties.

"Hello, Mother."

"Hello, daughter."

"How are you?"

"Hanging in there. Where are you?"

"Heading home from work."

"In your car?"

"Yes."

"I thought it was against the law to be on the phone while you drive." *This again.*

"It's fine if you have a Bluetooth. I have a Bluetooth."

"A what tooth?"

"Mom, we're on speaker phone, don't worry about it, okay?"

"Well, okay, you're the one driving."

"That's right, I am."

"I heard that even with the speaker phone people are too distracted to drive."

"Are we going to talk about the phone or do you want to have a conversation?"

"That's fine, honey, if you know what you're doing."

"I'm pretty confident at this point." Long pause. "Are you still there?"

"Yes, dear, I'm waiting for whatever you're going to say next."

"Mom, I'm returning your call! What's up?"

"I wanted to thank you for that sweet card. Just made my day, honey."

"Oh, good. Was thinking about you and thought I'd send it."

"Well, it's always nice to know your kids are thinking about you, especially the one that ran away from home!" Old joke.

Tessa smiled. "I haven't gone anywhere, Mom."

"Well, you have, but that's what kids do. Oh, I meant to ask earlier and forgot; what is this $600 check I got in the mail last week? I don't understand. What is a, let's see, what is this...'past-due investment refund plus some interest' business?"

"Just some money I borrowed from you guys a while back."

"I don't remember you borrowing any money."

"It's okay, Mom, it was a long time ago."

"Is this a trick?"

Tessa laughed. "Why would it be a trick? No, it's just something I should have taken care of a long time ago and forgot. Go buy yourself a new chair for the porch or something, okay?"

"That would be nice, wouldn't it? I always love sitting out there. When are you coming home again? It seems like it's been a very long time and I miss you. We could sit out on the porch together."

"I miss you, too, but right now is not a good time. I just got a new project at work and I'm already behind, so there will be no trips for a while."

"You could bring your computer and work from here, right?"

Oh God, why did I ever explain telecommuting to her?

"I'd like to see you some time before the good weather is over."

"I know, that would be nice, Mom, but I have to go to locations and interview people so this time it's a little more involved than just writing on a computer. But I'll try to get home for Thanksgiving. Or, hey, you could come out here for a few days, bask in a little California sunshine! How about that?" Tessa knew there was no chance, but the invitation had emotional merit.

"Oh, honey, thank you, that's so sweet, but I can't travel right now either. Darlene and I are in charge of the garage sale at the church and there's more to do than I ever imagined. Besides, Rome was very hard on me; I'm just not ready to get on an airplane again. So see if you can come home soon. We all miss you." Suddenly there was sniffing.

"Mom, are you crying?"

"I just miss him so much. Why does God take everyone away from me? He was too young and didn't deserve to die. Such a good man…a perfect husband and the best father you kids could've ever had. I hope you thank God every day for giving you a father like that. Do you, Tessa?"

Tessa squelched a retort. "I…I do, Mom, I do."

"That's good, honey. I just don't know how I can go on without him." Audrey whispered.

"Mom, I know you're sad, but it hasn't been that long. You just have to feel what you're feeling and try to do the best you can. There's really no way to hurry grief. It's a process." She was starting to sound like a self-help guru. If only she could apply half of what she said to herself.

"I know, sweetheart, I know. Darlene says I have to be strong.

I just don't want to be a burden on you kids, especially Michaela, who's just my little angel."

Tessa let that one go too. "Well, don't worry too much about being a burden. Just live your life and enjoy what you can. Listen, Mom, I'm pulling onto my street so I'm going to go so I can park the car without distractions. I love you. Let's talk again soon."

She arrived home to a message from Michaela with the name and number of the company: Thompson Transport, Evanston, Illinois, "ask for Brad." Michaela's tone on the voice mail was non-confrontational but lacking any particular warmth. Obviously another rapprochement would be necessary. Tessa would call Brad at Thompson Transport in the morning.

Her phone buzzed, text from David: "Out with guys. Home late. Hope U had a good day."

She texted back: "Yep, good day. Sorry again about last night. We OK?"

"We're OK. Sleep well."

Neither one texted "love."

FORTY-FOUR

His Two Big Girls – _First in a Series_
By Tessa Curzio

Clifton Brandenhall was dying an excruciating death. The pain and decimation of late-stage liver cancer had taken its toll on his mind and body and there was little left now but the shell of a man who had loomed large over a family that both loved and hated him.

Holly Brandenhall believed in love. She believed in family. Love and family informed, even dictated, every aspect of her life. From where to go to school to where to live upon graduation. From whom to marry to how to raise her children. Ultimately, from how to participate in her father's death to how to reconcile his life. And in each of these seminal decisions, she had to weigh the burden of how to forgive and even love a man who had convinced her, from the age of five until she left home to marry, that her body was his domain.

Clarissa Brandenhall was Holly's older sister. Though Clifton had inexplicably avoided any inappropriate contact with her, she knew he had systematically destroyed her younger sister with his perverse and seductive power, his blind emotional need; his insistence that her vagina, breasts, mouth, and soul were his to invade, to experience, to possess, with no thought to the irreparable havoc that would wreak. Clarissa hated him for his perversion and hated her sister for her willingness to forgive it. And as he lay dying under the care and ministrations of the beautiful, damaged Holly, Clarissa knew she could not *participate in the final chapter of this sick play and packed up her family and moved to Maine, a state as far away from California as possible, where she waited to hear that her father had died and her sister was free to finally acknowledge her own destruction...*

Tessa felt wrung out by this story. She had met separately with these two women, both of whom were now living in Los Angeles and, though not speaking to each other, had mutually agreed to have their story told. After listening to their brutal memories, and gathering and going over her notes, Tessa wondered how some children survived their parents.

She also couldn't help but feel her own story diminish in the gravity of theirs. And that's exactly what she'd told Vivian she wanted to avoid – unavoidable comparisons. But here she was, knee-deep in it now, pondering how she could be so wounded by nasty journal entries when their father had literally ripped these two apart. No easy answers there.

Before she shut down the computer for the night, she acknowledged the tremendous satisfaction she felt at taking on this project in spite of the internal conflicts. It felt important, at least meaningful, and she could sense that spark of inspiration, dormant of late, sputter to life. She was starting to envision the scope of the articles, how they'd work together to create an arc on the topic, how each would expose and explore a different avenue of the experience of fathers and daughters, and she was grateful for the challenge. It might help her forget her own.

FORTY-FIVE

About an hour after Tessa's first visit to the gym in almost two months, eight days after the unfortunate nightclub debacle, and just as many since they'd done much more than text each other, David made it through the condo door at a reasonable hour. A kiss, a pat, a quick smile, then, unexpectedly, he sat down across from her in the living room with a doleful stare.

She looked up from her book. "What?"

"We need to talk."

There's a hated phrase. She warily slid the book off her lap and sat up. "I know. It's been weird, I agree. And I miss you, David; I want to make things better. I'm working hard to figure out why all of this has hit me so hard, and I hope you understand that I just –"

"Tessa, I understand about as well as I can, but I've been thinking about a lot of things myself these last few months – what I want out of life, out of a relationship; what's important to me, how I want to share my life – all those sorts of things."

Tessa felt an alarming clutch. "Okay. I understand." *Understand that no prologue with that litany could possibly harbinger anything good.*

He continued: "I think we've been together long enough to have an idea of where we're headed and if we're headed in the same direction. And after a lot of honest thought, I've come to the conclusion that we're not."

Direct, clinical, no hemming and hawing; so very David. She kept her cool, her face held in the calmest expression she could muster. She was silent long enough that he cocked his head.

"Do you have a response?"

"I'm thinking about what my response should be."

"And what is it?"

"I'm curious; upon what criteria are you basing your opinion?"

"About us?"

"Of course. About how we're not headed in the same direction." She might even agree but definitely wanted to hear his opinion before she revealed her own. She also wanted to encourage enough dialogue to hopefully quell the hysteria she felt building.

"Tessa, you know I love you. I think you're amazing and talented and beautiful and all those things. I really do. But I think these last few months have clarified our differences in ways I hadn't seen before, all of which leads me to believe we're not really walkin' down the same road."

She hated it when he got all folksy, dropping his g's to feign casualness. "But I'm still curious as to what you're basing that opinion on. Was it the thing at the club?" Actually, she was pretty sure this had something to do with that fucking marketing job.

David, never wild about emotional dissection, appeared hesitant. "No, that was an unfortunate blip, I get that. I think our issues go way beyond uncharacteristic bad behavior at a dance club."

That was generous. "Then I presume it was the job offer."

He stood up, moved across the room, and positioned himself as if he were going to give a speech. He reminded her of Duncan in that moment. Which was not good. "Look, Tessa, I like being a corporate guy. I like the idea of working in a structured environment, dealing with strategic planners and good minds from the business sector. I like accruing a portfolio, building reserves, having a pension plan, working towards a showplace home and a luxurious lifestyle. I plan to achieve all that ethically and honorably,

I want to be as charitable and giving as I can afford, but I don't want to limit myself and my life to some idealistic notion of what's noble and worthy…the way you do."

What? "And this assessment is based on my not wanting the marketing job?" She was struggling to keep her voice modulated.

"No, but that was a piece of it. I get that you love writing but I cannot, for the life of me, understand how you could turn down what could ultimately be a mid-six-figure job with benefits and retirement and paid vacations and all that for a freelance position with a marginal online magazine. No offense to Vivian, I think what she does is brilliant, but there's no money in it and never will be. You're looking at forty, Tessa, I'm already in my forties, and I just don't think we have time to live like college kids so you can feel noble and artistic."

"And that's why you think I didn't want the job? Because I want to be noble and artistic?"

"I think that's part of it."

"Well, maybe artistic but noble? I don't even know what that means. But the main thing is that, unlike you, I *don't* like being the corporate guy. I have no problem with you being a corporate guy so why should you care what the fuck kind of guy *I* am?"

"Please don't get hostile. I'm trying to explain my thinking, to get you to understand how all this hits me. I don't want to get beat up for it."

"And I don't want to get beat up for being what I am either. Fine, you think we're not walkin' down the same road; is the only remedy for that ending our relationship?"

"Certainly not in every case, but I honestly think we may be too different in the way we see life to get over this hump."

"I'm having a very hard time listening to you talk so matter-of-factly about our relationship as if it were some sort of clinical subject you were analyzing. You *fuck* me, David! You put your cock inside me and feel my breasts and put your tongue in my mouth and tell me you love me and none of that is some dry, unemotional, clinical thing to be analyzed!'"

David was clearly uncomfortable with the road they were walkin' down now. He came over to the couch and put his arm around her. "Tessa, please calm down. I'm not negating that part of who we are. I do love you. I love what we have between us sexually, but that isn't enough in a relationship and you know that."

She yanked away from him. "Don't patronize me, David. And don't tell me to calm down, I fucking hate that."

"Fine." He moved over slightly.

"And I don't need you to tell me what is or isn't enough in a relationship. I think I know what a relationship is or isn't," she countered clumsily.

"Really? Do you?" That got him up and pacing again. "From what you've told me, this is an area you've struggled with most of your life so I'm not sure you *do* know."

"Oh, I see, but you do? One marriage, one divorce, some serial monogamy and you've got it all figured out?"

"At least I had the guts to commit to a marriage. It may not have worked out but at least I tried. You've obviously never felt that kind of commitment was necessary to get what you wanted out of a relationship."

The condescension resonated in some ancient, familiar way. Then it struck her. He was channeling her father. She'd let him read one journal, she'd told him the Trevor story, and now he was spouting Leo-speak. "What do you mean by *that*? Are you also going to tell me what a failure I am, how I use men, how I'm a complete fucking disappointment? When do you get to that list?"

David was honestly stunned. "Whoa, Tessa, do *not* go there! That is seriously dangerous territory and this is not at *all* about what your father said. It's me talking here and I'm just saying – based on things you yourself have told me about your past choices, your past relationships – that you might not have all the answers, that's all. I'm not saying I do, clearly I don't, but please don't try to pretend you do."

"Why are we debating this stupid issue? I never said I did! If you want out of the relationship, David, just have the balls to say it without all this bullshit about what I am or what I'm not or whatever the fuck you're rambling on about, okay?"

"But that's the point, isn't it? This relationship isn't working for me *because* of what you are or are not. That's the reason. You can be whatever you want to be but I want to be with someone who sees the world a little closer to the way I do."

"How do you think I see it?"

"I don't think you really care how I think you see it. I think all you care about is hanging on for dear life to some personal philosophy that is, to my mind, counterproductive and, frankly, pretty outdated."

Tessa's head was swimming. "I don't even know what you're saying right now. I think you're taking very personally the fact that I didn't want to work at your precious New Strand International. I think it's that simple."

"Well, it's too bad you think it's that simple. I guess reducing it all down to that makes it easier for you to just close your mind to any option outside of your narrow little worldview."

Tessa couldn't believe they'd come to this. She'd always felt David's complete support for who she was and what she did. She was stunned by this bizarre and seemingly sudden turnaround. Unless it wasn't sudden. "So have you always felt this critical of my worldview or have you just been struck by some sort of corporate-loving lightning bolt?" She was trying to be glib but it wasn't working. Her heart was pounding faster than it should and her ability to behave well or process information maturely was gone. "Why don't you tell me all about my narrow little worldview and why it is so fucking unacceptable to your brilliant, evolved, corporate ass-kissing self, David?"

Whatever decorum he started with had also evaporated. "You really want to know? Okay, I'll tell you. I think you believe you've got to suffer and grovel and wear this mantle of tortured artist to be truly you. I actually feel sorry for you in some ways. You live like an art victim, an art martyr. Like somehow you don't deserve to succeed or win or have wealth or happiness unless it's from your art. And if that doesn't happen – and odds are it won't – you'll just live a lesser life, that's part of the bargain. To me that mentality is bullshit and is probably the reason you *haven't* succeeded. I hate to say this because I know it's going to send you round the bend, but there was one line from the journal that *did* stand out to me – that you're endowed with so much talent but you haven't used it for anything useful. Maybe that's where your father *was* right."

BOOM. Like a bomb dropped from on high. Ripples of heat swept off that comment, cascading over them both. Tessa closed her eyes and from there, everything he said was a blur. He saw the blowback as it happened and tried quickly to recover.

"Jesus, that's not what I meant…I meant – come on, you know I don't agree with anything your father said – not about the useful part – obviously you've been useful, obviously." Stupidly, he continued. "And you *are* talented, Tessa, everyone in your life thinks so, but you have to admit, it seems like you want to play with the scrabblers of life; the freelancers, the no-commitment, don't-tie-me-down artist types who just can't face their fucking adulthood. Sorry, that's just how I see it. I thought you were the most dynamic, incredible woman I'd ever met but if you're willing to squander it all for a mid-level, unambitious, ain't goin' nowhere life, yeah, I guess I do see myself going down a different road."

He finally, thankfully, belatedly, stopped.

Tessa had retracted into a ball on the couch, her face hidden in the circle of her arms. David looked stricken. The room was very quiet.

"I know I just really hurt your feelings and I honestly wasn't planning on that. But truth is truth. Time we both face it. I'm sorry, Tessa."

He grabbed his coat and walked out the front door. It took a good ten seconds before Tessa realized she was holding her breath.

FORTY-SIX

It wasn't until hours later, laying in the darkness of Room 314 in the Hacienda Inn up on Sepulveda, that she could review the verbal napalm rained upon her. She hadn't felt this battered since Trevor. Disassociation was the only remedy that made sense so she spent the first hour or two watching hotel TV and thinking about the article she was working on; ultimately normal activity would be unsustainable.

After David left, Tessa had stayed in her ball on the couch for a good fifteen minutes, part of her hoping he'd come back and throw himself on his knees, declare his love, rescind his words and beg her forgiveness. Another part simply couldn't move. When she could, she got up, every muscle aching, her heart and lungs as heavy and congested as if pneumonia had struck, and tried to assess the damage.

At that moment she couldn't reconcile the man she loved with the judgmental person who just annihilated her in a few blunt paragraphs. It was now impossible to think of anything but getting out of there. She realized she wanted no late night reconciliations, no further arguing, no pathetic silence and pretense. She needed to get out.

Staggering through the condo it was clear that packing would be easy. The two chairs in the foyer were dispensable. Other than that, there were only a couple of wall hangings, a number of forgettable kitchen items, and the contents of her closet and dresser. She dragged her suitcases out of the storage space and hastily packed all her clothes and personal belongings. After lugging them down to the car, she grabbed one old picture of her singing at some bar in Hollywood, her computer and printer, a few of her books from the living room, and left a note saying: "Anything I've left you can have. None of it matters. I think I've got everything that does. We'll sort out remaining bills later. I'll put a forward on my mail as soon as I have a place. Until then, please hang on to it and I'll come by and pick it up when you're not around. Good luck."

She didn't sign it. He knew who she was. Or not.

FORTY-SEVEN

The first two days at the Hacienda were spent in a cycle of fitful sleep, anxiety and pacing, unrestrained sobbing, imbibing of whatever was in the mini-bar, followed by occasional retching and frantic searching for an apartment. The only things Tessa ate were the cashews and granola bars in the courtesy basket. Even that felt too much for her curdling stomach. She called no one, answered no calls, did not check her emails and generally kept the TV on mute. The lights never went on, except in the bathroom, and she never left the room.

By the beginning of the third day, she was exhausted enough to lie quietly in her thrashed bed – she'd had a "do not disturb" sign on her door since arrival – and examine more thoroughly what had just happened. David had extracted her. Her David. The man she so deeply loved, the man she'd lived with for over a year – the man with whom she imagined spending the rest of her life. She felt an ache of loss so deep it was difficult to breathe; she moaned and pushed her fists into her stomach as if to force the air out. Everything she knew that had been awkward and distancing and incompatible between them was gone; all she could think of now was how his smiling eyes looked at her when she said something that made him laugh. Their quiet, peaceful driving trips that took them to enchanting inns and mountaintops she had never seen before. The intensity and passion of his lovemaking. His strong, powerful body she so loved to curl into. His protectiveness and sense of propriety toward her. She was his woman, his girl. He loved her and cherished her and couldn't live without her.

Except he could. And now he wanted to. Because she didn't want to work in the marketing department at New Strand International. *That motherfucker.*

The more she rolled through that line of thinking, the more her grief transformed into rage. Running through the conversation and all its horrible, terrible, diminishing statements, she wanted to beat his head into a wall or drive an ice pick through his heart. So strong was the impulse that she heaved herself off the bed, picked up the desk chair and threw it into the coffee table with a roar. Luckily nothing of value broke, but the magazine display rack flew across the room, magazines flapping through the air, and hit the sliding glass door with a force hard enough to threaten breakage. The phone rang and she was sure it was the front desk calling to say someone was concerned about her sobbing or screaming or furniture tossing, so she didn't answer. But she did quiet down, realizing that a visit from security would do little to improve her state of mind. Curling back into the bed, she fell into a ragged sleep, a migraine descending.

By the fourth day the headache was so bad she started thinking she might need an emergency room. She couldn't stop throwing up and she was pretty sure it wasn't just from grief or alcohol anymore. She'd stopped drinking the night before, sipping only bits of water, but couldn't keep even that down. She wasn't sure she'd ever felt as wretched, and the headache, with its brain disturbance and unrelenting, nauseating pain, seemed to mirror her emotional agony. Not sure what to do, she lay on the bathroom floor and hoped it would pass. After fifteen minutes of erratic sleep, she knew it wouldn't. This was bad. Really bad. Her heart pounding, her stomach churning, she could barely open her eyes for the pain of the bathroom light; even the sound of doors slamming down the

AFTER THE SUCKER PUNCH

hall made her wince. This must surely feel like death.

She dragged herself out of the bathroom, climbed up on the bed, and pulled her phone to her. Time for help. She called Kate.

"Oh, my God, Tessa, where are you? We've all been so worried! I didn't know where you were or what was going on…my God, I didn't know if you'd driven yourself into a wall or what! Are you okay?"

Tessa could barely whisper her response. Kate finally wrangled the location and was on her way.

After two hydrating IVs, injections of some intense painkillers, and an admonishment from the urgent care doctor to never again wait that long to get help, Tessa felt at least well enough to get up off the gurney and stagger to the car with Kate's help. Back in the room, which had been attended to in their absence, Kate got Tessa tucked in and, after a quick conversation with the front desk, who needed assurance of better behavior to come, sat and watched her friend finally fall asleep.

193

FORTY-EIGHT

A couple of hours later Tessa awoke. Kate, quietly tapping away on her laptop, looked up and smiled, not without some reaction to Tessa's current state.

Tessa reached up to her hair. "That bad?"

"Well, you've probably lost some weight – one good thing." A standard joke.

After ordering some light fare from room service, little of which she could get down, Tessa relayed the whole story. Kate, always a good listener, didn't interrupt until she was done. "Well, I knew some of what happened, at least David's version. He called when he got back that night and you were gone. I think he was shocked that you packed up so quickly."

"Did he actually think I'd stick around after that?"

"I think he figured he'd have a chance to soften the blow. He was pretty shook up."

"He should be. He said some monumentally unforgivable things."

"Yes, he did. I'm so sorry." Tessa curled deeper into the bed. "So what are we going to do with you?" Kate asked, somewhat rhetorically.

"I don't know. Find me a place to live…I don't know. God, I hate my life."

"And you don't think he was just being dramatic, saying a bunch of crap he might have said differently if he'd thought about it a little more?"

"Don't think so. He seemed pretty calm and collected, like he'd been putting it together for a while. I think it's over."

"Really? Not worth a fight?"

"Kate, I know you're an optimist and you think people should fight till the bloody end, but I think this was the bloody end. I don't think you get to come back from here. Not in my book, anyway. Truth is, he's probably right about us being on different roads; we would've lost it at some point, regardless."

"Then I'm sorry, sweetie. I thought you two were in for the whole show."

"Me too." With that she crumbled again.

After about fifteen minutes of sobbing mixed with Kate's soothing consolations, Tessa fell back asleep. When she awoke, it was 4:30 in the afternoon and Kate had to leave for a dinner meeting up in North Hollywood. She offered the guest room in their house but Tessa couldn't imagine going through this hell in the presence of people who actually knew her. "Anonymous hotel guests are all I can handle right now, Kate. I don't want the guilt of annoying you and Todd during my deconstruction…not after Ruby's extended stay."

"You wouldn't, but I understand. Get some sleep and I'll check back in the morning. Call me – no matter how late it is – if you find yourself going down the rabbit hole again."

Tessa promised, knowing she wouldn't. Call, that is. The rabbit hole was less assured.

FORTY-NINE

Day Five arrived with sunshine and the unexpected urge for coffee. Though Tessa could feel the migraine ghost hovering, she could also feel some semblance of normalcy creeping back in. She finally checked her messages to discover Vivian had called five times, Ruby ten, Kate – prior to hearing from her – had called eight. Oddly non sequitur, Brad at Thompson Transport also left a message. David had called and texted seventeen times, at first just wondering where she was, then more frantic – worried about her state of mind, if she was all right, could they please talk – followed by fervent apologies, attempts at revisionist clarification of statements made, declarations of rethinking it all and arriving at different conclusions, and so on. By Day Four he sounded positively terrified, begging her to call, revealing that he had contacted everyone they knew and might soon call the police. He had, however, refrained from calling anyone in her family, which was odd but appreciated. Aunt Joanne had called several times. She sounded less frantic but certainly concerned.

Tessa felt a wave of gnawing obligation. She now had to call them all back. *Fuck.* She wasn't up to it. She attempted to eat but couldn't do that either, though the coffee proved doable. She wrote a bit on her article, which made her feel guilty about not calling Vivian, so Vivian she called.

"Well, kiddo, I'm glad to finally hear from you. I was concerned after David left a rather hysterical message making it sound as if you were teetering on a bridge somewhere. I had faith you'd survive. How are you?"

"Awful. Haven't felt this battered since…well, in a long time."

"Bastard. Give me the nutshell."

Tessa ran it down as briefly as she could, graciously omitting David's harsh assessment of *Edge+Reason*, and was sobbing by the end of the conversation, something she'd never done in front of Vivian. "I'm sorry, I feel like I've been crying for a year. I am without equilibrium."

"It's understandable. Give it some time, you'll snap back. Personally, I'd like to drop-kick his bony ass across the universe, but for the moment I'll just hate him on your behalf."

"I don't hate him, I love him. Which is why this feels like such shit."

"If that's true, then I really am sorry. He doesn't deserve your love, not after that assault. All I can say is, once you get some distance, you'll be able to see him for what he is…and you'll probably be grateful he dumped you."

Tessa couldn't help but laugh. "You have your way with words, don't you?"

"Well, I'm sorry, but he's a schmuck."

Tessa conceded to at least that, leaving out any thought to her own schmuck-quotient. They wrapped up the conversation with Tessa's agreement to stay in touch and stay on track with the first article of the series. Once off the phone, however, she headed back to bed unclear if she could honestly do either.

Just as she was drifting off, the room phone rang. Startled, she answered it, presuming it was the front desk. It was David; clearly Kate had outed her location.

"Tessa, it's me; please don't hang up!"

"What do you want, David?"

"I'm sorry, I wouldn't have disturbed you but you're not going to believe who showed up at the door this morning."

Fucking Ronnie. Poor, stupid, inconsiderate Ronnie had decided he ultimately *did* want to visit his sister in Los Angeles, but rather than call ahead to make sure it was a convenient time, thought it'd be "fun to just show up." Not so fun. Not so convenient.

The exceedingly brief conversation with David ended with Tessa's permission to send Ronnie to the hotel despite her intense desire to suggest he get back on a plane and fly home.

She hated all men.

The only bright spot was when she stepped on the scale while brushing her teeth and discovered that she had, indeed, lost eight pounds. *One good thing.*

FIFTY

As she waited for Ronnie's arrival, she started returning her other phone calls. Luckily Ruby was at work so she was able to leave a quippy message about doom and double dates now that they were both single. She called Aunt Joanne, also not available, and left a brief message suggesting they get together the following week. She checked in with Kate and left a message saying she was doing okay and would be babysitting Ronnie for a few days. Finally she called Brad at Thompson Transport in Evanston, Illinois. Brad was the owner. Brad was not helpful.

"The boxes still aren't there? That's strange; those shipped out a while ago. They should've been there by now. Well, I'm assuming they'll get there soon."

"You're *assuming*? It's been over three weeks. Don't you have a tracking method?"

"Yeah, but right now that truck has been diverted."

"What does that mean?"

"The original truck broke down through Colorado and we had to transfer everything to another truck. I'm still trying to find out what got delivered and what didn't, where the new truck might be, that sort of thing. All I can say right now is that I should be getting some information later today so if you want to call later – or maybe tomorrow, that'd probably be better – hopefully I'll have some news for you."

Tessa could not believe this was the company Michaela had entrusted to deliver several boxes of irreplaceable family history. All she could do was agree to call in the morning. As she hung up the phone, a loud knock confirmed the arrival of her new roommate.

She opened the door to a bedraggled, unshaven, and obviously inebriated Ronnie. She felt like punching him in the face. Instead, she smiled weakly. He straggled in and flopped on the bed.

"Well, sis, I guess now we drink."

So they did.

FIFTY-ONE

Tessa then did something she had never done before. She abandoned all responsibility, all obligation, and proceeded to spend the next two days drinking with Ronnie. As with her first few days at the hotel, the slew of phone calls rolled in and, once again, she refused to answer a one. She missed her deadline for Vivian and, in some distant recess of her brain, felt really bad about that one. But right now, in this moment, at this time of her life, she wanted nothing to do with deadlines, phone calls, or demands on her time and energy. She was commiserating with her depressed, alcoholic little brother. Her poor, damaged, vulnerable little brother who needed her more than anyone else in the world and, for once in a very long time, she needed him back.

At some point he went out and hit the local liquor barn for a supply of Jack Daniels, Captain Morgan Rum, Diet Coke, limes, Chardonnay, a few six-packs of Samuel Adams, several bags of chips and nuts, bananas, and a pack of salami. This would be their sustenance for the next two days. Despite the threatening return of her migraine, despite her good sense and innate knowledge that this was the last thing either of them needed, this is what Tessa was determined to do. Because after days of pondering, she'd come to the conclusion that, despite her wild child years, she'd always been a really good person (factoring in the nuances of subjective moral codes) and it seemed clear that being a really good person came with very little upside. Your father still didn't like you, you still didn't get to be a rock star, and your boyfriend still broke up with you. *Fuck 'em.* Maybe a run of Bad Girl would be empowering.

So she pulled out the sleeper sofa, yanked shut the blackout drapes, turned off her computer and she and Ronnie drank, snacked, cried, and talked about Fucking Leo, Fucking Wendy, and Fucking David.

"I have to say, Tess, I never really liked the guy. He always sounded like a big, fat pussy. Way too wimpy for you."

"He wasn't wimpy. He was…normal."

"Like oatmeal. Didn't you say he wore Dockers?"

"Whatever, he's a dick."

Ronnie roared, "Yes! David is a dick. Dicky David in Dockers. What the fuck did you ever see in him anyway?"

"Dammit, Ronnie, you don't get to ask questions like that."

Ronnie glanced up from his bottle to see tears and was immediately stricken. "Oh, Tess, baby, I'm sorry. Forget that question, forget it. What do I know? My wife left me for bein' a loser and I *still* love her. We can't help who we love." *Wisdom from a drunk.*

"He was kind. He treated me like I was precious. He made me feel loved. All those things. I knew we were really different but I didn't think that would be a deal-breaker. I still can't believe it." Her tears ratcheted up until she was sobbing. "Who's gonna love me now, Ronnie? Really, who? I'm an old, wrinkled art martyr." He grabbed her and held tight.

"You're none of those things, Tess. And someone will love you, just like you told me. Someone will. We both gotta believe that."

But she didn't. Not anymore. She was almost thirty-seven, working as an independent contractor for a "marginally successful online magazine"; she had no home, no furniture, no retirement fund; she paid for her own insurance, her car had a broken airbag, she was only average-looking (though certainly now thinner), and could not remotely predict when she would ever again feel stable in life. Not exactly a catch.

By the time the mixed nuts were gone and they'd exhausted the conversation, she was able to sleep, comforted by Ronnie's presence. Around three in the morning she awoke with such a start she literally threw herself off the bed. Ronnie jerked awake, peering through the dark at his sister on the floor.

"Jesus, Tess, what are you doing down there?"

"I don't know…it's where I landed." Her heart banging in her chest, veins flooded with adrenaline, she assessed that she was in one piece and leaned against the wall. "I just slammed awake like the house was on fire and ended up here, have no idea why. Sheesh, might be time to lay off the beverages."

He crawled over to her. "You are a bit of a lightweight."

"Well, you're a tough act to follow."

"I do set a high bar." He leaned against the wall next to her. "That happened to me a bunch after Wendy left; I'd jolt awake all jacked up with this weird sense of doom or something. I Googled it and it's some kind of physic shock."

"Psychic shock…that sounds about right." She leaned her head on his shoulder. "I hate this, Ronnie. I just want to be happy. Why does that seem to be so hard for us?"

"I don't know, maybe it was having a crazy mother. Maybe it's the genetic anti-cheerfulness we inherited from Pops."

He pulled her close and their knees banged together the way they had when they were kids hiding down in the basement to escape whatever family onslaught was in progress upstairs.

"You want something to drink?" he asked.

"Are you kidding? My stomach lurched just hearing those words."

"Look, Tess, if my experience with this heartbreak stuff is any gauge, this is gonna take a while. You just gotta ride it out and be ready for some rough nights. I mean, if it's knocking you to your knees, this is no small shit."

"Why do you make it sound so ominous?"

"It's 'cause you're just out of a relationship, less distracted; that's usually when the Startle Demons swoop in."

"Startle Demons?"

"That's what I call 'em. Even happened to me sometimes when we were kids. I'd wake up freaking out that something terrible was going on, then I'd look around and everyone was sleeping, the house was quiet; nothing. Weird shit. During the divorce those fuckers'd sometimes wake me up two, three times a night. Doesn't happen much anymore. It's probably just anxiety. Maybe old childhood crap – fear of hell, fear of getting your ass kicked, you know, all that good stuff."

"Couldn't it just be that my boyfriend broke up with me?"

"Maybe. But I bet the Dad thing is pulling the strings. I mean, what have you been obsessing about since he died, since you found the journals? Did he love me? Did he think I was a good person? Was I redeemed?"

"How pathetic if that's true." She put her head in her hands. "Of course it's true. My dad thought I was a failure, boo hoo, I don't know if he loved me so now I'm going to be a crazy person with Startle Demons...what the hell? I have no reason to be this crazy, do I?"

"You're not crazy, you're just sad. I think it's good that you're getting the journals. You'll read them and maybe find something that helps you get past all this shit and on with your life." He pulled her closer. She leaned into him...*dear clumsy, wonderful Ronnie.*

FIFTY-TWO

The next morning Ronnie woke to see Tessa showered and dressed for life, sitting at her computer with a cup of coffee and the rental lists up. Her face was pale and drawn but she was at least upright and somewhat functional. He groaned. She turned from the computer as he burrowed further under the sheets.

"Nope, get up. Time to stop this. I feel like shit and I can't keep fucking up. People are counting on me."

"I never let that stop me," he said from under the covers.

She didn't laugh. "Get up, I mean it."

He sat up and shook his head. "Damn, girl, what's gotten into you?"

"I can't keep doing this, that's all. Turns out I don't do Bad Girl all that well. I need a place to live, I need to get some work done, and I can't do either with you here shoving Jack Daniels down my throat." She managed a painful wink.

"Oh, you do not get to blame this on me!" He threw a pillow at her and, thankfully, missed.

"Please don't. I think even that pillow would shatter my head right now. And seriously, it's time for both of us to get moving along, okay?"

"You're actually kicking me out?"

"Yes! I can't live in a hotel…I'm going broke! I have to find an apartment, you have to find a job, and we both have to take some responsibility for our lives. Besides, don't you have some birds to attend to?"

"Yes, you're right, my peeps, shit, gotta go." He rolled his eyes and got out of bed. "I've got my peeps covered but don't you worry, sister, I know when to hit the road." He started throwing things in his duffel. "And I certainly wish you good luck and hope you can get past this whiny-assed, self-indulgent loser stage of your life right quick." He smiled that big goofy grin of his.

"Asshole. By the way, I'll let you know when I get the boxes, *if* I get them. Damn Mickie."

"Yeah, I know, but give her a break. I think she was just trying to save you some money."

Tessa turned to him, incredulous. "Did I just hear you defend Michaela? You, Ronald James Curzio, defended Michaela? Did hell freeze and no one told me?"

Ronnie actually blushed. "Yeah, I know. Maybe I've mellowed a bit. But there's actually a reason."

"Do tell!"

"You're not going to believe this, but she kinda offered me a job."

Tessa practically dropped her coffee. "Really? Why does that just amaze me? What's the job?"

"Nothing huge. I guess the school lost their IT guy and they had some major tech stuff jamming them up. I ran into Mickie at Mom's a week or so ago and she asked me to come by and see if I could do anything with this one specific thing they needed fixed right away. It was actually no big deal and I got it taken care of pretty easily – which their other guy apparently couldn't do – so they were sort of impressed. Then later that night, when I was having dinner with her and Randy as sort of a 'thank you,' they offered me the job."

"Astonishing. And sort of unbelievable, considering it's Mickie."

"Well, let's be real clear here. She didn't say it out loud, but she hinted pretty clearly that it's all on me to keep my shit together and show up on a day-to-day basis. All very grown-up stuff and not necessarily in the wheelhouse of Mr. Nuts and Bolts these days."

Tessa got up and gave him a gentle hug. "You're going to be fine. Just do the best you can; I know you can make this work. It would be so good if you could make it work, right?"

Ronnie had no smart comeback, more somber than usual. "Something you said a few minutes ago – 'I can't keep fucking up, people are depending on me' – that struck me, y'know? Nobody's really depended on me in a long time. I mean, sure, at all my various dumb-ass jobs, but nobody who really cared about me, nobody I didn't want to let down. Not in a long time."

"I know, Ronnie…"

"I'm not tryin' to make you feel all sorry for me, sis, it's just the truth. When I planned this trip I figured I'd have one more good blow-out, spend some time tearing up the town with you, just let it all go before I got back on the program and made a decision about the job."

"Well, beyond the fact that we didn't tear up anything but this hotel room, how does it feel now?"

"I guess what keeps hitting me is that if Mickie's willing to trust me, to give me a chance at something worthwhile, well, that's kinda big, isn't it?" He looked so young and vulnerable at that moment Tessa felt a sob rise in her throat. Poor battered Ronnie; just wanted to know he was a good guy and could be counted on by people who would love him either way.

"Yeah, it kind of is."

He got up, shaking it off. "Obviously I should've called before I came but maybe it's good that I didn't. I wouldn't have come then and I'm glad I was here to help you get through the weekend. You've always been there for me; felt good to be able to return the favor."

Tessa didn't point out that his ministrations had been limited to drunken conversation, sloppy hugs, and an endless supply of booze and bad snack food, especially since she realized his being there, however deleterious to her health, actually *had* gotten her a few steps along in the grieving process. She also didn't mention that she had no idea he'd ever been in a program of any kind. But what she was absolutely blown away by was Michaela's offering him a job. *That* Michaela she didn't know and it touched her deeply to realize she existed.

At five that evening Tessa dropped Ronnie at the airport with a kiss and a wish for him to make the absolute best of this opportunity. He promised he would and she hoped, from the bottom of her bruised and broken heart, he would be true to his word. She drove back to the hotel and, unable to maintain her stoicism a moment longer, crawled into bed and cried herself to an early sleep.

The Startle Demons woke her at midnight, but after the ten minutes it took her to calm down, she was able to fall back asleep for the rest of the night.

FIFTY-THREE

Vivian had left several conflicted messages, anger mixed with sympathy, and Tessa could no longer put her friend and employer through this mess. She slipped into the office barely noticed by the others, but Haden, working with Glen across the room, looked up as she stopped at her workstation. His face told her he knew. It also indicated how tragic she must look; his expression was that of someone viewing an accident victim. He raised his hand in a cursory wave and she smiled wanly in return. She knocked on Vivian's door. Vivian looked up, surprised and slightly stern. She motioned her in. Tessa put a pen drive on her desk then sat down, anticipating the lecture.

"I presume this is the piece?" Not a speck of humor in Vivian's voice. "You couldn't have just emailed it to me?"

"I'm sorry, I could have but I know it's late so I wanted to be absolutely sure you got it. If you can figure out how to get it in the next issue, great. If you want me off the project, I completely understand."

"That might be best."

Tessa was stunned. "Really?"

"Tessa, I'm sorry you're going through such hell, obviously. You know how I feel about you. But I am running a business here and if you can't do the work, at least have the fucking courtesy to

209

call and tell me. I held up the entire run waiting for your piece and not getting it on time inconvenienced a lot of people who I respect equally. I want you to figure it out, get your life together, and we'll talk about it later." Vivian was not kidding around.

"Are you telling me to leave?"

"I'm telling you to decide *what* you want to do. You want to take some time to sort out your life, I get it; then do that. You want to write for this magazine, you show up. End of story. I'll love and respect you either way. But I need a writer. If you need time, I'll find someone else to write this series. Up to you."

Tessa stood up, grabbed her bag, and raced from the room, slamming the door behind her. Everyone looked up as she stormed across the office and marched out. By the time she clamored down the stairs and got to the front door of the building, a wave of sanity, mixed with a big dollop of shame and some stone-cold weariness, crashed over her and she sank to the bottom step. She sat there, calming her ragged breath, once again embarrassed with herself. Miss Drama Queen. *Fucking Leo and his nicknames.*

Footsteps came from behind and before Tessa could look up, Vivian plunked down next to her. "As far as you got?"

"Apparently." Tessa looked up with chagrin. "I'm sorry. I'm a mess. This is why I should never be allowed in an office."

Vivian put her arm around her. "Sweetheart, I don't want you off the project. I want you happy. I want you feeling yourself. It's my magazine; I can run the damn story whenever I want. I was just annoyed that I wasn't hearing back from you. I know you're going through hell but I'm on your side."

"I know, I'm sorry. I'm not thinking clearly these days."

"I understand. I just had the idea of getting the series up in time for some East Coast consideration that had deadlines and I didn't want to lose the opportunity."

"Oh, no…is it too late?"

"It is, but it'll still be a great series and I'm sure you've done a masterful job on this first one. We'll run it next week."

"I'm so, so sorry and really do appreciate your support, it's just been so…" She couldn't even finish.

"Go home – "

"To my hotel – "

"To your hotel. Get some rest, feel better; I'll make it right upstairs."

Tessa left realizing that while she loved Vivian, she didn't much care how right she made things upstairs, especially with Haden. Somewhere after slamming the door and making her ungraceful exit, she realized the buzz was gone. The man she wanted was not the one upstairs; it was the one who'd just broken her heart.

FIFTY-FOUR

Morning brought the dawn of a new day. Or so she told herself. Tessa was so determined to turn things around that she took time throughout the day to form and update a mental checklist that went a long way towards making her feel more organized. That most of it didn't actually get done was less relevant.

1. An hour spent crying with Ruby, plotting their respective recoveries, talking about apartments, small boys, the mystery of love and how neither of them could hold on to it. Ruby offered her the guest room; Tessa deferred, claiming a temporary lack of tolerance for toddlers. Ruby understood. It was a cathartic conversation and Tessa made note of what good friends she had.
2. Thought about calling Aunt Joanne. Didn't.
3. Thought about calling Ronnie. Didn't.
4. Listened to her mother's interminable message about how no one had heard from her and would she please call soon. Couldn't.
5. Realized she'd forgotten to call Brad at Thompson Transport. Needed to get that done.
6. Marked a few apartment listings to check out when she could. That wouldn't be today.

7. Checked and ignored her notifications on Facebook and Twitter, her updates on LinkedIn, and her comments on Tumblr.

8. Ate a small omelet with broccoli, so there was progress on the nutrition front.

9. Answered when Kate called. They discussed possible living arrangements with a friend of Kate's; talked about Todd's new job and their sudden income increase (Kate promised to take her and Ruby on a spa trip once things settled down); debated where the journals might be and what options there were to track them. It was a calming exchange and Tessa found herself ready for bed.

Curled under the covers waiting for sleep, Tessa decided not to ponder the illusion of today's accomplishments. There *was* the omelet. She quickly drifted off, only to wake at two in the morning with a pounding heart. She sighed, rolled over, and accepted that the Startle Demons had, once again, been assigned to keep her company.

FIFTY-FIVE

Apartment hunting was much like shopping for jeans: sweaty, frustrating, and nothing much fit. Tessa called Martina at her old place and, much to both their disappointment, the errant tenant who'd earlier threatened to leave ultimately decided to stay; apparently the loser boyfriend moved to Petaluma with another girl. Martina suggested a couple of other places that Tessa checked out; the one near her old neighborhood was great, another in Culver City was potentially worthy, and she put a call into a decent duplex in West Los Angeles. The plan was to lock down something this week.

After a day of phone tag with Brad at Thompson Transport, the latest call revealed that no one had any new information on the location of the replacement truck or, more ominously, what had actually made it onto the truck and what hadn't. This was a new wrinkle and certainly not good news. When Tessa asked if it was standard procedure to check the cargo area of a disabled truck to make sure everything had been loaded off, the only answer she got was that the truck had been moved to a repair lot in another city and it was unlikely anything had been left inside. Since Brad wasn't there at the time, the gentleman she spoke to suggested she call back at the end of the business day, but when she did, Brad was still not around and no one, again, seemed clear on where the replacement truck was. After every phone call Tessa silently cursed her sister.

Aunt Joanne. The one person Tessa had managed to avoid for over three weeks was the one person she most definitely needed. After her room service meal of the night (followed by a gnawing realization that her credit card would soon be hitting its limit), Tessa finally returned her aunt's phone calls. She found her in her office.

At first she thought Aunt Joanne sounded terse, a result, Tessa presumed, of her erratic and persistent stonewalling. But as the conversation continued, Tessa decided she was reading something into it that wasn't there. Her own guilt was more likely at play.

Aunt Joanne, in fact, listened sympathetically to the story of David's breakup and Tessa's subsequent dislocation and misery. Though she queried the wisdom of the weekend binge with Ronnie, she was glad to hear Tessa had survived her brother and sent him home to a program and a job. She shared frustration regarding the mystery of the detoured journals and said they needed to talk more about why the urgency surrounding them had ratcheted up. Tessa told her about the Startle Demons and Aunt Joanne's take was that they were repressed pockets of past anxiety stirred up by recent events.

"The main thing is, how do I get rid of them?"

"I think we need to keep talking, keep pulling memories out from under the covers so you can reexamine them, release that anxiety, and maybe find truths you hadn't seen before. If we can do that, I believe it will help you banish those demons and reconstruct your memories, your story, so to speak. Particularly now that the old story has been so shattered by what you've learned through this journal you gave me. Which is something else we need to talk about."

"Did you read it?"

"Yes, several times. I have some thoughts I'd like to share with you, but unfortunately I have to get to a meeting right now. I'd also rather talk about it when we can get together."

So they booked time for the following week, Tessa explaining that her immediate priority was finding a place to live before her credit ran out. She hung up realizing there was comfort in knowing her aunt was prepared to take on her demons. Somebody had to; she was exhausted.

✴

FIFTY-SIX

The girls were lunching together for the first time in a very long time. It seemed that life had convulsed into a completely new form since those easy days before December, when chatting about jobs and men and their latest projects was the norm. Now it was all about parental loss, potential divorce, an unfortunate breakup; lost journal boxes, midnight terrors, and now Kate said she had something to tell them, which could only be some new tragedy given the trajectory of late.

Quite the contrary. She was pregnant.

Much screaming, hugging, and crying ensued, enough that the waiter, with raised eyebrow, asked if they'd like to be moved to a private area, which they didn't. Once they settled back down, the next thirty minutes were spent grilling the new mother-to-be, eliciting the following information:

1. Kate was twelve weeks along.
2. They were going to clarify the gender.
3. No names had been picked.
4. Todd was over the moon.
5. Kate had not thrown up yet but expected to soon.
6. Yes, she was going to have to have amniocentesis.
7. No, she wouldn't circumcise a boy.

8. Yes, they would vaccinate.
9. The families were thrilled.
10. The house would need even more remodeling.
11. She was grooming her assistant to take over during her leave.
12. And no, nothing had ever made her happier.

"I waited till the first trimester was over so I could be sure before I made my big announcement. I almost feel selfish telling you guys about this, both of you have been through such hell lately, but you were also the two people I most wanted to share it with." Kate reached out and grabbed both of their hands. "Maybe we can look at this as the beginning of better times, okay?"

"Absolutely," Tessa concurred. "There is nothing I'd like more than to look at this as the beginning of better times!"

Ruby agreed. They made some sort of girl-oath to really be there for each other through the good and the bad, then proceeded to toast with sparkling cider and the third drink Tessa had consumed so far today. Life could only get better now that a baby was on the way.

But back at the hotel Tessa sat in a whirlpool of conflicting emotions. She *was* happy, sincerely happy, for her dear friend, yet enveloped in a new envy/despair mix. She couldn't help but view her own life and realize her chance for love and family was edging slowly beyond reach. Of all the men with whom she'd ever been involved, David was closest to "the kind of guy you marry and have children with," as she'd once described him to her father. Now he was gone, off to be a stable corporate guy, and the only person on her horizon was a good-looking computer geek who probably had unframed rock posters on his walls and a refrigerator full of beer and string cheese.

Thoughts of David triggered a non sequitur: what if the journal boxes had already been delivered to the condo? She'd given Brad at Thompson Transport the address at the hotel, but considering his general cluelessness, efficiency was unlikely.

My God, what if the boxes have been sitting in David's foyer, just sitting there, and after trying to reach me for three weeks he finally gave up?

The more this illogical thought roiled around, the more feasible it became. She was going to have to call David. Or at the very least check all her voice mails from him. Or maybe she should just go over there. If the journals *were* there, she'd damn well like to get them as soon as possible.

She was pouring her fifth drink of the day when a new thought emerged: *What if the journals have been delivered and David purposely hasn't called? What if he's ignoring them in some punitive effort to engage my attention? That would be so unlike him, but who knows these days?* She never figured he'd say half the things he did so maybe subterfuge *was* in his playbook. She picked up the phone and, before she could talk herself out of it, called.

"Tessa! I'm surprised to hear from you. I've tried to call – "

"I wasn't up for a conversation, David." She could hear the surf in the background and pictured him out on the deck. Which gave her a pang. "Listen, did the boxes with my dad's journals ever show up at your place? They were originally supposed to be delivered there and since no one seems to know where they are, I'm wondering if you already got them."

"No. I would have called you if I had."

"I haven't exactly made it easy to get in touch with me."

"I realize that, but obviously I would've told Kate or Ruby if I couldn't get through to you. And no, of course not; there haven't been any deliveries for you. Some mail, but no deliveries."

"Fine, just wanted to check. I know you think it's dumb that I'm bothering to get them but – "

"I never said it was dumb. I'm not sure we actually talked it out completely."

That sparked something. "Oh, we did; we did, David, you probably just weren't listening. Or maybe you were too busy internalizing your negative judgment on the topic to actually hear me."

"Okay, be mad at me for what actually happened. You don't need to make stuff up."

"That's right, I'm just a loser who loves to be a martyr, I forgot."

David sighed. "If you want to talk, Tessa, that's fine, but I don't see any point in doing this right now."

"YOU DIDN'T EVEN COME TO HIS FUNERAL!" She surprised even herself with this outburst. Up until the words flew from her mouth, she hadn't consciously realized it was an issue. Apparently it was. Or at least it was in this charged moment.

He was as stunned as she was. "Tessa...God...you know I felt bad about that. I wanted to come, I really did; I just couldn't figure out how to make it work at the time. You said you understood; you said you knew it was unavoidable. You even said it was probably easier if I *didn't* come."

"Those are just polite things people say! I was in shock, for God's sake, you should have known better!" She felt on fire, digging deep into this new, convenient pocket of rage. "The one time, the one fucking time I would *ever* have to go through such a thing – a father's death, a father's funeral – and you couldn't figure out that regardless of what I *said* in my attempt to be the undemanding girlfriend, it was your job to be there! To be by my side, helping me through one of the most shattering moments of my life. But where were you? You were at a management-training seminar for people who sell sneakers. SNEAKERS, for fuck's sake! You and your fucking sneakers! You missed my father's funeral for sneakers." Even she was amazed at how many times she got the word *sneakers* in.

David was floundering. "You're right. I should have been there. Thinking about it now it was ridiculous that I wasn't. I'm sorry. For what it's worth, I'm really sorry."

A brief moment of consideration, but she was too far gone to stem the tide. "A little late for that, David. Maybe when you're reviewing your new corporate candidates for your next relationship, you can make sure none of them actually expect you to show up for the important moments. Because while you were busy judging me and my pathetic worldview, you forgot to realize what a shallow, meaningless, unforgivable prick you are." With that, she hung up.

She thought she'd feel triumph. Instead, she felt incredible shame. *Once again, Miss Fucking Drama Queen takes a bow.*

FIFTY-SEVEN

The hotel era concluded and by the middle of the following week Tessa was moved into her new place, a small but charming one-bedroom near her old neighborhood in Hollywood, only higher up the hill. There was something both regressive and comforting about being back where everything was familiar and recognizable. Although there was no ocean, no pelicans, and no salty breeze, her bedroom window overlooked a sweet little fenced-in yard where night-blooming jasmine flung its scent around and flowerbeds and tall grass lent a country feel. After the beige sand and treeless environs of her beach neighborhood this was a good trade. She was delighted to have use of the picnic table and lawn chairs that were artfully positioned around the yard and decided this would be where she would do most of her writing. Once she got settled.

Getting settled, that was the challenge. With no furniture (though he insisted, she refused to take back the chairs she'd left at David's) and only a selection of such basics as utensils, towels and garbage cans, repeated shopping trips to big box stores filled her schedule. Kate and Todd gave her a new bed and chair as rather generous housewarming gifts, Ruby donated a few essentials from her garage, which helped fill the gaps, but it was clear this would be an ongoing process not an overnight success. After the décor abdication at David's, Tessa felt eager make this place her own, to fill it with old band photos, family portraits, quirky artwork, anything and everything that was testament to her good taste and creative sensibilities. The fact that she was missing a couch, a coffee table, and most incidentals was less important than the fact that it was all *hers*; the rest would come with further time and income.

Now that she'd landed, continued avoidance of her aunt just seemed rude. Tessa had canceled their last session due to her moving schedule, but there had been three awakenings in the past week and she was forced to accept that they were compelled by something worth discussing with a wise and willing listener. Whatever their cause, she sensed they were not going away on their own. Another session was scheduled and she was determined to get there this time.

Thompson Transport continued to disappoint. The replacement truck had arrived in Los Angeles during the previous week and, unbelievably, there were no journals onboard. Neither of the two drivers had any idea why not, nor where the journals might be, and when Tessa drove out to the warehouse where they'd unloaded, nobody had any answers. After a furious phone call to Evanston, Brad called back with news that he had finally tracked down the original truck and was sending one of his guys out to see if anything could be found.

"How could this possibly have happened?" Tessa tried hard to keep from yelling but was close to failure.

Brad didn't even try to defend himself. "I don't know, I really don't," he mumbled. "This has never happened to a load we took out. All I can say is, it's possible someone got sloppy transferring things from one truck to the next and your boxes didn't make it on."

"Really? Is there anybody else who didn't get what they shipped?"

"Unfortunately, yes. A woman shipped some clothes boxes from Chicago and I think her daughter said they weren't on the truck either. I don't know what happened but obviously I wouldn't be in business if this kind of thing was the norm. I'll get to the bottom of it and let you know as soon as I have something."

"You have to find them. I cannot express more emphatically how important those boxes are. My family's entire heritage is in them, and if they're lost, it's going to be – I don't know – just really bad for a whole lot of people."

Brad, genuinely mortified, assured her he would do everything in his power to track them down. Tessa wanted to call Michaela and annihilate her, but now that Ronnie was in her care and, from what had been reported, doing well, the greater family dynamic trumped Tessa's urge to flog.

There was one other issue nipping at the edges of her brain (and trying to ignore it was getting problematic). Tessa found herself sipping Chardonnay on a more regular basis than usual, which, recently, had become mighty regular. Since her binges both before and after Ronnie, semi-inebriation became her most reliant state during this particularly trying time, and though she never allowed herself to get to bona fide drunkenness (putting aside the anomalous meltdown at the club), a distracting buzz definitely made life more endurable. Given her gene pool, her mother's on-and-off issues, and the witnessing of Ronnie's downward spiral, the folly of this choice was apparent, but for the first time in her life she began making excuses to herself about drinking every day.

Miss Drama Queen, meet the Bad Girl.

FIFTY-EIGHT

Re:	**my marital status!!!!**
From:	**Ruby Kapinos** rubykwednesday@gmail.com
To:	**Kate Hamilton** kateh@thegreatgift.com
Cc:	**Tessa Curzio** tessacurzio@EdgeReason.com

Girlies!!

The divorce is off! ☺☺!!

I don't know if I'm crazy and this is really stupid, but I have to go with my gut and my gut says it's the right thing to do. So he's moving back in this coming weekend. Why, you ask? We just missed each other too much, it's that simple. He said the separation gave him lots of time to experience life without me and it turns out he didn't like it much! You both know I didn't, so I'm ready to try again.

And I know you're dying to ask so I'll just tell you: yes, he admitted he did "share some time," as he put it, with this Margo woman. Makes me want to puke. I seriously CANNOT picture Ethan touching another women and don't know how to get over that hurdle (!!!!!), but given my own transgressions I can hardly be a bitch about it, right?!?

Anyway, I love him, I missed him, he's the father of my kid, he says he loves me and missed me too, so here we go...on to the next chapter of the Ruby and Ethan Show!

I know you both thought I was an idiot about this so I have absolute faith you'll think this is a good idea. Either way, wish me luck, ladies ☺ ☺ ☺!!!

Love you both TONS!!!

Rubes ☺ ☺ ☺!!!

Ruby loved her emoticons.

While this development was not totally unexpected, Tessa was ashamed to realize it gave her the tiniest jolt of disappointment. In the weeks since the breakup with David, she and Ruby had talked almost nightly, commiserating over their hurt and anger, discussing their views of men in general, as well as their particular ex-men (*not* of the super-hero category). They took in movies on nights Milo was with Ethan or his grandmother; they did yoga class, hiked Mount Wilson, even rented bikes and tooled around the Sepulveda basin on days when the air wasn't brown. While Kate was busy gestating and running her gift basket business, Ruby and Tessa had been über-bonding as only two single chicks can.

Now Ethan was on his way home. With single-chickdom fast

concluding for Ruby, Tessa would be stranded in her unwelcome status as fifth wheel. Of course she was delighted for her friends, authentically hopeful they would get it right this time, but any way she looked at it, fifth-wheel status sucked.

Tessa spent the day of Ethan's return painting her bathroom. Epoxy white in an enclosed shower was surely a route to pulmonary disease, but she felt nesty and compulsive about bringing her new home as close to the luxury of her previous as possible (*not so possible, but still...*). The bathroom was clean and sparkling by the time it was done, and she was pleased to note the day had concluded in the meantime. Ethan was now firmly re-ensconced and she would make herself stop thinking about how weird it was that both her best friends were happily married women and she had just epoxied the shabby bathroom in her new one-bedroom all by herself.

FIFTY-NINE

<u>Love Her to Death</u>– *Fourth in a Series*
By Tessa Curzio

*The power of a father's love is so potent that if its balance is off in any way –
either offered in miserly bits or showered with hurricane force – the recipient is,
likewise, either starved or overwhelmed. Sarah Hoppe was one of those
overwhelmed by the unlikely affliction of father-adoration, the state of having
been so completely doted upon and adored as a child that adulthood's imminent
arrival left her incapable of finding any man able to live up to the standard set
by her father. Though this initially sounded unfathomable and even cloying,
after interviewing Sarah, who appears almost infantilized at the age of forty-one,
this writer came to realize that, certainly in Sarah's case, endless and
overweening expressions of love and attention can cripple almost as much as no
love or perverse love.*

*As described by Sarah, she grew up as an only child with a father who
awoke her each morning with the tinkling of wind chimes, the drawing of a
bubble bath, and the serving of a hot and handmade breakfast. He braided her
hair, ironed her uniforms and, though an accountant by trade with a busy
schedule, never failed to pick her up from school. From there he'd accompany her
to the park for exercise and fresh air, then get her home for a dinner religiously
prepared with at least two vegetables, always one green. Her mother was a
timid, bookish woman who receded somewhere into the background of Sarah's*

life, willing to abdicate all parenting to her more obsessive husband, while never once questioning the wisdom of his crippling attentiveness to their daughter.

Sarah escaped briefly during college but was forced back when a good job did not immediately materialize upon graduation. When her father unexpectedly died in her twenty-sixth year, she found herself incapable of relating to her mother and ultimately, and finally, moved into her own place. More damaging and irreversible was her conviction that meeting a man who could understand her, much less provide the attention she had grown so accustomed to and now so desperately needed, was impossible. Little did her father realize how he had doomed his daughter to a life of loneliness and unnatural isolation simply by loving her too much...

It was hard getting this article to the desired word count, given that Tessa found Sarah Hoppe to be a difficult subject and a decidedly unlikeable person. Their interview, which had been rescheduled three times due to Sarah's supposed "conflicts," had been strained and uncomfortable throughout. Tessa kept wondering why this very odd woman had ever agreed to do the story, given her reluctance to answer questions or offer insight. In truth, Sarah Hoppe's conundrum was so atypical Tessa felt a distinct lack of sympathy. She didn't like herself for this but, as ridiculous as it was, and she knew it was ridiculous, it actually annoyed her that some woman was struggling in life because her father had loved her too much. *Please.* She delivered the article on Tuesday, relieved to get it off her plate.

When she got to *Edge+Reason*, she found a flyer placed near her station announcing a party at Haden's. No reason was stated so she tapped on Vivian's door to ferret out the details.

"Glen said he just finished remodeling his place and wants to celebrate. Are you going?"

"Of course not."

Vivian looked up sharply. "Why do you say it like that?"

"It's just weird. He made a pass a while back and it's awkward, that's all."

"What are you, twelve? He made a pass, so what? You should be flattered. Most women I know think he's pretty hot."

"Really? Who? Meagan? What is she, like, twenty-five?"

"Thirty-two. Besides, what's age got to do with it?"

"I've never been into younger guys."

"I don't think he's that much younger."

"I'm not in much of a celebratory mood anyway. Besides, I can't imagine whatever Haden's done to his place could be all that exciting. I mean, really, what? Lava lamps and a new touch-screen TV with the latest version of whatever boys are playing these days? Yippee."

"From what I've heard, he's got quite the place."

"Nice. Twenty-something tech-head saves up freelance fees to get the Studio City bach-pad of his dreams. Just my kind of guy."

"Wow – have I said this before? – you are an elitist bitch. And what's with the snark? Not exactly your style, my dear."

"I'm trying a new style…whaddaya think?"

"Not lovin' it."

Tessa finally sagged into a chair. "Yeah, I know. Me neither."

"We can presume it'll pass soon?" Vivian winked.

"A girl can hope. Look, I'm sure Haden's a really nice guy, but it's just a little pathetic to me that the only man hovering on my perimeter is a cute geek who knows how to fix computers. You'd think I'd be in a slightly different league at this point of my life."

"First of all, though I'm not remotely pushing him on you and, in fact, think you'd be completely wrong for him, you're incredibly off-beam about the delightful Haden Pierce."

Tessa shifted slightly. "What does that mean?"

"As for age, I don't know exactly how old he is but he's at least in his thirties; a minor detail but since you asked. As for what league he's in, perhaps you've misunderstood his involvement here. He actually *owns* the company he works for; has a franchise here, one in Seattle and a third in Chicago. He developed software for Microsoft several years after college and opened the stores with his earnings; apparently did extremely well. His business not only sells and repairs computer systems, some of which are quite sophisticated and specialized, but he personally designed two award-winning pieces of software. One is related, I think, to financial management, the other has something to do with virtual museum tours. He's only been here helping us because he's training Cecilia and he and Glen go way back. He won't be here much after this week. So get over yourself, Tessa. He's quite a well-respected guy…with a very cute ass to boot." Vivian's eye sparkled with mischief.

"Then why am I completely wrong for him?"

"You're too old, too bitter, and completely unstable. He deserves better." With that, Vivian swept out the office door with Tessa following close behind, flyer firmly in hand.

SIXTY

Aunt Joanne was a patient and compassionate woman but by the fifth time Tessa called to cancel an appointment, her pique broke through. "Tessa, I appreciate that your life is tumultuous of late, but I cannot continue to prioritize your schedule at the expense of others who need my time. You get a lot of leeway as my niece, but let's be realistic about this. If you no longer want to meet for these sessions, just tell me and we'll put this on hold for now." She sounded like Vivian.

It wasn't that Tessa didn't want to talk to her aunt; she actually *needed* to talk to her aunt. It was more that she felt so tired and enervated these days that the drive to Thousand Oaks loomed as an obstacle. Even the drive from Hollywood to Sherman Oaks was getting prohibitive (*how had she ever managed it from the beach?*) and that took a third of the time. "I'm sorry, Auntie, I know I'm being really inconsiderate."

"The greater issue for me is that I think you could really use the time. Are you still having the awakenings?"

"Yes, sometimes, but not as often." Which was a lie. They were actually happening now on a nightly basis, sometimes several times a night and were, in no small part, responsible, along with the daily alcohol consumption, for her lethargy. But for some reason, she felt reticent to admit either.

"Well, I'm glad to hear that. But I'd still like to discuss my thoughts on the journal, so why don't you give me a call when things settle down and we'll try again when you're more apt to keep the appointment."

Guilt reigned. How do you deceive and manipulate a person whose only intent is to help you recover from the worst crises of your life? Tessa couldn't possibly answer her own question and limply agreed to be in touch. She pretended not to notice the immediate urge for a drink.

SIXTY-ONE

Later that night, Tessa received two pivotal phone calls. The first came as she sat watching *Dirty Dancing* for the twentieth time with a tub of over-salted popcorn in lieu of dinner. David. They had not spoken since the meltdown about her father's funeral and though there'd been several times she felt the impulse to call and apologize, she held off, fearful of losing her cool in the heat of another conversation.

She picked up with feigned nonchalance. "Hel-lo."

"Hello, Tessa."

"Hi, David."

"Listen, I'm sorry to call – I doubt you want to hear from me right now – but I've been thinking a lot about you lately and didn't want to let any more time to pass before calling to apologize."

She felt her stomach lurch but maintained the glib tone. "For something specific or just all of it?"

"Look, I can't take back the things I said, but I wish I could. I wish I could literally erase them all. Knowing what you've been through, it's clear what I said was unconscionable and I'll regret it until the day I die." His sincerity was undeniable.

Tessa had to smile. "Well, I appreciate that. It was pretty brutal hearing all that from you."

"The worst part is, I didn't even mean it."

"Any of it?"

There was a slight hesitation. "I think we both know things had changed between us. I'm not sure why. Maybe it was the pressure of what you were going through mixed with my frustration that I couldn't help much, I don't know. It did seem like we pulled away from each other; that was true. What *wasn't* true was all that stuff about you being a martyr to your art and not being able to accept success, all that. I'm not good when it comes to breaking things down and defining what's going on with me and I think I just struck where I knew I'd hit pay-dirt. Pretty lame, I admit, which is why I wanted to apologize."

"David, I'm – "

"I still think you're amazing and, in truth, I *do* have faith that you could be a big success with your writing. I really do."

Tessa was taken aback. She could think of no reason why David would bother with this retraction if it weren't true. "Thank you. It hurt to think you meant those things."

"I know, sweetheart."

Sweetheart?

"I'm so truly, deeply sorry and I hope you can find a way to forgive me at some point."

The uncharacteristic hyperbole was touching. "I'll try, David, I'll really try." An awkward silence followed. "So…how are you?"

"I'm good, I'm good! How about you?"

"Well, it's been a pretty difficult time, I have to say."

"Yeah…of course."

"But if we're handing out apologies, I have one, too. All that awful stuff I said to you about coming to my dad's funeral was just mean and really unfair, especially since we did talk about it beforehand."

"Well, thanks, I appreciate that. But obviously I understood. I wish I had handled that whole situation a lot better."

"It was a weird time for both of us, I guess."

Again, silence, then David suddenly blurted, "Shit, Tessa, can you just come home?'"

She sat back, stunned. "What are you saying?"

"I made a really big mistake here. I got all caught up in thinking about the perfect plan for our life together and forgot to factor in the specifics of who you are and what you'd want. So, yeah, when you turned down the job I felt like you were rejecting me, rejecting the life I pictured us having together, and it all went downhill from there. I don't need you to be a 'corporate guy.' I've always loved exactly who you are. I just felt so impotent and frustrated; I guess my fucked up solution was to blow it all to hell. But that's not what I want…what I want is you back home."

"But how do we just walk back into our lives together like nothing happened? I honestly appreciate your apology but, for me, there was some serious damage done. I can't just hit re-set like nothing happened. How can it be so unequivocal for you?"

"I get why you'd feel that way, but, yeah, I feel clearer than I've ever been. I miss you; I want our lives back. I want you, Tessa, I love you. That never stopped for me."

Unbelievable. And strange that in this particular moment, one she couldn't possibly have anticipated, she felt…nothing. Not a thing. Not relief, not anger, not happiness. She didn't have a clue what to say. "David, I need to think about this. I've been through so much these last few months I have no idea what I want or if I think we should get back together, I really don't. If you can accept that, then we should talk about it again later. If you need an answer tonight, I'd have to say no."

"Of course you can think about it. How could I expect anything else under the circumstances? And believe me when I say I'll respect whatever decision you make. I just wanted you to know how I felt before it was too late."

They agreed to talk again; Tessa promised to think about it all very seriously. She hung up wondering what "too late" meant. Another girl? A change of heart? *Interesting.* And before she could mull that further, the second pivotal call of the night came in.

Haden Pierce.

"Tessa, hey, how are you?"

"I'm fine. This is an unexpected call!"

"I know. I asked Vivian for your number; she didn't think you'd mind if I called. Do you?"

Damn Vivian, Tessa thought with a smile. "No, of course not. What's up?"

"I don't know if you got the flyer I left at your station, but I'm having a party Saturday after next and I'd love for you to come by."

"Oh, thanks, yeah, I did see that. I'm not sure what's on my schedule but I'll definitely check and let you know." She had absolutely nothing on her schedule and the flyer was prominently tacked to the bulletin board.

"The other reason I called is I wanted to make sure I didn't completely blow things that day when I asked you to come out to Doug's. Frankly, I *didn't* know you were in a relationship at the time or I might not have asked, but either way, it really was just a friend thing. I thought you might enjoy seeing Doug again and that's all there was to it. I think maybe I upset you a little and I didn't want that to get in the way of our being friends."

Reminded of her overwrought reaction to his invitation, Tessa felt a stab of chagrin. "You know, Haden, it's me who should apologize. I think it had just been so long since anyone but my boyfriend asked me out under *any* context, I got flustered and overreacted. You were perfectly fine and I wish I had gone with you. It *would* have been fun and I would have enjoyed seeing Doug."

"He'll probably be at the party so if you can make it you'll have another chance."

"That's great; I'll really try to get there."

There was a pause, then, with a quick breath: "Look, Tessa, I'm not going to lie, there's more to this call than all that."

Tessa smiled. *This guy is so damn sweet.* "And what's that?"

"Truth is, I actually would like to ask you out…and yes, *that* way." They both laughed a bit awkwardly. "I know you just got out of a relationship so this is probably premature, but if not, I'd like to take you to dinner whenever you've got a free night." Slight pause. "Have I completely jumped the gun?"

"Haden, I'm flattered, I really am, but you probably have. At least a little. I don't think I'm ready to get into anything with anyone right now; it has nothing to do with you. But thank you for asking and if things change up ahead, I'd love to share a meal or see a movie sometime."

It was a graceful rejection graciously accepted. She promised to stop by his party and after they hung up she sat in the tumult of her emotions. Odd that both conversations came on the same night; odd, too, that both followed a similar template – apology trading, admissions, more apologies; more admissions. But, however odd, it was lovely to be the focus of so much attention. She felt vindicated by David's call, titillated by Haden's…and as confused about men as she'd ever been.

SIXTY-TWO

Crickets were louder in the hills. Louder than the crash of surf in Manhattan Beach, louder than the stream of traffic on Highland Avenue, louder, even, than the clamoring noise of the old Chicago neighborhood. Tessa lay in bed staring at the swaying eucalyptus outside her window, listening to her crickets and their chirping, rhythmic soundtrack, feeling less anxious than she'd been in a while. She knew it was because of David's call. His entreaty had calmed her and put the ball back in her court, giving her a merciful semblance of control over her situation. But she wasn't kidding herself; it was a temporary reprieve and not necessarily one she could immediately determine. Still, it was nice not to feel so rejected tonight.

Her thoughts shifted to Leo. So distracted and distraught over the loss of David, she hadn't thought about her father as much lately but was amazed at how quickly he swarmed back into her consciousness. Tonight she actually *wanted* to think about him. She wanted to remember him. She closed her eyes and tried to picture him, feeling almost as if she'd forgotten his face. But he came back to her: his dark, wavy hair much like her own, his serious brown eyes and handsome face. She remembered being so proud of how handsome he was. She adored him the way little girls adore their fathers. As a younger child, she didn't consciously register his aloofness or feel his lack of emotional attachment. Until she was old enough to decode his signals of dismissal and disinterest, she looked at him with only loving eyes and the bursting, forgiving heart of a child.

She lay there now trying to remember the way he looked at her, the way he talked to her, the sound of his voice. She searched through her jumbled collection of memories for something that would stick, a sense of what emotions, what attitudes and opinions, he transmitted by way of tone and body language. Except as a passing observer, occasional organizer, or the purveyor of punishment, he didn't appear to have much of a role in her memories. The presence of absence. There was nothing she could remember right now that convinced her of anything beyond the words of his journal, which loomed like a curse.

She'd read about people who couldn't love their children; lately she'd written about some. Not all were monsters; some were simply inept, incapable parents. They fulfilled their obligation to their children – provided for them, kept them dressed and well fed, made sure they got to school and learned good manners – but did it all in the absence of authentic love. She wondered if Leo was one of those people. He said he felt obligated to love her but obligation wasn't love. Was he one of those fathers who regarded honor and duty more highly than real emotion, saw responsibility to his family as a sacred vow more than a response to true affection? Felt emotion was negotiable but obligation wasn't? It was hard to know.

She could ultimately live without knowing, she could certainly succeed without approval, but as the child of a man so spare with his emotions, she was tugged by the urge to dissect and define the few he had shared. So tonight she just thought about the man. Leo Curzio. Her Dad. Father. Daddy. Suddenly the memory of a look. His eyes met hers, for just a moment. A quick smile.

What was that, Dad? What made you smile? Did something funny happen? Did I do something that pleased you? I hope so. I miss you, Dad. I miss hearing you say my name.

SIXTY-THREE

A Beautiful Child – *Sixth in a Series*
By Tessa Curzio

Olivia Sandapat was one of those beautiful children, the kind perfect strangers stopped to gaze upon and admire. The kind who elicited offers from talent scouts and modeling agents who waved business cards and smiled a lot. The kind of beautiful child who awoke each morning from dreams of ballet dancing, white stallions on a beach, golden princes to love and…shooting her father to death.

Until the day of her thirteenth birthday. That day she got up from her dreams, walked downstairs to her father's gun cabinet, took out a small handgun, then proceeded to her parents' bedroom where she deftly made dreams come true and put a bullet through her sleeping father's head.

He had never touched her, nor had he touched her two sisters, but on too many days of her life he had beaten her mother so ruthlessly she'd lost most of her hearing, many of her teeth, suffered brain damage from repeated concussions, and had an arm so often broken it hung in the awkward shape of limp, twisted rope.

Olivia Sandapat was now thirty-nine and not one day goes by that she regrets pulling that trigger…

The series continued to spark tremendous response from the magazine's readers, either slamming Tessa for surely exaggerating the facts or congratulating her for so honestly reporting them. Many women wrote to thank her for mirroring the torments of their own experiences ("You made me feel like I wasn't alone in the prison of my memories."); other readers wanted follow-up stories, or stories about sons and mothers. Several men wrote wondering why only bad fathers were being profiled. One angrily queried: "Why no stories that celebrate someone who got it right as a father?" Tragedy porn, he called it. Tessa found herself agreeing with at least some of what he had to say. She gave Meagan the assignment to find at least two, preferably three, good father/daughter stories. Balance was needed.

She was on her way home, Etta James playing softly in the background and traffic doing that heinous thing it does on Friday nights. She mulled the two conversations of earlier in the week, confused about what to do with either David or Haden. For whatever reason, she wanted to get through the gauntlet of the journals before she made any life-altering decisions about anything, particularly men and relationships. The continued, frustrating delay of their arrival left her in limbo, one of her least favorite states-of-being.

As the road-worked Hollywood Freeway South snaked its way from four lanes to two, her phone rang. Brad at Thompson Transport. He didn't sound cheerful. "I'm afraid I've got some bad news."

"What?" she said, immediately alert.

"Unfortunately, it seems there *were* a few boxes mistakenly left on the original truck. I guess it was pouring that day and it was probably late enough that visibility wasn't good, so I guess the guys were rushed and missed a few things." Lots of guessing going on for Brad.

"But it's good that you found them, right?"

"Well, not exactly. It turns out they were left in the truck while it sat out by the side of the road for a few days and, like I said, it was raining and, uh, I guess the truck's roof leaked. Anyway, when they finally got it out to the repair yard it sat there for a few more days and by the time the guys got in there to clean it out, everything was soaked and pretty much destroyed...so they just chucked it all."

"WHAT!?" Tessa's fist inadvertently hit the horn, causing the driver ahead of her to glance in his rearview mirror with a frown. "They *chucked* my family's boxes? Are you fucking kidding me?" No pretense of decorum was possible at this point.

"Ma'am, I'm really sorry – "

"Don't call me ma'am – "

"Sorry. All's I'm saying is, I'm really sorry; I don't know what happened. Obviously we'll reimburse you for the goods and – "

"You can't reimburse me, Brad! How can you reimburse me for almost fifty years of my father's life? How do you do that? Not possible, Brad, not remotely possible." She was suddenly struck by a desperate hope. "Is there a chance they didn't throw everything away or maybe it wasn't my stuff?"

"Didn't you say your stuff was a bunch of boxes with spiral bound books in them?"

"Oh God, yes...fuck..."

"Yeah...sorry. The guys there said that's what was in the boxes they tossed, those kinds of books and some clothes; I guess that was the other lady's."

"But they had plastic covers! How could they have been completely destroyed?"

"I guess it rained a lot those few weeks. I heard it was bad enough that it took 'em way over their seasonal average. Anyway, the truck was left unlocked and people had been in there going through everything – there's lots of homeless people in that area – so the boxes were ripped open and everything was all over the place. I guess most of it was covered with mildew and dirt by the time they cleaned out the truck. I asked them if there was any way to salvage anything but it was thrown in the dump over a week ago and it's been covered over by a ton of garbage since then. I don't know what to say…I'm just so sorry."

He sounded as mournful as if someone had died. Which was not far from the truth. Leo had just suffered another death. Homeless people had ripped open his guts and strewn his private thoughts all over a filthy, dirty truck, the remains thrown into a mountain of garbage and covered up forever.

Tessa was speechless at this point. She snapped her phone off, unable to say one more word to the mortified Brad, and before she could blink, slammed good and hard into the BMW in front of her.

SIXTY-FOUR

It wasn't necessarily appropriate for passersby to give an injured woman the finger but this was, after all, the Hollywood Freeway on a Friday night. Tessa's ill-timed fender-bender would likely make the majority of south-bound Los Angelenos late for whatever they might have had planned for the evening, so she was definitely persona non grata…albeit persona with a mild concussion.

Sitting on the shoulder of the freeway, dizzy and pained, she watched the show as it swooped by in a blur of muted sound; lots of motion and moving lips but no idea what was being said. She wondered if anyone had been hurt or cars had been damaged, then remembered she'd smacked her own head on the steering wheel upon impact (*never got the damn airbag fixed*), after which she hazily disembarked for a frantic, apologetic conversation with Russell Doretsky, the semi-good-looking and very hirsute driver of the BMW. His bumper was significantly bashed but it was her car that took the brunt of the impact. Smoke curled from the leaking radiator and the hood was bent at an alarming angle suggestive of stiff body shop bills.

She and Russell exchanged the necessary information and made that awkward small-talk people do while waiting for the authorities; about twenty minutes later the police and EMT truck arrived. Reports were made, vitals were taken, ambulances were refused and tow trucks were called. A cold pack was applied to Tessa's head and she was encouraged to pay serious attention to unwanted symptoms. It all took about forty-five minutes, after which the EMTs left, as did the tow truck with her car in tow. The police asked if she had anyone she wanted to call; she thought about David but decided the intimacy of rescue was more than she was willing to grant him at the moment, so she accepted a friendly ride home from Russell. They stopped along the way at Joseph's, a Greek taverna not far from her neighborhood, and, on this night, after this day, she drank until she willfully surpassed buzzing to the state of full-blown inebriation and, before the night was over, fucked the brains out of the hairy man she'd just rear-ended.

SIXTY-FIVE

The morning-after arrived with sunshine, blue skies, and as many morning-after discomforts as possible.

The first thing Tessa did was throw up, conveniently in the bathroom. While huddled over the toilet bowl, she couldn't help but notice a discarded condom in the garbage; this both repulsed and relieved her. Once digestively unburdened, she surveyed her face and made note that her continuing weight loss was useful in offsetting morning alcohol bloat. The angry red protuberance on her forehead was not attractive but, considering the throbbing state of her head, smaller then she'd have expected. She brushed her teeth, took a washcloth to her weary privates, fluffed her hair to affect a sort of insouciant sexiness and, as she headed back to the bedroom, realized she no longer got migraines as a matter of course after drinking. After head-butting the steering wheel, yes, but not drinking. That this likely meant her body was adjusting to her new level of consumption was not something she wanted to reflect upon just now.

Russell was awake and half-dressed and, as is unavoidable in these circumstances, exhibiting the post-sexual, now-sober awkwardness of being in the bedroom of a stranger. They smiled at each other and once again she couldn't help but notice how hairy he was – Alec Baldwin hairy. Not that this bothered her. She remembered thinking he was very cuddly and teddy-bearish in a handsome Soviet bodyguard kind of way. She wasn't sure now whether to crawl back into bed or demand that he leave. She had never in her life allowed a man she didn't know into her home, much less her bedroom, and there was no part of her that didn't recognize the inherent risk of the situation. Which was sort of exciting. She acknowledged that this worked well with the Bad Girl motif, adding sex with strangers to a list already stocked with daily drinking and irresponsible appointment breaking.

Thankfully, he broke the ice. "Good morning. It's Tessa, right?"

She went for the crawl back into bed option. "Yes – Tessa. I remember your name, Russell, because I make a habit of never forgetting the men I crash into." They both laughed, if a little stiffly. "Would you like breakfast?"

He got a sultry gleam and pulled her to him with just the right amount of caveman. "I would like *you*."

Making love to a stranger sober is a great deal different than doing so drunk. She liked the way he felt and particularly the way he felt her, but it had been so long since anyone but David's hands had been on her body that his very different way of doing things was initially distracting. He didn't seem remotely interested in oral sex, quite the departure from David and his luxurious tongue, but Russell's caressing was so passionate and committed that she couldn't help but get aroused. He seemed profoundly fascinated with her nipples, rolling them between his fingers, pulling them, sucking and nipping them with his teeth. She alternated between titillation and pain, but he couldn't seem to get enough. By the time he climbed on top of her she was gamely into the unfamiliar romp, but just as he was about to penetrate, he rolled over and swung her on top of him in one fluid motion, making her feel rag-doll light and agile as a porn star, a strange and potent combination. Except now she was looking down at the face of a man she knew nothing about other than his name and license plate number and that felt...perplexing. Nonetheless, she'd gone too far for interruptus, so without quite the sensorial abandon of moments earlier, she did her part to bring things to their natural conclusion. After sweet postcoital kisses, they each made their way from the room and through their various, and unavoidably self-conscious, morning ministrations.

Shortly after, as they sat at her table with coffee and toast, she tried to determine whether she wanted to know more about this man, if he was someone she should invite further into her life. He seemed content to scan the paper with occasional smiles in her direction. She couldn't tell if this was comfortable silence or continued awkwardness.

"So, Russell, where do you live?"

He put down the sports section and sat back. "Pasadena. Bungalow Heaven...you know that area off Orange Drive with all the little '20s and '30s bungalows?"

"I do. I used to write with a girl who lived out there. It's a really sweet neighborhood."

"So you're a writer?"

With that they finally started talking to each other. By the end of breakfast he knew she'd recently broken up with a man she assumed she'd marry, she used to be a singer but currently worked for an online magazine; came from Chicago, was one of six kids, and hopefully would have a couch by the end of the week. He had three siblings, grew up in Anaheim, and worked as a financial consultant. He was thirty-two, divorced with one five-year-old son, and dating someone, but only casually.

After twenty minutes of conversation he had to get going, but they agreed to stay in touch. She apologized again for the accident and as he waved goodbye at the door, they both joked about her needing to come up with a less assaultive way of meeting men.

Still awkward.

SIXTY-SIX

By mid-morning the distractions of the day and the lingering warmth of friendly sex could no longer occlude the cold reality that the journals were gone. By noon it hit Tessa like a tsunami. The first layer was outrage at the stunning incompetence of Thompson Transport. She called a lawyer she knew to discuss whether it made sense to sue. He wasn't there but she left a detailed message that only served to stoke her anger. She next called Michaela, who was also not there, and left a terse but controlled message about the situation, choosing not to mention the fact that this would never have happened with FedEx.

Within the hour her anger shifted to despair. It was all gone: the opportunity, the history; the one lingering connection to this man who was such a mystery and now always would be. Tessa was overwhelmed with loss and regret and, before long, her disbelief swelled, followed by the kind of panic one feels when something important and irreplaceable has just slipped from their fingers.

She paced around the apartment trying to figure out what to do about all this. Waves of anxiety crashed over her with a ferociousness that signaled trouble. Wild-eyed and panting, she ran down to her garage only to remember she had no car. She yelled loud enough that the gardener came from around the corner to see what was going on; she waved him off with a bark and ran back to the apartment. She thought about calling the car rental place her insurance company suggested but realized she would not make it there before becoming unhinged. And what did she need the car for anyway? *Oh, right…Aunt Joanne.*

Frantically dialing her aunt, Tessa felt a sensation of such foreboding, such doom; she knew that surviving it was going to take some immediate and professional intervention. Her heart was beating so hard it hurt, there was a sharp and growing pain in her back, the burning in her throat was odd, and it seemed to be getting harder to breathe.

What is this? An anxiety episode? A nervous breakdown? A heart attack? How the hell did I get here, from a happy, in love, beach-dwelling success to this drunken, car-crashing, stranger-fucking, lonely, jealous loser screaming at the gardener? FUCK, where is she?

Tessa left a frantic message, realizing that even if her aunt could drive down to Hollywood, it would likely be over an hour before she could get there. And this was dire.

She could hear Kate's voice in her head, something about breathing and calming herself, finding her center and quelling the irrational thoughts cascading. She sat cross-legged on the floor in the proper position, eyes clenched, fingers and thumbs touching, breathing evenly and visualizing the word "love," but as the minutes ticked by and her heart seemed only to speed up, all she could think was, "Fuck Zen."

She leapt up, pulled a bottle of Chardonnay from the refrigerator, and poured herself a tumbler full…this was no time for dainty. She bolted it down like a boozer in a bad movie and took the bottle to bed, hoping to be unconscious before the buzz hit.

The next thing she heard was a loud rapping at the front door. It was dark and she was so disoriented she couldn't begin to remember what day it was or why she was in bed with an empty wine bottle. She hobbled from the bedroom, aware of being both woozy and drained of the earlier panic, and was most grateful to see her "non-habit forming" aunt standing at the top of the stairs.

SIXTY-SEVEN

The living room was dark and cool and felt like one of those places people came to sit quietly and not talk. As if in cooperation, the neighborhood was unusually still that night, with only the sounds of occasional traffic and the introductory chirps of the evening crickets to break the silence.

Aunt Joanne was seated on the floor, mostly because there was no couch but also because that was just where the night had landed her. Tessa lay curled on the rug across the room, tea mugs and tissues cluttering the space in between. She'd spent the first thirty minutes on the loss of the journals. It remained unfathomable and, in fact, seemed to have grown in importance since the call from Brad at Thompson Transport. At some point, Aunt Joanne suggested that their loss might have triggered the greater loss of her father's death, grief she'd aborted back in December after finding the journal. Tessa accepted that as a possibility but kept her focus on the travesty that was Thompson Transport and the sister that was Michaela, ranting about both until she'd run out of epithets.

Finally, weary and wrung out, she sat up and took a sip of tea; with a grimace, she remarked, "Ironic that tea would make me queasier than cheap Chardonnay."

Aunt Joanne took note of the ugly knot on Tessa's forehead. "What happened there?"

"I rear-ended a guy last night. Thank God I never got that airbag fixed or I might have hurt my neck," she snorted sardonically.

"Were you drinking?"

Tessa shot her a look; just the thought of being seen as a drunk driver was mortifying. "Not until afterwards. Come on, Auntie, I'm not that far gone."

"Why do you think you've been drinking so much lately?"

"Doesn't my life seem ripe for that sort of misbehavior?"

"I don't remember that being part of your particular playbook."

"Me neither, but all previous paradigms are off...I'm forging a new way."

"And how's that working for you?"

Tessa's doleful stare made the point. "Don't worry; it'll be short-lived, this drinking thing. It's just a part of my 'fuck you' to the universe. Frankly, I'm not wild about wine and Jack Daniels kills me. Never could hold my liquor."

"We find our self-censors where we can."

"Yes, I'm nothing if not a self-censurer," Tessa dryly acquiesced.

"Tell me more about what happened with David."

So she did. She went over the whole thing again but in greater detail, including the addendum of his recent phone call. Aunt Joanne seemed most interested in dissecting the comments of David's that mirrored the accusations of Leo's journals.

"Do you think he meant those things?"

"No, actually, I don't. I mean, maybe there was a smidgen of truth in some of it. We are very different people with very different styles, that part he probably meant. But the really cruel stuff? I think he said all that because he knew there was nothing that could hurt me more."

"Because they were similar to things Leo said in the journal?"

"Of course. That's what we do; we go for the jugular. It's the way people fight, Auntie. It's all Sid and Nancy without the knives and tattoos. It's not nice, it's not admirable, but it's what we do."

"I don't completely get the reference but how could I forget the night of the funeral? Perhaps a better way of fighting could be considered. Are you thinking of going back to David?"

Tessa couldn't help but smile. "It does sound pathetic given the context, doesn't it? Right now I can't even think about it." She stared off for a long, silent moment, then straightened up in a quick mood shift. "Anyway, I'm doing much better at this point, so thanks, really. I think all this talking has helped…I can't tell you how much I appreciate it."

"I'm glad you're feeling better, Tessa, but since I'm here – "

"And I'm so sorry I dragged you out. I know what a long drive it is."

"It's not a problem, I wanted to see you anyway. But it's still fairly early so why don't we talk a bit more?"

"Actually I'm pretty wiped out."

"Tessa, we've talked about disassociation quite a bit, yes?"

"Yessss…why are you bringing that up right now?"

"I think it bears discussion given what just happened."

"What just happened? We've been talking – "

"Yes, but you also just completely detached from your emotional state – I saw it. Earlier this evening you were so panicked and overwhelmed you called me in sheer terror that you might be dying. Now you're acting like it's all fine, no problem, snip snap, I'm better."

Tessa shifted uncomfortably. "Look, I understand why you'd be worried, but that's just me. I'm a mood swinger. Probably get that from my mother. I get all hysterical then I'm fine."

"I don't think you are fine. Your awakenings tell me you're not fine, your drinking tells me you're not fine, even your mood swings tell me you're not fine. You shut it all down, Tessa, you detach. I think this is how you survived your childhood. When it got too painful you just removed yourself emotionally. That may have seemed like a workable solution when you were three or six or fourteen – maybe your only solution – but now you've got other options. I'm asking you to take advantage of the fact that I'm here to help you face what you're feeling."

"But I have been, haven't I?" Tessa was genuinely confused.

"Tell me what you were feeling right before you said I could go."

Staring down at her hands clasped in her lap, Tessa said, "I can't."

"Why not?"

"Because I don't know."

"Are you sure?"

Tessa thought for a moment. "Seriously, I don't know. I just felt…sort of…blank."

"Can you try to reach past that to what you were feeling right before the blankness?"

"I don't know…really…I don't get a sense of anything. Maybe I just don't want to get any deeper into what I'm feeling."

"Why is that?"

"I might not ever be the same afterwards." She laughed uncomfortably.

"Why would that be?"

"I don't know."

"And would that be so bad?"

"Wouldn't it?"

"It depends. It's possible if you face your pain in all its naked truth you might find you're stronger than you know. And that strength and truth could help you towards a better, more functional set of strategies for your life. It might also allow you to reclaim more of your memories – without needing your father's words to fill in the blanks. So, no, I don't think 'not ever being the same again' would be such a bad thing."

"Auntie, I really appreciate what you're trying to do here but to be completely honest, I'm just exhausted. It's been a really long day."

"I understand. So I'll go and you'll run off and have another drink, then go to bed to be startled awake by anxiety."

"Okay, okay." Tessa's reserve crumbled. "What do you want me to do?"

"First, I want you to listen." Aunt Joanne picked up her bag and pulled out *2002*. She held it up. "I have a couple of thoughts about this, okay?"

"Okay…"

She opened the journal to a marked page. "Did you read this entry called 'The Pros & Cons of Neighbors'? Odd that he titled this one – did you read it?"

"I don't remember it specifically. If I didn't see my name, I probably didn't."

"Your name's not in here. It's not about you, but I believe it tells us a lot about Leo and I think that's worth looking at. Can I read part of it to you?"

"Sure."

Aunt Joanne read out loud:

June 8, 2002 – The Pros & Cons of Neighbors:

Our relationships in Chicago have been unintentionally a laboratory for my ideas about friendship and the worth of people. Let me illustrate by naming couples with whom we've made friends (though not all close friends); the characteristics whereby we would or wouldn't be attracted, and my opinions of why sustaining close friendships may not be attainable with these people.

1. Mr. and Mrs. Albert Matthews—Pros: Catholic, family, neighbors; intellectual compatibility. Cons: social stature, financial position.

The degree of the "Cons" outweighs the "Pros" here because their concern for social and financial status requires considerable effort on their part and therefore would necessitate occupying large portions of time and thought. This has been the case here and the result is malnutritioned intellect.

Let me also explain that, with each example, I am dealing with four human beings and there exists a possibility of wives liking each other and husbands not, or vice versa. However, in marriage, couples should be regarded as a unit; this is the basic characteristic of a successful marriage and, may I add, a successfully married couple would be the only type with whom we would attempt a close friendship.

Tessa snorted.

Aunt Joanne looked up. "What, specifically, are you reacting to?"

"The whole 'a successful married couple would be the only people to be friends with' or whatever the hell he said. How bizarre is that? Like, single people aren't valid enough for friendship? No wonder it bothered him that I wasn't married!"

"Indeed. Let me go on." Aunt Joanne continued reading:

2. Mr. and Mrs. Clayton Anderson—<u>Pros:</u> Catholic, neighbor, social stature, financial position; intellectual compatibility. <u>Cons:</u> No children.

It is with this couple that I anticipated the greatest potential of friendship, but the difference of "no children" has proven too large an obstacle. Being childless, they are simply not of our ilk.

When a couple does not have children, there exists a home with no one to dirty it and a husband and wife with a multitude of time to clean it. The result is over-fastidious people who avoid contact with "careless people," or, as they might see it, people with children. The obvious attempts to avoid close ties with us would indicate this is true for the Andersons. Unfortunate, but their loss.

"Oh, for God's sake!" Tessa shook her head. "We spent plenty of time with them and they loved all of us kids. What is he talking about?"

"Let me read one more." Aunt Joanne continued:

3. Mr. and Mrs. Roy Berendt—Pros: Catholic, family, neighbors, social stature; financial position. Cons: Intellectual incompatibility.

Perhaps here my opinions reek of stultification, but I believe this couple suffers from a condition that afflicts many poorly educated people. That is, the foisting of their intellect and opinions upon everyone, to the point of literally shouting down others around them. In matters of intellect, I believe that it should be adjusted to those around you; that is, if I am in the company of a person of greater intellect, I should attempt to raise up my thoughts to him and he should lower his to me. If in the company of one with less intellect, then I should go halfway to meet him.

In the Berendt's case, I feel our intellect is higher than theirs (through no great effort of ours), but they refuse to come up to meet us. Roy especially demands that we come down to his level. This does not breed a close friendship.

Aunt Joanne put the journal down. "It goes on and on but I think you get the idea. What do you think of all that?" she asked.

"Strange, pompous, incredibly judgmental. A truly bizarre way to analyze your friends."

"So you know who all these people are?"

"Of course. These were our closest family friends. The Andersons are Duncan's godparents; the Matthews were my parents' weekly Bridge partners. These were the people who came to our Christmas dinners and First Holy Communions and backyard barbecues. It's actually shocking to hear my dad be so condescending, especially about Roy Berendt."

"Why Roy in particular?"

"He was Kate's dad, my father's best friend. They talked on the phone and played tennis together every week. I even remember when my dad accidentally hit this neighborhood kid when he was backing out of our driveway – I think I was about nine – and Roy was the person right there with him during all the craziness that followed. He truly was his best friend. Or so I thought. I guess not."

"But he *was* his best friend. I knew Roy. Before I left Chicago I used to spend time with the two of them when they'd come downtown and they were like two peas in a pod, literally inseparable. When Roy died your father called me in absolute stunning grief and talked to me for over an hour about what a stellar man this was, what a singular loss, what a true, unforgettable friend. And yet a few years earlier he's writing in this journal about how Roy's lack of intellect 'does not breed close friendship.' What does that tell you?"

"That my father was a prick?"

Aunt Joanne gave her a look. "Yes…he may have been, but the correlation I'm trying to draw is this: for some reason your father used these journals to vent emotions and frustrations he couldn't tolerate or communicate in real life. Rather than talk about his issues – whatever they were – with the appropriate person, he'd sneak away to these very controllable, non-responsive journals and leave his feelings there. Quite a cowardly way, I think, of asserting one's superiority. Maybe Roy was annoying him for some reason. Maybe he didn't like a book Leo thought was important, maybe they argued about church dogma or how to discipline your children. But instead of accepting that someone he loved might have a perspective different from his own, Leo decides it's an intellect problem. And because this condescending opinion wasn't something he could comfortably communicate to his best friend, probably didn't even believe, he spouts his criticism in the journal – again, as a way to vent and feel superior without fear of consequence. I think Leo struggled with tremendous self-doubt and self-loathing."

"Really? I saw a pretty self-assured guy who seemed mighty comfortable throwing his weight around."

"That is what you'd see as his child. As his sister, I saw things differently. Frankly, I think there were two Leos. One was the quiet, patient guy; sympathetic and understanding. He accepted life for what it was and worked hard to support his family as best he could.

He used to tell me he'd sometimes finish his work in a half-day just to get home to help your mom. I believe he loved you all and truly did his best to protect and provide for you.

"I never said he didn't, I –"

"Let me finish, Tessa."

"Sorry."

"My point is this: despite that first Leo, there *was* the other side of him. The side that was frustrated and stymied; maybe because, regardless of how much he wanted a big family, having one came at a tremendous price. I think he was jealous of the freedom others had to pursue their dreams. He certainly had his – yet chose to leave them behind. He might have been bitter about that, angry about your mother's fragilities, resentful that our parents could ill afford to help him out financially. I think he had a hard fight with himself and felt he had few people to talk to or confide in, particularly with your mother too emotionally unstable to be that person for him and me someone he typically kept at a distance. The only outlet then was the journals, where he could express himself and nobody could talk back, nobody could debate him. And some of that played out in his cruelty toward the people he loved, particularly his children. This is a pattern I found over and over in the pages of this journal and is, no doubt, in all the others as well. Do you see what I'm getting at?"

"I'm not sure."

"Tessa, I think a man who could snidely put down a friend he loved, analyze his own son as a pathetic loser, and comment about his beloved wife as if she were a piece of property – all things I read in this journal – was also profoundly capable of looking at his powerhouse of a daughter, the one who perhaps most reminded him of himself, the one who went after the dreams he didn't, and see her struggles as mirrors of his own. And because of that transference, he just might vent his personal despair and resentments in her direction. Does that make any sense?"

Tessa got up and slowly walked to the window, staring out.

"Kind of. Interesting idea anyway."

"My perception, Tessa, knowing him as I did, knowing you as I do, and seeing how those dynamics played out, is that what he wrote in this journal isn't really about you, it's about him. Horrible way to communicate his insecurities, but true, I believe, nonetheless."

Tessa turned to her with anguish. "That sounds good, Auntie, a good theory that makes sense, I guess, but I'll never know if it's just your interpretation or if it's actually true. I have no sense of it myself and that's why I wanted to read the other journals. Without that, I'm forced to choose an interpretation – maybe yours, maybe Ronnie's – and just have faith that it's correct. But I'll never actually *know*. I don't think I can do that, have that kind of faith. Maybe you can – well, clearly you can; you're a nun who has faith in things I can't possibly fathom! But I have no faith in what isn't concrete. We've been over that. Your theory has merit, but it's just that, a theory. The journals would have been concrete."

"Yet still requiring interpretation. You could read his words and presume what he meant, but no one but your father would actually know. Your analysis of the journals could be no more accurate than mine, but if you decided it was true, you'd be basing your decision on faith in your *own* interpretation. Not unlike spiritual faith, I might add."

Tessa looked up, puzzled. "What do you mean?"

"Do you think a believer knows any more about the concrete truth of God or life after death than you do?"

"I thought that was the point."

"They have faith, that's all. They have analyzed a set of beliefs – the Bible, the Koran, the Torah, the teachings of Buddha, Neal Donald Walsch, Seth; whoever – and decided that something resonated for them. They *felt* something, so they choose to believe and embrace that philosophy. That's faith. The choice to believe. The nuns at your grade school weren't necessarily wrong about that; they just went about it the wrong way."

"Okay, interesting, and probably worth about a five-hour conversation, but what does any of that have to do with my father and the journals?"

"Tessa, I want to give you another assignment. Are you up for it?"

"Oh, God…" Tessa's eyes rolled.

"Now, stop that and listen. There are no journals. You can't investigate what your father wrote in hopes of figuring out what he thought or believed about you. So you have a choice: you can either believe that he literally meant every word he said or you can choose to believe my analysis. Without the backup of the other journals, you are going to have to rely on your own memories of his relationship with you."

"Then give me an F right now because I have very few memories of him and me, and the ones I have are typically shitty and most of them you've heard."

"Disassociation is designed to remove memory because it detaches you from the moment you're in, even, sometimes, the good ones. Difficult to remember what you're removed from, yes? So your assignment is to go back and retrieve some of those good memories."

"How do I do that?"

"You talk, you look, you remember. You open your mind, meditate, and practice getting beyond the automatic rejection of what you come upon to see if you can find a few. I think you will. Ask your brothers and sisters, ask your mother, even ask your friend, Kate, who lived that period of life with you. Go after it like you're researching a good story, only this one is your own. See what you can piece together: make lists, columns, like 'The Pro and Cons of Neighbors.' Only these will be your own pros and cons."

Tessa took a deflated slide to the floor. "You're asking me to do a pros and cons list of my own childhood, my own father. How pathetic is that?"

"I don't think it is. Follow his lead in a way. He analyzed his friends in that format and as misguided as the analyses might have been, it wasn't a bad template. You don't have to write anything down, just think about it with the idea of looking at both the good and the bad. I believe you will find some…*good*, that is."

"It's too fucking complicated, Auntie. I just wanted an answer, you know? I don't want it to be so hard, figuring it all out. I don't want to make mental lists! I don't want to analyze my relationship with my father like some kind of generic event. I just, I just…" Tessa felt a knot tightening in her stomach; her hands went to her face. Aunt Joanne moved closer.

"What's going on right now?"

Tessa shook her head wearily. "I don't know, I don't know. I'm so sick of myself but I can't seem to change anything."

Her aunt gently pulled her into an embrace. Tessa stiffened, not certain she wanted the contact, but Aunt Joanne didn't let go, pulling Tessa closer until she was almost cradled against her shoulder. Aunt Joanne caressed her hair, like a mother comforting a grieving child. The gesture cracked something inside Tessa, bringing the unvarnished sobs of a daughter's broken heart. "I just wanted to know my father loved me, that's all. I just wanted to know." Over and over. Aunt Joanne never let go.

SIXTY-EIGHT

Russell Doretsky called a few nights later and left a message inviting Tessa to dinner. Casual Girlfriend was apparently more casual than advertised. Tessa considered the request for a moment (they *did* have a dramatic "how'd you meet?" story), even thought about asking him to Haden's party, but decided that would be bad form. Things were too complicated to bring a new character into the mix anyway. She called and begged off; said her old boyfriend had re-emerged (*true*) and she was going to explore the possibilities (*not sure that was true*). He was so gracious and understanding she wondered if she should keep him on-call in case Ruby and Ethan didn't work out – Ruby liked hairy men – then decided that kind of thinking was counter-productive to her friend's Marriage Reconstruction Project. She did put his number in her contacts, however.

After Aunt Joanne left that amazing night, Tessa had spent a good half-hour trying to imagine what it would be like moving back to David's. Beyond the fact that she really liked her charming hillside apartment, it was getting harder to conjure up a scenario that felt doable. But again, maybe she was still too focused on the Leo investigation to give the idea a fair shot. She sent David a brief email, told him she hadn't forgotten but was still sorting through everything. He responded that she should take all the time she needed.

Everyone was playing nice.

Aunt Joanne's assignment stymied her. Every time she'd attempt to conjure up instructive childhood memories, all she could find were various scenarios of brothers and sisters, friends and relatives, Audrey and Aunt Joanne, even some with Leo in the periphery but not much involved. When she tried to remember him in moments of one-on-one, particularly involving joy or love or acceptance, she came up empty. At first she wondered if Aunt Joanne was right and she'd disassociated away their relationship, but after repeated attempts she began to fear that, maybe, there was nothing there, nothing to be discovered, and Leo really was just a cipher. She thought about asking various siblings for help in shaking free some new memories, but considered their significant biases on either side of the aisle and rejected the notion for now.

Audrey. It was time to talk to her mother, a woman with a preternaturally detailed memory about almost everything that happened prior to Leo's death. Lately she claimed she could barely remember lunch.

"Of course I remember your childhood. I was there, for God's sake! What kind of silly question is that?"

"Mother, I have something very specific I want to ask you and you have to really focus and try to avoid judgment, okay?"

"Is this going to be one of those 'I hate you, Mother, you ruined my life' kind of things Ronnie's so fond of? I don't think I'm in the mood for that sort of foolishness right now."

"No, Mom, it's not. I've forgiven you for all that."

"You've forgiven me for what?"

Oh dear God. "Mom, this isn't about you, this is about me and Dad. Can we talk about that?"

"I suppose so. I just tend to feel like a dartboard every time I get into a discussion about our family and the horrible childhoods you all supposedly had."

Tessa ignored that. "You know about Dad's journals, right?"

This elicited a poignant pause. Audrey struggled with the fact of the journals, finding it difficult to believe the "perfect father" she'd chosen for her children could have done anything so heartless. As Ronnie commented one night, "fact fucked with fantasy."

"Of course I know he wrote journals. He was a wonderful writer and I don't know why that man never got anything published. My God, half the stuff I read can't hold a candle to – "

"Mom, focus. I don't want to critique his writing style or discuss his failed career; I want to ask you about memories, good memories, of me and Dad."

"Why on earth do you need me for that? Your father adored you. You can't possibly need me to tell you that!"

Tessa picked *2002* off the table and held it up to the phone as if her mother could see it. "Mom, I want to read you some of the things Dad wrote about me in his journal, okay? I'm not going to change a word, and I just want you to listen and not say a thing until I'm done, okay?"

Audrey exhaled a deep, obvious sigh. "Fine. You're going to read it no matter what I say so just go ahead."

Tessa read each earmarked passage with the gravity deserved. Words and sentences piled on top of each other like tumbling rocks. Even Audrey couldn't miss it. When she was done, Tessa paused for a moment, waiting for her mother's response. None was forthcoming. "Well, Mom, what do you say to that?"

"What do you want me to say?" Her tone was petulant.

"I want you to tell me if Dad really meant all of that. And if he did, how do you feel about him writing those kinds of things in a journal he wanted me to read?"

"I think if your father wrote all that – "

"Oh, *if* is not what we're debating. He definitely wrote it, it's his handwriting!"

"The point I was trying to make before I was so rudely interrupted was, if he wrote it, assuming he wrote it, he must have been mad about something you did at the time."

"He wrote those passages over a year's time. He was mad at me for a whole year?"

"See, this is what always happens!" Audrey snapped. "Parents are blamed for the critical things they say about their children but no one ever wants to admit the children might have done something to deserve it."

"Really? So you think when I was a twenty-five-year-old woman, trying my best to build a career for myself, struggling financially but making my own way and being a good, honest person, I deserved to have my father make fun of me and say he didn't like me and call me a failure and a disappointment? I *deserved* that?"

"I thought you said this wasn't going to be a 'you ruined my life' conversation? I'm just not good at this; I don't know what you want me to say."

"This isn't a riddle, Mom. Just tell me what you think."

"Well, of course you didn't deserve it! Your father could get mad and say stupid things just like the next person. Why he chose to leave all that in his journals, I don't know. But remember, Tessa, you did have quite a few problematic relationships with difficult men. You weren't always a very good judge of character when it came to your boyfriends, so he was probably very worried about that and your crazy Scientology stuff and that's probably all it was."

"Oh, it sounds to me like he had a lot more concern for the difficult men than he did for me, Mom. He basically insinuated I was a gold digger. How do you think that makes me feel, coming from my own father?"

"For heaven's sake, Tessa, I don't know what he was thinking and you're really putting me on the spot. I just know that he loved you dearly and was proud of everything you accomplished."

"Was he?" Tessa sincerely asked. "How would I know that? He never told *me*."

"But he did, in his own ways. He used to tell me that you depended on language too much. He'd say, 'words aren't always the best way to communicate feelings,' and now hearing what he wrote in his journal I wish to God he'd listened to his own advice. But he *did* love you, of course he loved you, and he expected you to understand that."

"Why? Because he'd say 'I love all my kids' once in a while?"

"No. Because he worked so very hard to provide you kids with everything you needed. Because he took the time to take you places and introduce you to things like music and theater and books, all things that you, Tessa, most loved, more than any of the other kids. I don't know, honey, there were hundreds of memories, I can't list them all for you. But if you'd stop hating him for one moment and put down that damn journal and just remember the person – his acts, not his words – you might come away with something."

"Mom. Give me one. Just one tangible moment that might stoke my memory. I'm truly, honestly, humbly asking for your help."

Audrey quieted down. "All right, sweetheart, I'll try." Tessa could almost picture her mother leaning back in her chair, scrolling through the backlog of family images and moments that filled her own psychic coffers. Then Audrey's breath caught at something. "All right, here's one I remember. You were in third grade and had Sister Carmelina – do you remember her?

"Yes, choir teacher."

"That's the one. She invited you into the church choir where Michaela and Suzanna were already singing. This was a big deal, you see, because very few younger children sang in the Sunday choir. But she thought you had a lovely voice, so much so that she decided you should join the alto section and sing harmony – the really good singers were given that honor and no third grader had ever been selected. Well, it turns out Michaela, who was also singing alto, got very jealous about this and after practice told Sister Carmelina that you shouldn't be an alto because your voice was too high and you weren't good at harmony. Apparently, she was so convincing that Sister changed her mind, thinking Michaela was looking out for you, and put you back with the sopranos. At the dinner table that night, when your father asked how your day went, you choked up telling him about the situation. He looked at Michaela, absolutely furious with her, and told her to go to her room. Then he pulled you out of your chair, told me to come along, and we drove straight to the convent. He rang the bell and asked for Sister Carmelina and when she came to the door, he explained why he was there and said something like 'this child sings like an angel and deserves to be in the alto section and if you can't tell when an older sibling is jealous, then you shouldn't be leading children.' I was so proud of him. Sister was absolutely embarrassed and promised you'd be singing alto the very next day and you were. And Michaela was grounded for a week. You must remember that!"

Tessa had a clear memory of the event, mostly of being furious with Michaela, but the players were different in her own version. "I remember you talking to Sister Carmelina, not Dad."

"Oh goodness, no! The nuns terrified me and I wouldn't have had the nerve. Your father, on the other hand, didn't let anyone intimidate him."

Strange. But if it *was* him, it was a wonderful thing to have done. That she couldn't remember that detail was regretful, but it remained a significant story. "Thank you, Mom, that's an excellent memory."

"I'm glad I passed the test," Audrey sighed.

"No test…but you did good."

"I just hope you know how much *I* love you. You really are a special girl, Tessa, you are. All my kids are special. And you all turned out to be such lovely people…in spite of me."

There was no tinge of melodrama in her voice. Tessa was taken aback and felt an instant pang of…what? Vindication? Sadness? Pity? "Mom…come on…you…" She had no idea what to say.

"Oh, honey, I know who I am. It may not seem like it all the time but I do. If nothing else, your father insisted I be crystal clear about my impact on the world."

Really? That was not a trait Tessa ever noticed in her mother's arsenal.

"Ronnie's right," Audrey continued. "I probably shouldn't have had so many kids, but which one of you shouldn't I have had? Which one?" She was now edging back toward drama.

Tessa leaped to avert the trend. "Look, it's obviously ridiculous to talk about which living, breathing child you shouldn't have had, let's not go overboard here. I think Ronnie – "

"Ronnie knows exactly who I am – I probably was a terrible mother, just like he says. I'm ashamed of hitting you kids. I had no patience and got too angry. It's a regret of mine. Maybe I did ruin all your lives."

Tessa was nonplussed. Her mother had never before so clearly and unequivocally taken responsibility for the havoc she wreaked and it seemed there should be trumpets blaring or a choir of angels singing somewhere. All she could offer was, "You didn't ruin my life, Mom, but I appreciate the apology, it means a lot. You did a lot of good things, too."

"Thank you, honey. I'm glad you remember the good with the bad. I just hope you can do the same for your father."

That struck a chord.

"I'll give it a go, Mom. And I do know you love me. I love you too." She meant it.

Afterwards, Tessa mulled this poignant conversation. Her mother's honest contrition had been unexpected and welcomed. It didn't wipe the slate clean, but it certainly offered some emotional course correction.

But the Leo memory? She tried desperately to readjust her own version, to feel something different about it, but no deep emotion was forthcoming. *What good was a memory if you couldn't feel it?* It was her mother's memory then, not hers. Here, now, was already an example of the faith requirement: if she chose to believe it, it had merit. If she didn't, it meant nothing; it was just something her mother told her. *Faith. Gotta have faith faith faith.*

SIXTY-NINE

The Fate of a Good Father – Ninth in a Series
By Tessa Curzio

It was sometimes easier to pretend her life was as difficult as those of her friends. When they cried over their parents' divorces, raged about groundings and faces slapped, crumbled in fear over grades not met, honors not accrued, or talent contests lost, Cindy Maloney cried and raged and crumbled in sympathetic tandem, even though she had no personal knowledge of what they were going through. Because Cindy Maloney had the curious fate of a completely functional family with a loving mother and a father who got it right. In a world where many of her friends came from broken homes with shattered, overwhelmed mothers and fathers too distant or outwardly focused to see or care enough, Cindy was an anomaly who couldn't risk losing the camaraderie of friends she cherished by sharing too much of her authentically lovely life. At least, that's how it seemed in eighth grade.

It wasn't until her first year in college that Cindy began to truly realize how fortunate she was. Working as a clerical assistant in a rape clinic for job credit in her women's studies class, she couldn't help but notice the stunning percentage of young women whose rapes seemed a cruel response to the self-hate they had already learned at their fathers' hands. She discovered that girls who are abused, sexually or otherwise, often suffer from a traumatic and profound lack of self-esteem, leading them to engage in disempowering and self-defeating behaviors that put them at higher risk for rape. Within a three-month period, she helped process paperwork for two rape victims who had been molested by their fathers as children, another who repeatedly ran away because her father was a violent substance abuser, and one whose father had abandoned her to poverty at the age of six. It was almost impossible to reconcile her own experiences as a daughter with the horrifying realities of these damaged, assaulted women, the shock of which left her with a sense of survivor's guilt. After she left the job, she made a commitment to not only continue working for women's causes, but to seek out other women, other daughters, who had also been blessed by birth into healthy, functioning families with strong and loving father figures; an effort designed, among other reasons, to create needed balance in her sense of herself and her right to celebrate her good fortune...

Meagan had, as requested, unearthed three interesting women with good father stories, stories that offered some counterpoint to the tragedies explored in earlier articles. Cindy's story, with her quiet, unspectacular, but completely joyful relationship with her father, a man she considered a mentor and guide, originally seemed too benign to be a page-turner in this particular series. But after talking to her and getting a sense of her passion for what she did – she founded The Core, a community center for at-risk girls – Tessa wanted to continue. She pushed harder, asked more questions, scratched further below the surface, but what she discovered was a well-adjusted, contented woman, not without some quirks or regrets, but a woman who had learned to embrace her good life, be grateful for it and, in response, give something back. Tessa found her inspirational and particularly enjoyed hearing her reminisce about her father. By the end of their interview, she even thought of asking if she could meet Mr. Maloney, so desirous of making the acquaintance of a man who helped deliver a sane, happy, powerful woman to the world, but decided it was outside the purview of her reporting.

As she closed her computer for the night, Tessa thought more about the series. There could be no denying catharsis had occurred.

The gravity of the stories, some in particular, had initially overwhelmed her, leaving her depleted and feeling petty, but as the series evolved and she met with each subject, analyzed each story with its particular characters and outcomes, her perspective evolved. She came to appreciate that everyone's pain is as deep as they feel it. Regardless of how invisible the wounds, pain is simply not a comparable entity. It's relative and subjective and though everyone may have a ten, no one's ten can be weighed against another's. And somewhere in all that developing thought, she allowed that her personal pain was as valid and real as Olivia Sandapat's or Holly Brandenhall's. A small step of reconciliation but an undeniably healing one.

Tessa pulled the pen drive out of her computer and put it in her bag. *There...a good father story.*

SEVENTY

Michaela finally called, leaving a sincere apology for her culpability in the demise of the journals. No excuses, no defense, just a clear, "I'm sorry for making such a stupid decision about something that was important to you." Tessa appreciated it. The only thing she didn't appreciate, at least not yet, was Michaela's conclusion that it was probably a blessing in disguise.

There was some kind of financial settlement being negotiated between Thompson Transport and her attorney, something she intended to split amongst the sibs. When word trickled out that the boxes had been irretrievably lost, each person in the family had their reaction, shared in their typical series of phones calls to Tessa.

Suzanna: "Ding dong the witch is dead, which old witch, the wicked witch…"

Ronnie: "Sorry, Tess, but sometimes karma gets it right."

Duncan: "It all comes down to our own memories anyway."

Izzy (weeping): "Oh my God, they would've been so precious to us!"

Audrey: "What a slap in the face to a man who only wanted to recount his life and times for those he loved!"

Suzanna: "I just told her, 'Mother, look at it this way; we've been emancipated from the burden of Dad's perspective.'"

Izzy: "She didn't appreciate Suzanna's comment, which I

thought was sort of hurtful, but, of course, that's Suzanna."

Ronnie: "Then Izzy got all mopey, walked out of the restaurant, I tried to calm things down with, 'Mom, you can now burnish the legend without the inconvenience of his actual words.'"

Duncan: "Yeah, not sure that helped much…"

And on and on. Truth be told, from the perspective of family history it was quite a loss; from the mental health angle, likely a reprieve. Audrey carried on for about a week or two, but without a specific person to target for the disaster (Michaela, after all, being her angel), her outrage finally sputtered. In her more introspective moments, Audrey must surely have acknowledged that she, too, had been delivered, in a way, from the responsibility of facing and explaining Leo's words to his wounded children. Sainthood was assured; the rest would now always be conjecture.

SEVENTY-ONE

Settling in for a night of good cable and better pizza, Tessa was momentarily annoyed when the phone rang. It was Vivian. Odd, she had just been there that afternoon. "Talk fast, boss, pizza's getting cold."

"You shouldn't be eating pizza anyway."

"This from the doughnut queen."

"Listen, I wanted to pass this on." There was a buzz of some unfamiliar excitement in Vivian's voice. "Are you sitting down?"

"Don't do that, just tell me."

"Okay, remember when I said I wanted to start this series at a certain time and was disappointed when you got me the first story so late?"

"Must I be reminded of my personal failings?"

"I mentioned then that I was on a particular time-table, but what you didn't know was that it was because I was in conversations with Echolane Media – you know who they are, right?" Echolane was on a par with Conde Nast or Wenner Media but with a mission statement more exclusively focused on women.

"Of course I know who they are. Their imprints are some of my favorites. Carry on."

"They'd been looking at various online magazines with certain demographics and branding, ones that were drawing a level of attention that suggested expansion potential, and we were one of those being considered."

"That's very cool."

"Yes, it is. They were quite complimentary and though they passed at the time, said they'd keep an eye on us. Then, lo and behold, this series of yours starts and suddenly we're bombarded with letters and comments and traffic all over the place, and as of this afternoon, we are back in conversation. It now looks very likely that we may have a syndication deal with one of the biggest publishing companies in the country. How does that sound?"

Tessa felt a tingle of something sharp and visceral but kept it in check. "Um…amazing?"

"Yes, wise not to get too excited just yet. No details have been worked out and we both know how these things can go. But boy, if I had to base my confidence on the two conversations I had earlier today, we'd be popping corks."

"Dare I ask how all of this – assuming it happens – would affect the group working there now?"

"Everyone stays, we get a bigger space and we just start adding people. And of course, you – well, they're absolutely wowed by you and though I'm not supposed to say anything yet, they intend to discuss a lovely arrangement for the managing editor job. Good money – way better than I'm paying you – full benefits, all sorts of expansion possibilities; you'll still write, but you'll work with the other writers and have input over content and style, which is quite excellent, I'd say."

"I would too." Tessa felt the warmth of potential good fortune roll over her. It was slightly unfamiliar and very, very nice.

"Now, this isn't going to be huge to start with, but it means tremendous advertising support, a wider demographic base, a much bigger international presence, and the rest we'll just see. Could be a game changer and if we do it right, who knows where it might lead? And you know what was the first thing that crossed my mind when the conversation got to you? Just how great it will be when you can rub it in David's face that your damn freelance writing career just hit the jackpot!"

Tessa was surprised – and pleased – to realize that *wasn't* the first thing that crossed hers. Second or third, maybe…but not first.

SEVENTY-TWO

Just when she started to think moving back in with David might actually be possible, it struck Tessa that, more than anything else, she wanted her foyer chairs back. She thought about why the chairs had suddenly become essential, particularly since she had made several grand gestures about not wanting anything she'd left behind, but the desire would not abate and no amount of analysis could disguise the fact that this was not a harbinger for reconciliation.

"David, I want my chairs back."

"Okaaay…I guess that means we're not talking about you coming home."

"I'm sorry. I guess not."

"Well, I can't say I'm completely surprised; I was just hoping."

"I know, David, I'm sorry. I tried to picture it and couldn't make it work."

"Can you tell me why?"

"Not really…I don't know for sure. But I thought about everything you said, about wanting me back, and I came to the conclusion that it really wasn't about me."

"Really? Well, who else would it be about, Tessa?" His voice got edgy.

"Please don't get upset, David. What I mean is, you probably do miss the idea of a relationship, of planning a life with someone, but I honestly don't believe it's about me specifically."

"Well, that's ridiculous. Of course it's about you. You're the one I've been in love with for over a year, the one I want to plan a life with. I know I screwed up and said a lot of things I didn't really mean, but I thought we got past that already. Didn't we?"

"I believe you *think* you didn't mean them."

"What does that mean, Tessa?"

"David, you're a good man and I don't think you intentionally meant to be cruel to me. But the truth is, you *do* have the right to live the life you want, with the kind of woman you want, and I don't think I'm ever going to be that kind of woman."

"But I said – "

"I don't even mean from your perspective – you might actually think I *am* your kind of woman. I mean from my perspective. You were right about us having different worldviews. We do. And that's not bad; it's just different. But I know over time it would kill us. I don't know when or how quickly, we might even be able to make a decent life for a while, but it would eventually kill us. And we both deserve better than that."

"Obviously you've thought this out. I appreciate that. But I'm telling you, I think we could make it work if we were both willing to start over."

"I guess that's it, David. I'm not. A lot has changed for me since we broke up; I'm a different person. And my feelings for you are…different. I hate to say this, because no one knows better than me how awful it is to hear but…I'm not in love with you anymore. And I am so sorry."

And so she ended it, without a raised voice, without tearful anguish, and without saying a word about Echolane Media. Because proving to David that she was more than a mid-level, success fearing, life scrabbling, don't-tie-me-down artist type was no longer required.

Neither, apparently, was her drug of choice. It had been four days since she'd wanted a drink.

SEVENTY-THREE

Vivian convinced Tessa that going to Haden's party as her and Glen's guest "removed the taint of arriving alone and exuding the desperate single-woman stigma that would inevitably follow." Vivian was typically, and amusingly, eloquent on the point; Tessa appreciated the lifeline and they set out.

It was the golden hour, that late summer dusk that turns the hills into postcard vistas and paints everyone with the burnished glow of California and all its sensuous clichés. It was early for a Saturday party but Haden insisted they come in time to enjoy the sunset.

As Glen maneuvered his Volvo up the narrow winding streets of the Studio City hills, Tessa took a moment to reflect on the surprise she felt at being reintroduced to this very appealing part of the valley. As with her thoughts on Haden himself, she realized how very presumptuous she'd been about so many things and resolved to be less so in this new, transformative era of her fabulously successful life. They arrived at the valet station at the top of a long, curved driveway that led to a house that looked like something out of *Architectural Digest*. With its white stucco walls and California-cool lines, the house beamed of chic. Lush, colorful landscaping framed like a backdrop and the overall impression was one of simple, unfussy beauty. Tessa was appropriately dazzled and wondered how much Haden had to do with its design.

Inside was more of the same. Wide, expansive windows made up the bulk of the living room and the steps down to a cloud-like flokati rug with its furry white hipness made the room almost float in the surroundings. Every single piece of furniture, every wall hanging and accouterment, contributed to a well-balanced, undeniably artful whole, with not an unframed rock poster or alley-retrieved chair in sight. *Wouldn't you know it? Feng shui exemplar.*

As Vivian and Glen grabbed plates and dived into the hors d'oeuvres, Tessa scanned the room to see if Haden could be spotted. Within minutes he emerged from a downstairs location with a bag of ice and Doug Reynolds, her old sound guy, right behind. Before Tessa even noticed Doug, she took in Haden Pierce. Out of his work grubbies and into well-cut slacks and a linen shirt, he was simply stunning. Tessa felt an actual jolt as his sparkling blue eyes found hers and crinkled in a radiant smile. "Tessa! You made it! Look who I've got with me!"

Doug roared and grabbed Tessa in an unchecked bear hug and, once extricated, she couldn't help but be delighted at seeing her old band chum. "Dougie, I didn't realize I missed you until just now," she teased.

"My God, Tessa, you don't look a day older. How do you do that?" Doug *did* look a day older, actually several days older, and Tessa was reminded of his unrestrained way with blow and the bottle. But his warmth remained and as he smiled and refused to let her go, she felt something sweet and familial for him.

"All it takes is the failing eyes of old friends," she laughed. Haden, satisfied that he'd done his job, slipped off to supervise the grill while she and Doug settled in for a good catch-up. She noticed he was drinking Pellegrino and joined him. Doug wanted to know everything about her last five years and she his, so they traded stories until they arrived at the present.

"Tessa, you've got to come down to my studio – it's a fantastic space. We're doing a lot of great things there and I'd love you to see it. And if you're planning to do any recording yourself, I'll make you a killer deal."

"Oh, I think that era is pretty much over for me."

He looked at her with raised eyebrows. "Blasphemy! You cannot tell me you're not going to sing again? Come on! That's ridiculous. Even if it was just some backups or a jingle or two, it would be fun. And how great would it be to work together again?"

She couldn't tell Doug that jingles and backups were nowhere to be found on her current bucket list, so she begged off with claims of unforgiving work schedules and out of shape vocal cords.

"Okay, okay, I get it. But someday you're going to write a song again and when you do, and you want to record it, you better give me a call." She promised she would. And as quickly as she was able to change the subject, they were thankfully summoned to the deck for dinner.

The party was a smash. Perfectly choreographed music played on cue: soft jazz during the meal, chunky blues at dessert, and by after-dinner drinks and coffee, the funk was on and the deck was rocking. Haden drifted in and out of her circle, wherever her circle happened to be, and she could feel his eyes on her, his attention wrapped around her, and it was intoxicating.

Vivian and Glen eventually announced they were both exhausted and ready to go but had arranged for Doug to give her a ride home. She was grateful and hugged them with a giddiness that bordered on girly. Vivian made hilarious note, but Tessa was unflappable tonight. She'd made a decision about David, she'd gotten at least one good memory from her mother, she'd been sleeping through the night, and she could feel her anxiety about the journals abating. Success was quite possibly just around the corner and Haden Pierce liked her – *that* way.

After another hour of dancing, the party moved into the quieter, late-night discussion phase. Doug was embroiled in some debate with a very good-looking woman inexplicably arguing the merits of Rush Limbaugh; Tessa figured that would be a while.

Haden was out on the porch talking to various guests making their slow exits, so Tessa wandered down the stairs to see the rest of the house. The large and well-furnished open space below overlooked the valley, with a separate bedroom area bordered by a bookshelf and an ornate, well-placed Asian room screen. Tessa noticed a guitar leaning against the bed. She sat down, picked it up and strummed a few chords. It had been so long since she'd played that the action of it felt supremely clumsy, but after a few minutes muscle memory took over and she was able to get through a shaky version of one of her songs. A wave of weariness rolled over her and she lay down in the quiet of this hidden space, the muffled sounds of the remaining party made a pleasant white noise to lull her to sleep.

Minutes later, or maybe an hour later, she didn't know which, she felt motion and woke to find Haden seated at the edge of the bed. Before she could say a word, he moved the guitar from her side and slid down next to her. She had an impulse to get up but it was short-lived; his arms wrapped around her, pulling her into a lush, provocative kiss. Haden's lips were soft and warm and his tongue found its way into her mouth exactly as a new tongue should. She arrived swiftly at a level of ardor that was slightly feverish; her desire for him, for his touch, was immediate and intense and she felt no compulsion to quell it. Nor did he. He was all caramel sweet and slow, thoroughly enjoying her warm, silky mouth. He pulled away briefly at one point and looked down at her. The pause and his pace both surprised and intrigued her, so used to rushed passion and the frantic removal of clothes and inhibitions.

He smiled and said in a husky bedroom voice, "I thought I might find you down here."

"You did, did you?"

"Yes. I hoped you'd fall into my trap, leaving the guitar nearby." He smiled wickedly. "I had a feeling you might not be able to resist."

She got up on her elbow and looked at him for a minute.

"Haden, why are you so fixated on getting me back into music?"

"I don't know…selfish, I guess. I love your voice and I'd love to hear you sing again. Maybe because I knew you in that context before I knew anything else about you. I don't know. It just seems like such an essential part of who you are, that's all."

"But what if isn't anymore? If I don't want to do it anymore? Would that disappoint you?"

"*Do* you not want to do it anymore?"

"Would that disappoint you?"

"No, not if you were completely happy with the decision. Is that the case?"

Tessa thought for a moment. "No, not really. It was just the direction things took. I loved that part of my life; it was my calling, my biggest dream. But for a lot of reasons I don't want to get into right now it ended and I could never figure out how to put it back together. So I moved on."

"You must miss it, though."

"Of course I do. Like a phantom limb. It's not that I don't want music in my life; it's just that it became more important to be happy…and music and everything surrounding it just stopped being happy for me. So I started doing something else I love and can actually have some control over and, well, here we are."

"I get it, it makes sense. And I think your writing is phenomenal. You just had a certain spark, I guess, as a performer. It'd just be nice to hear you sing again someday, that's all." He leaned over and kissed her. "But bottom line, no, it doesn't matter to me. You're perfect just the way you are."

Perfect answer, too. She pulled him to her, warm and ready, reached for his belt and began to slowly slide it open when his hand inexplicably stopped her.

"There is nothing I'd rather do right now than make love to you…"

"Okay…" She nuzzled into his neck. "There's nothing I'd rather do either." Again she reached for his belt and again he stopped her. This time she pulled away, immediately embarrassed. "Sorry, I'm clearly misreading the signals."

"No, *I'm* sorry, the signals are mixed."

She sat up, doing her best to keep hurt from creeping in but it did anyway. "What am I missing?"

He sat up too; they faced each other cross-legged. "Here's the thing, Tessa…normally I'd just pounce. Just throw myself into it and jump you. That's what I've been thinking about since that first day at the office and nothing's changed since then."

Oddly sweet. Titillating. Confusing. "Okay."

"And this is going to sound trite, but I think there's more to this than a one or two-night hook-up and I don't want to screw it up. It's not my typical style to think things out that much, but you're already special to me and you've gone through so much lately, I don't want to rush into something that would only throw more confusion into the situation."

A mix of appreciation and disappointment descended, stranding her between the thought that he was a paragon of consideration and that sex sometimes just needs to be had, not discussed. *Yeah, like the night with hairy Russell. No caution, no discussion. Just hot, random, rutting sex that leaves you feeling wild and sated and…sort of disgusted. Yeah, that's just what I need. Another bloody night like that.*

Haden sat looking at her, waiting for her response, but random, distracting thoughts kept popping into her head: *Gold digger. Man-fleecer. User. Why wasn't I interested in him before I knew he was a man of means? Could my father be right about me using men? No! I'm walking away from David and he's plenty successful. Besides, I'm going to be successful in my own right soon, dammit. God…look at him, sitting there so handsome, waiting for me to say something.*

She shook off the urge to reach for him and decided to go with familiar detachment, shifting off the bed. "You know, Haden, you're probably right; it is too soon for any of this. Besides, truth be told, I should probably sign off men for a while anyway. Not exactly an arena I have any business trolling these days."

Now he was thrown. "I'm not sure what that means."

"Let's be honest, I'm shitty at relationships. I have no clue how to choose someone who might actually be right for me. I tend to muck it up with all sorts of family-of-origin, Daddy-damaged bullshit. I'm apparently terrified of commitment and I might now be entering the manic body-clock phase of female desperation. So, yeah, getting together with me would probably not be your best bet." She was tucking in shirttails and tying shoes somewhat frantically, eager to get away as quickly as she could.

"Wow. You just went a whole other way with this. I'm not rejecting you, Tessa, I –"

"Wait, do I sound rejected? I'm talking about *my* need to pull away, Haden. Because you're right, there's just too much going on. But trust me, I'm okay, I get it. I'm not some weepy little girl getting all dramatic because you don't want to have sex with me."

Except she was getting dramatic and he did want to have sex with her. He grabbed her before she could jettison up the stairs and pulled her to him so hard she gasped. He kissed her as deeply and passionately as he had moments earlier and now that they were standing, she felt her knees would surely buckle and drop her to the floor. But they didn't; he held her too close. And they kept kissing, until her head was swimming and his resolve began to crumble. But it didn't. He finally, reluctantly, stopped, but kept his face tucked into the curve of her neck.

"Tessa, listen to me," he said softly. "I want you. I think you know that. But I want to *know* you. And I want you to step into my life with a free heart and an unencumbered head and when you can do that, I will grab you with everything I've got, your stated flaws and all. Until then, I'd like to see you and talk and kiss and spend time together doing whatever we both feel like doing. If that's something you want, let's do that and leave it here for tonight."

The following eleven thoughts then ripped through Tessa's head like flashcards:

1.   *Yes, that's a perfect plan…leaving it here.*
2.   *Face it, he's gorgeous and I'm not that hot.*
3.   *Am I just being petulant?*
4.   *I can't believe he just rejected me!*
5.   *I'm so utterly embarrassed.*
6.   *What's with this singing thing anyway?*
7.   *WHY CAN'T I BE NORMAL!?*
8.   *I bet he thinks writing just isn't that cool.*
9.   *He's so sweet…I'm so insane.*
10. *So, what, we do lunch and act like friends?*
11. *I'm SO confused…I need to get out of here.*

It was clear #11 was her best bet.

She pulled out of his embrace, went back to adjusting her clothes, and with a tone that had just the slightest whine, made her point. "Look, Haden, I'm completely confused right now and, frankly, have no idea if any of that's something I want to do. I seem to know only so much at a time and when we got started here tonight, I thought I wanted you. I didn't want to sing or talk about singing. I didn't want to play that stupid guitar. I just wanted some closeness, specifically with you. But that's done now, you've set your boundaries, I'm properly contained, which seems like a good place to end this. So I'm going to take my confused self home and I'm sure we'll talk again at some point. Probably be best if it wasn't for a while. Thanks for the party; I really like your house."

With that she turned and ran up the stairs where the last remaining valet arranged for a cab that, as far as she was concerned, couldn't get there fast enough.

SEVENTY-FOUR

Three days went by and she did nothing but write, work on her apartment, comb memories for Leo stories, and feel really shitty about the way she left things at Haden's. Each activity had its own rhythm and sway, but at least she felt preoccupied. David had a friend drop off the foyer chairs and Tessa was quite pleased at their arrival. That she didn't have a foyer was less relevant than the fact that they were hers, they were here, and they lent a certain flair to the apartment that had previously been missing.

She wanted to talk to Ruby. Needed some girl grit. Wanted to know how things were going. Wanted to tell her about Haden, and though she wanted to hear nothing but good news about her friend's renewed marriage project, held hope for maybe just a little commiseration. No go.

"We're actually doing pretty good, Tessa, can you believe it? I mean, the jury's still out in some ways. There are moments when this new version of us is all transcendental and mature and stuff, then the urge to start ripping him a new one kicks in again."

"About what, specifically?" Tessa suspected it had to do with the issue of "other people." She wasn't wrong.

"I told him about Gym Guy. I know I said there was no point in hurting him with that, but ultimately it seemed worse to make him think he was the only one who strayed. But it's really hard; *I*

290

did it while we were still together and he didn't. That makes me the badder guy, you know?"

"Did he say that?"

"Badder?"

"No, dolt, did he imply you were worse because of the timing?"

"Imply? He damn well said it. But he *said* it, didn't yell it. We're all mature now, did I mention that already?"

Tessa laughed. Ruby just had a way about her, particularly when she was happy. And she sounded happy.

"We've spent weeks processing the information," Ruby continued. "It gets touchy but at least we're dealing with all the feelings involved. Sometimes I can forget we've both been with other people, other times it just makes me sick to my stomach. I'd say we're still very much a work in progress but, if nothing else, the separation made it clear to us how much we love each other so, at this point at least, we're both up for the challenge. Aren't you impressed with me?" Ruby smiled almost shyly.

Tessa was and told her so. She also noticed herself feeling less personally invested in how Ruby's life turned out, a budding confidence that whatever happened to her friend did not have to impact her own sturdier foundation. This was important and hard won. She hoped she could sustain it if and when the dreaded call came in that Ruby was on the mattresses in some hotel somewhere, screaming about the futility of love.

She decided not to tell Ruby about her hissy fit at Haden's. There was no point discussing the behavior of a stupid single chick when Ruby was trying to be a smart married one.

As for Kate, like always, everything was going swimmingly: the remodel on the house was moving along, her assistant stepped seamlessly into Kate's role, and a new hire made business easier and less demanding. The pregnancy was progressing without a hitch and she and Todd were having a "splendid time sharing every step of the journey from doctor's visits and birth training, to name books and endless trips to baby stores."

And Tessa found it all profoundly annoying. Kate's flawless life had lately made Tessa feel choked, as if there was nothing she could offer or say that could compare on any level and so she felt like saying nothing. She couldn't figure out if it was sheer, unadulterated envy or just some sense of distancing, but as their lives became more disparate, Tessa felt the chasm widen. She simply did not want to hear one more bloody word about Kate's perfect fucking life when hers still felt so unformed.

Kate must have sensed the growing gap. That very evening she showed up on Tessa's doorstep uninvited, loudly and repeatedly banging on the door.

"Tessa, this has gone on too long," she said as she marched into the now be-couched living room. "I guess I'm guilty of something since it's clear you're avoiding me, but this is ridiculous and I won't have it."

Tessa got the tea going and shouted from the kitchen, "I'm not avoiding you. I just have nothing to say to you."

"And why would it be, after a lifetime of friendship, that you have nothing to say to me?"

Tessa came in with a mug for each of them. "I don't know, Kate. I think it's a case of having nothing in common anymore."

"What ridiculous bullshit is that? What common threads do you and Ruby share, besides the past? She has a three-year-old kid, a prodigal husband, and a retail job. What part of that do you share?"

"For God's sake, Kate, don't be so dense. It's not about that; it's about connecting, about being there. I don't know, I just feel like you always make such a point of doing everything so to the hilt; like, every little step in place and adhered to, and sometimes that doesn't leave much room for us imperfect folk. Maybe the difference is, despite what's going on in her life, Ruby always finds the time to make time."

Kate puffed up like a blowfish. "What in the living hell are you talking about? I've called you three times this week alone! You rarely return my calls and when you do, you sound positively disinterested. I find out from Ruby you've got this amazing thing happening at work but not one word of it has been shared with me. No discussion about the journals being lost, the David decision, not one mention of this random Russell guy, and certainly nothing about Haden." *Fuck, Ruby covered it all.* "What am I supposed to think?"

Tessa took in her friend's red-rimmed eyes, the plaintive tone in her voice, the big, pregnant belly heaving with each angry word, and all of a sudden she couldn't help herself; she burst out laughing. She had never seen Kate so thoroughly unglued and at the same time so completely endearing. As Tessa's laughter bubbled, Kate looked at her with growing exasperation, until she slammed her foot on the floor and charged for the exit.

Tessa quickly gathered herself and stopped her at the door. "Kate, Katie, my God, you are so fucking cute. It's ME! It's me, for God's sake; it's not you. I just look at your life sometimes and get so fucking jealous. I'm shallow, I know, and it embarrasses me, but I'm nothing if not embarrassingly human."

Kate cocked her head in that sweet, compassionate way she had and grabbed Tessa in a hug. "Thank you for being so honest, but please, PLEASE don't be jealous of my life. It looks good on the outside, and it *is* good, but just like everyone else I've got all my own shit. I've come to realize that everything is a trade-off, from relinquishing control of my business to accepting the burgeoning mountain that is my ass. It's all something to be dealt with, and I'm doing the best I can and am truly grateful for all I have. Particularly my beloved husband who is currently driving me nuts with his picayune bullshit about how this nursery should be built and why I should quit working right now to preempt any ankle explosion on my part, apparently a fanatical pregnancy fear of his. This is my life, Tessa, please don't be jealous of it."

By then they were both laughing and the rift was done and

they got to catching up on everything. Kate was surprised but pleased about the David decision; she reminded Tessa that she had never felt they were a perfect match. Tessa assured her she had never forgotten. Kate was thoroughly disgusted with the Russell episode, having never approved of this sort of behavior. Even when they were younger and everyone and their brother was hooking up, Kate never did. Which is probably why she was now happily married with a baby on the way. Tessa got off that topic as quickly as she could. Kate was intrigued but cautious about Haden, suggesting they come back to further discussion of him when they were done with everything else. Then the journals; Tessa told her the whole story, right up to Aunt Joanne's assignment.

Kate's eyes brightened. "She actually said to ask me about it?"

"She said you were there during my formative years and maybe you could help me remember things about Leo I've forgotten, things that might make it easier to come to some kind of resolution about what my damn father felt about me."

Kate sat quietly on the couch, using her belly as a shelf to balance her tea mug. The sun was setting and neither made a move to flick on the lights, the ambiance growing dusky and cocoonish. Kate recalled their childhoods, those years in Chicago when their homes seemed interchangeable and welcoming, when friends and family mixed like good stew, when life, however complicated, was also simple and unfussy. Kate talked about witnessing Audrey's rages and how, though they always left her terrified and appalled, she could never stay away when the mood pendulumed back to ebullience; forgiveness was always easy to muster.

"Why is that, though?" Tessa wondered. "Why was it easier to forgive her than my father?"

"I don't know, maybe because your mom was completely transparent. No matter what state she was in – excitement, rage, happiness; violence – you always knew exactly what was going on with her; there was no mystery. As awful as it was when she'd lose it, at least you knew it would be short-lived and she'd get back to being wonderful Audrey at any moment. And wonderful Audrey was...wonderful. More wonderful than any mom I knew, including my own in some ways. With your dad – wow – I don't know. Subterfuge. No one could've been sweeter to my father than Leo, then I hear this stuff about how my dad was too stupid to be his friend."

Tessa wondered if, perhaps, it would have been kinder to refrain from sharing "The Pros & Cons of Neighbors."

Kate continued. "How do you explain that or figure it out as an adult much less a vulnerable little kid? You don't. You also don't know what any of it means: the love, the coldness, the protectiveness; the disdain. It's all a mystery because the code is unreadable. Show me love than disappear from my life. Show me love then write about what a loser I am. Show me love than tell me I'm an idiot. Which is real? I don't know. It's maddening."

"Which is why I need you to help me find a memory, decipher a code that might confirm that he actually loved me."

"Of course he loved you." Echoes of Audrey.

"Why do you say that so unequivocally?"

"Because he did."

"But how do you *know* that?"

"Because I was there. I was a witness to your life, Tessa. Not all of it, not all the behind closed doors moments, but a lot of it. And I know that your dad, however enigmatic he was, loved you."

Tessa felt something unclench, the tremor of some slight letting go. "Okay. You were a witness to my life." *A lovely description of friendship with Kate.* "What can you tell me that I might have forgotten? What pictures swing to mind when you say that so definitively?"

Kate stared out the darkening window for a moment. "I saw you as this loud, crazy Catholic family, all high-strung and inspired, something that didn't exist in my very contained and elegant household. I remember always wanting to be there, at your house, because someone would undoubtedly be doing something fun and imaginative. I *loved* being there. Do you remember when you were in the church band?"

"Of course I do. It may have been the only thing I ever liked about church!" Tessa laughed.

"You guys would always be in the living room playing guitars and singing, you leading the way with that voice of yours…I felt like your groupie."

"You were quite the backup singer, as I recall."

"Oh please, I was a horrible singer but it didn't matter; it was all so fun! Or how about Valentine's Day, when your mom would have all of us lined up at your big dining room table making those handmade cards we passed out to the neighbors? I loved that…I think I still have one of those. Or the times Duncan cast us in his basement plays or Ronnie made us be the audience for his dumb stand-up shows!"

"God, he was always so funny. Or how about when Mickie and Suzanna made those weird costumes and we wore our yarn wigs for weeks on end, 'member that?"

"Of course! I kept my princess yarn wig for years. I said I was going to wear it for my wedding!" They both laughed. "When I think of your house, the main thing I think of is activity and fun that was so constant you could almost forget the dark stuff. But that was there, too."

"Yeah, I have no trouble conjuring up the dark stuff. It's the good stuff with Leo that's most elusive. That's what I need you for."

"Okay, well, let's see…I can remember things like Leo coming into a room where we were all playing like little puppies and extending this sort of collegial nod to whatever non-Curzio was there. Which was usually me," she said with a smile. "He kind of scared me because he was always so serious, but then I also remember those moments when he warmed up. Like the time he took you, me and Suzanna to Ravinia to see the Joffrey Ballet, remember that? The whole way there he sang those goofy songs that had us peeing our pants."

Tessa smiled at the memory. "I remember that. It's a good one but it's not specific to just him and me and that's what we're looking for."

Kate leaned back on the couch and stared up at the ceiling. "You should get one of those bamboo fans for this room. It's going to get hotter here than at the beach."

"Kate. Focus." Tessa laughed.

"Okay, okay! Let's see…okay, you have to remember the time I fell down the basement stairs, right?"

"Of course."

"And how your dad got so concerned and came flying down to carry me up? He couldn't have been sweeter and I was so touched by that."

Leo had iced and wrapped Kate's sprain with the gentleness of a physician but, while that was also a lovely memory, Tessa again reminded Kate that it didn't demonstrate any clarity about Leo's feelings toward *her*, Tessa, specifically. So Kate, like a deep-sea diver determined to retrieve an elusive black box, took another breath and went back in to find something of value.

Something else came to her. She described a nondescript night after school. Tessa was at the Berendt's doing homework with her. As the adults sat around the living room over cocktails and conversation, the girls, ever curious about what it was their parents talked about, snuck behind the sofa to eavesdrop. The discussion was about how the girls were doing at school and at one point, Kate remembered Leo saying something like, "I think Teresa's extraordinary. Sings better than anyone I know, gets straight A's and on top of all that, she's a beauty. Not much anyone can do to hold her back."

As Kate relayed this memory, Tessa remembered the night too, remembered hiding behind the couch. As she ran it over in her mind, the memory gelled, particularly the phrase, "Teresa is extraordinary." She remembered it because, at the time, it had struck her so viscerally, the idea that Leo thought she was extraordinary. The memory calmed her. It wasn't specifically *love*, but it was at least approval. Like a hungry child who'd just been fed something delectable, she wanted more. "Keep thinking, Kate, find me one more."

So Kate kept thinking, flipping through her remembered images, looking to find one that jumped out. One jumped. "Oh, this is a good one! Eighth grade. You were invited to participate in the parish short story writing competition, remember that? Sister Eugene made a big deal about this being 'an elite event and to be invited was almost as good as winning.'" Kate laughed. "Do you remember her, Sister Eugene? She was such a cheerleader!"

"Yeah, she was nice, wasn't she?"

"She was. Nice but very candid. I remember going to her afterwards and whining about not being invited and she flat out said, 'you're only an average writer, Katherine. Read more and learn to use adverbs correctly.' I was crushed. Anyway, I came home with you that night and distinctly remember when you told your parents about the invitation, because I saw Leo act like I'd never seen him before."

Tessa sat up, "Really? I don't remember. What did he do?"

"I can't believe you don't remember this! He lit up, got up from his chair, went over to you and gave you the biggest hug. Leo did not typically do those sorts of thing, at least not in my presence, so it was memorable."

Tessa closed her eyes and pictured the moment, trying to remember. Vaguely.

Kate continued, describing Tessa's short story about a crippled dancer who learns to dance in her mind. "I thought it was the most beautiful story I'd ever read, really; I was just amazed by you, so when you came in second to that idiot Eddie Maynard's stupid piece about a baseball team winning the pennant, I remember I was so furious!"

"Oh God, I remember Eddie's story. It was awful, but it

figures he won; the coach was one of the judges!"

Kate went on to describe Tessa walking up to the podium to receive her second-place medal. "I followed Leo to the side of the stage; you came over and just stood there shaking, trying so hard not to cry. I burst into tears myself when Leo put his arms around you and you just sobbed your little heart out. Then I remember him saying the sweetest thing, something like, 'Just keep going and don't ever let any prize you win or you lose get you off track. You made me proud and I love you.'" Kate looked up at Tessa wide eyes. "I remember him saying 'I love you'…I do. That's big, right? I also remember, verbatim, the line about, 'don't ever let any prize you win or you lose get you off track' because I thought it was incredibly wise…something that would be a meme in today's world. Do you remember any of that?"

Tessa closed her eyes and let the story wash over her, just as Aunt Joanne had instructed. And as she ran through the details, her own version slowly emerged. The haze of forgetting pulled apart, leaving a picture she could actually conjure: her younger self, the pink and black suit she wore for the awards ceremony, the image of twelve-year-old Kate, of the lectern where a jubilant Eddie Maynard celebrated his win. And there he was, her father, standing at the side of the stage with his usual stern expression, one that softened into the kind of look parents bear for their children, mothers for their sons, fathers for their…daughters. As she reached deeper into the memory she could almost feel her tear-streaked face burrowing into his scratchy cheek, his smell, his arms encircling her, and then, ever so slowly, as if coming from a distant place outside of herself, she could remember his words, just as Kate remembered them: "You made me proud and I love you." The feeling behind them was unmistakable…love, sweet love. For her. Just her.

Kate and Tessa sat in silence for a while. It was only later, after eating dinner and talking more about Haden and laughing over the list of baby names, that they finally returned to it and acknowledged its simple but illuminating importance. Tessa had found a strong, salient, irrefutable memory. It didn't answer all the questions. It answered one. Her father loved her.

SEVENTY-FIVE

Tessa decided she'd been wearing too much black eyeliner. It was an edgy look, certainly, but there was a softness creeping into her psyche that demanded a palette shift; she switched to something brown and less aggressive. But as she pulled a black jean jacket out of the closet and readied for her day as a woman with memories, she made mental note that no amount of personal transformation would ever get her into pastels. Some things remained non-negotiable.

Aunt Joanne was thrilled by Tessa's assignment report and scheduled a get-together for the following week. As Tessa hung up the phone, she took a moment to think about her aunt: how this remarkable women, from the same gene pool as her father, had somehow found an interpretation of their religion that included compassion and love devoid of the terror of Leo's. The disparity was as inexplicable as why one twin has red hair, the other blonde. She made Catholicism palatable, even understandable, and though Tessa would never be drawn to it, she'd been gifted now with an ability to at least view it through a more tolerant, forgiving prism. Whether that left her open for some future foray into another kind of spirituality, she didn't know. But she knew she was grateful for Aunt Joanne.

She stopped by the office briefly and found a note at her

station from Haden. "I'll be at Starbucks downstairs at 3:30. Would you meet me there?" It was 2:30 now.

Do I want to hang around till then…do I want to face him at all?

Since she felt incapable of making an immediate decision, she headed into a meeting with Vivian to discuss the Echolane proposal – it was moving forward undeterred, something both women quietly cheered. By the time they wrapped up, it was 3:26. Tessa decided to make her way down for a latte and some unavoidable music-facing. She didn't mention it to Vivian, however, because the topic of Haden Pierce had become one of those things they couldn't share for the time being. Vivian thought Tessa was wasting a tremendous opportunity and Tessa thought Vivian should butt out for just once. There had been a minor but heated conflagration in the office kitchen, after which they declared it to be a category similar to politics and religion: untouchable, except in cases where the parties agree. They didn't so it was off the table.

When Tessa got to Starbucks she saw Haden already seated with a coffee, nonchalantly flipping through the newspaper as if he had nothing on his mind. She decided to forego the latte and its unavoidably loud announcement and proceeded directly to the table. He looked up and by the genuine warmth of his smile she could tell he hadn't expected her to come.

"Hey, I'm glad you made it!"

"The timing just worked out."

"Did you want to order a coffee or something?"

"No, that's okay."

"Okay…"

She sat down. He took her in for a moment, his eyes reflecting some of what they'd stirred up that night. Tessa was both relieved and annoyed; how could she wrangle this unwieldy situation if he kept looking at her with those twinkly eyes? He took a sip of coffee and left her to break the silence. She finally did. "Look, I'm really sorry about my exit speech the other night. I seem to have lost my ability to behave like a normal person, particularly when it comes to you for some reason. I'm honestly sorry. I acted like an ass."

Haden smiled. "Well, there were certain ass-like components to it but I remain convinced there is a normal person in there somewhere."

"Don't be so sure."

"Tessa, obviously our timing has been off and maybe we do need to step it back a notch, but I still believe there's something good between us and – "

"Haden, yes, the timing is off, but it's more than that. This year has been a minefield like no other and it's not just about ending a relationship. It's a long story and even though there's been a bit of a breakthrough lately, I'm far from solid ground. Maybe some day I'll tell you the whole thing but, suffice it to say, I've been about as discombobulated as a girl can get and acting accordingly, much to my embarrassment. I'm not typically *this* crazy and I'm sort of sad we met at a time when I am." She was flushed and earnest and he couldn't help but grin. Her brow furrowed. "What?"

"You're cute, that's all. Hyperbolic and self-flagellating, but cute."

"And he likes the crazy ones!" She rolled her eyes.

He leaned in seriously. "No, I *don't* like the crazy ones, but I happen to know you're not crazy. I have a small idea of what you've been through, courtesy of our mutual friends, and based on what little I know, I can only imagine the roller coaster you've been on. I'll look forward to talking to you about it when the time's right, but I'm glad to know you're doing better."

"Thank you, but it concerns me a little that you're always so unperturbed. I don't think I've had one rational moment around you."

"Okay, let's be clear: yes, you acted a little pissy at our first coffee event and you were slightly histrionic the other night, but so what? If I thought that was all you were about it would be different. But I know you to be a pretty spectacular and talented person who happens to get under my skin. Which one wins in my book? Not hard to figure. Would I prefer you *not* act like a hysterical teenager? Sure. But we all get a pass and you got one – two – from me. Believe me, when you see me lose my cool one of these days, you won't think I'm so damn unperturbed." He sat back. "There, is that better?"

She smiled. "Yes." A pause. "Now what?"

"Well, I figured if we got through this conversation, I'd invite you to an event coming up in a couple of weeks. No pressure, just a really nice event."

"Daring of you but go ahead, tell me."

"My parents have a big ranch above Cambria and every year they invite family and all sorts of friends for a big end-of-summer bash. This year we're also celebrating Cecilia's engagement – "

"Please tell her 'congratulations' for me."

"You could tell her yourself. I'd love for you to come up and just spend a couple of days with me and about fifty other people. We do beach walks and roast a pig and sing around the campfire and all that other corny stuff, and I think it would be one of those great opportunities to spend some time together in a nice setting free of pressure and expectation."

"Really? Meeting your family is free of pressure and expectation?"

"It's not an official 'meeting the family' thing. It's a gathering with a large group that happens to include family. The nuance is inescapable. I guarantee you'll have a blast; it's impossible to come to this event and not have a blast, so if nothing else, we'd –"

"Have a blast!" They both laughed.

"What do you say?" Haden asked.

"It sounds fantastic, but I think I need to stay on this path of quiet for a bit longer. I hope you can understand."

"I do." He squeezed her hand. "But a little fun wouldn't hurt either. Under the right circumstances, it might actually help."

"It might, but it's too soon to tell. And truthfully, I'm just not ready to meet a bunch of new people yet; I'm not ready to meet your family yet. I'm too raw. Imagine me having a meltdown with hot marshmallows over an open flame; the options for catastrophe are endless!"

"We're a tolerant bunch," he persisted with a grin.

She felt his pull and the sweetness of it touched her. "I have no doubt you are. You are nothing if not tolerant. If we're still talking to each other next year, will you ask again?"

"Of course." He stood up and put on his jacket. "I'm heading up to Seattle for the next couple of weeks, then I'll be off to Cambria from there. I may have to head to Chicago right after that so I won't be around for a while. I hope you'll stay in touch."

"I will," she promised.

"I'll be thinking about you, Tessa." He touched her cheek then turned and walked out the door.

Tessa felt like maybe, just maybe, she'd never see him again.

SEVENTY-SIX

"But why don't you want to pursue it?" Aunt Joanne asked, genuinely puzzled.

Tessa sat across from her aunt a lighter, less burdened woman, and realized, for the first time in a long time, she was talking about something other than Leo, the journals, or David. She was talking about her life beyond. Which now included Haden. This was surely progress.

"It's not that I don't want to pursue it, it's more that it's bad timing. Even he said that."

"He sounds like a pretty great guy."

"He *is* a great guy. I don't know; it's lots of stuff. Reluctance. Fear that there's some remnant of damage, of commitment aversion. Fear that I'll fuck it up somehow. All of that."

"Tell me, how do you typically choose a relationship?"

Tessa had to think about that. "I don't. It typically chooses me. Some guy likes me and I'm flattered and don't want to waste it so I leap. On good days the guy has enough redeeming qualities, but not always, I have to admit. But it's never about me making a choice; it's about me reacting."

"What do you mean, you don't want to waste it?"

"Don't want to waste the opportunity of someone liking me."

"Like that's so rare?"

Tessa couldn't help but smile. "I know, it seems weird; lots of boys liked me, just ask my dad. But it's probably some kind of pathetic 'don't want to be in the same club that wants me' low self-esteem 'you really like me' kind of thing."

Aunt Joanne laughed. "You are the wordsmith, aren't you?"

Tessa felt oddly pleased that she'd made her aunt laugh. "Truth is, I'm always surprised when someone wants me. The paradox is hard to explain: popular but pathetic. But I've never felt like I was the one making the choice. Even with David; he came to me."

"Yes, but you had to make a reciprocal choice and you did. You had reason to make that choice. What was it?"

"I was mostly drawn to how nice and sane he was. Trevor had been my bar, my last serious relationship, and I thought nice and sane would be a balm after him. I chose David for those reasons."

"Weren't they good ones?"

"At first. But ultimately not enough. As nice and sane as he is, David wasn't right for me; he was a reaction to Trevor rather than an active choice. It's *always* some kind of reaction, not a choice."

"So with Haden you feel like it's just more of the same? He's a reaction to David?"

"I don't know, maybe. I don't think so."

"Or is your equation that, because he likes you, you don't want to waste it, but you also want to do things differently?"

"Probably closer to that."

"So because you didn't choose him, he chose you, you'd rather reject it than risk it being more of the same? Something like that?"

"Pretty much. I don't know. Even you make me sound insane!" They both laughed.

"Well, think for a moment about why you're drawn to Haden. Clarify it for yourself. And for me."

Just bringing him to mind made her smile. "Well, besides being very sexy and handsome, he's different. He's thoughtful and sweet but also impulsive. That's kind of new for me. David was always so planned and regimented. Haden has something really simple and good about him. I feel like we live on the same planet and for some reason he seems to get me, all of me, even the parts that aren't around anymore."

"What do you mean by that?"

"He remembers me as a singer. My absolute most precious dream. No one in my current life – except Kate and Ruby – has any notion of that part of me and how much it all meant. He does. And that touches me. It's meaningful. So I guess I don't feel like it's a reaction to David or Trevor or anybody else. He's just his own lovely person."

"A nice person to have chosen you. Now make your own choice."

"But why wasn't I interested until I knew he had money and wasn't this geeky little slacker boy. How pathetic is that? If he's so great, why didn't I see it before I knew he owned a showplace in the hills or ran a conglomerate? Is it possible my dad *was* right?"

"What do you think?"

Tessa didn't answer immediately. This was a troubling question, not something to gloss over. But enough had happened; enough had been revealed in the last few months that she knew more of who she was now than when she'd first read the 2002 journal. "No, I don't think my dad was right. I actually think I was so concerned about choosing consciously this time that when I thought Haden was just this sweet, little undeveloped boy, it didn't seem wise. Knowing he was further along in his life changed that. It made the choice seem wiser."

"So it wasn't that he was financially successful, it was that you determined he was more mature, more evolved, more capable of participating in an adult relationship than you originally believed, yes?"

"Yes. That's true."

"I would say that's a very functional, very sane thought process. You might want to acknowledge that and let yourself off the hook."

"Okay, I will, thank you." Tessa smiled. "But then there's still me, isn't there? I feel like I'm still sorting *me* out and have no business getting involved with anyone else, wise choice or not. It's not like I'm all cured and fabulous now and ready to move on, is it?"

"First of all, you've done some good work here, you've had a breakthrough or two, and I think that's important to celebrate and acknowledge. But, yes, in some ways you're right; a lifetime of emotional patterns is unlikely to restructure itself in a matter of months. It takes time and a commitment to slog through it all. You've come a long way, but you can expect occasional setbacks, old stuff to come up, most likely the awakenings will come and go for a while. You might question things you thought were already handled. It's not a linear process, Tessa. Sometimes it can take longer than you'd expect, longer than you'd like. We can continue with this work. If you want to transfer to a more objective therapist at this point, I have some wonderful people I could refer you to. But if you want to stay with me, I'm ready and able and believe we can get a lot more done if you're willing to continue the journey."

"I am. And with you, definitely." Tessa replied firmly.

"Good. I'd like to continue as well."

Tessa leaned back on the couch, restless.

"What is it we're still not getting at?" Aunt Joanne asked.

"I'm just not sure how I'm supposed to be now. How do I live my life in the meantime? You say this is not a linear process and I accept that, but I can't put my life on hold forever. What do I *do*?"

"You just live your life, Tessa. You continue to be yourself. You go after what's meaningful to you. You'll make mistakes and we'll talk about them here but you simply move forward, with thought but without hesitation."

"Even relationships?"

"Certainly. You can learn as you experience. And as you learn, your experiences will take on more meaning. It can be a concurrent process."

"Okay." She sounded tentative.

"Live your life, Tessa," Aunt Joanne repeated gently. "What's on your current agenda?"

"Well, I'm writing a song I have to finish up…haven't done that in a long time."

"Good."

"I've got two more stories to write for the series; that'll keep me busy."

"That's good."

"I've got to get home to see my mom soon, probably for Thanksgiving."

"I might be coming back then, too. Perhaps we can travel together."

Tessa brightened. "That would be great."

"Anything else?"

"I still have something I need to write in regards to my father. I haven't fleshed it out completely yet, but I have to do it."

"Then do it, Tessa, do all of it. Live your life. And if you are inclined to explore something with Haden Pierce, do that too."

There it was, what she wanted. Aunt Joanne giving her the peace of permission.

SEVENTY-SEVEN

Tessa had expected Haden to send the address for the family event...or at least try one more time to convince her to come. He hadn't and now she was disappointed. She started getting that compulsive, fretful feeling of rejection but, as the new poster child for functional living, got herself to a bike-riding Meet-up with its series of "bikes and hikes" instead. Very invigorating.

On the work/friends/family front, she stayed admirably on-task:

1. Wrapped up her latest story about a woman saved from the streets by an adoptive father, confident it was her best piece to date and, after sending it off, was reminded by Vivian of the next meeting for the Echolane deal. Very exciting.
2. Talked to Kate and Ruby, both happily focused on Kate's rapidly approaching motherhood. It was a boy and his name would be Henry.
3. Returned a call to Ronnie, who was now dating a driver's ed teacher from a nearby public school and, astonishingly, was continuing to do well both at the job and the program. Life never ceased to amaze.
4. Spoke briefly to Suzanna, who was planning a weekend trip to Los Angeles later in the month; they'd get together.

5. Texted Izzy and Duncan, both too busy to respond to either phones or emails.
6. Sent a warm, perky email to Michaela asking about the family and updating her on the latest in her own life.
7. Called Audrey to confirm her planned trip home for Thanksgiving.

But most momentous, on the afternoon of a completely unremarkable day, she drove down to Doug Reynold's studio and for the first time in over five years, recorded a song she wrote. And it felt, like so many things did these days, transformative.

Later that night, while sitting at home finishing up her Leo project, a text came in: "No pressure, leaving address in case you change your mind. 5953 San Simeon Creek Road, Cambria. 101 North to Cambria, right on San Simeon a mile past town. Hope to see you but either way, be well. HP"

The rush of relief was powerful. She had no plans to attend; in fact, she had no idea what to do about Haden Pierce in general. All she knew was that he was worth the mental exploration. She hoped he wouldn't disappear before she figured it out.

SEVENTY-EIGHT

Dear Dad,

    I knew I was going to write something to you a long time ago, but it's taken me a while to figure out what I wanted to say and how I wanted to say it. At first I wrote volumes that listed every transgression, every hurt, every distortion; then I'd turn around and reduce it all down to a paragraph. One minute I wanted to defend myself on every point, then I came to realize my life would have to be the evidence of who I am. In death as in life, it seems you and I have a hard time communicating to each other. I don't know why, Dad, but it ends here. I'm done being fearful. I'm done hiding instead of speaking. I'm done being angry and hurt. Though I'm sending this letter without complete conviction that it's all I want to say, I'm certain it's enough.

She wrote all Friday night. Editing and rewriting, deleting then adding paragraphs. At some point it finally felt done; she signed it and declared it so.

    On Saturday morning she sat at the dining room table with eight padded envelopes and eight CDs stacked neatly beside them. She stuffed the CDs into the envelopes, then pulled a stack of letters out of a file and folded each one, putting one letter inside with each CD. She hand-addressed each envelope: Duncan Curzio, Michaela Curzio Height, Suzanna Curzio, Ronnie Curzio, Izzy Curzio, Joanne Curzio and Audrey Curzio. The last envelope remained on the table as she thought about the address. Finally she shook her head and got on with it, filling it in with a smile: Leo Curzio, The Next Life, Heaven. It was a gamble she was willing to take.

I've been angry with you on and off my whole life, but for most of this last year that anger overwhelmed me. When you died I felt such grief and loss I wasn't sure I could endure it, but I did. Mostly because those cataclysmic emotions were trumped by the ones that followed when I read your 2002 journal. I don't know what you were thinking when you wrote all that. Maybe you had some notion that chronicling your life – and ours – would authenticate all that we had experienced together. But somewhere along the way you lost track of that purpose and became hurtful.

Maybe you meant for us to read them while you were still here and could talk to us about it. How interesting it would have been to confront you when actual dialogue could have occurred. But most of us didn't know you wanted us to read them; some of us – Izzy – didn't even know they existed, so it's hard not to think they were most decidedly meant to be found after you were gone. Reading what I have, I can actually understand that. How could you ever have explained them while you were here?

Cowardly, though, to have hit and run. Don't you think that now, looking back?

Tessa put a sufficient number of stamps on each of the eight packages, though Leo's was just a guess, then slid them in her bag. Reaching into the closet to grab a jacket, her eyes glanced at a box on the floor, one she'd moved over from David's house months ago. She crouched down and opened it up, pulled out the picture of her and her father she'd so painfully discarded after the funeral. She brushed off the dust and set it on the bed table.

After a quick adjustment of her jacket and a fluffing of her hair, Tessa took a moment to look at herself in the mirror. Thirty-six (thirty-seven in four days), five-feet six-inches, 135 pounds, dark brown hair with a slight wave, hazel eyes like her father, and a face that took it all in. She had survived. Intact. Perhaps even a few pounds lighter...*at least some good came out of this*, she smiled to herself.

My biggest hurt? Realizing you didn't know me, at least not in 2002. Instead you conjured up some caricature that was laughably far from the truth. Except it wasn't funny. Children need to know their father loves and values them for who they truly are, but you diminished me; you made fun of my struggles, you dismissed my fears. You reduced me to a series of blunders and pathetic mistakes. You depicted me in ways that were so off-beam as to reach the level of distortion. Can you understand how painful that was to read? I do wonder if you ever came to realize how wrong you were. I can only hope you did in later years and later journals.

I also witnessed the pain your words inflicted on my brothers and sisters. I watched my mother struggle to explain your words. I longed to read more of them in hopes of understanding the person behind them, hoping there would be more loving words to follow. So much heartache and hope and anger swirling around your damn words. Ironic that they would end up in a landfill covered with rotting garbage and bird shit. No matter what I might have wanted, the Fates made their own judgment about what was to happen to them.

Pulling the car out of the garage, she noticed that the flowers she'd planted her first month there were still going strong, the grass was green, and the leaves were ever-so-slowly starting to darken…nice place, her home. She took the winding canyon road down the hill to the post office. The line at the drop-off box was long, longer than usual, and the parking lot was full. She drove down a few more streets to another branch where there was plenty of parking and she could walk to the box. Some ceremony was warranted, she decided; a quick drop through a drive-by just wouldn't do.

But here's where it gets tricky for me, Dad, probably for all of us. How do we reconcile the father we loved, the father we thought loved us, with the man who wrote those words? How can both those men exist in the same human being? But they did, somehow they did. And I thought if I could discover who you really were, who you were in relation to me, how you actually felt about me beyond the cruel, inaccurate things you wrote, maybe then I could reconcile those contradictions to form a cogent impression of my father and my own childhood. With the journals gone, that wasn't easy.

This might make you smile: your sister, Joanne, a person I never had a moment of time for until this past year, has been my salvation from the two-headed monster that was your death and your journal. I mean it when I say she saved my life. Literally. I'm not sure exactly what I mean by that, given that I'm not the suicidal type, but she is a phenomenal, loving person who saved my life; we'll just leave it at that. She asked me to dig deep and I did. I cried and drank and slept badly. I broke up with my boyfriend, one you actually liked, and I had – and still occasionally have – anxiety awakenings that Aunt Joanne is sure will ultimately stop. I hope she's right. We talked about all of it, Dad, and when I felt emptied, I was left with what remained. What remained was you. I still needed to find a version of you I could live with for the rest of my life, one that convinced me you loved me. What I needed was emotional evidence.

Tessa pulled in the lot, turned off the car and just sat, immobilized, suddenly unconvinced about what she was doing. Really, why was this so important? Certainly she could understand sending the CDs and letters to her family. After the brouhaha surrounding her getting and losing the journals, they deserved to know what conclusions she'd come to. And the new song was just a good share. But the envelope to Leo?

I can remember happy, loving memories of so many other people in my life but finding you in any of those was difficult. Finding memories that actually involved you and me was impossible. I had to ask others. About my own life. Strange, isn't it? Mom remembered one with Sister Carmelina. I don't remember the same details she did, but what a lovely thing you did for me. Thank you. I asked Kate Berendt to help. You remember her, right? She was my best friend throughout my childhood and still is. Her father, Roy, was your best friend. (I know you remember him…) I asked Kate to see what she could remember because she has been a witness to my life and Kate remembered an important one: the writing contest in eighth grade. Do you remember it, Dad? Amazingly, I did. It was a good memory that gave me hope. I'm struggling to remember more of those. Clearly I'll need more than one to get me through a lifetime but it was a start.

She shook off her hesitation, grabbed the bag with the eight packages and walked resolutely to the box just outside the post office door. One by one she dropped them in. She paused for a moment with the last package, Leo's package, and tried not to feel foolish. She realized that, ultimately, she didn't. She felt profound. She knew it would end up in a dead-letter box somewhere, either ignored or discarded, but she also knew it was essential for her to mail it. Her last communication to the man whose presence and absence loomed large in every corner of her life. She needed to know it went out into the ethers; where it landed was less important. She held it for one last moment then…dropped it in.

Here's what I do know: You were a good man. You had moments of warmth and kindness and you took good care of us. When you laughed it was golden. You loved a good book. You appreciated creativity and personal expression. You understood passion and you somehow made me feel like I could find my path in the world, that I had the courage to step outside of convention to go after bigger things. You encouraged my artistic self even if you didn't understand it. You had your own dreams and you understood their value. I know because you were the one who gave me the eyes to dream in the ways I still do. You gave that to all of us, and it is a gift so treasured. When other fathers, perhaps more loving, more expressive, more emotionally available fathers, couldn't begin to see the value of such things, you did. It isn't enough to exonerate you but it does allow me to find a way back to some clarity.

Tessa pivoted quickly and walked back to the car, a perceptible bounce to her step. She opened the trunk and threw the empty bag next to a new guitar and the small duffel packed for a girls' overnight at Kate's. She pulled out of the parking lot and headed east with a clear mind, curious about what was next. She didn't know for sure but she knew she wanted to celebrate her birthday in the company of friends. She wanted to let go of everything she'd put in the letter and walk into a new, less burdened reality. She wanted to play guitar and sing again, write like there was no tomorrow, and open her heart to the unknown future.

She waited at the light before her turn, watching as people crossed the street. She looked over at the little neighborhood market, listening to the song on the radio and smiling at the warmth of the day, when it suddenly struck her.

What I discovered in my search for you, Dad, is a stronger sense of myself. It's fragile, occasionally teetering, in need of much support and reinforcement, but it's there. I even wrote a song about it, the first one I've written in over five years. I'm sending it to you with this letter because it's about you and me. About how, in trying to find you, I finally discovered who I am. The real me. The true girl. The one who survived your sucker punch, survived my own mistakes and evolved into who I am, not the stranger you wrote about. Your words didn't define me; my life does. That is a monumental accomplishment. I'm holding on to it for dear life. And I hope you like the song!

Mostly? I know you loved me. No matter what you said in that journal, I know you loved me. As I loved you. And in accepting that, I've come to accept you as the flawed man you were. I've forgiven you for that man, as I've forgiven you for hurting me so deeply. I've also come to accept you as a loving father who relished life and cherished his family. Can those contradictions exist in the same person? Yes. Because I've chosen to believe that. And that choice gives me faith. Faith that you loved me. And that's just going to have to do.

Love, your third daughter,

Tessa

The feeling was sharp and clear as a bell; filled with such tangible emotion she was stunned. Because she knew, right then, that whatever else was next, whatever else she wanted; whatever else might be expected of her, in this luminous moment with the sun shining and the music playing, one thing was certain.

She wanted to kiss Haden Pierce.

She didn't want to analyze it. She didn't want to discuss it. She surely didn't want to talk herself out of it. Because…she just knew.

So when the light changed, instead of turning right, she turned left, onto the freeway. She slipped her CD in the stereo, cranked it up loud, and drove north. North to Cambria.

EPILOGUE: TESSA'S SONG

<u>My Search For You</u>

You were puzzled by my need for clarity
Maybe you thought I depended on language too much
But there were volumes you didn't say or I never heard
I know you thought the way you loved was surely enough

So elusive, I wonder if you ever figured out?
How your silence always made me feel a little loud
So convinced if I sang and danced and jumped up and down
You would see me, just me, and maybe be a little proud
And sometimes I know that you heard me
Sometimes I know that you cried

CHORUS
But you left me in early December
You loved me but we both knew our time was through
Now I stand here and try to remember
The girl I discovered in my search for you

They say love doesn't ask for more than what it gets
So why did I always want a bigger piece of you?

320

In the crush of life I was sometimes lost in the crowd
Never sure if I ever came completely into view
But somehow I learned to be stronger
And somehow I'm certain you knew

CHORUS
But you left me in early December
You loved me but we both knew our time was through
Now I stand here and try to remember
The girl I discovered in my search for you

BRIDGE

You gave me the passion to find my way
You gave me the eyes to dream
If we squandered the time we had
You've got to know
That what I searched to find in you
I finally found in me

CHORUS
You left me in early December
You loved me but we both knew our time was through
Now I stand here and surely remember
The girl I discovered in my search for you

THE END

To hear and download song,
input the following link into your browser:
https://soundcloud.com/tessa-curzio/my-search-for-you

[My Search For You by Lorraine Devon Wilke & Rick M. Hirsch]

READING GROUP/BOOK CLUB GUIDE

The themes, questions, and talking points that follow are intended to enrich your group's discussions about *After The Sucker Punch*, Lorraine Devon Wilke's irreverent look at father/daughter relationships through the unique prism of family, faith, cults, creativity, new love and old, and the struggle to define oneself against the inexplicable perceptions of a deceased parent.

The story of *After the Sucker Punch*:

They buried her father at noon, at five she found his journals, and in the time it took her to read one-and-a-half pages, the world turned upside down: he thought she was "a failure."

Every child, no matter what age, wants to know their father loves them, and Tessa Curzio – thirty-six, emerging writer, ex-rocker, lapsed Catholic, defected Scientologist, and fourth in a family of eight complicated people – is no exception. But just when she thought her twitchy life was finally coming together – solid relationship, creative job; a view of the ocean – the one-two punch of her father's death and posthumous indictment proves an existential knockout.

In the flip of those pages, all childhood memories and her most basic sense of self are thrown into question. Tessa struggles through the funeral weekend with its all-too-familiar sibling chaos and the never-ending drama that is her mother, and though she tries to "just let it go," as her sisters suggest, the weight of hurt and confusion cracks her resolve. When she finally flees back home to

Los Angeles the fallout hits.

First to go is David, the good man in her life. He loves her but cannot fathom the depth of her crisis and their relationship implodes under the weight. Long-time friends, Kate and Ruby, swoop in to circle the wagons as they always do but ultimately they're busy, they have their own problems, and there's little they can offer beyond comforting words. When even Tessa's work at a successful online magazine loses its luster, her always inspiring boss, Marcia, assigns a series on father/daughter relationships, hoping to encourage Tessa to draw off her own pain to infuse her writing. Initially reluctant, Tessa is piqued enough to send for the rest of her father's journals under the guise of research… what she really hopes to find is some kind of redemption in his later entries.

Convincing the family of her intentions becomes challenging, particularly when her mother puts up a mighty resistance, convinced Tessa's out to destroy her father's legacy. Repeated calls to siblings only result in driving Tessa further from familial good will, and when adored but troubled little brother, Ronnie, arrives in Los Angele at exactly the wrong moment, her quest becomes a mission, taking her to uncharted territory and unexpected people. Her most significant relief comes in her regular sessions with Aunt Joanne, her father's sister, who is a Catholic nun and therapist, an arrangement that lends unexpected clarity to Tessa's confusion.

And into this swirling eddy comes Haden Pierce, a wildly intriguing man who remembers her from earlier singing days and seems hell-bent on reminding her of her better self. She's skittish and smitten, confused enough to push him away while deconstructing in a rebellion of drinking and indiscriminate hooking up, uncharacteristic rage against all that's happened. But when the entire library of journals is lost somewhere between Chicago to LA, Tessa finally hits bottom.

It's then that Aunt Joanne emerges as the clearest voice in the din. With her compassion, guidance and deeply felt empathy, she helps Tessa reclaim both truth and memories; enough to gain a more authentic view of herself and the flawed, but ultimately loving, man who was her father…opening the door for forgiveness, hope and, just maybe, another crack at love.

Suggested Questions for Discussion:

1. The inciting incident of this story is a daughter finding her father's journals and learning — at least at the time he wrote them — that he thought she was a failure. How would it impact you if you had a similar experience? Would your father's words alter your sense of self in the present, or could you categorize them as "specific" to that time and era of your family's life and not be affected by them?

2. The Tessa's family plays a big part in this story, weaving in an out of her life, mostly via phone calls. Family is an almost universal element of most people's lives; how much is yours involved in your current life and do you find yourself resisting or resenting their involvement or cherishing and welcoming it?

3. Some in the Curzio family seem to be unwilling to believe the father could be as cold and cruel as his written words convey. Often times, one person in a family has an experience with a family member that others do not. Would you find it difficult to believe your sibling if they felt your parent was doing something cruel or hurtful and you had not experienced or witnessed that sort of behavior?

4. A prevailing theme in the story is the depth and breath of

Tessa's hurt and confusion, and the fact that her boyfriend, David, doesn't seem to grasp the totality of that crisis. Do you think Tessa is being too emotional, too demanding of David, or is David remiss in not paying enough attention, or making a greater effort to understand Tessa's emotions?

5. Religion has had an overriding impact on Tessa's life, particularly her early childhood experiences in a very fundamentalist, rigid Catholic environment. Did you find that discussion offensive or off-putting? Were Tessa's confusions and concerns related to her burgeoning sexuality, the weight and terror of sin, and the seemingly insurmountable demands of being a good Catholic girl something you could relate to or did this surprise you?

6. In addition to Catholicism, Tessa also spent time in the very controversial "religion" — or cult — of Scientology. Were you at all familiar with Scientology and some of its philosophies and tenets? Did you find Tessa's experiences fascinating? Could you understand how and why a young person seeking truth and spiritual solace might be attracted to a group such as Scientology?

7. Another repeated theme is the troubling issue of domestic abuse, first in the form of an emotionally erratic mother who used violence as a way to exorcise her own frustrations, as well as, purportedly, to discipline her children. What are your thoughts on parents who hit their children? Do you subscribe to the differences between "spanking," "hitting," and "beating," or do you believe any physical impact on a child is a form of violence and abuse?

8. Additionally, Tessa unexpectedly finds herself in a romantic relationship with a man who is an abuser. Given her

commitment to "make it go right," a Scientological mandate, she hopes to change this man enough to stay with him. Ultimately she cannot and she leaves. Have you ever been in an abusive relationship? Could you understand Tessa's rationale, how her background with her violent mother positioned her to endure more, perhaps, than others might? Did this help you understand better how a woman might end up in an abusive relationship?

9. Tessa's relationship with her aunt, a Catholic nun, turns out to be pivotal to her emotional transformation. Given her rejection of the Catholic faith, did this surprise you? Were you interested in the juxtaposition of Tessa's experience with the religion and the very different attitudes of her aunt? Did you enjoy this character?

10. One of Tessa's struggles is reformulating who she is and where her true honor as a person lies after reading her father's painful words. Can you identify with any of her concerns, particularly in how she views men, her merit and her choices as a creative artist, her values and integrity as an artist, an employee, a friend, and a sibling?

11. There is much discussion in the story about the creative life versus the more corporate, conservative life. Do you have any experience with those kinds of choices? Do you think it was fair for David to criticize Tessa for not wanting a corporate job and all its benefits, or do you understand her feeling that being motivated by creativity and art is of more value, at least for her, than being motivated by money? Have you ever made the less conventional choice, regardless of money, to follow your heart or your Muse?

PRAISE FOR AFTER *THE SUCKER PUNCH*

"A realistic and profound journey of realization and forgiveness... a solid novel that admirably explores the fragile, fraught relationship between parent and child." **Publishers Weekly/BookLife**

"With bare-bone honesty and fiery dialogue, Wilke explores the loaded relationship between parents and their adult-children, examining the brave and lonely journey of self-discovery, reinvention, and healing... raw and brave — a great read." — **Tracy Trivas, author of The Wish Stealers (Simon & Schuster)**

"A keenly executed character study. The novel is tightly structured and holds its complex elements with a sure and skillful grip. The dialogue pops... a thoroughly engaging and enjoyable read." — **Junior Burke, author of Something Gorgeous (farfalla press/McMillan & Parrish)**

"A great, sweeping, beautifully written, page turning read, gripping from page one. A family saga with ambition and class. Meant to be read in bed; absorbed, over time, savoured by lamplight."
— **Mark Barry, author of Carla and The Night Porter (Green Wizard Publishing)**

2014 indieB.R.A.G. Medallion® Honoree

2014 Best of Summer Reading List Selection — Fran Briggs, publicist

For other reviews of After The Sucker Punch go to Amazon.com/author/lorrainedevonwilke and click book link

A "THANK YOU" TO MY READERS

I want to thank you for choosing *After the Sucker Punch* amongst the many literary titles available for readers today. I loved writing Tessa's story, one that gave me the opportunity to tap into much of my own experience, as well as explore and imagine so many areas of meaning and interest to me; I sincerely hope you enjoyed it.

Certainly for independent authors like myself the involvement and support of readers in getting the word out about books they like is essential. In that spirit, and if you are so inclined, I invite you to leave a short review of *After the Sucker Punch* at the page where you made your purchase. Positive feedback goes a long way toward advancing the cause of independent publishing and I thank you in advance for your contribution!

I always love hearing from readers for whom the book resonated, so feel free to get in touch via info@lorrainedevonwilke.com.

ACKNOWLEDGEMENTS

When you're a decidedly late bloomer (as I am), by the time you get to your first acknowledgment page you've accrued a hefty list of people who've played pivotal roles in the trajectory of your career. For this page, I want to acknowledge those who played specific and appreciated roles in my writing career, all of which collectively contributed to the fruition of this book.

First, I must start with my family, with whom I have all that is most precious to me. To my son, Dillon Wilke, who is not only the most spectacular person I know, but will always be the best thing I've ever done; thank you for encouraging me to write this story. I loved your title suggestion even if we ultimately went another way! To my stepdaughter, Jennie Wilke Willens, thank you for being there for me in ways I will never forget. And, always and forever, thanks to my beloved husband, Pete Wilke, my good, good man who has supported me in every way imaginable, never forgotten who I am, and still thinks it's funny when I dance to TV theme songs. It doesn't get much better than that!

Next up, my incredible sibs – Peg, Mary, John, Paul, Tom, Eileen, Gerry, Louise, Vince and Grace Amandes. Their lifetime of interest, involvement, creativity, and support has been extraordinary and invaluable. A special thanks to Tom, my rock in ways both personal and artistic, who has, as far as I know, read this book more times than anyone else and always offered clear perspective when needed most; to Louise, my earliest designer and always empathetic sounding board; to Grace, whose talent was tapped to create my beautiful book cover, and to my parents, Virginia and Philip Amandes, whose greatest legacy was inspiring our appreciation of art in all its many expressions.

There is no limit to my gratitude for the teachers, friends, associates, and colleagues who have read, edited, shared, shopped, requested, optioned, encouraged, guided, referred, bought, produced, consulted on, or published my work, many of whom contributed directly to this book: Mrs. Beth Scamehorn (my first and most influential writing teacher); Fred Rubin, Bill Stetz, Judd Parkin, Penny Peyser, Jean Abounader, Penny Perry, Tina Romanus (distinguished for being ATSP's very first reader and knowing exactly how often to email with comments while she was reading!); Joyce DiVito Jackson, Patricia Royce, Barry Caillier, Susie Singer Carter, Don Priess, Nancy Capers, Barbara Tyler, Minda Burr, Katerina Alexander, Rikki Kapes, Jake Drake, Steve Brackenbury, Marian Hamlen, Cindy Ritt, Wendy Treptow, Cris Carroll, Carolyn Sutton, Debra Sanders, Lane Aldridge, Maureen Haldeman, Susan Morgenstern, Suzanne Battaglia, Dr. Joan Rankin, Sandy Wilson, Nancy Everhard-Amandes, Caroline Titus, John Merline, Arianna Huffington, Saralee Rosenberg, Shirley Lipner, Tami Urbanek, Herby Beam, Tessa Lena, Ellen Shanman, Pamela May, Dr. Lauren Streicher, Louis Rosen, Jason Brett, Brenda Perlin and Mark Barry. To my editors Erin Reel, Diana Rosen and, especially, Laurie E. Boris, who, along with Martin Crosbie, gave me invaluable counsel on the art of independent publishing. And to the late, beloved, and very missed Lisa Blount, who was one of my biggest champions and a brilliant editor who contributed greatly to the early development of *After the Sucker Punch.*

From my music world, thanks to Rick M. Hirsch, my co-writer and the co-producer/guitarist on Tessa's song, "My Search For You."

My deepest thanks to you all ... more as we go!

ABOUT THE AUTHOR

Writer, photographer, singer/songwriter, **Lorraine Devon Wilke**, started early as a creative hyphenate. First, there was music and theater, next came rock & roll, then a leap into film when a feature she co-wrote (*To Cross the Rubicon*) was produced by a Seattle film company, opening doors in a variety of creative directions.

In the years that followed, she wrote for and performed on theater stages, developed her photography skills, and accrued a library of eclectic and well-received feature screenplays; *The Theory of Almost Everything* was a top finalist in the 2012 Final Draft Big Break Screenwriting Contest; *A Minor Rebellion* was a 2014 quarter-finalist in that same competition. She kept her hand in music throughout – songwriting, recording, performing – leading to the fruition of her longtime goal of recording an original album (*Somewhere On the Way*). Accomplished in collaboration with songwriting/producing partner, Rick M. Hirsch, the album garnered stellar reviews and can be found at CDBaby and iTunes. She continues with music whenever she can (which, she maintains, is never, *ever*, enough!).

Devon Wilke's current life is split between Playa del Rey and Ferndale, California, and is shared with her husband, Pete Wilke, an entertainment/securities attorney, her son, environmental engineer and web designer, Dillon Wilke, and stepdaughter, educational administrator, Jennie Wilke Willens and family. She curates and manages both her fine art photography site and personal blog, *Rock+Paper+Music*, is a regular contributor to *The Huffington Post*, writes a column for the award-winning Northern California newspaper, *The Ferndale Enterprise*. And invites you to enjoy her essays and journalistic pieces @ Contently.com. Her dramatic short story, "She Tumbled Down," was published in 2014, and her latest novel, *Hysterical Love*, will be published in April of 2015. You can follow her journey with this, and all her other book at her book publishing website, *AfterTheSuckerPunch.com*. Links to all the above can be found at her website, **www.lorrainedevonwilke.com**.

Contact: info@lorrainedevonwilke.com.
General information and links: www.lorrainedevonwilke.com

LORRAINE DEVON WILKE'S OTHER BOOKS

Hysterical Love: *a novel* *(available in paperback and e-book)*

Dan McDowell, a thirty-three-year-old portrait photographer happily set to marry his beloved Jane, is stunned when a slip of the tongue about an "ex-girlfriend overlap" of years earlier throws their pending marriage into doubt and him onto the street. Or at least into the second bedroom of their next-door neighbor, Bob, where Dan is sure it won't be long. It's long.

His sister, Lucy, further confuses matters with her "soul mate theory" and its suggestion that Jane might *not* be his... soul mate, that is. But the tipping point comes when his father is struck ill, sparking a chain of events in which Dan discovers a story written by this man he doesn't readily understand, but who, it seems, has long harbored an unrequited love from decades earlier.

Incapable of fixing his own romantic dilemma, Dan becomes fixated on finding this woman of his father's dreams and sets off for Oakland, California, on a mission fraught with detours and semi-hilarious peril. Along the way he meets the beautiful Fiona, herbalist and flower child, who assists in his quest while quietly and erotically shaking up his world. When, against all odds, he finds the elusive woman from the past, the ultimate discovery of how she truly fit into his father's life leaves him staggered, as does the reality of what's been stirred up with Fiona. But it's when he returns home to yet another set of unexpected truths that he's shaken to the core, ultimately forced to face who he is and just whom he might be able to love.

Author Lorraine Devon Wilke brings her deft mix of humor and drama to a whip-smart narrative told from the point of view of its male protagonist. *Hysterical Love* explores themes of family, commitment, balancing creativity, facing adulthood, and digging deep to understand the beating heart of true love.

Publication date: April 7, 2015.

She Tumbled Down: a short story *(available in e-book):*

New Year's Eve. It's late, well past the midnight hour. A woman looking for respite from noise, champagne, and tensions with her boyfriend steps out to clear her head. She calls out that she'll be back shortly and heads down the quiet neighborhood street... and never comes back.

A man who's had too much to drink, driving too fast a car, roars by on that same darkened street and, in a flash of motion and impact, is stunned to see the face of a startled woman smash into his windshield. When the car stops he shakes in silence, waiting for... something. But when no one approaches, no cars go by and no inquiring lights flick on, fear and panic take over and he makes the unfathomable decision to drive away... and never look back.

"She Tumbled Down" follows the ripple effects of this tragic hit-and-run attempting to answer that unanswerable question, "Who could do such a thing?" From that first fateful moment through the months and years that follow, the narrative weaves through the lives of seemingly disparate characters, threading the initial event into another story, a love story, that ultimately links to the tragedy in unexpected ways.

"There is lightness and there is dark. The story travels around to both sides. As a reader I wanted, hoping to know everything would turn out okay but guessing it would not. I was left to guess as I read at a feverish pace."

"Rarely, if ever, have I read a short story that was so incredibly good that after finishing it, after drinking a cup of tea and reflecting on it, I sat down and read it all over again. But that's what I did with this one, and now three days later I find myself STILL thinking about it; still talking about it to every bookaholic I know. It's a story that begs for discussion, so provocative is the subject matter and story line."

"I was engaged right from the outset, and this was one story I couldn't put down. I liked how the author played with time, and covered a very sensitive subject that ended up being satisfying in its conclusion. Secrets have a way of tumbling out, and the results are not often predictable, as Lorraine Devon Wilke shows in this gripping drama."

For other reviews of "She Tumbled Down" go to Amazon.com/author/lorrainedevonwilke.

Connect Online With
LORRAINE DEVON WILKE

Website: www.lorrainedevonwilke.com

Blog: www.rockpapermusic.com

After the Sucker Punch Blog: http://www.afterthesuckerpunch.com

Twitter: https://twitter.com/LorraineDWilke

Facebook: https://www.facebook.com/lorrainedevonwilke

FB Writer's Page:
https://www.facebook.com/lorrainedevonwilke.fans

Photography website:
http://lorraine-devon-wilke.artistwebsites.com

SoundCloud Page:
www.soundcloud.com/lorraine-devon-wilke

CDBaby: www.cdbaby.com/cd/wilke

iTunes:
https://itunes.apple.com/artist/lorraine-devon-wilke/id119681867

Huffington Post:
http://www.huffingtonpost.com/lorraine-devon-wilke/

Article Archive: https://lorrainedevonwilke.contently.com

Email contact @ info@lorrainedevonwilke.com

CPSIA information can be obtained at www.ICGtesting.com
Printed in the USA
LVOW10s1938230315

431670LV00007B/1194/P

JAN 2 8 2016